T0418441

AS THE STORM CLOUDS GATHER

Also by M.B. Henry

Novels

ALL THE LIGHTS ABOVE US

AS THE STORM CLOUDS GATHER

M.B. Henry

SEVERN
HOUSE

First world edition published in Great Britain and the USA in 2025
by Severn House, an imprint of Canongate Books Ltd,
14 High Street, Edinburgh EH1 1TE.

severnhouse.com

Copyright © M.B. Henry, 2025

Cover and jacket design by Nick May at bluegecko22.com

All rights reserved including the right of reproduction in whole or in part in any form. The right of M.B. Henry to be identified as the author of this work has been asserted in accordance with the Copyright, Designs & Patents Act 1988.

British Library Cataloguing-in-Publication Data
A CIP catalogue record for this title is available from the British Library.

ISBN-13: 978-1-4483-1553-6 (cased)
ISBN-13: 978-1-4483-1554-3 (e-book)

This is a work of fiction. Names, characters, places and incidents are either the product of the author's imagination or are used fictitiously. Except where actual historical events and characters are being described for the storyline of this novel, all situations in this publication are fictitious and any resemblance to actual persons, living or dead, business establishments, events or locales is purely coincidental.

All Severn House titles are printed on acid-free paper.

Typeset by Palimpsest Book Production Ltd.,
Falkirk, Stirlingshire, Scotland.
Printed and bound in Great Britain by
TJ Books, Padstow, Cornwall.

Praise for M.B. Henry

"An author to follow"
Heather Morris, author of *The Tattooist of Auschwitz*

"WWII like you've never thought of it before. And D-Day like you've never thought of it before"
Adriana Trigiani, *New York Times* bestselling author, on *All the Lights Above Us*

"Well-researched and gripping . . . Fans of WWII fiction and women's fiction won't want to miss these inspiring stories of courage and survival"
Historical Novel Society on *All the Lights Above Us*

"Not to be missed. Written in confident and evocative prose, Henry has crafted a remarkable novel that belongs in the canons of thought-provoking World War II literature"
Anita Abriel, international bestselling author, on *All the Lights Above Us*

"An apt multifaceted portrait, not just of World War II, but of any 'good war'"
New York Journal of Books on *All the Lights Above Us*

"A brilliantly crafted work of historical fiction . . . a compelling and entertaining read from cover to cover"
Midwest Book Review on *All the Lights Above Us*

About the author

M.B. Henry is a lifelong student of history, especially military history, having visited battlefields and historical sites all over the world. She has a degree in Cinema and Comparative Literature, and has served as a historical consultant and researcher on films and television in Los Angeles. She lives with her husband and three cats in Indiana.

www.mb-henry.com

*To love, our most powerful ally.
And to every grave marked 'unknown' in Flanders Fields.*

ONE
Ilse

May 7, 1915

Nineteen-year-old Ilse Marie Stahl leaned against the cold metal railing of the ocean liner.

It was one of the largest in the Atlantic, with almost two thousand passengers aboard. It was also one of the most luxurious. Her family's small, second-class cabin looked nicer and cleaner than their flat in New York City ever had. Fresh linens covered their beds every day. There was a porcelain sink with running water. Elegant tea china adorned a small counter. Handsome dishes too. In addition to all that, Ilse hadn't combed nits from her hair in weeks. All the food was fresh and hot, and the staff treated her well. They didn't narrow their eyes when she walked past or hurl insults at her about 'squareheads' and 'boche.' They didn't threaten her father's life or destroy his business.

New York had already seen to that.

Ilse wrapped her wool shawl tighter around her shoulders, while the early afternoon sun glowed down on her pale skin. The fresh sea breeze blew loose strands of yellow-blonde hair around her stern face. Her mossy eyes pierced the ocean.

On the horizon, the coast of Ireland had become visible, the Old Head of Kinsale jutting out into the sea. Soon, they would be safe and sound on dry land after a very intense passage, where talk of the war and German U-boats and sunken ships had haunted every square inch of space. Normally busy writing rooms and lounges had become ghost towns. Cafeterias typically filled with cheerful gossip and chatter remained eerily silent. Men of prominence puffed on cigars and spoke in anxious whispers, while their wives wrung their hands and tried to hide their growing fear. Even the bands in the dining room felt a bit dull, submarines prowling deep in the musicians' consciousness, just like they did in the ocean around them. Landfall would be a relief to everyone.

Everyone but Ilse, anyway. As her new life loomed before her, she thought of her old one back in New York. The place had its problems, but she was born there, and she had always called it home. It frightened her to face such a big unknown, with a whole new set of worries and trials. She yearned instead for the familiar routine and cozy things she always knew. Like how the sun beamed through the sparkling dust particles at the apartment's single window. The familiar creaks in the water-stained ceiling from her friendly neighbors upstairs. The floury dough her mother pounded into delicious bread every morning. The faded, yet charming, colors on the torn, sagging wallpaper in the kitchen.

And the people. How Ilse would miss her girlfriends from neighboring flats and the way they giggled and gossiped while they walked around the busy street markets. The grocers in her new neighborhood might not wink at her the way the old ones did, slipping her extra treats, asking after her mother while they tussled her hair. She had also left behind a good job at a clothing factory, where her talent with the needle helped her stand out, where she earned a nice living to help support her family, and where she had yet more friends and admirers.

New York had been a hard life with too much dirt and never enough food, but she and her parents were happy.

Well, mostly.

The sea breeze threw a chill over Ilse, and her happy memories clouded over. Instead, she saw her father stumbling in the apartment door while muffled shouts and yells came from outside. She remembered his torn vest, his rumpled hair, his shaking knees. The tears he wouldn't let fall glistening in his tired eyes. Ilse and her mother had stood slack-jawed while he told them he'd lost his job at the furniture shop.

He came from a long line of carpenters, and he crafted many fine things for his wealthy American neighbors at the shop, fetching exorbitant prices for his boss. But the war turned once-friendly co-workers against him. They accused him of spying and called him a traitor. They hustled him out of the warehouse, and it wasn't enough to take away his job. They chased him home and threatened to take his life too, if he should ever dream of returning to work.

He wasn't the only one. Ever since the big war started overseas, Germans and other immigrants were accosted on the streets. Sneering people accused them of stealing jobs from real Americans. One snarling man, when he overheard Ilse speak German at the market, grumbled at her to 'go back where she came from.' He stomped off before she could tell him she was born right there in New York.

Ilse sighed. It was true she was born in America. But people still went out of their way to make her feel like she didn't belong there.

As she wrestled with her mixed emotions, her father joined her on the ship's deck. He removed his hat to catch the breeze, which exposed a balding head with wisps of gray hair, and a stern face just like Ilse's. He also had the same green eyes, although a lot more crow's feet circled his. Age had hardened and firmed his jawline, and his lips were tight and pursed. He leaned over the railing and drew in a long breath of the fresh, salty air.

'It's a beautiful day,' he said with his thick German accent. 'A shame your mother gets so seasick. She can't even leave the cabin.'

Ilse giggled. 'Careful, Papa, your German is showing.'

'Quiet, girl. I'm a full-blooded American from here on out.' He poked the tip of her nose with his index finger. 'Just like you.'

Ilse glared. 'It's not a crime you were born in Germany.'

Her father sighed. 'I know, my child, but this is a British liner and war makes people a bit silly. This is only temporary, though. You'll see.' He threw her a sly smile and a wink. 'No one said that old Kaiser was perfect. Especially not me.'

'Well, we didn't start any war. We shouldn't have to leave America.'

'Of course not, but it's a complicated thing.' He propped his elbows up on the railing. 'War riles people up. They don't use their heads. They say and do cruel things.'

'Like tossing you out of your job.'

His face fell. 'It's not just the job, Ilse. It was frightening to witness neighbors beaten in the streets. Businesses smashed and looted. Our friends getting evicted. All this because one loudmouth neighbor with their own ax to grind accuses them of betrayal, or German spying, or being anti-American. And no one stops it because they don't want to be next.' He sighed. 'I'm sure it won't be the worst of it, either.'

'What do you mean?'

'The world is scary right now. I don't want anyone getting hurt.' He reached over to pet her windblown hair. 'Your mother's family is well off in England. They have a beautiful home in the country. Quite isolated. There's room enough for all of us and we will be safe. We can make it a new home until we're ready to go back to our old one.'

Ilse huffed. 'If her home is so nice there, I wonder why she left in the first place?'

'You have me to thank for that.' He winked again. The same sly smile. The same mischievous twinkle in his eyes.

Ilse raised her eyebrows. 'Charmed her right out of the British Empire, did you?'

He laughed. 'When your mother and I met in London, I knew it was meant to be. Especially when she told me how badly she wanted to go to America. Just like me.'

'Why though? Why . . . why leave your home?'

Sensing the tough transition his daughter now faced, he sighed a little. 'To make a new one, of course. One with more opportunity for a lower-class working boy like me.'

'And Mother?'

'She always loves a good adventure, no matter how seasick it makes her. Besides, she couldn't keep away from me, despite how upset it made her wealthy parents. So, America it was. There we made our new home.' He patted her head. 'There we had you.'

Ilse gazed over the azure water, sadness flickering across her eyes. 'Home . . .' Her lower jaw trembled with oncoming tears.

'What is it, Ilse?'

'I was born in America so I'm not German, but people in America say I'm not American. What does that make me?'

He turned her chin so she faced him. 'It makes you very special, little Fraulein, because you have both the worlds right inside you. The heart and blood of the old, but the mind and eyes of the new.' He draped his arm over her shoulders. 'Besides, you will always have somewhere to belong. To your parents, who love you.'

Ilse nestled into her father's shoulder, enjoying the warmth of his coat and the faint smell of cigar smoke in his scarf.

'Perhaps I will take you to Paris one day.' Her father smiled. 'When the war is over, of course. Then you could be a French girl.'

'Is it really as pretty as they say?'

He winked at her. 'It would be enough to satisfy even your sense of adventure, my little Chère-Amie.'

'What does that word mean?'

'It means "dear friend" in French. And that's what you are to me. More than just my daughter, you are my dear friend.'

The compliment burrowed deep in Ilse's heart, sparking a shot of warmth through her sea-frozen body. It reminded her what kind of father he was. He was no taskmaster who believed children should be seen and not heard. He let her have opinions and speak her piece, even in important family matters. He didn't scold her if she cried. He gave her options instead of orders. Ilse deeply treasured her father, more than anyone else she knew.

'Papa, will we ever see America again?'

He sighed. 'I'm quite certain you will at least. You're too much like me. Like your mother. You buckle under strict tradition, which means you won't last long in Britain.'

She laughed, which broke up her nerves and melted them away. She decided, right then and there, that as long as she had her father, life in England would hold just as much promise as life in America. They would figure things out, just like they always did. They would patch it all up. They would survive.

Together, the pair looked over the railing and out to the horizon. The deep blue water lay at a dead calm, the green of Ireland beckoning.

It was all so peaceful. Ilse inhaled deeply.

Then she noticed something odd. A mysterious trail of white bubbles zipping across the water's surface, beelining for the liner's hull. The bubbles made a perfect straight line, moving much faster than any sea creature could.

Ilse's father saw them too. 'Down, Ilse!' He grabbed her by the arms and threw her onto the deck.

A millisecond later, a giant explosion ripped through the side of the magnificent steamer, tearing the entire hull away as if it were made of paper. There was a horrific jolt, and a wall of blasting water suddenly appeared between Ilse and her father. It shot straight up into the cloudless sky, ripping off pieces of the railing and the ship's deck.

Ilse screamed as the burst of water knocked her down the boat deck. Her body slammed against the starboard railing and flipped over the side. Through the chaos, she somehow managed to grip the slick, frigid metal in her shaking hands and hold on for dear life.

The water geyser had to obey gravity, so it soon tumbled back over the ship and plastered Ilse with frozen ocean. Gasping for breath, she struggled to keep her grip on the liner's fragile, squealing railing. She looked at her feet dangling precariously over the churning ocean, at least sixty feet down. A perilous drop.

Above her, in a chorus of squeaks and screeches, the once-sturdy ship had already started a dangerous list to starboard. She heard the slam and clatter of objects inside pulling loose from their moorings. Dishware and chandeliers shattering. Furniture thudding and crashing through the walls. Luggage tumbling and turning in the rooms.

'Father!' Ilse tried to pull herself up, but her hands slipped on the wet rails. She screamed as her grip loosened, her fingers too cold to stay wrapped around the metal. Just when she braced herself for the fall, a strong pair of familiar, warm hands grabbed her own.

'Ilse!' her father yelled as he clung to her. 'I have you! For the love of God, don't let go!'

Ilse convulsed in her father's grip, and she wasn't the only one in shock. The once-quiet decks had devolved into a swarm of chaos. Hundreds of people clamored up and down the narrow passageways. Wails of terrified children cut the air. Baffled ship officers blew piercing blasts on their whistles, trying to bring some order to the masses. More ship officers stuffed sobbing, screaming people into life jackets.

Mobs descended in a fury toward the lifeboats. But the ship listed so badly the ones on the port side weren't even usable. The boats on the starboard side were swamped in seconds. Passengers had to leap across a dangerous gap to even make it aboard. Quite the challenge for women in long skirts and children with short legs. Officers shouted over the crowd, wrangled more people into the boats, and barked orders to lower away.

The horrifying sight made Ilse realize her own mortal danger. She locked her hands around her father's, and she fought like hell to pull herself up. However, the ship was listing at an alarming rate and she didn't have the strength to overcome it.

Ilse let out a shout. 'We're sinking!'

'Just hold onto me; I've got you!'

Ilse gasped as her fingers began to slip through her father's. 'Father! I can't hold on!'

'Ilse! Don't let go!' He strained his grip harder, gritting his teeth, trying to hoist his daughter to safety.

Ilse tried a final time to force her body over the side of the listing ship, but her muscles wouldn't obey. She screamed as her fingers left her father's. She saw his eyes go wide and his face fall in agony. She felt her own heart stop and her body begin its awful free fall.

Before she could take a breath, or do anything to prepare herself, she slammed back-first onto the water below. It felt more like landing on concrete than ocean, and the water sucked her down below the surface. She kicked her feet and thrashed her arms, but her heavy brown skirt pulled at her, weighted her, and dragged her down.

Ilse craned her head to spot the ocean surface, which already looked alarmingly far above her. Myriad jerking legs and arms shattered the ocean's sky-blue top layer.

She kicked through the turquoise water around her, punctured by the waving, golden bands of beaming sunlight. A few big air bubbles escaped her lips. She knew she was drowning, but it didn't scare her. It somehow made her feel . . . quite peaceful. So, she stopped struggling. Her body went limp, and the turquoise faded to midnight blue as she sunk deeper and deeper. Even the light couldn't reach her now. Death opened its arms for her . . .

Then Ilse's eyes flew open. Her face hardened with determination. Fierce, fiery determination handed down from generations of ancestors who had survived wars, famine, hunger, poverty, and everything else in between. She couldn't give up this easily. She knew she would die someday, but it damn well wouldn't be today.

With newfound resolve, Ilse fumbled with her skirt, then ripped it off her waist. Once it dropped away, her body broke from the water's pull. She began ascending, the blue around her growing lighter. The golden bands shimmered around her once again. Then, she burst to the water's surface, coughing and sputtering, water pouring out of her nose and mouth.

That was when she registered the cold. Her lungs seared with it. It stabbed her legs over and over again with a million tiny needles. Her fingers and lips turned blue, and her limbs jolted and locked with deathly, frigid cold. A hideous scream escaped her throat, but it got lost amongst the thousands of others.

So many others. Swarms of people, as far as the eye could see, kicking and struggling in the water. They fought like savages over piles of loose debris. They clamored for the handful of drifting, overcrowded lifeboats. They tackled people with life vests to keep themselves afloat.

Ilse's eyes drifted to the liner, now in its horrific death throes. It tilted almost completely on its side now, most of it already under water. The horrible squeal of collapsing iron came from deep within as the last of the ship slipped beneath the ocean waves. A massive debris field, a few lifeboats, and an entire island of struggling and screaming people were all that remained of the once-proud liner.

Ilse knew the scene would haunt her forever, but for now, she had to worry about surviving. Step one was to get her frozen limbs out of the water immediately.

She spotted a blown-apart barrel nearby, and she pumped her weak arms to get to it. It wasn't much, far too small for most people to bother with. But it would at least get her upper body out of the icy sea. She grabbed the barrel in her arms and tossed her torso on top of it. It took her several seconds of wrestling with both the tide and the flimsy barrel to keep from dropping right back into the water. Once she got situated, she scanned the massive crowds. Her eyes zooming over each person, desperate to find a familiar face.

It would be easier said than done. Because there were people everywhere, thrashing about, swimming away, splashing each other. They yelled for the boats, they cried for their loved ones, they screamed for help. They twisted and turned, writhed and wrestled, locked in an animal-like struggle to stay alive. Ilse could only take it in quick flashes. A bleeding woman here, a shrieking man there. A dead man in an expensive suit. A ship's officer floating face-down right next to her.

'Father!'

Completely futile, of course. No one could possibly hear her over the tumultuous uproar in the ocean. She had never heard so many people yelling all at once. One loud, awful chorus of voices, much like the yells at the baseball diamond when something went wrong with the team. Only these were not disgruntled fans; these were people in their final fight with death.

Ilse began to cry. Just a few feet away, a little girl with beautiful ringlets floated face-down in the water. Next to her, a woman with a bloody shoulder also floated face down. A man with cuts all down his back floated face down. A single teacup drifted on the surface; a red-stained life vest flopped in the tide. A woman's shoe bobbed in the blue, and a child's bloodied teddy bear rocked in the waves.

Then came the seagulls. With a bone-chilling, devilish call to arms, they dove among the corpses. They picked. They clawed. They ravaged.

Ilse screwed her own eyes shut and let out a terrified sob. With no warning whatsoever, her lunch came up from her belly and splashed into the water. She laid her face down against the wood of the barrel. The frigid water lapped at her feet, and slowly, eventually, the screams started to fade around her.

'Father . . .'

There was hope, she tried to tell herself. Hope that he had made it to a lifeboat or somehow survived. Unlike her mother, who was down in the cabin when the torpedo struck. It was unlikely she'd even made it to the deck before the liner sank.

Ilse had known that things would be hard when she left New York, but she hadn't even considered it could all be taken from her, when she was an ocean away from anyone who could help.

Sobbing at the thought, Ilse ran her hand weakly down the side of the barrel. Her fingers came to rest over the stamped black letters . . .

RMS *Lusitania*.

TWO
Roland

July 30, 1916

Twenty-two-year-old Roland Seybold Hawkins strolled down the streets of Manhattan. Businesses had closed hours ago, leaving all the buildings dark and shuttered. Walkers had mostly abandoned the streets for their quiet homes and comfortable beds. As his work boots thumped on the concrete sidewalk, the bright summer moon was his only real company.

He glanced at his rusty pocket watch, which showed a few minutes past two in the morning. Which made him yawn and yearn for his squeaky, cozy fold-out bed in the living room of his family's brownstone. He also longed to change out of his heavy work pants and dusty, dirt-stained work shirt.

He plucked the hat from his head, running a hand through smooth walnut hair that matched his sparkling eyes. His partially unbuttoned shirt showed tanned skin interspersed with developing muscles and manhood. His father's frayed old pants sagged on his boyish hips, a constant reminder that he couldn't quite measure up to his proud father in many ways. Because Sam Hawkins was one of the most well-respected detectives on the New York City police force. He threw a shadow over most people. He was that big of a man, and that admirable too.

It made Roland anxious to leave his own mark on the world. So, he always held his chin up like he thought a man should, and he tried to speak in the same bold voice as his father. He took care of his younger brother, Bernard, much like a father would a son. Bernard, two years his junior. Such a shy and quiet boy who always needed a gentle push.

Not so with Roland. He felt restless and ready to make his own way, to be his own man. While he hadn't found a wife or his own place to live yet, he had found his own job in the big city. After various part-time jobs, he landed a position at a furniture-making shop in Manhattan, taking a spot recently vacated by an older man returning to Europe. Fleeing America, going back to where he came from.

Good.

Roland whistled as he walked along, feeling pretty damn lucky, and fueled by the happy buzz in his stomach from the spirits he had just enjoyed with his work mates. He lived in one of the finest cities in the world. He had wonderful, healthy, and loving parents who could see to his every need, and he had the sweetest younger brother who felt like a built-in best friend. He was safe here in New York, where war hadn't called in years.

Which certainly wasn't so for the rest of the world.

Roland glanced up at the moon, watching a somber cloud move over it. He wondered what a new day would bring overseas. Countless people had died, while countless more people were broken, wounded, and homeless. Armies from across the planet had dug Europe into a snarling system of trenches. Artillery screamed across the continent, and U-boats prowled the icy waters of the Atlantic, bringing their own pieces of war to American shores. It was just a year before that German U-boats had sent the *Lusitania*, a British liner packed with helpless civilians, including some Americans, down to the bottom of the frigid Irish Sea.

Just like a sore throat signaled a coming cold, Roland thought the *Lusitania* was just the beginning. The government clung to neutrality in this great war like a life raft, but after the *Lusitania* was hit, they couldn't do so much longer. Not with anger smoldering all over the country, and Germans still running amok in the streets. Always making Roland nervous with their hard stares, piercing eyes, and mischievous language.

They made his father nervous too. Detective Sam Hawkins had a full-time job sniffing out German espionage in the city. He had broken up violent plots, he had busted multiple spy rings, and he had shut down protests in support of the Kaiser. The work earned him approval and promotions on the force, and trembling fear in the German sections of the city. But it might not be enough. He might end up in the trenches across the water. Now that he was of age, Roland might too.

He began whistling to calm the sudden flutter around his rapidly beating heart. He couldn't think like that. New York was safe. It was sound. It was home.

Then, something like a loud peal of thunder suddenly rocked the night air. A forceful concussion rumbled the sidewalk and pushed Roland to his knees, where he scraped his skin on the hard concrete. He covered his head as the windows up above shattered, and shards of glass rained down, clinking and clacking on the streets and sidewalks.

It took several moments for the rumbling to stop and the glass to settle. A plethora of police sirens soon cut through the air. So did shouts and curse words from the people in their flats up above. A nearby dog let loose a deep-throated howl, answered in kind by other resident canines.

Roland, a bit shook up, crawled to his feet and brushed loose glass off his shirt. He noticed an ominous orange glow on the distant horizon, and he detected the sharp odor of smoke in his flaring nostrils.

He suddenly got a sinking feeling in his gut. One that he couldn't quite explain.

'Father . . .'

Everyone else's fears soon drowned out his own though. People stumbled out of buildings in their pajamas. They held up flickering oil lamps and looked up into the glowing night sky.

'Was it an earthquake?' someone shouted.

'A bomb?'

'What happened?'

Nervous neighbors wandered through piles of glass. They checked in with friends to make sure they were all right. They shouted for family members they couldn't locate in the dark.

Roland finally kicked his legs into high gear. Thoughts of his own family set his brain on fire like whatever had just exploded in the distance. He shoved through the crowds and broke into a sprint. All the while, his heart pumped cold and his hands went clammy.

'Father!'

When he spotted the familiar brownstone that had housed his family all his life, he noticed a single candle in the upper story window, the amber flame providing the only light in the otherwise ominous black street.

It called out to him like a beacon in the night, flooding him with relief. His mother had lit that candle. It's how she always signaled him home after a long day. A tradition so wonderfully familiar on this night filled with chaos. Making him feel like everything would be all right.

* * *

As The Storm Clouds Gather 13

The candlelight still glimmered in Roland's brain the next morning, when he sat on the small sofa in his living room, his thoughts fused to all the hope that flame had brought him just the night before.

He remembered the embrace of his mother when he had come in last night, and the lilac smell of her perfume as she pulled him into her bosom. 'Roland, thank God you're home.'

'Where's Dad?'

She buried her face in his hair. 'He's been out with the force all night. He should be home soon, and he'll be glad you're safe.'

Twenty-year-old, wiry Bernard, trembling and pale in his striped night shirt, also looked glad to see his brother. He wrapped his scrawny arms around Roland. 'Did you hear the big explosion?'

'Yes, it knocked me clean off my feet.'

'Did a bomb go off or something?'

Roland shook his head. 'I'm not sure.'

Bernard turned to his anxious mother. 'When will Dad be home?'

'Soon, darling. Soon.'

The trio had retired to the living room to wait. The candle burned bright in the picture window, casting dancing shadows all about the room. Bernard pulled a silver mouth organ from the breast pocket of his night shirt. He played a few notes to lighten the air.

At every creak of the walls, or bird on the roof, or shout from outside, they all jumped. They turned their hopeful eyes to the door. They waited for proud, decorated, and strong Detective Sam Hawkins to make his bold entrance into the family brownstone.

Dawn arrived with no signs of Hawkins Senior. Mrs Hawkins saw to a light breakfast and tea for her sons. Outside, city maintenance crews swept away the glass from the night before, and New York moved on with its day. Newspaper boys shouted about an explosion from a 'manufacturing accident' on Black Tom Island, which hushed all the nervous whispers. People went back to their jobs at city skyscrapers, back to their picnics in Central Park, back to their busy, hurried lives.

But it didn't ease Roland's nerves. His father was a cop, so he could smell a spin when the papers tossed one out. He also knew Black Tom housed munitions scheduled to be shipped to the Allies. Any explosion there wouldn't be an accident.

And still, Sam Hawkins did not return. No one came to the

brownstone until almost the lunch hour, and then, it was the New York City Police Commissioner.

By then, the family had feared the worst. Now, in the safety of his living room, Roland sat across from the fully uniformed commissioner. The official poured a brandy for Mrs Hawkins, while she sobbed into a cloth handkerchief. He held her frail hand and assured her the force would be there for her during this difficult time.

Bernard sat next to Roland with a vacant look on his face. He fidgeted with that silver mouth organ. He played a somber note, since he didn't know what else to say or do.

As for Roland, he focused on that candle. The melted wax framing the windowsill, dripping onto the floor. Only a charred, dead wick stuck out of the pearly-white remnants. Just like his father, the light had gone out.

Roland looked down at his hands. He wasn't sad, not really. He knew that sadness would probably come, but for now, he just felt angry. He knew what his father's job was. He also knew that look in the police commissioner's eyes.

Black Tom was no accident. The German agents had gone to blow up those munitions, and Sam Hawkins and his crew went to stop them. The ensuing foray had added Sam's name to the list of American war victims, a list that would only get bigger.

The espionage, and the lies about it, boiled Roland's blood. So did his new enemy that had no face and no name. It was just an idea. A whole group of people. Murderous people who hadn't contented themselves with killing everyone on land and sea in Europe. They had to take his father too.

Germans.

Roland's eyes blazed, and his insides turned to steel. He balled his hands into fists.

He would make them pay.

THREE
Ilse

July, 1917

Two years after the *Lusitania* sank, working as a nurse in Flanders, Ilse Stahl still cringed whenever she smelled smoke. It threw her back in time, to a horrible day when she woke up alone, naked and shivering, wrapped in a moth-eaten wool blanket in the hull of a crowded fishing boat.

The sailor, a bushy-bearded, middle-aged Irishman, had pulled dozens of people from the *Lusitania* debris, stuffing them into the tiny, creaking cabin of his practically dilapidated boat. His crew stoked up the wood stove to keep the survivors warm. It filled the tiny, pitch-dark room with eye-watering, nose-piercing, lung-searing smoke. It made Ilse cry and tremble in her blanket, traumatized at what she had seen, scared for what had become of her parents, and embarrassed to be without her clothes on a boat full of lusty fishermen.

No one harmed her though, and they eventually dumped her, and the rest of the survivors, ashore in Queenstown in County Cork. While the fishermen were poor and couldn't give her any money or food, they at least gave her a blanket to wrap around her waterlogged underclothes, which had been stiffly dried on the wood stove in that crammed boat.

Ilse stumbled about Queenstown in a daze, where survivors of every caliber had been brought by officials and makeshift rescue teams. People with vacant eyes, roughed-up life preservers, and ragged hair filled the streets. Churches flung open their doors so people had a place to sleep. Impromptu soup kitchens opened up in the city center. The Queenstown citizens vacated rooms in their homes for the torpedo-weary *Lusitania* survivors.

Morgues opened up too, in warehouses and factory floors. Scores and scores of bodies piled in from the ocean recovery teams. Rows and rows of sheet-covered forms, frozen figures, some half-decomposed and picked apart by sea creatures. Harried volunteers and medical personnel marked down anything they could use to identify them – soiled clothing, sea-stained jewelry, stopped watches, and waterlogged belongings.

After a hot meal at one of the many soup kitchens, and a fresh change of clothes from a church, Ilse tried to locate her parents. She went to every shelter and hospital. She pounded on the doors of people's houses. She combed the faces of strangers on the street. When all of that turned up no fruit, she took a deep breath and stepped into one of the makeshift morgues.

Which is where she found her father. His lifeless face stared back at her from underneath a ripped sheet. Frozen in the same horrified expression she'd seen when her grip had slipped from his back on the ship. She couldn't even cry as she looked down at this dead man who had once loved her. She could only reach out and brush her fingers against his icy hand. A hand that would never hold hers again, or dry her tears, or pet her hair. Or hug her.

She bit her lower lip as a nurse approached her from behind, clipboard in hand.

'Do you know this man, love?'

Ilse froze. Staring at her father's haunted gaze, she remembered all the warnings he had given her. The admonitions to never admit her German heritage. Not in England. Not in Europe. Not until the war was over. In those frozen eyes, she saw the same fear in his face that he had when he came home from the furniture shop, scared and hurt while his coworkers hollered outside.

'*It's a scary world*,' he had said. A scary world where Ilse tumbled into the Irish Sea and emerged into a war-torn continent with no papers, and no verification of who she was or where she came from.

So, she didn't answer the nurse's question. She just scampered out of the morgue and admitted the one thing she had dreaded since she landed in Queenstown.

Ilse Stahl was probably on her own now. Especially since more searching failed to turn up any signs of her mother, whose family was supposed to harbor them for the duration of the war. She was gone now, and so was any safety net that Ilse might have had.

There was nothing she could do but stumble from charity to charity in search of aid. She visited newly formed survivor foundations for food. She slept in churches or cold, windy alleyways. She had no idea what to do from one day to the next. Especially when most of the other survivors moved on, and the aid societies began to close down.

The fear and uncertainty would have paralyzed most people, but Ilse, from the moment she had snapped to action in the depths of the ocean, was determined to survive. She was so hell bent on it that she crammed the heart-shattering loss of her parents deep down into her soul. Far down in a place where she would never think of it again. Callous, perhaps, but she had no other choice. Because the minute she stopped or even slowed down, she knew she wouldn't be able to go on.

And going on was hard enough. After weeks shuffling through Queenstown trying to survive, one of the last charities for *Lusitania* survivors arranged to transport her to England. She wasn't keen on boarding another ship. Especially one loaded down with traumatized *Lusitania* steerage survivors, some still clinging to their sea-stained life jackets.

The liner's personnel crammed them all into a saloon converted into a barracks hall for the extra human cargo. They spent the entire voyage staring through lifeless eyes. A few of them took pulls from complimentary glasses of spirits, while others tried to soothe themselves with tea and scones. Any time the ship creaked, or someone shouted, or a seagull squawked, their eyes darted and their muscles locked. A few hid under their blankets. Some strapped on their ragged, torn, *Lusitania* life preservers and kept them on for the whole voyage.

Ilse spent most of the journey in a deep sleep, one she almost didn't care to wake up from. But she did wake up, because she had to survive, and her troubles were just beginning.

After she arrived in England, Ilse Stahl experienced firsthand what her father had so carefully warned her about. Anti-German sentiment lurked on every street corner, in every business, and every soup kitchen. Her overtly Prussian features, coupled with the fact that all her worldly possessions, including her papers, were lost at sea, made her life more than difficult. The people here weren't as willing to clothe and feed her. Her pleas for a meal or an extra coin garnered hard glares more than human sympathy. Most churches sent her away empty-handed. Citizens in a hurry practically kicked her out of their way.

The authorities were no help either. The American Embassy turned her away when she tried to claim citizenship with no papers. She went to British authorities next and told them about her mother's family, but she had no idea exactly where they lived. She had never seen the place with her own eyes. It didn't paint an honest picture. The British suspected her of using the *Lusitania* tragedy to her own manipulative, German-spying advantage. When they mumbled amongst each other about placing her under arrest, she took off.

Ilse didn't get help until days later. Starving and alone, shuffling around Liverpool, she found a humble, plain booth manned by lively women in medical uniforms. They had strung up a large banner with 'Hospital Personnel Wanted' printed on it. One girl yelled at passers-by to help the hospital efforts in France and Belgium. Money or manpower. They would take either one.

Ilse didn't know much about nursing, but she was a fast learner. She was also hungry and desperate. She volunteered her services on the spot.

The women drilled her with dubious eyes.

'Where you from, lass?'

'America.'

One of them snorted. 'America, my foot. Not with your looks and a name like Ilse. You're more German than a spiced bratwurst.'

'I was born in New York City.'

'Well, listen to that accent. You sure speak like a Yank, I'll give you that. Where are your papers then?'

Ilse couldn't say it. She couldn't even think it. Because if she did either one, she would freeze. And she had to keep going. She had to survive. 'Lost. I was involved in a . . . um . . . incident while crossing the ocean.'

That piqued the recruiter's interest. 'A U-boat incident? You and a thousand others these days. What barbarians that German race.'

The comment felt like a needle prick on tender skin, but Ilse had to swallow it.

'How do I know you're not a spy if you haven't got any papers?'

Ilse beckoned to her filthy, rumpled clothes, her tangled hair, and dirty skin indicating she hadn't bathed in days. 'Do I look like a spy?'

'Look there. You've got the motor of a Yank too. Do you have any nursing experience?'

'No, but I'm a hard worker. I'll do whatever you ask.'

The woman considered. 'We're a civilian operation, strictly volunteer, not military. Funded by some of Britain's wealthiest families. So prior training isn't a large requirement, unlike the more official corps. However, I'm not so sure I trust you.'

'Please. You don't even have to pay me. Just feed me and let me have a bath.'

Ilse's determination wavered the doubts of these nurses. They turned away from her and exchanged a few whispers.

One turned back to her. 'We'll be honest. We're not sure about you, but we like the cut of your American jib anyway. We'll give you a trial period. If you prove yourself, you can stay. If not, we'll have you arrested. Agreed?'

Ilse's eyes widened. They could decide any time she hadn't proved herself. And if they were indeed a civilian corps, they didn't have to answer to anybody or even have an official inquiry. They could just send her straight to the authorities, no questions asked. The experience she had with authorities so far told her that wouldn't be good.

It scared her to place her fate in such unreliable hands. However, she had to survive, and she had no room to be choosy.

'Agreed.'

FOUR
Roland

August, 1917, Belgium

Once the grief over his father finally arrived in Roland's heart, it never left. It just churned and strengthened into a ripping hunger for a fight, eventually growing so strong that it propelled him across the water to a land so far from his own, just so he could finally do something to right the wrongs.

Now, he stood in a wooden box car rumbling and clattering along rusting tracks. He wore the drab olive uniform of a British 'Tommy' private soldier. A tin helmet tilted over his head and covered his slicked hair. His eyes glowed out from beneath it like windows to his troubled soul.

The cars hurried across shell-riddled Belgium to deliver him to the front lines, where he would get his first real taste of the real war. He would finally see what he had only imagined when he sneaked aboard a Britain-bound steamer in New York Harbor all those months ago, desperate to make his way into a fighting army.

Rash, perhaps, but there wasn't much else he could do after his father died. Because after Hawkins Senior had left the world, the rest of Roland's life unraveled pretty quickly. His mother, despite a growing cough, threw herself into whatever work she could get. Roland also went to work every day, while Bernard took care of the house. It was a lot of work, but it wasn't enough. Only Sam's police pension kept them from losing their home all together.

Their dead father haunted them both, but Roland especially. Sam Hawkins lingered in his blood and whispered to him while he slept. On his way to work, he looked with savage bitterness at the windows Black Tom had left boarded and covered over. That was when his grief began to change, morphing into an anger and an energy that was all-consuming. Lethal, even.

He decided to go to the war, but at that time, America was still stuck in neutral. The *Lusitania* had generated plenty of smoke (along with plenty of political huffing and puffing), but no fire had caught.

Which made Roland feel like a mighty lion with its jaws clamped shut. He craved so badly to settle his score with the world, to fight the German infection polluting his own home shores. However, the only way he could fight for now was turning up his nose at Germans. He avoided their pubs and neighborhoods. He refused to fill orders from German customers.

By January of 1917, Roland had gone crazy with waiting. Poring over newspaper accounts of British gains had worn thin. He had a long conversation with Bernard and explained what he needed to do, and why. Bless his heart, Bernard took it in his stride, just like he had everything else thus far. So, Roland left the house and his mother under his brave brother's care, then he quietly crept aboard an England-bound steamer. After a week of bad food, submarine scares and throwing up on the rough seas, Roland stepped ashore in Liverpool, where he wasted no time visiting the various recruiting stations.

Although many wouldn't take a Yank from a neutral nation, the London Fusiliers had no qualms about it. Eventually.

Roland remembered sitting across from that stern-faced recruiter. One he had been told was a little more willing to thumb his nose at neutrality than most. The recruiter, a properly mustached man with a stiff, shiny uniform, broad shoulders, and very loud breathing, picked through Roland's American passport with a stern glare.

'You're American.'

Roland just nodded.

'You know that means I can't take you. Neutrality laws and such.'

'What if I was half Canadian?' Roland said with a wink. 'Eh?'

The recruiter was not amused. 'Suppose I went along with that. Because I could look the other way. I'm desperate for men, after all. But why in the world are you so desperate? Why in blazes would you want to get involved in this mess if you don't have to?'

Roland's eyes had gone steely then. His jaw set firm. 'Revenge.'

The recruiter shrank back from that a little bit. Then, without a smile, a smirk, or anything else, he slid a form across his desk. 'Sign here, please.'

So, with a few broken rules and some little white lies, Roland got into the British Army. Just for the Americans to officially declare war that April.

What luck.

Back in the present, Roland leaned against the rattling wall of his '40 hommes 8 chevaux' box car, one that could fit forty men or eight horses. However, many more than that now stood shoulder-to-shoulder in the tiny sweatbox of a train car. The only light and fresh air came from narrow slits near the roof. Men weighed down with combat gear shuffled and bumped into each other. A cough sounded here. Grumbling emerged there. Crass passes of gas, along with a smattering of giggles, polluted the already stifling air.

Roland kept a sharp eye on his fighting gear to distract himself. His rifle, extra ammunition, a gas mask, rain gear, iron rations, and a shovel, all of which made him dozens of pounds heavier and unsteady on his feet. As he struggled to keep his balance, his bayonet jabbed the man next to him.

'Hey, mate,' the soldier said in a stern, British accent. 'I'm no dame, so watch that poking device.'

Roland smirked. 'Sorry, Vernon.'

Vernon Thomas, a witty corporal the same age as Roland, with a boyish grin and goldenrod hair, grinned. Under his tin helmet, his steely eyes sparkled. 'Well, I'll forgive you this once, but I'll keep you clear of my sister, that's for sure.'

Roland scoffed. 'You told me she's ugly anyway.'

'A perfect match for you, then. You won't even need my father's approval. It'd be too hard to find his bones in the Somme.'

The comment poked Roland in a soft spot, reminding him how much he and Vernon had in common. Both had lost their fathers. Both had a younger sibling in their care, and both had never seen combat with their own eyes. It forged a bond between them during training.

Now, the train inched them closer to the dreaded Ypres Salient. Dubbed 'Wipers' by most British Tommies, the place had an awful reputation, with other nicknames that proved a lot more telling. 'A sacrificial ground,' 'a slaughterhouse,' 'a mud hole.' The soggy fields of Flanders had been fought over since 1914. It had become infamous as one of the worst battlefields in the war.

The train came to an abrupt halt in a chorus of screeches and groans. Boys pitched every which way, while the doors slid open and officers barked orders into the chaos.

'Come along then, out you go.'

'Move it. Don't slouch.'

'March! And march!'

The boys poured out of the boxcar and stepped onto a muddy,

partially bombed-out platform. A sign had been stuck in the dirt, with 'Poperinge' written on it. It pointed in the direction of the small town nearby.

Roland held his helmet with one hand and gripped his rifle with the other. He took in the gloomy, ashen sky and the gutted, carob earth. Splintered wagons, rusted barbed wire, and dead horses littered the outskirts of Poperinge. Yet the rest of the town tried to go on like normal. A few pubs were still in business. A church spire stood out. And, of course, there were the buildings that had been commandeered for hospitals. There were ambulances, army troops, refugees. All of them shouting and yelling at once.

Cool sprinkles of rain splatted on Roland's flushed cheeks, and the sound of rumbling thunder met his ears. At least that's what he thought it was at first. When the rumbling didn't stop, and the flashes of light on the horizon caught his eye, he realized nature wasn't the one who was rumbling. The guns of Flanders were.

On the other side of the bombed-out platform stood a host of British Ypres veterans. Mud drenched their uniforms. Filthy, blood-crusted bandages speckled their arms, legs, and faces. One hobbled around on crutches. Another rocked back and forth with his arms wrapped around his crossed ankles.

'Look there,' one of them said. 'Replacements for the cemetery.'

'Don't listen to him,' said his buddy. 'They hand out more decorations on this line than any other. The coveted wooden cross.'

They burst out laughing.

Roland felt his throat stiffen as he glared in their direction.

During training, he had shown the likes of those seasoned boys something crucial. Roland Hawkins was no typical recruit. He learned fast, pushing through every obstacle, mastering his rifle in record time. He finished first in almost every drill. Even the officers acknowledged him with respectful nods and salutes. He was ready to prove himself once and for all. Those grizzled old soldiers would be left in the dust by his prowess, and he took a step forward to tell them so.

But the smell hit him before he could open his mouth. A horrible, putrid odor that invaded his body and stabbed at his stomach. He doubled over and scrambled for a handkerchief in his piles of gear.

His misery drew more laughter from the hardened soldiers across the platform.

'You don't like the smell of dead people, mud, and shit all mixed into one? That's too bad because it's what your rations taste like.'

Vernon grabbed Roland by the elbow and hurried him along. 'Just like the farm back home. You'll get used to it after a while.'

'Mighty Lord, how can you stand it, Vernon?'

'Did you think war would smell like a basket of roses?'

'We're still miles away.'

'So, imagine how bad it will be when we get there. I say enjoy the fresh air while you have it.' Vernon pushed him forward once more.

Roland didn't budge. He buried his face in his handkerchief and tried to quell the nausea deep inside him.

Vernon glared. 'Come now. All that banging on during training about the medals you'll win and the Germans you'll kill. Here you can't even handle the smell.'

This time when Vernon pushed Roland, he forced his legs to obey, and the two marched along with the rest of the recruits. They formed clean rows of four and moved down the squishy road in columns. Their boots got weighed down by the sloppy mud. Their heavy rifles rubbed their shoulders raw, and their gear clanked loudly together with each step.

As they reached the town outskirts, Roland noticed a little stone house that the war had mostly left alone. It still had its charming picket fence, a sprawling front lawn, and a pleasant thatched roof. The sounds of hammers and wood saws emanated from behind it. The owners must have been carpenters of some type.

Roland found out exactly what type when the backyard came into view, where two men labored under the shadow of their finished products – piles upon piles of wooden crosses. There must have been close to a thousand of them. Crosses stacked against the house, heaped up in the yard, and leaning against the fence . . .

One of the men noticed Roland. He gave him a nasty grin and a mock salute.

Roland ripped his eyes away and glued them to the backs of the soldiers in front of him. The rumbling of the guns grew louder, the flashes more frequent. For the first time since he came to Europe, he felt a little more afraid than angry.

But his fear had come too late. He couldn't turn back now, nor did he want to. No matter what, Roland Hawkins was going to war.

FIVE
Roland

A sharp whistle blast cracked through the rain-drenched, mud-soaked, corpse-strewn battlefield. It rang through the maze of lip-to-lip shell craters, resembling the uneven surface of the moon. It startled all the rats growing fat off the bloated corpses, scattering them in a dozen different directions. It rippled through the slog and water puddles, tinted a greenish yellow from lingering remnants of poison gas.

The whistle also signaled the weary British soldiers. The ones still alive anyway. It was time to scramble over the top in another ridiculous assault on the enemy trenches. Ironclad German positions that hadn't yielded all summer, no matter how many British bodies the commanders threw into their merciless machine guns.

The soldiers emerged from battered shell craters, mud heaps, and piles of barbed wire. They had barely stepped onto the battlefield before the *rat-tat-tat-tat* of German guns cut through the smoke, mowing them down like weeds under a scythe. German artillery shrieked across the gray sky and smashed into the earth, kicking up sooty, inky geysers of mud and water, tossing handfuls of soldiers into the gooey muck. Weeks of shelling and relentless rain had turned Flanders into a giant bowl of frothy, sloppy, practically liquid mud.

One boy splashed knee-deep in the goop, pushing through a hastily carved-out path, with globs accumulating all down his pants. He suddenly slipped on the lip of a shell crater and splashed into a muddy sinkhole, where the mud gurgled and wrapped around him like a monster's tentacles. It glued his legs together and swirled up around his waist, pulling him down, down, down. He thrashed and splashed, kicked and screamed, and cried for help as soldiers flew past him on every side.

No one stopped. They wouldn't dare. Because zinging enemy bullets would put a quick end to any rescue mission.

Meanwhile, the mud crept up to the boy's chest and pulled down hard on his legs. He wailed again for help, and at last a man stopped.

Under the layers of filth and grime, a hint of Roland Hawkins still poked through. His brown eyes were hard and fierce, and his jaw set with determination. A few days in combat had turned him into a man all right.

He held out the end of his rifle to the panicking soldier. 'Grab hold, Collins.'

Collins tried to grasp the rifle with his muddied hands, but the suction was too strong. He couldn't get a firm grip. 'Help! It's pulling me under!'

Roland anchored his feet to give the boy a better chance. He heaved on his rifle while the kid hung on for dear life, the mud creeping up his body, wrapping around his collar bones.

'Help me, Hawkins! Help me!'

'Don't let go of the rifle. You hear me, Collins?'

'I'm getting pulled under!'

Roland let out a determined groan and gave another heave. In the damp and muddy weather, his hands slipped off the wooden rifle and he splashed back into his own pit of mud.

Collins went into hysterics when the mud curled around his neck. 'Shoot me, Hawkins! Shoot me! Shoot me!'

Vernon, or what was left of him, sloshed through the field to Roland's side. He fished Roland out of the mud, then he picked his rifle up and dug into the soggy ground around the screaming boy. He tried to create an escape path, but the sinkhole was worse than quicksand. He just turned up bones, body parts, and debris from past battles.

It was no use, and it had grown too dangerous. Bullets whizzed by their ears like wasps, and the debris from shell bursts sprayed them from all directions. Men ran by them in swarms only to be thrown to the ground by the vicious fire.

Vernon grabbed Roland by the collar. 'We have to move.'

'Shoot me!' Collins screamed again. 'For God's sake, shoot me!'

Vernon and Roland chanced one last look.

The mud had really caught Collins now, and they knew he was done. Drowning in mud had claimed too many soldiers in Ypres, and it was more than unpleasant to watch. It would be merciful to shoot the boy like he wanted, but neither of them had the courage to do it.

Vernon thrust Roland's rifle into his hands. 'Let's go.'

The boys tore off through the earth-shattering shells and screeching bullets. Soldiers splashed into the earth all around them. Men still on their feet moved forward in a daze. One was so distracted he didn't even flinch when his friend went down next to him. He didn't stop to help either. He just kicked his mate out of the way, like an angry dog, all his focus zeroed in on the carnage. Heartless, perhaps, but when that whistle blew, some men went into a war coma. They didn't know anything but the fight and their pending objective.

Today, their objective was a forward German rifle position. The sharpshooters in there had made hell for any Brit who dared venture his head out of the trench. Fed up with the extra deaths, the company captain had ordered Roland's small unit to take them out.

Well within range of the German trenches now, Roland noticed a band of rifles and bayonets popping through the mud like weathered wildflowers. He also saw a row of helmets that looked more German than British.

He ground to a halt and tapped Vernon on the helmet, pointing at the pocket. Vernon nodded; no words necessary. Combat had been a strong weld for their friendship. Usually with little communication, they each knew what they had to do.

Roland made it to the trench first. It was sturdy, miraculously so for the infamously soggy Ypres terrain. Even so, Roland dove into the muddy mess, landing right on top of some startled Germans. They were so drenched in mud he couldn't even see their faces. Which was fine, because it allowed him to dehumanize them. Turn them into the 'kill or be killed' army targets. Without faces, he could also blame them for his father's death. He could tell himself they deserved what they got.

Vernon pitched into the trench right after Roland. While his fierce American buddy took on the Germans one at a time, he pulled an old ration jam tin out of his pocket. He knelt to the ground and stuffed it full of loose powder, bits of metal, and spent bullet casings. He created a makeshift fuse out of torn fabric from his coat. He also rifled through his pockets and found matches. With shaking fingers, he struck one.

Meanwhile, one of the Germans emerged from the squirming pile of bodies and put a cocked pistol in Roland's face. '*Hände hoch,*' he screamed. '*Hände hoch!*'

At the same time, Roland put his loaded rifle right between the eyes of the squealing German. If either pulled a trigger, both would die. 'Drop your gun! Drop it!'

'Hände hoch!'

Only Vernon broke the intense stand-off when he tackled Roland and pressed him to the hard ground.

A half second later, the explosion from his improvised jam tin bomb sent hunks of hot metal and debris flinging through the entire entrenchment. It ripped holes in the wooden beams and pierced the hard skin of the vulnerable enemy soldiers.

As soon as the mud settled, it left quivering Roland and Vernon, along with a heap of bloodied Germans. About half of them had been killed outright, and the rest were too incapacitated to be a threat. The one who had almost killed Roland suffered a severed artery in his thigh. Blood spurted from it like a fountain. His body shuddered, and his eyes went wild. It didn't take long for death to call him home.

Roland turned away and glared at Vernon. 'Are you crazy? You could've blown the both of us up.'

Vernon brushed the dust off his arms and Roland's words off his back. 'You always were a little hothead with thin skin, weren't you? It was the cleanest way to take them all down at once.'

'It was still nuts.'

Vernon and Roland stayed down for a few seconds to catch their breath, then they heard a second shrill whistle blast.

Retreat. Another assault had failed.

Roland and Vernon climbed out of the trench and stumbled their way back across no man's land. They went the same way they came, so they wouldn't slip off into uncharted territory and unknown mud pits waiting to drown them. As they scrambled across the field, chased by machine guns and enemy artillery, Roland caught sight of an awful land marker.

Collins was gone. Only the top of his helmet and a small, lifeless tuft of hair remained.

The pitiful remains of Roland's company stood before their captain that evening, in trenches built from nothing more than a few shell craters knotted together. Men had dug sleeping holes into the muddy walls. Mountains of sandbags were piled here and there. Slime-covered duck boards served as an unstable, wobbly walkway.

The men standing on them were nothing but pillars of mud, with blood-soaked bandages wrapped around their heads, hands, or legs.

A few of them puffed on soggy cigarettes as they stood at attention. Others dug into cans of bully beef and crackers smeared with mud. Toward the end of the line, Roland and Vernon stood next to each other with their faces forward.

The captain's uniform looked spotless, with its fancy markings and crisp folds. A symptom of the better accommodations he and other officers shared, probably in a house with beds, water, and even heating. He held a chart and clipboard in his clean, unbruised hands, and he walked with precision down the line of muddy soldiers.

'Smith,' he said.
'Here.'
'McKenny.'
'Here.'
'Matthews.'
'Wounded.'
The captain looked up. 'Status?'
The man who had answered for Matthews took a long drag off his cigarette. 'Shot in the face. Took one of his eyes out. Hope the stretcher team got him.'

The captain made a mark on his chart and continued. 'Collins.'

Roland started at the name, the sound of the shrill screams, the pleading to be shot, and the gurgling of the mud all crash-landing into the front of his mind.

'Collins,' the captain repeated with a bark.

Roland let out a grunt. 'Dead.'

The captain froze for a split second, although he heard this word often enough. He made another mark on his chart. He walked down the line and stood across from Vernon and Roland. 'You boys managed to take out the front segment of the rifle unit?'

'Yes, sir,' they replied.

'By yourselves?'

'And a little help from luck, I suppose.' Vernon gave Roland a nudge with his elbow.

Some snickers sounded off across the trench, and even the stiff captain cracked a smile. 'Roland "Lucky" Hawkins. The nickname suits you after all the stunts you've pulled. You have wild cowboy blood or something?'

'No, sir.'

'You just want to get killed then? Why else do you always want to take on the whole German army yourself?'

Roland didn't answer. He just stared straight ahead with a distinct hardness in his eyes.

'Well, fine then. I guess I should thank you two. Those snipers have been a bane for days. Perhaps a decoration might be in order.'

Roland's chest puffed up at the thought, but Vernon just scoffed. 'I'd rather have a hot meal.'

More giggling.

The captain wasn't amused this time. 'All right then, let's get on with our assigned work details. McKenny and Smith, trench repair. Jackson and Burns, guard duty. Hawkins and Thomas, listening post.'

Roland and Vernon exchanged annoyed glances. Listening post topped the list of the most dreaded work details. It involved taking what amounted to a giant stethoscope up into no man's land, where they crawled through the soupy mud and listened for mining activity deep in the ground below. It exposed the unlucky workers to gunfire and snipers along with the other displeasures of the battlefield at night. Like rats, dead bodies, and the atrocious, sickening smell.

Vernon glared at the captain. 'We had listening post last night.'

'Then you've had loads of practice for tonight, haven't you?'

'We shouldn't have to do it twice in a row.'

'Orders are orders, Vernon, and this is just the way it was assigned tonight. We all have to do our work details. Off you go. And don't forget your hot meal.' The captain tossed them a few cans of bully beef.

As soon as darkness fell, Roland and Vernon gathered their rifles and the clunky listening apparatus, then they climbed up the trench fire step.

Star flares screeched through the night sky, bathing the whole battlefield in a fizzing, white-hot glow, transforming anyone caught in the open into a perfect target. The smattering of guns raged for however long the star flares stayed alight. More men fell, the flare faded out, then all was quiet until the next flare went up. Sometimes minutes, sometimes hours later.

Even without the star flares, the darkness was still hell. Mainly because of the wounded, crying out through the vastness. Their shouts for mother, for home, and for water echoed all over the battlefield. In the dark it was like listening to ghosts, disembodied haunts warning the living of what their inevitable fate would be.

Then there were the corpses. So many of them, tangled and swinging in the rusted barbed wire, awaiting burial at the lip of the trench, picked apart by hordes of rats. Bodies and body parts all over the field, soggy and gory, riddled with bullet holes, faces gaping into the night. Some had even died bayoneting each other, still propped up on each other's rifles. Blood reddened the water at the bottom of certain shell craters, indicating that more bodies were buried underneath. There were older bodies too, soldiers that went over the top in 1915. Reduced to muddied bones and rotted shreds of outdated uniforms.

In the midst of all that, Roland carved a clean path in the slime while Vernon ran the listening cone along the liquid ground. He pressed the hearing piece to his ear.

'Like we'll hear anything in this mess,' Roland said. 'Isn't there any way around the damn mud?'

Vernon tilted his head to get a better read. 'Oh, come now, all that hell fury in your blood, I thought you enjoyed yourself out here.'

Roland dropped his eyes to the ground. He didn't know how to tell Vernon that a few days in combat had put a permanent halt to his crowing, braggart training days. Because when he had imagined the war back then, he saw banners flying, drums rolling, and mud-free, shining uniforms. He saw men charging each other with gleaming swords and jangling boots across a field of honor.

Instead, war was a world of poison gas and bloody attrition. None of the uniforms glowed or gleamed under their layers of mud. Generals just threw more men at the hungry machine guns and hoped they would somehow break through. It required no skill, no prowess, and no man-to-man battles. It was all luck and nothing more. Either a bullet would find Roland or it wouldn't. When it did, he would vanish in the mud, never to be seen or heard from again. There would be no medals, no funerals, and no traces of him for his family to mourn.

It was no way to save anyone, least of all his family back home.

Especially Bernard. How would he save Bernard? The baby brother whose frequent letters still smacked of innocence and were devoid of war fever. However, he would get sucked into this hell soon enough, now that their own country had finally declared war . . . just a few months after Roland had signed on with the British.

Vernon brought Roland's thoughts back to their work. 'So quiet all of a sudden. Looking forward to reserve like the rest of us then?'

Roland glared. 'You don't get medals sitting in the reserve trench.'

'Oh, Christ, you and your medals. You've proved your point, boy. You hate Germans and you're good at killing them. But even your luck is bound to run out. So, what is it you're really after anyway?'

Roland just dug in the mud a little harder.

Vernon took note. 'Are all the Yankees as hot-headed as you? We're in for a real treat if so.'

Roland just rolled his eyes with bitterness. He didn't need yet another reminder that if he had just held out a little longer, had a touch more patience, he could have gone to battle under his own flag. Maybe beside his own brother. Now he sat in British fatigues in a mud hole he had never imagined. So far away from home and anything that felt familiar.

Which forced him to think about some unpleasant realities. Like why he had come here in the first place, and why it really mattered. Because it certainly hadn't satiated him the way he thought it would. There was no scratching the itch for revenge here in this mud hole, facing down shells and machine guns every day. Being a number instead of a name, which felt so futile and meaningless.

Perhaps, he had thought to himself more than once, it might mean more under his own flag, with his own people. Fighting for his own home. His own brother. They were thoughts that had made him decide that he would find a way into the American army, one way or another. It would hurt to leave Vernon behind. Yet he had to make this mean something. He had to find a way to fill the emptiness. To get out of the mud and make a real difference.

Surely the US would want him, given his experience. He might even get a break from the fighting while he switched uniforms, and wouldn't that be nice? They also might have him train some of the new boys or even lead his own regiment. Something that would feel like a real purpose in a war that seemed to lack purpose above all else.

But he had to wait for his moment. After all, he had illegally joined up with a foreign army. A form of treason in some people's eyes. It couldn't hurt to earn some credentials before he knocked on Uncle Sam's door. Hence the desire for medals.

Another star flare shot up, and Roland and Vernon ducked into the mud. They froze in place while the flare crackled above them, washing the battlefield in light. Gunfire came from the German trenches, then came the screams of British patrols caught in the open. After the flare fizzled out, the pair went back to their work like nothing had happened.

Vernon clenched his teeth as he ran the cone over the mud. 'You know I haven't seen a shred of green in this soil for weeks.'

'I can't imagine you will either.'

'There's just mud, rats, and more mud.' Vernon mopped some slime off his forehead. 'Maybe when I see my first bit of color, the first poppy or the first shoot of green. When I dig in the mud and pull up something other than bones, I'll know the war is coming to an end.'

Roland smiled. 'That's a pretty romantic notion for someone so surly.'

Vernon went to answer the retort, but both boys locked in place as footsteps cropped up nearby. Some eerie whispers in a German dialect accompanied them.

Roland's eyes widened and he made a grab for his gun, but Vernon clamped a hand over him.

'Hold your fire.'

'What the hell for?'

'You don't know how many there are. If it's a full patrol, we'd be outnumbered and dead before you crack one shot off.'

Roland burrowed a little deeper into the mud, and Vernon did the same. They hunkered down like ground moles in no man's land, trying not to move or even breathe too loud.

The footsteps came closer, and Roland could now hear some German words. While he didn't fully understand the language, he got the distinct feeling the Germans were aware of him and Vernon. He tried to keep still despite the mud tickling the back of his neck.

The footsteps were just a few feet away now. In seconds, the Germans would step right over them. They would put a bullet in their heads before they could even signal for help. Just like that, it would all be over. No medals, no American army, no nothing. He'd never see his home again. Never see his brother again. And his mother . . . what about his mother?

Roland's heart slammed in his chest. He closed his eyes. He held his breath, and he waited for the fatal shot to find him.

Then, one of the Germans slipped in the mud and splashed into a water-filled shell hole.

'Donner and Blitzen!'

The accident garnered ruckus laughter from his German patrol mates, which attracted the wrong sort of attention. A British machine gun homed in on them and opened fire.

The German soldiers scrambled for cover. They dove into shell holes, behind piles of debris, and even behind dead bodies to hide from the spray of bullets.

As for Roland and Vernon, they had been saved by a lucky tumble into a shell hole, and they decided right then and there that the listening post was done for the night. Careful to dodge the buzzing hail of lead and glaring tracers, they packed up their equipment and picked their way back through the mud on their hands and knees. They fell into the safety of their trenches a few minutes later, breathing heavily and marveling that Roland's lucky streak had held once more. He laughed along with his troops as if he hadn't been scared at all.

But inside, he felt chilled and heavy. It was the closest he had come to death or capture, and it chiseled yet another small fissure into his arrogance.

Perhaps Vernon was right. No one's luck could last forever in the war to end all wars.

SIX
Ilse

August, 1917, Flanders

It didn't take long in the nursing world for Ilse to really prove herself. Especially when it came to driving ambulances. As she drove one of the lumbering, sputtering, squeaky vehicles around the bombed-out soil, relishing in every bump, jostle, and shake, she felt like nothing but a natural. This despite being one of the only women in the entire ambulance training program.

'Hard right,' the instructor said to her, clinging to his seat in the rough terrain.

Ilse jerked the wheel. The vehicle protested a little, but she quickly forced it to obey her command. Working the gear shifter just right. Not hovering her foot over the brake pedal too much. Pumping the gas, clutching the wheel, and keeping that vehicle on the straight and narrow. The same skill she had demonstrated all morning through her final test for certification to drive and operate an ambulance on the front lines.

Even the instructor couldn't help but be impressed, nodding his approval. 'Now left.'

Ilse jerked the wheel again, unafraid, unapologetic. Which surprised her just a little. After all, she had every reason to be nervous. Before taking these courses, she had never driven a vehicle before in her life. She'd barely even pedaled a bicycle, let alone tried to maneuver around in a big car. Yet the second she sat in the driver's seat of that ambulance, she felt nothing but excitement. That, and control. So much control. Being in the driver's seat meant that she called the shots. She made the decisions. She was master of her own fate.

For once.

Ilse wheeled the car back around the makeshift obstacle course, designed by an actual ambulance corps to test her skills. Weed her out. Prove to her that she couldn't measure up to the rest.

But Ilse could measure up all right, and she would damn well show them. Just like she showed the nursing corps how quickly she could learn and make herself useful. Within weeks of her arrival in war-battered Belgium, she was one of the finest nurses at her hospital. Although, she didn't quite fit in with the other girls as much as she'd hoped. They all seemed to keep her at arm's length. They left her out of things. They gave her questioning glances and harsh looks sometimes. Still, Ilse was good at what she did, and she put her whole heart into every task. Even if it was more menial things like changing bedding and mopping up mud.

As far as training for actual nursing duties, Ilse absolutely flew through the worst that they could throw at her. She may have had no prior experience, but she quickly mastered the basics, like tying off wounds, cleaning open cuts, and administering basic first aid. She did so well, so quickly, that she moved up the ranks rather fast. It wasn't long at all before she was assisting in more important duties like triage and minor surgeries, in addition to her other tasks like cleaning up muddy soldiers and keeping up with paperwork.

But she still didn't earn many friends. Except the matron, who seemed to like her and her skills well enough. One day, she came to Ilse and suggested she sign up for the driving courses.

'But it's all men,' Ilse had said.

'So?' The matron challenged her. 'They'll need women sure enough when the rest of the men go to the trenches. So, go and show them what you're made of, Ilse Stahl.'

The driving instructor cut into Ilse's thoughts. 'KABOOM!' he shouted. 'A shell just hit the road! What do you do?'

It was pretend, of course. A shell hadn't really hit the road. But it very well could someday, and that's just what the instructor was trying to train her for. Ilse didn't disappoint him either. Without a single shred of nerves, and just like she'd been taught, she pumped the breaks and turned the wheel over hard. Ensuring that were this the real thing, she would have maintained control of the vehicle yet also dodged the worst of the concussion blast and debris.

A masterful bit of driving.

The instructor nodded again. 'Well, young lady, you're very talented, aren't you?'

Ilse just gave him a haughty sniffle in return, easily pulling the vehicle back onto the road. Of course she was talented. She knew she was talented. Perhaps that was why she had taken to the entire medical field like a duck to water. Maybe the *Lusitania* had prepped her for it all somehow. Hardening her, turning her into a survivor. Which obviously translated to being an excellent medical team member.

Yes, her skills were undeniable, and they had at least got her enough respect to stay at the hospital. But the friendship door stayed firmly closed, with an impenetrable wall put up too.

Ilse knew what the wall was, of course. It was the big, Kaiser-shaped elephant in the room. Her heritage was an open secret. Even if the matron had looked past it because of her talent, the other girls didn't trust her, and they didn't seem willing to try.

Yet Ilse really wanted them to try. She wanted to be their friend. So, she worked harder, faster, and tried to be smarter. She covered shifts when other girls were tired. She took care of them when they didn't feel well. She even taught them things, since she wound up so far ahead of them in training. All so she could prove herself and earn their friendship.

She was certain she would earn it eventually. Because it wasn't like she was the only stranger to be found at the hospital. On the contrary, she was lumped in with quite a random crowd that came from a range of different backgrounds and countries. While the vast majority of the nurses were English, some were French, a sprinkling were Belgian, and a handful even hailed from America. Some came from mansions with marble halls, some had donned the silken robes of noble ladies, and more than a few had worked their way up from the poverty-stricken coal and factory families. Some of the women had proper schooling, while others couldn't even read.

So many different women from so many different places. They were in fact so varied that it seemed their only common link was their urge to help, which allowed Ilse to stop feeling like a misfit. While she couldn't boast even one real friend, she at least became part of the furniture instead of a weird foreign centerpiece, which helped her feel like she belonged in at least some little way. Not to mention, it helped her, through all the craziness, to discover her real self. A hard worker. A worthy human. A talented woman.

A survivor. Despite everything life had tried to throw at her.

Ilse returned her attention back to the road, whipping the jalopy ambulance around a tight curve. As the mechanical shed where it lived came into view, she slammed on the breaks. At first, it felt like the vehicle would tip. The instructor cursed and held on accordingly. But Ilse brought it under control at the last minute, landing it perfectly outside the mechanical hut. With a flare, she killed the engine, then she sat back in her seat and grinned.

The instructor brushed himself off, then frowned in her direction. 'So, you have a wild streak? Is that it?'

'Something like that.'

He shook his head. 'Well, the only woman on this team or not, there's no denying your skill. I'm going to recommend you for front-line service. I'm thinking a shuttle between casualty clearing stations and hospitals further back. Would that suit you?'

Ilse smiled.

Yes, that would suit her just fine. As did the rest of her life in the medical service. New York City, her mother and father, even the *Lusitania*. It all felt like another time. A bad dream. Pages in a dusty book she couldn't throw away, but couldn't open either. Any thoughts she had of finding her mother's family had faded away under the mud and rain of Flanders. This was her life now. People needed her here, whether they wanted to admit it or not. And what she had needed more than anything else was a purpose.

Now, she had found one.

SEVEN
Roland

The morning after their listening post shift, Roland and Vernon watched the battlefield get soaked under yet another rainstorm, which brought all of the fighting to a sopping standstill. Occasional sniper bullets snapped down unwitting victims. Single artillery shells, from the few mounts that weren't waterlogged, screeched here and there. Other than that, the battlefield was quiet. One could almost call it peaceful.

Especially since the rain had put a halt to work details, with soldiers burrowing in their cubbyholes instead. Some tried to write letters home on soggy paper. Some played cards with their bare butts inside German helmets and their pants around their ankles. Some took their shirts off, plucked all the lice, and mashed them between their fingers. Still others raced fat rats for a little excitement, cheering and kicking their chosen racers down the trench.

Roland and Vernon spent their downtime digging into ration cans, watching a group of younger boys standing at the lip of the trench. They squealed with laughter while they pushed and shoved each other.

'I bet Simmons will drop first,' one said.

'Sod off, mate,' Simmons replied. 'I've nerves of steel.'

The third boy cackled. 'Becket is going down first. I've put my last earning on it.'

When the whistle of an incoming shell cropped up, the boys braced and stood still as statues. They didn't duck for cover like everyone else. They just jabbed and sneered at one another. Seconds before the incoming shell burst, a few of them bowed to their instincts and dropped. The explosion rattled the trench, caved in some walls, and displaced a few heavy guns. Then the debris settled, and the boys still on their feet howled with laughter. Money changed hands from those who had ducked to those who hadn't.

Roland and Vernon watched the childish shenanigans while they leaned on each other's backs to stay dry.

'It won't be so funny when they're buried alive,' Vernon said between bites of food.

'At least they found something to do, I guess.' Roland chomped on some bully beef. 'And made some money to boot.'

'You're so fond of it, why don't you go over and play?'

'You don't get medals playing chicken with the artillery.'

'You and your goddamn medals. So pathetic.'

Roland chewed his lower lip in reply. After all this time, he still hadn't told Vernon the real reason why he needed medals. It made him feel cold inside. Because since basic training, he and Vernon had stuck to each other like glue. The little corporal would be upset when he learned Roland wouldn't see him through to the end.

He sighed. 'Vernon, I need to tell you something, pal.'

'You've finally given up on glory then? Well, I don't blame you.' Vernon scooped another bite of bully beef. 'Although if you ask me, a bullet to the face could only improve your looks.'

Roland laughed. He would miss that wit when he went away. He would also miss Vernon's uncanny ability to keep his over-inflated ego in check by reminding him what was at stake. Not medals. Not glory. Just his life.

He hesitated, twiddling his thumbs. 'I have another reason for needing those medals.'

'Lord, Hawkins. You're sick in the head.'

'It's not about glory.'

'What then? Are those American lassies so hard to impress?'

Even in the heavy rain, Roland's hands got sweaty with nerves. Facing the German guns felt easier than disappointing his closest friend. 'The Americans . . .' He trailed off and hung his head in frustration, while a stream of curses rolled through his mind.

'The Americans . . .?' Vernon nudged him. 'Spit it out, old boy. You sitting on some juicy gossip I haven't heard yet?'

'Vernon, this unit has been good to me, but . . .'

Vernon read his mind and his eyes went dim. 'Oh Lord, my Lucky. You're leaving us, aren't you?'

Roland didn't look up, but he could still feel the sting from Vernon's sharp gaze. 'I wouldn't have signed on here if I knew the US was joining. I blame them for waiting so damn long.'

Vernon couldn't conceal the mist in his eyes, no matter how hard he tried to.

Roland knew it wasn't from the rain. 'Come, Vernon, you understand, don't you? My brother will get conscripted. He'll need my help. Wouldn't you do the same for Celia?'

Vernon somberly stirred his bully beef around. 'Please. She doesn't need my help. She'd scare the Germans off with her ugly face.'

Roland chuckled to break the ice.

'And the medals? What has that got to do with it?'

'I broke a lot of rules to join this regiment. Told some lies. Signed on some dotted lines that I probably should have looked at a bit closer.'

'What, like treason?'

Roland shrugged. 'Maybe to some. Either way, if I want a transfer to a US unit, it couldn't hurt to have a bit better service record.'

Vernon wolfed down another bite of his rations. 'And how do you figure on getting out of this unit in the first place? Didn't you sign on for the duration of the war?'

Roland looked out into the rainy battlefield. 'I haven't figured everything out yet, but I will. And soon. Because I have to, Vernon. I have to go home.'

After a moment of icy silence, Vernon put a limp hand on his friend's shoulder. 'Well, no need to explain yourself to me, mate. But don't expect me to be happy about it.'

A sniper bullet suddenly buzzed through the air and cracked into the group of boys playing chicken, clipping one of them right through the forehead. He sprawled back through the trench and splashed into the water at the bottom. His body twitched for a few seconds then lay still.

Vernon shoveled another bite of bully beef into his mouth. 'I suppose they'll count that as ducking.'

Roland went to reply, but shouts laced with cursing came from somewhere down the trench. He threw his rations aside and got to his feet.

From around the corner, a small group of soldiers, soaked to the bone, barreled down the sloppy, narrow trench. Behind them came a raging wall of flood water, sweeping away everything in its path. It tore down sleeping quarters, crashed through wooden barricades, and swiped away the duck boards. Even sandbags were useless against the mighty tide.

Some soldiers made a mad grab for any equipment they could, while others scrambled and bunched around the ladders in droves, shouting and screaming as the water came for them like a mighty, roaring wildcat. A few who didn't move fast enough got yanked into its beastly claws. As for the rest, they hurried up the ladders or climbed over the slimy trench wall *en masse*. Once up top, soldiers cursed and tried to mop up their soaked uniforms, pushing and shoving for a position in the middle of the crowd, trying to shield themselves from enemy bullets.

But they shouldn't have worried so much. Because across the torn barbed wire and mud holes of no man's land, the Germans were too distracted battling the exact same problem. They shrieked and howled in German. Some labored in the pounding rain to pull equipment up from the water, or heave weakened soldiers out of the mess.

Amid the turmoil, another river suddenly rose up on both sides – one of tension and fear. German and British soldiers hesitantly looked at one another, unsure of what to do. Some put a nervous hand on their guns, drilling their eyes into the soldiers across from them.

A knot appeared in Roland's stomach. He wrapped his hands around his rifle, his grip so tight his knuckles showed white. Fear flickered in Vernon's eyes. A few men next to them nervously shuffled their feet and reached for weapons. Just when it looked like a mini battle would break out in the rain, a peel of laughter erupted from the German line.

A stocky soldier of the Kaiser, with an impressive build that strained his leather belt, stepped forward. He shook water off himself like a stray dog. He pointed at both his comrades and the enemy, and he bellowed with laughter at the fix they were all in.

It quickly became infectious. Giggles scattered down the rest of the German line, then they all began jabbing and teasing one another. They helped brush loose sand and mud off uniforms. They squeezed trench filth from their hair and skin.

Their silly attitudes broke the heavy tension like the shells broke the earth. The British soldiers relaxed a little. A few smiles pulled on their cold, blue lips.

Only Roland couldn't relax. He still glowered at the soldiers across the way, his hands glued to his rifle, his stomach boiling over. These German soldiers, who found their awful situation so hilarious, had caused immense pain and suffering throughout the world, even in his own living room. He didn't find that even a little bit funny. In fact, that familiar fire surged through Roland's blood like the floodwaters through the trenches. So did temptation. All those enemy soldiers ripe for the picking, well within range. His fingers flirted with the lock on his rifle. He pulled it back to the firing position.

The stocky German squinted through the rain and noticed the dangerous look on Roland's face, the active mode of his rifle. It just made him laugh even harder. He pointed his own gun at Roland with a playful sneer. Then, he let out a yell of sheer exhaustion. A yell that said he was tired of killing people in the rain and mud, while the people who started the war were safe and warm in their palaces, far away from the misery. With one fluid motion, he whirled his rifle up over his head. Then he smashed it against the side of a battered piece of concrete from a broken pillbox. A loud crack echoed across the battlefield as the rifle shattered into pieces.

There would be no more killing with that gun.

The Germans broke out into cheers, surrounding their comrade, pummeling him with hugs and claps on the back.

Roland just stared at the crazy German, still dancing around with his comrades. Everyone, British and German alike, now doubled over with smiles and laughter. They had deadly differences, but they could all unite under one banner – they were fed up with this filthy old war. Fed up with being the cannon fodder for imperialistic rulers and haggling politicians. Fed up with generals who treated them like nothing but expendable numbers.

It cracked the veil over Roland's war-crazy eyes. Back in America, newspapers had fed him a full diet of grisly stories about the German race and their atrocities. He lived in fear of their spy rings in the city, and their submarines in the oceans. He had watched their antics snuff out his father's life. He had grown to hate them so deeply it felt poisonous. He had been told, and seen with his own eyes, that German soldiers were hard men who wouldn't back down from a fight. They would kill in the name of their blood-lusting Kaiser until the last man.

But then came this dancing soldier who had just smashed his rifle on a rock. He and his friends were done fighting.

For today anyway.

That was something, wasn't it?

The rain finally stopped late that afternoon, and the flood waters slowly receded. Once it was safe, the boys dropped back into their trenches and, like a well-oiled machine, they began repairs. They slopped gooey mud back into place. They pushed the drowned corpses out of the trench. They stacked waterlogged sandbags, and they reformed the holes where they slept.

Roland worked in silence alongside Vernon. He noticed the little corporal wasn't as talkative as usual, avoiding his eyes and constantly turning his back. It made him fear his attempt to stay honest had put up a wall between them. He tried to think of a witty remark, but a low, steady drone from the gray, sullen dome stopped him.

Roland tilted his head back and saw a single English biplane wobbling its way over no man's land, drifting and bumping along on the sharp air currents.

Back stateside, Roland had known nothing of the newfangled art of aviation. He had never even seen an airplane. Aviation had only cropped up in the occasional news story on the back page of small-town papers. Here, aviation was headline news. Vast and widespread. Entire patrols of a dozen planes flew over any time the sky allowed for it. Roland had even seen actual dogfights from his hiding place in the trenches.

'Is it the bloody Red Baron?' one of the soldiers nearby asked. 'Coming to pick a fight with us, is he? Someone get me a gun!'

His buddy huffed and smacked him across the back of the head. 'Are you blind? Of course it isn't the Red Baron. Like the most famous pilot in the war is going to come flying over a British trench and get shot to pieces. Besides, this plane has British markings.'

The first soldier ignored his buddy. 'Ooh, I'd love to see the Red Baron. Just one glimpse of that scarlet biplane!'

'Oh, come off it. He's German. You ought not to root for a German.'

'It's different in the air war, you know that. They're all heroes.'

The Red Baron. Different in the air war. They're all heroes. It gave Roland a flutter of longing in his muddy chest. Because that soldier was absolutely right. Airplanes were the personal war he had craved when he came over here. Man against man. A place where skills mattered as well as smarts and prowess. Not to mention, pilots like the Red Baron didn't eat dry beef and hard crackers out of tin cans. They got real meals, and clean beds with clean sheets. Mud didn't invade every facet of their lives. Rats probably didn't, either. Both sides of the Atlantic treated their pilots like modern-day knights. Their exploits, their kills, their lifestyle, their women, all of it got splashed across the front pages of the newspapers.

Roland had never flown an airplane before. Hell, he had never even sat in one. But things he excelled at now had all been brand new when he arrived here. He didn't see how learning airplanes would be any different. He wondered if the US troops would start up their own air corps. If so, they would need legendary knights of their own to offer up to their public.

Perhaps, someday, Roland Hawkins could be one of them.

EIGHT
Roland

Roland locked his cold hands around the wooden ladder to keep his balance on the side of the dugout. His helmet strap locked his chin in its stinging, leathery grip. A heavy, damp rifle hung off his shoulder, practically wrenching it out of place.

Peering over the lip of the trench, he saw loops of rusted barbed wire, spread out like a wheat crop across the field, speckled with the white bones of long-dead soldiers. Steam rose up from the old shell craters, while British artillery made new craters, screaming across no man's land and smashing into the German lines. The repercussions shook the trenches and thundered deep in Roland's chest, pulling and tugging at his jostled innards.

He hoped this artillery barrage would do more damage than the previous ones, but he had seen with his own eyes the elaborate, reinforced enemy trenches. He knew the German soldiers were waiting this out safely underground, with little more than dust displacement in their caves. In reality, the shells probably did more damage to British nerves than anything else.

This was evidenced by the dozens of soldiers who had bunched up behind Roland at the base of the ladder, standing still and rigid. Hearts pounded and hands shook. Fingers picked at imaginary mud and gripped slimy rosary beads. One man held a prayer book with a picture of the Savior on it. *With Jesus in the field*, the cover said.

A sobbing, wailing young boy in the back of the huddle, fresh from the replacement line, pressed his hands to his ears, while a urine stain appeared on the front of his pants.

A hardened old vet with a sergeant stripe tried to talk some sense into him. 'Get a hold of yourself, lad. Crying won't chase the Jerries off. Come now.'

'Talking won't do him any good,' another soldier said. 'Try a hand across the mouth.'

'I already did. That's what set off the waterworks.'

'Got any liquor ration?'

'If only. Those quartermasters drink enough to float the British

Navy and leave barely a tot for us.' The sergeant put his arms around the sobbing boy's shoulders. 'Come now, there's a good lad. It will be over in a wink, just you wait and see.'

Roland turned his eyes back to the battlefield. Perhaps he hid his nerves better than that boy, but fear still exploded with the ferocity of those shells, deep inside his gut. His whole stomach churned, and he felt like he too would soil his pants if the shelling didn't let up soon.

He reached into his pocket and pulled out a dirty, crinkled envelope. His thumb ran over the seal, and the return address from his brother, Bernard. The first mail he'd had in weeks, but he wouldn't open it. Not yet anyway. He had decided with grim determination that he would save it until after the assault. A letter from Bernard would give him extra reason to not give up on the battlefield, no matter how hopeless it looked.

He gave the letter a final squeeze and pocketed it, swallowing the cannonball that had cropped up in his throat. As he shifted position, he carefully avoided Vernon, who clung to the ladder rung just below him. Exhaustion had dulled the corporal's eyes, and his hair had turned brown from layers of dirt and mud. He reached behind his neck to scratch at the merciless lice. Then out of nowhere, he leaned over the side of the ladder and tossed his breakfast.

At long last, the echoes of the explosions died away, leaving a battlefield marred in smoke. Then came the captain's piercing whistle blast.

'Over the top, boys!' he screamed. 'And give them hell!'

Roland led the entire company in scrambling up over the ladders and stomping out into the battlefield. As soon as he made it up top, the mud yanked at his ankles like quicksand. He hugged his rifle and sucked in his gut to dodge the rusty claws of the barbed wire. The cold, damp wind blasted his cheeks and stung the tops of his ears. Sulfurous smoke from the shells roiled his nose and stomach.

With his company, he threaded through the barbed-wire fields and fanned out across no man's land. As they approached the German trenches, he saw that, as he had feared, their cruel bombardment hadn't deterred the German machine gunners in the slightest. Bullets flew across the scattered ranks, and a soldier right in front of Roland went down hard, the side of his head ripped off. Somehow, he was still alive when he hit the ground, although it was no doubt a fatal wound. It was just cruel enough to not take him instantly. He could linger in pain for days. Maybe weeks.

Another British soldier stopped to examine the wound, despite the atrocious fire. With one hand, he smoothed the boy's hair and talked to him in cooing whispers. With the other, he pulled a pistol out and cocked it.

Roland knew it was the merciful thing to do, but he couldn't stay and watch the rest. So, he pressed on through the madness, glad the raging battlefield dulled the single pistol shot behind him. He couldn't think about it. He had to keep moving. Moving targets were harder to hit.

From within the thick smoke, the lines of the German forward entrenchments materialized. The haze lifted as if parting the curtains for a dramatic play, and a pair of German soldiers emerged. One held a long tube in his hands, while the man behind him held some kind of tank. They both sported eerie masks, built to sustain some serious heat.

Before Roland could ask any questions, or wonder what the heck kind of weapon this was, the German with the tube pulled a trigger, and a stream of neon orange liquid fire gurgled out of the tank and sprayed out of the tube. It instantly melted anything it touched into red-hot, roaring flames, transforming the ground from a cold mud pit to a raging inferno, blanketed in choking, black smoke.

Just in time, Roland screeched to a halt, covered his head, splatted into the slimy mud and ducked for cover. The soldiers next to him weren't as quick. They ran right into the newly erupted fire wall and instantly broke out into hideous screams. The chilling sound of sizzling flesh seared the air as the flames dissolved their bodies, plopping their liquefied skin to the ground.

It was the dreaded *flammenwerfer*, one of the worst of the German death tools. Roland had heard plenty of rumors, but until now he hadn't actually seen one in action. He trembled in the mud as the shrieks and howls of his burning comrades tore his nerves into splinters. Sweat poured from his core, his body locked with dread, and he braced for another lethal blast from that awful weapon. He closed his eyes tight and wondered what it would feel like to burn alive.

Just as the German prepared to pull the trigger again and send Roland to his doom, a British rifle unit crashed out of the smoke from just behind him. They dropped to their knees to avoid the flames, then they opened fire. Their bullets whistled through the air, cracking into the guts of the unfortunate Germans. Another spray belched forth from a flamethrower, and the heat singed Roland's back as he lay face-down in the mud.

After a few more seconds of vicious gunfire, the flamethrower quieted and clattered to the ground, and the remaining Germans made a mad dash into the fog. The angry riflemen took off in hot pursuit. A chorus of battle cries rang through the field, then faded into the mist. Soon enough, Roland could only hear the pitiful cries of the dying, and the distant cracks of gunfire. With quivering shoulders and legs, he finally dared to look up.

The flamethrower's fires had died out fast, burning too hard and too hot for the smoky air to keep pace. Only blackened, scorched earth remained now, along with the random crackling of small, non-lethal, leftover flames.

And the bodies. Just in front of Roland lay a pile of charred corpses and black, grinning skulls. Moments ago, they were living, breathing men who had hunkered in the trench with him, readying for an assault. They threw back their rum ration as the sun came up, having no idea they wouldn't see it go down. They had felt the wind in their hair as they ran across the muddy battlefield, the drops of rain on their faces, the pounding fear in their hearts. All of it was gone now. With the press of one button. In the blink of an eye.

Roland ripped off his helmet, letting the cool air spill down his neck, and he took a moment to collect himself. Then, his face hardened and he jumped to his feet. With a snarl on his lips, he jammed his helmet back on and stormed toward the nearest German trench in a rabid, blind rage. Without a second thought, he jumped into it and landed right on top of a lone German soldier. A wrestling match ensued, but Roland quickly gained the upper hand. With a roar of fury, he pinned the squirming soldier to the ground and brought his bayonet up for a killing stroke.

'*Kamerad*,' the soldier cried. '*Kamerad! Nicht schiessen.*'

Roland smacked the German with the butt of his rifle. 'Turn around, you son of a bitch. I want to look you in the eye when I kill you.'

The German wriggled onto his back and showed Roland his face. His clear face, his pale eyes, and his trembling lips.

Instead of inspiring a frenzy of murder like Roland thought, a lightning bolt of reason struck through the clouds of madness around his mind. His heart slowed just a little, and something like a voice of calm broke through.

This soldier was just a kid. His wiry body struggled to fill his uniform. He held his smooth hands up, and tears streamed out of his youthful eyes. He babbled something in German, his voice squeaking with coming manhood.

Roland's shoulders slumped a little. He still held his bayonet in killing position, but for some reason, he couldn't jab it into the boy's body. He just couldn't bring himself to end a kid's life, no matter how mad he was.

The trembling German soldier reached into his pocket and pulled out a prayer book. He handed it to Roland. '*Bitte öffne. Ich habe familie, mein bruder . . .*' He gasped for air through his choking sobs, tears still running in rivers down his face. '*Ich wollte nicht kämpfen . . .*'

Because he didn't know what else to do, Roland took the book. It had the exact same cover as the one he saw minutes ago, back in his own trenches in the hands of one of his own men. It had the same picture of the Savior, only this one said: *Mit Jesus auf dem Feld*. The exact same prayer, just in a different language. Both sides, German and British, prayed to the same God. Something about that pierced Roland like a knife.

With shaking fingers, he opened the cover of the prayer book. Inside rested a photo of a young boy. It couldn't be a son, because this boy fighter was much too young to have a kid that age. Which only left one real option.

'Your brother . . .' Roland said in a mumble.

Roland looked down at the shaking boy. So young, younger than Bernard even. He released the most violent stream of curse words he could think of. Then, almost against his will, he lowered his bayonet and climbed off his prey.

Without a second thought, the boy scrambled to his feet and started in a sprint down the trench.

Roland called after him. 'Wait!'

The boy soldier, his face tear-stained and soggy, froze. His shoulders rose and fell with his terrified breathing. When he turned back to Roland, his eyes were like dinner plates.

Roland tossed the prayer book at him.

The boy caught it without taking his eyes off Roland. When he was finally convinced that his life had been spared, he gave a humble bow of his head. Then, he wheeled around and tore off down the smoky, abandoned trench.

Roland stood there for a long moment afterward. He had let an enemy live, something he once swore he would never do. Something he was under strict orders not to do. It didn't make him feel very good. Anxiety trickled into his stomach, and the word 'coward' started flashing through his head.

He swallowed hard, trying to think the whole thing over. If what he had done was some form of cowardice, he at least knew he wasn't the only one to crack under the pressure. Unable to stomach more suicidal human assaults against machine guns, many men had mutinied and refused to go over the top. Some boys collapsed in complete insanity. Some soldiers screamed in hysterics in the middle of the night, and vomited up everything they ate. It happened to any man who stayed on the line long enough. Their spirits just hit a breaking point.

Then, instead of the medical care they needed, they got arrested and sent to military court. Punishments ranged from extra work detail to days tied to a wagon wheel and left to suffer in the trenches. Some men got the worst sentence of all. Because of their nerves breaking down under the strain, they were blindfolded, marched up against a brick wall, and shot by their own troops.

The thought turned Roland's heart to lead. He looked down the trench where that boy had disappeared. Would anyone find out what he had done? Did a blindfold and a brick wall linger in his own future? What could he even say in his defense? Because he didn't know why he had let the boy go. All the boys in both armies were so young. It hadn't stopped him killing before.

As he stewed in his mounting anxiety, Roland heard the sharp blast of the retreat whistle. But he remained in the German trench, his eyes darting back and forth. Someone might have seen him let that German escape. They may have already reported it to his superiors. Perhaps when he got back, the military police and a pair of shackles would be waiting for him.

A few machine guns burst to life nearby. A sharp reminder that while trouble could be waiting for Roland in his own trench, a worse fate would find him if he stayed here. So, he climbed out of the German entrenchment and ran back across the battlefield. Back through the flamethrower's carnage. Back through the mud holes and barbed wire. His thoughts reeled and his legs felt heavy, only this time it wasn't because of the mud.

A few German shells chased Roland across the field, although he quickly noticed the projectiles didn't detonate. They just plopped into the mud with a sloshing noise, some kind of liquid splashing around inside them. He wondered if there could really be that many dud shells in the German army.

But then the battlefield started to grow foggy, hazing up in a yellowish mist. A cloud slowly enveloped him, and Roland's eyes teared up. His nose and throat burned.

Poison gas.

Roland quickly reached down for his gas mask, but he only felt an empty space where his pack should have been. He ran his hands all over his waist in a frantic search, but it came up fruitless. He must have lost it in his tussle with that German. He would never find it in this fog either. The one thing that could save his life was gone.

His heart slamming inside of him, Roland made a mad dash for his home trench, but the gas moved faster than he did, wrapping up his body and shutting down his lungs. Breathing already felt harder, and his vision had gone cloudy. He still had his ears, and with them, he heard the banging of sticks onto empty shell cases coming from his own trench. The gas alarm.

'Gas! Gas! Gas!'

Roland began to lose his balance, stumbling through the fog with his hands at his throat. It felt like he had swallowed shards of glass, while his exposed skin burned as if it were dipped in acid. A hard, deep cough racked his lungs. He felt his steps slow to a crawl as the poison spilled into his blood, restricting his breath, paralyzing his muscles.

He dropped to the ground, splashing in a bubbling puddle of liquid mud like a fish out of water. He gasped for air and his body and lungs wheezed. So close to his trenches. He could see a line of faceless British soldiers in their eerie gas masks, with tube respirators and buggy plastic eye holes. They looked like something out of a ghost story.

He tried to call to them. 'Help me . . .' But his voice came out so weak the nearby rats wouldn't even hear it.

He coughed again, so hard he thought he would vomit. He crawled through the mud which sucked him down with every bit of progress, billowing up around his knees and thighs. He kicked his legs and dragged his body forward. He had to keep moving. Keep going. Keep breathing.

'Help me . . .'

Of all the ways to die in the trenches, gas was rumored to be one of the worst. Now, he understood why. He felt like his entire body was being axed apart from the inside out. Soon, he could no longer struggle. The mud purled up to his waist and squished about his abdomen. A sticky, burning, gooey discharge from his eyes mixed with his tears and seared hot against his face. There would be no smiles from his mother when she got this letter. No hero son. She wouldn't even have a grave to visit. And Bernard . . . What about Bernard?

He tried to reach for the letter in his pocket, but his fingers were quivering. His whole hand shaking. Panic, combined with the gas, had locked him in place.

'Help me . . .'

Out of nowhere, Roland suddenly felt a strong pair of hands grab him by the shoulders. With a severe jolt, someone yanked him out of the mud and dragged his limp body across the sloppy terrain. A heavy rubber gas mask got slapped against his face and slipped over his head.

The world became even more blurry through the scratched plastic eye holes. It also reeked of rubber and sweat inside the mask, and the restricted airway felt suffocating. In a fury, Roland clawed at the mask to get it off.

'Leave it on.' The gruff voice came back muffled because of the heavy mask. 'God damn it! Leave your mask on! That's an order, you hear me?'

Roland's eyes rolled back into his head, and the corners of his vision went dark. Blackness started moving over him like a shroud.

'I can't breathe . . .' He said as he lost his grip on consciousness. 'I can't breathe . . . can't . . .'

The mud and shell holes of Ypres faded away. In their place, he saw the dark streets of Manhattan. Shards of glass glittered in the moonlight. People wandered around in their pajamas, holding up glowing oil lamps and speaking in urgent whispers.

Through the confusion, a single candle went up in the window of his familiar brownstone. The orange flame flickered through the night. A bright bit of color in a world of black and white.

A wave of peace washed over him.

'Roland,' came his mother's voice in a delicate whisper. 'Time to come home.'

NINE
Ilse

Ilse pulled her lumbering, squeaking ambulance toward a hectic casualty clearing station, located just down the line from the British reserve trenches – although it wasn't a safe place in the slightest. In fact, the guns of Flanders could be both seen and heard, roaring so loud that people had to shout over them. The only real shelter from stray shots was the bullet-splattered medical tents, manned by uniformed and overworked military doctors and nurses. A small ward stood apart for emergency surgery, where a harried doctor sawed the leg off a screaming soldier. A few nurses held the wounded boy down and tried to dose him with morphine.

More wounded flooded the other tents and surrounding fields, all screaming for treatment at once. They lay on stretchers, blankets, and stacks of hay. Some were shot up with bullets. Some had tied-off stumps where their arms or legs used to be. Others coughed up chunks of blood and gore into handkerchiefs. They all had pencil marks on their forehead indicating what treatments they already had. 'M' for morphine, 'T' for tourniquet, and so on.

Nurses trotted around and examined each soldier, determining who could handle a rough ambulance trip to the nearest hospital. Off to the side, a team of ambulance corpsmen stacked dozens of rickety, rattling stretchers inside the waiting ambulances, cramming in way more than could properly fit in each vehicle.

Ilse hopped out of her own ambulance and took a solid look around. Just like when the *Lusitania* sank, various images came to her in flashes. One man with half his face shot off, holding his jaw in his hands. A man with bits of gravel and shrapnel embedded in his face. Another man with his own severed arm on his lap, and a bloodied stump sticking out of his torn uniform. Another man gone so insane he kicked and screamed at the top of his lungs, while two other wounded men held him down and tried to keep him quiet.

As she walked closer to the madness, Ilse's throat tickled and her eyes watered. She let out a deep cough, fanning her eyes to keep them from watering too much. Poison gas had been used again. Probably mustard.

Sure enough, she soon spotted the ever-familiar human train of gas victims. Each wearing damp blindfolds to ease the burning in their eyes, resting a hand on the shoulder of the man in front of them. Some poor medical corpsman had probably led the human train from the trenches, receiving quite the earful any time someone slipped or lost their footing, as it put the whole train off track. Those too poisoned to walk sat up on stretchers with big yellow blisters on their exposed skin, hacking and coughing up parts of their lungs. A swarm of nurses and military medics were hard at work decontaminating the lot of them – scrubbing them down, bandaging their eyes, dousing their hair.

One of the patients in particular caught Ilse's eye. He sat on the ground apart from the rest, a blindfold over his eyes. In his hands, he clutched an oxygen mask that had helped save his life, but it obviously hadn't spared him any suffering. Small, bubbling blisters had already appeared on his hands, and a trickle of blood ran down the corner of his forehead – probably from the rough and tumble scrub job they had done on his hair and clothes. Yet, he didn't squirm, yell, or put up the least bit of fuss. Something about the stoicism moved her. And he had other appeal the Flanders filth couldn't hide. Like dark-brown hair, and carved, toned muscles that made her gut flutter.

Ilse put a hand to her tummy and rolled her eyes. She had seen thousands of men in the last two years, some much more handsome than this one. Yet she had never fallen under their spell. Even when they showed interest in her curving hips, her sparkling eyes, or her pretty face, she didn't reciprocate. She just didn't have time for such nonsense. Yet now, the sight of this man had somehow reminded her that her feminine desires, though long dormant, were still intact. Which was annoying more than anything.

She timidly approached the man and knelt next to him. Brushing his cheek with her fingers, she checked his forehead and noticed it was blank. 'Sir? Have you been treated?'

'Just decontaminating. Whatever the hell that means.'

Ilse's eyes flew open wide. The attitude didn't surprise her. Plenty of these wounded warriors were quick to cop an ornery streak. But the distinctly *not* English accent sure threw her for a loop. 'You're not British.'

'Well, neither are you, from the sounds of it.'

Ilse glared. As well as her feminine desires, her pride was still intact too. She wouldn't stand for it being beaten down by this man or any other. 'I understand you're in pain, but if you want taken to a hospital, I'll thank you to act respectful.'

'Ambulance driver, are you?' He paused to let out a raspy cough. 'What kind of woman can do any driving?'

'Me, as a matter of fact. Name and rank?'

'Private Roland Seybold Hawkins. I'm an American.'

An American! Ilse drew in a sharp breath and put a hand to her fluttering heart, trying to tamper down her blooming excitement. Like the rest of the medical personnel in Europe, she had heard the boys from her homeland had finally declared war on the Kaiser, and just like everyone else, she had celebrated when she heard, which surprised most of the people around her. After all, they all knew her heritage. One half of it, anyway. They didn't seem to get it that she didn't consider herself German. She considered herself an American of partial German descent.

Sure, some of the people in her old German neighborhood back home hadn't felt that way. Many of them had supported the Kaiser and rooted for Germany. Ilse didn't. Ilse loved America, despite its faults. Like her father before her, she viewed it as a work in progress, but one that was well worth fighting for. 'Making the world safe for Democracy' was something her father definitely would have believed in, so Ilse believed in it too. Which is why it relieved her that the Americans would soon be coming to Europe in droves. With them, they would bring fresh troops, fresh supplies, fresh energy, and fresh life. They would bring a faster end to a terrible war. A prospect so wonderful after so much bloodletting, it actually kept her going on the especially bad days.

But, so far, she hadn't seen a single American soldier. Neither had anyone else, and the continued delays had aroused some hostile bitterness in the European medical tents. Nurses and doctors the world over constantly complained about the slow-moving Yanks, and how they must be waiting for everyone else to die before they finally came on over to help.

Now, she knelt face to face with an honest-to-God American soldier. A real Yank. The first she had seen thus far, and the first, she prayed, of many. 'The Americans have finally come over, have they? Oh, my goodness, it's such wonderful news!' She put her hand on his shoulder. 'Please, sir. Can you tell me how many—'

He rudely cut her off before she could say anything else. 'American armies aren't over here yet. I came over off the books before they officially got in on the fight.'

Ilse's stomach sank like a stone in a river, and the happy buzz in her veins quickly deflated. 'Oh.'

'What do you care anyway?'

'Well, I'm American too. My parents immigrated just before I was born.'

If Ilse hoped their shared American heritage would ease his surly mood, he sorely disappointed her. At the word 'immigrant,' he frowned. 'Immigrated from where?'

'Well . . . that's not important. American is American, yes?'

He glared. 'Unless they came from Germany. Because you know that makes you at least half boche.'

Ilse's eyes hardened and she got back to her feet and brushed off her skirt. It was easy to see there would be no cracking this soldier.

'Well, sounds like you've had enough chit chat. Let's get you loaded into the ambulance.'

TEN
Ilse

A sopping, windy Flanders rain shower blew its way into the station, which shattered Ilse's hopes of a smooth, timely ambulance load. While the rain soaked through her already waterlogged clothes, and the wind whipped at her hair and face, she squished through the mud with the other medical corpsmen, loading men on stretchers, heaving them into her ambulance, wheeling them inside, and stacking each stretcher on top of another in tall, metal stacks. Once she insisted they couldn't possibly fit one more patient, she administered first aid where needed and made a few bandage adjustments. All the while, the men shouted and cursed, screamed and yelled, miserable with the combination of rain and their painful wounds.

Things didn't improve once they finally started for the hospital. In the awful weather, the road had deteriorated into a soggy quagmire, just waiting to snare unwitting drivers. Vehicles stuck and tires spun out everywhere, holding up all the traffic behind them, flicking globs of mud at other ambulances and troops of soldiers marching by. Before long, the road was a total log jam of dim, flickering headlights, squealing horses, and swarms of muddy, marching columns. And the constant thundering artillery only added more casualties and more obstacles.

It was well after dark when Ilse finally pulled her ambulance, filled with wailing cargo, to the open doors of her hospital. Her company had commandeered an old bombed-out chapel for the constant influx of Ypres patients. The place did its job, but it wasn't large enough to fit everyone. In addition to that, shell damage had left the sanctuary susceptible to water and mold, not to mention the damp, bitter air. The nurses had scattered hay on the stone floor in an attempt to keep it dry, but days of rain and constant foot traffic had turned it into slop.

As Ilse's vehicle squeaked to a stop out front, nurses and ambulance corpsmen burst out the church doors and helped her offload her patients. The boys didn't come quietly, roughed up and angry from the long, arduous journey. Many had vomited all over themselves. Wounds had ripped open, and bandages had snapped. A couple of men had even died en route.

Ilse and her team hurried the survivors into the church and out of the rain. It took another hour to get them all checked in, fed, and marked with big yellow tags showing their injuries and previous treatments. Urgent cases went straight to the line for surgery, and the rest got a place to sleep and await evacuation to an official hospital further back. If they were lucky, they got a cot. But most were forced to huddle under blankets on the hard, stone floor. Still others lay in a leaky, breezy medical tent outside. More than a few still suffered directly in the elements.

However, sleep wouldn't come easy wherever they wound up, because nighttime wasn't peaceful in the hospital. Flashing oil lamps cast demonic orange shadows along the dark, dripping walls. The occasional strike of a match illuminated eerie silhouettes of the strained nurses and harried personnel on the move. From somewhere in the sanctuary, a shell-shocked patient moaned and babbled. Someone else whistled the tired strains of a haunting church hymn. Others sobbed in the dark, calling out for their mothers or sweethearts. Still others lay in their cots with their eyes glassed over, starting their journey to the next world.

Ilse walked her way through the chaos on her final round, administering some last-minute aid before she retired for the night. Her boots felt extra heavy as she leaned over dozens of lumped figures buried under their blankets. She longed for the bathing bucket in her quarters, since her damp clothes had left her skin slimy and her scent musty.

She was just about ready to head to her sleeping quarters when she noticed a familiar face in the back of the sanctuary. He was wide awake despite the hour. A set of fresh gauze patches covered his eyes. He had been stripped of his gas-contaminated combat clothes and draped with hospital clothing. Someone had also left his shirt open to air out the oozing gas blisters on his yellow-tinted skin. Every few seconds, he let out a horrible cough. In his hands, he held a dirty envelope. A letter that hadn't been opened.

Roland Hawkins. His open shirt and exposed bare chest reminded her how handsome he was. However, his bitter attitude and slur against her roots had quickly overshadowed her physical desires. She prepared to leave him to his business, but she caught him picking at his bandages.

Damn it. She couldn't avoid him now. 'Don't take those off. You could blind yourself if you do.'

Roland turned his face every which way, trying to calculate where the voice had come from.

Ilse let out an annoyed exhale and took a step closer to him. 'It's all right. I'm a nurse.'

He tilted his head. 'Your voice sounds familiar.'

'I drove you here from the trenches today.'

'Oh, the Hun driver. How delightful.'

'All right, then. Get well soon.' She turned on her heel to storm off, but his scratchy voice stopped her.

'Wait.'

'What? More nice manners?'

He held up the envelope in his hands. 'Actually . . . well, I got this letter and didn't get to read it before . . .' He let out a nasty cough, accompanied by a terrible rattle in his lungs. He coughed so hard that he soon started gagging, and he made a quick reach for a pan next to him. He snatched it just in time for a nasty, red-tinted glob of fluid to wretch from his mouth and join the large pile of them already in the pan.

Ilse winced and looked the other way. She knew that couldn't feel or taste good.

When he finished, Roland cleared his throat and put the pan aside. He took in a few raspy gulps of air to catch his breath.

Ilse softened. 'Are you all right?'

He beckoned to the pan. 'Would you call that all right?'

'Well, you sure seem all right enough to keep that mouth running.'

He again held up the envelope in his trembling hands. 'Yes, but not my eyes for the moment. Would you read this to me?'

'No, thank you.'

'What, just because of the Hun remarks? I was only teasing you.'

'Is that how you tease? You belittle people because of their roots? Sounds a little cruel to me.'

'I'm just surprised they let Germans nurse this side of the line, that's all.'

'Well, I told you, I'm *American*.'

He scratched the back of his bandaged head a little harder than necessary. 'Right. Look, I've just had a rough go lately. It's made me forget my manners. I have no other excuse to give you.'

'Then maybe you should just apologize.'

He winced, as if the concept of apology had never been properly wired into his system. 'I'm sorry,' he said in a dry tone. 'Will you please read my letter now?'

Ilse glared. She still didn't feel like doing him any favors, but she knew that a big part of her job entailed being kind to the patients, even the mean ones. So, she walked the rest of the way over to him and made a grab for the letter. At the same time, he tried to reach through his blindness to give it to her. In the confusion, they brushed hands. The contrast between her smooth, soft touch and his rough, calloused fingers jarred them both. It also sent a hot shower of sparks through her tired, chilled insides.

Frustrated at the second reminder of her physical desires, Ilse yanked her hand out of the entanglement, rubbing it on her apron to expunge the butterflies.

'Sorry.' He scratched his scalp again. 'So how does a Ger . . . er . . . American girl wind up in a place like this?'

Ilse's jaw tightened. She hated it when anyone pried into her background, much less a man who had a sore spot against Germans. 'I wanted to help.'

'They're not hard on you?'

'Not as hard as you.'

His shoulders drooped and he twiddled his hands.

Ilse continued. 'I may not have earned everyone's trust just yet, but I have at least earned their respect. As for the rest, I use a French name that seems to hold them at bay.'

'Oh yeah? What nickname?'

Ilse suddenly found herself annoyed. Her nickname wasn't his business. She didn't owe him anything, least of all her back story. After all, she had never told anyone her back story, not even the people she worked with every day. Not a soul knew she had survived the *Lusitania*. And if she had her way, they never would. Because they still weren't her friends. Colleagues, perhaps, but not friends. As much as they didn't seem to trust her, she didn't really trust them either.

She especially didn't trust their questions. So many questions from so many people. It often left her numb. Reporters in Queenstown. Morgue officials. Ambassadors. Doctors. Patients. So many questions, but she always dodged them. Not just to protect her identity, but also to keep her feelings in check. Her losses still weighed so heavy on her, and she couldn't let the tragedies of her past pull her down to the depths again. So she didn't speak about it. And she tried really hard not to think about it. She knew that if she did, she would never stop.

So when people pressed Ilse for her back story, she lied. She played the patriotic card easily and often, claiming she just wanted to help. She wanted to do her bit. She couldn't sit at home while people died. She had to do right by the boys. Which was at least a partial truth. Ilse had always supported her American homeland. As for her German heritage, well, she loved her father, but not his homeland. How could she love them after what they had done to the *Lusitania*? To her family?

No, Ilse considered herself wholly American, especially after that, and she would fight this war accordingly. Even if, after all she'd done to prove herself, she still had hardly anyone to count on. Just the matron, who probably liked her more for her talents than her heritage. In fact, it had been her idea to use a French nickname to try and win people over. 'You should use another name, so the boys treat you better,' she had said one day. 'The boys like French girls, so how about something Parisian?'

At the mention of Paris, a name had popped into Ilse's head like a phantom from the mist, along with the feelings she had when she first heard it. Warmth, family, and love. She even thought she smelled a hint of her father's cigar smoke wafting around her. In that instant, she knew no other name would suit her.

'Nurse?'

Ilse snapped back to Roland.

'Your other name?'

She clenched. 'Chère-Amie.'

She waited for him to mock her, balling her fist in anticipation, ready to give him another reason for needing a hospital.

Instead, he only smiled. 'Dear friend . . . right?'

The name had always been an emotional touchstone, but hearing Roland say it turned Ilse into a puddle for some reason. The pretty, reflective kind of puddle that a spring shower leaves in a green field. It was something about the tenderness in his voice. The playful smile on his lips. She suddenly felt very glad he couldn't see her.

She quickly changed the subject. 'What about you? Why do you fight if you don't have to?'

He shrugged. 'I wanted to kill Germans.'

The air around Ilse violently shifted, and she instantly went from warm and fuzzy inside to feeling like she had been stabbed with a knife. She took a giant step back accordingly.

He must have sensed he owed her an explanation. 'Germans killed my father. So, I hated them all instead of just the ones responsible.'

Ilse forced a nod. 'I see.'

'But I guess you could say I've rethought some things.'

'How do you mean?'

'It's a little more complicated than that, isn't it? War, I mean. Being in those trenches, living in a pig pen and seeing what this has all devolved into, well . . .' His hand fumbled around the blanket until it rested on the letter. He handed it to her. 'Would you read it for me? Please, Chère-Amie?'

Ilse snatched the envelope and glanced at the writing on it to keep herself distracted from the second round of butterflies. 'It's addressed from New York. Is that where you live?'

'Yes.'

'Me too.'

He managed a grin under his bandages. 'Small world, isn't it? I wonder how things would be different if we'd met there instead of here.'

Ilse smiled at the glimmer of flirtation. He was rough around the edges, that was certain, but there just might be a decent man in there. She suddenly wondered if he had a wife or sweetheart back in New York. She didn't know why she cared. Maybe she felt sorry for him, or maybe his good looks had permanently clouded her judgment. Either way, she wanted to read the letter and get out of there. As quickly as possible.

She tore open the envelope.

'*Dear Roland,*' she began. '*I hope you're safe. I think of you often, especially when I put the candles on at night. I pray you will see them and find your way home. Although, I don't know what home you have left. I'm sorry to bring you bad tidings, but our mother passed from the consumption. That's both our parents, so we're orphans, I guess. Some of Dad's old police buddies came to see her off; I thought that was real swell. I've sold the house, and I enlisted. The police force helped me get into a decent regiment which was nice. I will be at training camp when this letter reaches you. So use the enclosed address when you write. Your loving brother, Bernard.*'

Ilse finished reading with an awkward clear of her throat, placing the letter back into Roland's waiting hand.

News of his mother's death had quickly dampened any remaining sparks of Roland's arrogance or attitude. He put his head down, turning away from Ilse, probably so she wouldn't see his trembling jaw.

But she did see it, and it broke her heart. Because if anyone knew the hard sting of family deaths, it was her. And no matter how mean he had been to her, she couldn't help but empathize. 'I'm so sorry,' she whispered.

'That my mom died? Everyone is dying. What difference does it make?'

Ilse didn't know what else to say, so she just reached down and squeezed his hand. She ran her thumb across his sandpaper, scratched-up knuckles. Then, she came to her senses and decided to get on with her night.

But he tightened his grip on her hand to hold her back. 'Pray tell . . . What is your real name?'

She chewed hard on her lower lip, unable to resist his firm grip. 'Why do you care?'

'Why wouldn't I?'

'You certainly didn't a minute ago.'

'Well, this is the war to end all wars. A lot can change in a minute.'

It was a fair enough answer. Quite poignant actually. And honest. Ilse sighed, looking this way and that before turning back to Roland. She leaned in a little closer so she could whisper. 'Ilse.'

'Ilse.' Roland smiled. He paused for a brief moment, still holding her hand. '*Danke schön*, Ilse. For reading my letter.'

The restless flock of butterflies pressed down on her tummy and made her hands quiver with nerves. A thank you from Roland for anything seemed far-fetched. A thanks in her father's native tongue was an extreme gesture, one that indicated he wanted to make nice, even if her feelings for her father's homeland were a bit complicated. She again felt relieved that he was blindfolded, so he wouldn't see the scarlet flush in her cheeks.

'*Bitte schön*,' she said back to him. Then she broke her hand out of his and quickly skirted away.

After she left, Roland settled back in his cot and tried to rest.

From out of the shadows behind him came another nurse. Her eyebrows slanted down hard, suspicious of hearing German words in her midst. She glared in the direction Ilse had gone. Then, she slipped back into the darkness.

ELEVEN
Roland

A rough few weeks lay in store for Roland Hawkins, even if they didn't start out so bad. In fact, when he awoke at the casualty clearing station after swallowing poison gas, it seemed like he'd dodged the worst of it. He only noticed some itchy skin and watery eyes. He could still see, and his lungs, although weak, felt like they would recover quite quickly. He had no burns, just a little pink tint to the most exposed parts of his skin.

Roland almost laughed at the time. If this was all he had to show for it, poison gas certainly wasn't as bad as everyone said. He began hounding all the medical personnel to quit fussing over him and return him to his troops, but no one paid him any attention. They just ordered him to wait with all the other gas victims for evacuation to the rear.

'I don't need to go to the rear,' Roland said in a firm voice. 'I feel fine. I need to get back to my boys.'

The medic just huffed. 'Make yourself comfortable. It will be a bit of a wait.'

A bit of a wait indeed. A few minutes turned into several, and things got worse in the meantime. While he picked and scratched at his prickly skin, burning more intensely than before, Roland felt small, sore blisters starting to crop up on his hands. And the coughing. Deep, rasping coughs that came from somewhere way down in the pit of his lungs. His eyes had begun screaming in pain and trickling with itchy, burning fluid, which made it much harder to see. Still, he wanted to return to his men, to get back to Vernon and make sure he was all right. So, again he asked the medic to release him.

This time, the medic looked a bit more alarmed on examining Roland. Especially when he noticed the yellow blisters. 'Just as I thought . . .' he said in a murmur.

Roland frowned. 'Wait . . . what did you think? Should I be worried?'

The medic sharply commanded Roland to sit in the mud. He

soaked some pads with a strange, sharp-smelling solution, then stuck them to Roland's eyes with tightly wound bandages, throwing him down into a chilling world of darkness, with the wraps hugging his cranium so tightly he could already feel the throb in his temples. A heavy mask was slipped over his face, and a burst of oxygen coursed down his throat. It was so strong, it almost made him gag.

'Decontaminate,' the medic barked.

With that, two nurses came to the scene and began scrubbing Roland everywhere – his scalp, his skin, even his clothes.

'The clothes have to come off,' one of them said.

'We don't have any more to change him into; it will have to wait until he gets further back.'

'They'll burn his skin.'

'We'll mark him priority and get him evacuated faster.'

As the two nurses argued, they wrapped more bandages around Roland's head, and Roland drew in a sharp breath.

He took the mask off and let out a cough. 'Please, could you loosen them a little?'

When Roland reached up to fix them himself, the nurse nudged him. 'Trust me, you want them tight.'

'Will you please tell me what the hell is going on?'

The nurse just scrawled on a yellow tag and draped it over Roland's neck. Before he could ask any more questions, the lady driver loaded him into a stuffy ambulance, and off he went to the hospital.

His symptoms worsened a great deal on the way. The coughing got harder and more painful, and he was pretty sure he tasted speckles of blood in it. The blisters on his hands got bigger. Behind his thick bandages, hot fluid poured from his eyes, which burned him with searing pain. Still, he somehow managed to convince himself he would be fine. That he would be back with his unit in no time. That the rough ride in the ambulance had just aggravated his condition.

After all, it was a rough ride indeed, blanketed in total blackness thanks to the brain-squeezing bandages around his head. The orderlies stacked his and some other stretchers on rickety metal racks in the hot box of an ambulance, packing them all in like sardines. Roland's cot wound up being toward the bottom of the rack, and he became quite claustrophobic when he realized the cot above him sat just inches from his face, which didn't allow him to reach out or even turn over. And he really wanted to turn over, because the whole stack of stretchers jolted and jerked with every movement of the vehicle. Blood from someone up above dripped on his forehead. All the wounded men smelled just as bad as the trenches. Except, in the trenches there was moving air. In this tiny ambulance, air had nowhere to go except right into his damaged lungs. He only got relief when the burning in his nose blotted out the foul odor.

When the torturous trip ended, a swarm of nurses whisked him into the dank, musty-smelling hospital. They ripped off his head wrap, but to Roland's dismay, he still couldn't see. Air hitting his face made him scream like a rabid animal. They quieted him by pressing another oxygen mask against his face and pumping him full of more air – even if it just made him want to cough harder. More medical personnel flushed his eyes with a chilled, smelly fluid. They put more solution-soaked bandages on his eyes. They ripped his clothes off and put him in a loose-fitting hospital garment. Then, they rubbed an oily salve all over his chest, face, and hands. All while shouting about decontaminating, and coughing and sputtering from their own exposure to the fumes.

After the mad dash to rid him of as much poison as they could, nurses planted him in a cot somewhere in the back of the sanctuary. After Ilse, his ambulance driver, read his letter, which didn't improve his spirits, Roland slipped into a light sleep. When he awoke in the middle of the night, he discovered he could barely breathe. Fluid came up from his lungs and out of his mouth every few minutes. He vomited anything the nurses tried to feed him. When they tried to change his eye bandages, he howled uncontrollably with pain.

In the morning, orderlies rushed a still-blindfolded Roland to the overworked doctor. The surly man brushed his fingers over Roland's yellowed skin. He probed the large, yellow blisters which had doubled in size overnight. Blood and clots now came out every time Roland coughed.

'It wasn't this . . . bad last night,' Roland said as his lungs wheezed in pain. 'What's . . . happening to me?'

The doctor sighed. 'Heinie got mean with his gas. They send a burning agent over first to get the throat, make you cough and take your mask off. Then they send the real stuff over. So you probably inhaled a lot more than you think. From the looks of you, I'd say it was mustard.'

'Not . . . phosgene?'

'Phosgene may be the deadliest gas, but mustard is dangerous because its effects are delayed.'

'You mean . . . I'm going to get . . . worse?'

'Symptoms increase and peak over three or four days. Just try to be strong until then.' He gave a heartless flick of his wrist, and orderlies removed Roland from the exam table. With a line of wounded soldiers out the door, he had no time for questions.

It was fine by Roland, because he didn't trust those damn doctors anyway. Especially the ones in these privately run hospitals. They were ponies fresh out of medical school, or still trying to complete their lousy, over-priced medical degrees in the first place.

But this doctor's prognosis proved right on the money. Within just twenty-four hours, Roland was suffering so much he actually wondered if it was better to die than to live. He vomited up blood clots all day. From head to toe, his skin felt like it was on fire. Red, scaly burns shriveled the flesh on his chest and hands. The yellow blisters filled to capacity and ruptured in a burst of burning ooze. He couldn't eat, he couldn't speak, and he couldn't see. Every breath felt like inhaling volcanic ash. So, he held his breath for as long as possible, which only caused more burning in his damaged lungs.

Roland figured that hell itself couldn't be worse than what he endured under the spell of mustard gas. He writhed in agony on his cot, unable to even lay down, as the nurses insisted he had to stay propped up. He wanted to cry, but his salty tears mixed with the poisoned discharge and burned his entire face. He could only clench his ratty blanket in his shaking fist and let out pitiful, scratchy moans once in a while.

It wasn't just physical suffering, either. In the poison's tormenting grip, Roland fell into an emotional agony that none in his life had matched. He often flashed back to that terrified German soldier, who had sobbed so hard for his life. Not because he wanted to live, but because he *needed* to live. He had a younger brother to look after.

At the time, Roland feared it was cowardice or the final snap of his nerves that led him to spare the boy's life. Now, he knew it was just his human side. That young, optimistic man he thought he had left behind in New York. That young man had somehow survived, even in such a terrible place, and now he was forcing his way to the surface. Shoving a path through layers of war mud and battle fever. Showing Roland just how wrong this entire thing was, and how wrong he had been to want to get in on it. How truly abhorrent it was to kill anyone, much less a young boy like that. A boy with whom, underneath their different uniforms, he actually had many striking similarities. More in common with each other than the overlords they were allegedly fighting for.

The jarring thought solidified over the next few days. Especially under the care of Roland's nurse, Ilse. He had never seen her face, yet he felt something angelic in her, something the screaming newspapers back home had assured him no person of German descent could have. Her voice calmed him, and her presence comforted him. Her touch, when she changed his eye pads and put salve on his burns, was gentle. Whenever she was around, he felt the healing energy bubbling up from deep within her. He felt the tenderness in her spirit, the caring in her treatment. She put things back together that his own hands had torn apart.

It made him feel so horribly guilty.

It was like the gas had sprung his long-dormant conscience from its muddy, war-battered prison. People like Ilse, that boy in the trenches, the mud-splattered soldiers he had already killed – they weren't the enemy. This was a top-down problem. Corruption of political leaders. The warped minds of conquerors and colonialists. Because no cause these politicians yelled and screeched about could be worth the horrors in those trenches. No love of homeland should rip the earth into crater fields and masses of trenches. Nationalism that made his skin blister, and his lungs bleed, and his eyes sear with pain, was misguided and murderous. He should have known that all along. But it took a deadly brush with mustard gas to break the shackles of his war fever. He vowed that if he could ever see again, it would be through different eyes.

After several days of mental and physical suffering beyond what Roland thought he could endure, gentle rays of mercy slowly started to poke their way through. Like the first pillars of sun after a streak of cloudy days. The blisters on his skin dried out and receded. The nasty red burns faded into peeling, pink, healing flesh. His stomach even settled enough to allow some broth from Ilse, the first food he had held down for some time, which gave him back some little spurts of energy.

One crisp, cool morning, he sat up and stretched his stiff, weak limbs for the first time in days. He exposed his bare chest and faded burns to the fresh air. This time, contact with the elements didn't cause his skin to sting.

He could finally feel things other than pain. Relief, lightness, hope. Especially when someone cranked up a gramophone nearby. Strains of a man and a woman singing to each other soon echoed through the open church sanctuary. Lovers crooning about being the only boy and girl in the world, and how wonderful that would be.

Someone sat down next to him just then, and his cot gave a creak and jolt.

'Hello, Roland,' a familiar voice said. 'It's me.'

'Ilse?'

'Yes.'

He fumbled for her hand on the cot.

She took it and gave it a squeeze. 'You're doing better today. How do you feel?'

'Not my jolly old self yet,' he said with a laugh that turned into a cough.

'Yes, it will take some time to heal completely, but I do have some good news. The matron says we can remove your bandages.'

Roland's insides lit up at the prospect. How he had missed the use of his eyes! How he wished he could see the people around him, the blue of the sky, the walls of the church, and the light of the candles. And all that paled in comparison to what he wanted to see most. His mind blazed with curiosity about Ilse. He often lay awake, imagining what she must look like. Trying to picture a smile, a pair of eyes, or a healing hand. Despite his many efforts, he could never come up with a face to match that sweet voice.

That sweet voice broke into his thoughts just then, drowning out the two lovers and their singing on the gramophone. 'What do you think, Roland?'

'I'm ready to see the light. Take it off.'

He sat still as she picked at some of the residue holding his gauze in place. Once the adhesive dissolved, she unwound the bandages from his head, layer by crusty layer.

'Don't open your eyes until I say.'

Roland obeyed, no matter how hard it was. As the last piece of gauze peeled off his face, he felt a rush of cool, dry air against his hot complexion. Sweat collecting for days finally evaporated. With shaking hands, he put a finger to his face. It alarmed him when he felt piles of crusty, hard clumps in his eyelashes and eyelids.

'Roland Hawkins,' Ilse said. 'Don't touch!'

He quickly put his hand down, but a shot of fear had already knifed through his waves of excitement. The church suddenly felt hot and stuffy, like the walls were closing in. The voices on the gramophone became shrill, especially the woman with her high-pitched vibrato.

'If I were the only girl in the world, and you were the only boy . . .'

Roland knew people had gone permanently blind from gas, and he simply couldn't imagine a life without his eyes. Just the last several days had been unbearable. It would be torture if he had spent so many sleepless nights dreaming about the face of his caregiver, only to be denied the pleasure of ever seeing it. Not to mention all the other things he would miss.

'Nothing else would matter in the world today, we could go on loving in the same old way . . .'

Roland grumbled and tried to shut out the music, while Ilse took a damp cloth and wiped all the debris from his eyelashes. As she did so, she rustled up the familiar fire and sting of days past.

He winced and pulled back. 'It burns!'

'It's remnants of the poison.'

'Well, stop rubbing it then.'

'I have to. You don't want that in your eyes.' She again dabbed the cool cloth against his eyes. 'Now, be a big boy, hold still and let me finish.'

He snorted at her jab, then hardened his resolve and tried to withstand the pain. But the burning soon overpowered him. He let out another yelp and collapsed back onto his cot. He balled his hands into fists. He gritted his teeth to keep from screaming out loud. His eyelids grew red and pulsated with the pain.

She put a gentle hand on his shoulder. That lovely, angelic touch. 'Keep still now, I'm almost done.'

Roland struggled to relax his grimace to make it easier for Ilse. A few quiet moans escaped his lips as the stinging reached its peak. Just when he thought he'd rather be blind than endure a second more of this, the crust and fluid at last detached from his lids. After it was gone, so was the pain. He even enjoyed the feel of the cloth and the touch of Ilse's fingers against his face. The breeze felt cool again, and the music sounded better.

'A garden of Eden made just for two, with nothing to mar our joy . . .'

After what felt like forever, she put the cloth down and took Roland's hand in hers. 'You are still very swollen, but you may try to open your eyes now.'

He thought his eyes would snap open on her command, more than ready to see after days in the dark. But they remained nailed shut. Stubbornly so. It perplexed him more than a little. He had craved this moment for so long, and now it was like he was too scared. His stomach curdled at the thought of opening his eyes after all this time, just to find unending blackness. What would he do if he was blind? How would he live? How would he take care of anyone? Who would look after Bernard?

I would say such wonderful things to you, there would be such wonderful things to do . . .'

'Roland, did you hear me? I said you can open your eyes now.'

He squeezed her hand in response, but he still made no move to open his eyes.

Ilse leaned in closer and brushed her fingertips across his sweaty cheek. 'I know it is scary to think of being blind, but I know you, Roland. You are so strong. A warrior. You would adjust, just like everyone else. So, have courage now. Open your eyes.'

Have courage now. Roland took a deep breath and let his eyelids open as far as they could. Which wasn't far at all, thanks to the swelling. At first, he didn't see anything. Darkness swirled around his head. His stomach plummeted as he thought all was lost, but then a bright light poured in. Coarse and white, harsh and blinding. Overwhelming his fragile pupils. He gasped and put his hands to his eyes, wincing and blinking so hard.

'You've been bandaged a long time,' Ilse said, her voice unwavering. 'Give yourself a minute.'

Roland's shoulders rose and fell with panic, but he forced himself to try again.

A few more blinks of his lids took the light's harshness down a notch. Colors began emerging from the white, like figures appearing from a dream. He slowly made out things around him: a ratty olive blanket in his lap, smoky stone walls, a mud-covered floor, glowing candles, and the blob shapes of people hurrying around.

It was enough to tell him a vital truth.

He wasn't blind.

His limbs went weak and tingly with relief, and against his will, a sob burst out of his chest.

'A garden of Eden made just for two, with nothing to mar our joy . . .'

Ilse put her hand on his shuddering shoulder. 'Roland? Can you see?'

For the moment, he was too emotional to answer. Roland Hawkins would get to keep his eyes. His lucky streak in the trenches had held up even against mustard gas. He cried with the joy of it, and with the pain for those who wouldn't experience a rebirth like this.

He blinked his teary eyelids again. This time, his pupils came into detailed focus, and he beheld his first clear thing after days in the dark.

Never had he seen eyes so green. They reminded him of the greenest fields or the finest summer woodlands back home. More things came into focus too, like a head of yellow, golden hair. A face of smooth, blush skin. A soft little smirk comprised of luscious, rosy lips.

It took Roland several moments to realize this beautiful creature was Ilse, the woman he had known only by the sound of her voice.

'I would say such wonderful things to you, there would be such wonderful things to do . . .'

Her eyes sparkled with joy, reveling in the relief of her patient. 'You can see me, Roland Hawkins? Does my face meet your expectations?'

Once again, Roland couldn't even reply. He had already sensed her angelic heart in the dark, and how it overpowered him now in the light. A strong feeling, much stronger than any poison gas, washed over him, spilling down into his stomach and legs. His breathing went into a tailspin. Birds ferociously beat their wings inside him.

'If I were the only boy in the world, and you were the only girl . . .'

He reached his trembling hands out, which came to rest on Ilse's arms. He slid his palms down over her biceps, swept his fingers around her smooth, delicate wrists. As if his hands had to confirm that his eyes weren't tricking him. This was her. His nurse. His caregiver. An angel.

Ilse.

He slowly scooted a little closer to her, his face landing a mere few inches from hers. They stared at each other as the air caught fire around them. His breathing grew shallow. His chest felt like it would explode.

'If I were the only boy in the world, and you were the only girl . . .'

Roland leaned in closer. So close he felt her hot breath tunneling from her mouth and into his ear. His nose picked up traces of her scent – hay, sweat, wool. They all yanked on a switch low down in his gut. Electricity fired up and down his legs. A shocking pulse of life from within.

Ilse leaned in closer too. The skin just above her shirt collar had turned pink with agitation. Sweat beaded up in the pleasant dip below her throat. She licked her lips. Tightened her grip on his wrist. Put her mouth a centimeter from his.

But the gramophone suddenly screeched with the end of the record, which snapped her out of her haze. She quickly jumped up and pulled herself away. Her cheeks grew flush, and she straightened her hair to hide her embarrassment.

Across the room, the gramophone clicked lifelessly, waiting for someone to change the record.

'Well,' Ilse said in a hoarse whisper. 'I'm . . . so happy you can see, Roland.'

A tear dribbled from his brown eye, milky from lingering gas remnants. 'Yes. My God, you can't imagine how much I . . .' The frenzy of chemistry had subsided, but the feelings still surged unchecked through his blood. So many feelings. His hands began to tremble under their power. 'I can see. I see . . . I see it all now. Yes, I do.'

Ilse couldn't hide her smile. 'You're on the mend then. You'll excuse me.' She began to walk away, but just like last time, Roland reached out and grabbed her hand. Held her back. Kept her close to him for just a few moments more.

She raised her eyebrows. 'What is it?'

Looking into her beautiful face, her warm gaze, Roland felt a heaviness inside. A yearning and longing, but also a grave sorrow. The familiar chill of embarrassment, of shame, reddened his cheeks. Part of him wanted to hide from what needed to be said, but he knew better than that now. He had to be a man, a real one this time. He had learned a humble lesson and he would eat his humble pie. She, and many others he had wronged, deserved it.

'Ilse,' he said in a shy mumble. 'I . . . I'm truly sorry. I said terrible things the day we met. Dreadful things. And I have no excuse. Just an apology that I hope you'll accept.'

Ilse's face turned several shades of red, and she tried to loosen her hand from his. 'Roland . . .'

'You've taught me what real heroism is. In more ways than one, you guided me out of the dark. Thank you, Ilse. And I'm sorry.'

She blinked her eyes in confusion for several, heart-stopping seconds. Then, that smile. A squeeze of the hand. A wink that set his insides ablaze. 'There now, Roland . . . I accept your apology.'

With a humble curtsy, she disappeared into the sanctuary before he could say more.

Seconds later, he heard the gramophone start up again.

'Roses are shining in Picardy, in the hush of the silver dew, roses are flowering in Picardy, but there's never a rose like you . . .'

TWELVE
Ilse

Ilse suddenly found her hectic days were a little easier to handle. Before, she had felt so tired it was like the whole world pressed down on her shoulders. Her boots felt like cement blocks on her sore, blistered feet. Her body was sluggish and stubborn when she forced it awake at dawn, refusing to leave the cot and start another long day.

But energy now came from somewhere, a new well spring deep down inside. Perhaps because for the first time since she came here, she felt like she actually had a friend – a thought that got her through the days with a smile on her face and a newfound pep in her step.

Once Roland's eyes were better, the rest of his body caught up quickly, and they shared even more stolen moments together. Flirtatious banter, giggly jokes, and he even kissed her on the hand a couple times. Ilse soon found herself thinking of him at odd moments during the day – while out on ambulance runs, while doing rounds in the hospital, while trying to sleep at night. It was an amusing thing for her, really.

Although, it made her duty this morning even harder than usual. She nervously made her way to Roland's cot, clinging tightly to the discharge forms that she had known would come eventually, because they came for every patient who recovered as quickly as he did. The stack of paperwork that would send him back to the trenches, away from her, maybe never to see her again. And for more reasons than just the dangers lurking in no man's land. He could meet some other girl in some other place, and Ilse Stahl, the nurse who had brought him back to the light, would just be a fuzzy memory from a different time. Much like her own family felt to her now.

It was a painful reminder of why she had worked so hard to guard her heart. Not just here in Europe either. Back in New York, in a time not far distant, she knew little about what went on between lovers. She had never kissed a boy and there were few who had made her want to. They all seemed so obnoxious, so wild, and some of them were downright mean. The way they lashed out at girls, got too handsy with girls, and treated girls like their general playthings. It turned Ilse off young men and their antics completely.

And this didn't change after she became a nurse. While many girls fell prey to wily, handsome soldier boys, and their shiny uniform charms, Ilse kept herself on solid footing. She didn't allow any soldier to turn her head. She convinced herself she had no time for romance, and no room in her *Lusitania*-shattered heart to make any real human connection. Certainly not a romantic one. It seemed far too risky in a world at war. It could even be downright dangerous. Romance, no matter how magical it looked sometimes, would have to wait.

But then came Roland. His friendship in a place where she had no one else picked away at her resolve. He had ignited something inside of her, making her think about men in a different way, raising her curiosity for things other nurses whispered about when they thought she was asleep. She had no idea why her heart had singled him out, but she suspected it had something to do with their shared grief. Both had lost their parents. Both needed a friend in their increasingly isolated worlds. And while Roland had made some terrible mistakes, he had also worked hard to amend them. Ilse found that honorable, since most men who treated her poorly didn't seem to know the word sorry.

For this reason and more, Ilse found herself spending more time with Roland than with any other patient. Even after her soul-crushing long days, she couldn't go to sleep without sitting with him for a little while. Often in the dark, so no one saw when she held his hand, or noticed the way her body tingled at his touch. She didn't want girls gossiping about the way she and Roland looked at each other. Or the way they started off their talks shoulder to shoulder, but ended up forehead to forehead. Lips to lips . . .

But no kisses. Roland seemed to be leaving that entirely up to her, which made her even more interested in him. No other boys seemed that courteous. The mother he grieved must have raised him incredibly well.

That wouldn't do anything to save her from the dreadful moment at hand, though. With a deep breath, and the familiar pang of longing, Ilse threaded her way through the busy hospital and arrived at Roland's cot. She pulled the thin separator sheet around them, wrapping them up in at least some veil of privacy.

He looked up at her with a playful smirk. 'Hi, you. Time for a sponge bath at last?'

It crushed Ilse to think of the blow she was about to deliver him. She gripped the papers even tighter in her hands, leaving telling sweat stains on the sides of them. She tried to cover her worry with a charming smile. 'Feeling good today?'

Roland's eyes narrowed. He had instantly picked up what she had tried so hard to conceal. 'Ilse? What's the matter?'

With a gusty sigh, she put the papers on his lap. No use beating around the bush. 'I have your discharge papers here.'

Roland's whole demeanor shifted. His face went pale. He didn't lift a finger to touch the papers, treating them like a deadly, poisonous snake.

Ilse's lower lip trembled. 'I tried to fight it,' she said in an urgent whisper. 'I told them you still had a lot of complications, but they're so short of men, Roland. They're throwing half-sick and blown-apart men back in there.'

He shrugged. 'I'm not afraid to do my duty, Ilse.'

'I know you're not, but I am afraid for you.' The words slipped out before she even thought about it, and she immediately felt her face redden.

Roland rewarded her with a sly, almost arrogant grin. It would have annoyed her if he wasn't so handsome. 'You're worried for me?'

She turned away to hide her blushing. She didn't dare tell him all the things that worried her. Not only that he could get hurt or even killed, but also that he might move on with his life, find some other girl, and cast her out of his heart. If she even had a real place there to begin with.

Roland just giggled. 'Aw, don't you worry for me.'

'And why shouldn't I?'

'Because of math.'

'Math? What in the world does math have to do with any of this?'

'Math never lies, Ilse. My number already came up, and I survived it. Now I got nothing to worry about.'

She glared. 'You don't really believe that, do you?'

'Not enough to do anything stupid, I suppose. But I have to believe in something. Might as well be math.'

'Just math?'

Roland's face brightened. He finally seemed to know where she was going with this, and he chuckled. 'Why? Got any other ideas?'

Ilse ran her soft fingertip over the scars on his hands. She felt so many words swirling up inside of her. Honest, passionate words about what she could give him to believe in. But they all felt foolish in her anxiety-riddled brain. She couldn't say them to herself, much less to him.

She cleared her throat. 'America, perhaps. We just might tip the scales and end all this very soon.'

Roland looked like he wanted to burst into laughter. 'Hmmm, yes. The Yanks do love a good fight. Not sure that will keep me warm on the cold nights though.'

Ilse looked up to find him piercing her with a firm gaze. Almost demanding. Not in a threatening way, but an urgent way. Longing. Yearning.

The urge to spill her secrets pulsed harder and harder inside of her, soon becoming impossible to ignore. However, she still couldn't say anything. She struggled too hard for the courage to speak the truth in such a public place, busy and bustling just on the other side of that thin, ragged separator. Besides, it was such a vulnerable time. He was leaving. Perhaps for good. What use would it be opening her heart again just to have it ripped up some more?

She bit her lip and looked down, avoiding his eyes while she gave it her best shot. 'I know you'll be all right, Roland. But . . . but don't forget about me. OK?'

Once the words were out, the closest she would ever come to a confession, Ilse kept her eyes fused to the wool blanket on his cot. She could feel a strange tension bear down on her shoulders, trying to force her to look at him, but she didn't dare give in. Instead, she wanted to bolt to her feet and get the hell out of there. Just as she prepared to make her hasty, embarrassed escape, she felt a gentle touch under her chin. A strong hand gently guided her gaze up, helping her to look into his eyes. The hair on her arms stood up. Her stomach turned to jelly.

Ilse Stahl had patience for almost anything, but she couldn't take it anymore. She had to be brave. She had to tell Roland how she felt, stake her claim against the world. And she had no more time to waste.

So, she leaned in. She slipped her hands over his warm cheeks and she pressed her lips against his.

It was soft. Shy. Moist. It made her shiver despite how warm it was in the church. Especially when she felt his arm move in protectively behind her, his hand on the small of her back. The sweat on his palm seeping through her shirt, sending hot streaks down her body.

Before anyone spotted them, she pulled away, but she didn't turn away completely, because the shyness had fled. She stared right at him this time, challenging him to toss her aside and dampen the sparks they had just created.

Roland reached for her hand, brought it to his lips and kissed it. 'Well now, that is certainly something to fight for.'

They both collapsed into a fit of giggles, then Roland pressed his damp forehead against hers.

'Ilse . . . can I write you?'

She pinched his bicep with affection. 'If you don't, I'll put a worse hurt on you than any mustard gas.'

They kissed again. A little harder this time. More heat. The squeeze of a bit more life into the little time they had left together.

With a twang of nerves and anxiety, a twinge of self-doubt and fear, Ilse at last gave in to a little bit of romance.

THIRTEEN
Roland

September, 1917

In the Great War, things moved pretty fast sometimes. Just a single day after Roland's discharge papers came to him, a filthy trench and rats had replaced the clean bed and nurses he had grown so accustomed to. Fresh hospital food turned back into stale, canned, and muddy army rations. The infamous Flanders rain pounded down on his shoulders again, this time with no soft covers to burrow under and hide from it. A sheltered existence morphed back into one spent out in the elements, in the mud, under the sky.

Once upon a time, Roland was used to this kind of life. A disgusting existence drenched in mud and death, but it had somehow become the norm. It was just his duty, what people did in wars. A part of him had even relished it.

Now, fresh from a place where people healed instead of killed, he had too clear a memory of what life was supposed to be like. What humans were really filled with. Which was compassion, mercy, music . . . and love. That was what life was supposed to be, not killing each other in a mud pit far away from their homes, their families, and their humanity. It made the whole war feel awful and devastating, wrong and immoral. And it wasn't like he was a fresh-faced recruit anymore, newly brainwashed into thinking this was some grand adventure, or some proud bit of patriotism. Mustard gas had stripped those scales from his eyes, and many other ones to boot. Not to mention his lungs were still weak, and his skin still burned. A sharp reminder that his body wasn't in top form anymore. Work details he once sped through made his muscles throb and ache. Shovels and rifles felt heavier. The air seemed a bit colder.

This time, he only got a short spell in the reserve trenches, instead of weeks of training, to help him reacclimatize to it all. Companies were supposed to be rotated into reserve every week or so, to keep their nerves from coming apart. And Roland was glad to find his own company in reserve when he left the hospital. He hoped it would give him time to readjust and maybe get some rest. Time to catch up on things he had missed – like Vernon. Like Bernard.

However, Roland quickly found out there wouldn't be much downtime where he was going. Reserve may have sheltered him from full-on combat, but the captain kept his boys plenty busy with various work details. He organized ration parties to get food up to the fire trenches. He rustled up volunteers to serve as stretcher bearers. Some boys drew the unlucky lot of repairing the breaks in the barbed wire. Then there was the never-ending job of trench reconstruction. Shells and flood waters always made sure that some part of the trench needed slopped back together.

Roland and Vernon did trench repair more often than not, and he once would have complained about such drudgery. Now, he loved it. Trench repair was mindless work with minimal risks to his body. Just enough exercise to keep his damaged lungs on the mend and get his body back into some form of physical fitness.

Besides, Roland enjoyed being back with his friend after so long in the hospital, even if their reunion had a lot less fanfare than he expected. When he had crept up on Vernon from behind and tapped him on the shoulder the day before, grinning in anticipation, the tired corporal only greeted him with vacant eyes and a mindless hug.

Roland saw right away this wasn't the Vernon he had left behind. The cheery English pink had gone from his cheeks, and his skin had faded to ash. His shoulders slumped under the weight of the world, and his lower lip twitched. He often dribbled the watered-down tea he sipped in the afternoons. Something had pulled on a dangerous thread in Vernon's nervous system, and now the whole thing had started to unravel.

It pained Roland to see it, although it didn't exactly surprise him either. In trench time, Vernon was overdue for a breakdown.

He wanted to talk to Vernon about it, and a lot of other things too. After all, his own brush with death had left him with all these intense new feelings, and a deep longing for emotional companionship. He had the strong urge to open up about everything – his real thoughts on the war, his newfound mortality, and also his newfound love. It might make Vernon feel less alone.

But he held back. Because his struggles had at least earned him some time off the line. Vernon had been in the mud and shelling for almost a month straight. He didn't look well. Stories about romance and thoughts about death likely wouldn't do much to help him.

There was also the unspoken rule of the trenches, which was that boys didn't discuss their real feelings about the war. Although they talked about everything else. They complained about the weather, the rations, and the mud. They swapped lewd jokes about sex and women. They played poker, whist, and pranks to pass the time. They bragged about the latest care packages from family. More often than not, they even cracked jokes about death. Trench boys talked about everything under the sun, except the big, bloody, war-mangled and obvious truth. Feelings, their real ones, were off the table.

Which made it hard for Roland to keep Vernon on the right side of sanity, but he did his best anyway. He buddied up to him for their evening meals. He arranged for them to be put on the same work detail. He even consigned his daily rum tot and tea ration to Vernon, hoping the extra goodies would bring him just a little relief.

After a few days, Vernon slowly improved, but only enough to crack a few smiles and eat some extra food. The old Vernon remained just out of reach.

On a morning that was surprisingly warm, the two boys worked on yet another repair detail. A random, wayward shell had smashed into the trench at dawn, landing right on a large dugout filled with new recruits. None had escaped before the mud and wood collapsed in a pile of rubble. Frantic soldiers dug out what survivors they could, which was a precious few. As air ran out in the chamber below, the cries for help went quiet. The rescue operation halted. The captain assigned a work detail to clean up the mess, and everyone went on with their day.

Roland recoiled under the glaring reality he could no longer avoid. Shells killed people. It used to be so normal. Now, he couldn't let it go. Underneath that pile of mud rested a handful of men – real men. Back home, people would shed rivers of tears over each one of them. Yet the British army treated it like just another hiccup in their busy war schedule.

It was a crushing, emotional wound to grapple with, but one Roland couldn't reveal to anyone else. Certainly not these hard men, and certainly not Vernon. He could only grab his shovel and get to work. While the sun beat down on their backs, and the wind blew hot and heavy, he and Vernon shoveled, grunted, and piled up the bodies. Other than coughing fits from Roland, they didn't open their mouths.

Finally, after Roland coughed up some drops of blood, Vernon threw his spade down in a fury. 'Damn it, Lucky. They sent you back too early. Go report to the medic.'

'Why? Just to have them throw me right back in here?' Roland huffed and kept on digging. 'I told you my nurse did everything she could. They're too short on men.'

His nurse. Roland turned away from Vernon so his struggling friend wouldn't see the smirk on his face that Ilse's image provoked.

Vernon didn't notice at all. He just picked up his spade, which squished into something hard right beneath the surface of the mud. He sighed with disgust, knowing full well what it was. He tossed his spade aside and dropped to his knees. With trembling hands, he pawed the gravy-like mud until he came upon the obstruction – another dead body.

Roland winced and helped Vernon pick up the corpse. 'I thought we got them all.'

Vernon wrinkled his nose at the atrocious odor. 'This one isn't from today. He's not fresh enough.'

They lugged the body over to a pile of corpses, and they dumped their latest find on top. They noticed the infamous trench rats were already hard at work. They clawed their way up and down the pile, squeaking and gnawing through rotting flesh and bones. They didn't even flinch at the presence of living men nearby. In fact, a very chunky rat waddled onto Roland's boot. With a hostile squeal, it sunk its teeth into his fresh leather footwear.

Roland tried to kick it off, but he just irritated the creature, who glared at Roland with beady red eyes, let out a hiss, then retreated back to the pile.

Vernon shuddered. 'They're getting real fresh, those rats. I woke up the other night with one sitting on my face.' He scratched at the back of his head, where yet another trench pest fed on his flesh. 'Lord. If they don't end this war soon, the rats will be the death of us.'

'Or the cooties.'

The two started digging again.

'Did I tell you I was damn near buried alive while you were in hospital?'

Roland paused to give his friend a curious glance. 'No.'

'A shell come in just like this morning. Blasted me clean on my arse and next thing I know, everything around me went black. I heard voices but it was all muffled.' His lip gave a sharp quiver, and he forced a laugh. 'I could've sworn I was dead. But you must've left me some of your luck. I had an air pocket over my head. The boys dug me out.'

'Christ, Vernon.'

'Not as fun as being gassed, I'm sure, eh, Lucky?' He leaned on his spade and grinned. 'What say you? Is it really that bad?'

Roland shoved his spade into the mud a little harder. 'Worse.'

Vernon just watched Roland, a dark cloud moving over his face. 'It wasn't me that pulled you out, you know.'

Roland focused on his work to cover the sharp sting of his friend's words.

He had long wondered who rescued him on that awful day. He had always believed it was Vernon. They were best friends after all, and he couldn't think of anyone else who would risk it. But apparently Roland hadn't been worth the risk. It was jarring to hear, especially the way Vernon said it. Such a cold, remorseless tone, mixed with a dash of sarcasm.

If Vernon noticed Roland's hurt feelings, he ignored them. 'I thought you were done for. Didn't want to expose my good looks to the lead shower. Stark fished you out. I staked him a shilling he'd fail. He just ran out there, slapped a mask on you and pulled you in.'

Roland let out a painful exhale. 'Stark? I thought he cracked up.'

Vernon shrugged. 'Every man has his hero moment.'

'So, he's all better now?'

'His problems are over.'

'Well, that's good.'

'I mean . . . they're really over.'

Again, Vernon's attitude wasn't right. Like a door not set properly on its hinges. It still worked, but it made a god-awful squeak.

Roland gulped. 'He's dead?'

'Shell got him. Just a few hours after they cleared you out actually. Went off right next to him and I thought he was OK at first. He just stood there and stared at me. Then he fell to his knees and . . .' Vernon paused. It looked like he was about to cry.

Roland was almost relieved. This trembling boy on the verge of tears looked a lot more like the Vernon he remembered. 'And?'

Vernon wiped his eyes and rammed his shovel back into the mud. 'And his head fell off.'

'Jesus . . .' Roland whispered.

A fat tear rolled down Vernon's cheek and plopped into the mud. 'You know what I done after that, Lucky?'

'What?'

'I went over and fished my shilling out of his pocket.'

The two men stared at each other, the heavy air settling over their shoulders, along with the raw and quite potent emotions.

Again, Vernon broke the ice first, and this time, the door tipped back on its hinge. Just a gleam of his old self poked through. 'I'm sorry it wasn't me.'

'Who lost your head?'

'No. I'm sorry I didn't . . . I mean, when you got gassed . . .'

There it was. Remorse, feelings, pieces of the old Vernon still lingering inside this tortured old soldier. Roland closed his eyes and soaked it in. Then he smiled. 'Vernon, I'm glad you didn't come after me. It was too risky. Although . . .' He paused, gave his friend a smirk. 'Losing your head could only improve your looks.'

Vernon shot him a stone-cold stare, but then he burst out laughing, so hard he had to bend over and catch his breath. Color filled his cheeks. Sparkle came back to his eyes. More than anything else, it looked like he had needed forgiveness. That and a good hard laugh.

Vernon let out a strong exhale, passing away all the frustrations he had bottled up for too long. Ever since his friend had been away. 'I been meaning to tell you something else.'

'Oh yeah?'

'Your precious Uncle Sam is finally whipping up those American armies.'

'I told you.' Roland went back to his digging.

'Yeah, but that's not the whole story.' Vernon fiddled with his spade. 'I can get in real trouble for what I'm about to tell you, because the captain wants it all hushed all up.'

Roland glared. 'What are you talking about?'

Vernon did a quick check to make sure no one was listening. 'There's a rumor going round that the Yanks want all their boys over here to return. They're giving most of them commissions. No questions asked.'

Roland's jaw dropped down into the mud. The American line and a commission were two things he had wanted for such a long time. If what Vernon said was true, he could have them both, perhaps without that chest full of medals he had always thought he needed. Apparently, Uncle Sam found his experience far more valuable.

'Are you sure you aren't bluffing me, Vernon?'

'Oh, I could never bluff you. Although, I wasn't going to tell you right at first. I'm a selfish bastard who likes you right here. But since I left you to die, I figured I owed you one.'

'And the cap? Why would he keep that from me?'

Vernon narrowed his eyes. 'Why do you think? You've seen these lousy boys they pull in from Blighty. Not a hair on any of those chests, I'd wager, and that isn't their only shortcoming. The likes of you and me, the experienced ones, we're hard to come by nowadays.'

Roland couldn't deny it made sense. This war had drained Britain of its fighting men. Kitchener's 'Old Contemptibles' had all taken up residence under the ground or in hospitals. Of course his captain wanted Roland to stay. He couldn't afford to lose him.

Vernon went on before Roland could comment. 'You know the old man thinks you're some kind of hell demon. Maybe even a lucky charm. You're the last person he wants to part with.' He sighed. 'Of course, I know you've got that brother to look after, not to mention your mum.'

A shot of pain hit Roland like a bullet to his stomach. He sucked in a breath of air, then quickly turned back to his digging.

Vernon caught the shift in the winds. 'You're sore I kept it from you? I'm telling you now, aren't I?'

'It's not that.'

'What then?'

Roland focused on his shovel full of mud soup. 'She's dead. My mother.'

'Lord, Lucky . . .'

'Consumption. I found out in hospital.'

Vernon leaned on his spade and took a long look around. He beheld the knee-deep chocolate mud, the smoky, iron battlefield, and the twisted barbed wire. His eyes moved over the tilted and splintered wooden crosses. Brown and gray. Dingy and sad.

Colorless.

'Still no color out there.'

Roland huffed through his labor. 'Not from where I stand.'

'What do you think, Lucky? Our masterful human race has engineered its own destruction. We'll blast ourselves back to the Stone Age before this is over. God won't need to have his rapture. We've saved him the trouble.'

Roland sighed, Vernon's words hitting a horrific nail right on the head. The killing had indeed spread everywhere, not even contained to the battlefields any longer. Shells could reach across the continent. Planes brought war all over the globe and right to the doorsteps of innocents. Poison gas imitated the very fires of hell. It seemed the human race had indeed hastened their own Armageddon.

Roland tried to imagine a barren Earth devoid of all human life. He imagined silent cities, abandoned houses, and forgotten landscapes. He pictured birds floating over torn-up earth. He saw weeds and wilderness taking their planet back, blotting out any sign that humans had ever existed. Time would move on with no one to track it. Centuries would pass, and with them all the love stories, the progress, the promise, and the passion . . . all of it wiped away.

It pushed Roland to the brink of tears. He couldn't handle the thought of the entire human story coming to an end, all over the heartless greed of corrupted empires. Just as he went to slam his shovel to the earth in frustration, a pretty whistle pierced the air, echoing across the fields and the reserve trenches. It was nothing like the harsh, lethal blast of the assault whistles. Or the sharp screech of an incoming shell. It was gentle. Musical. A songbird nesting somewhere nearby.

Roland and Vernon both perked their ears.

It was the only bird he had heard in weeks, and its song flung Roland back in time. He saw the little sparrows chirping for food at the New York cafes. He saw the pigeons in Central Park, where he went on picnics with his family. He saw the blue jays, the red-breasted robins. All the winged beauties he once took for granted. Now, that songbird hearkened a time and place untouched by death and war.

'A songbird . . .' A smile tugged at Vernon's lips. 'You know, my father once took me to the Belgian villages as a boy. It was summer. Wildflowers bloomed all across these meadows. Red poppies, as far as the eye could see. And those songbirds, the very one you hear now . . .'

He couldn't hold back the floodgates this time. As tears leaked out, he knelt to the terrain and plucked a handful of mud. He squeezed it through his fingers, and the black dribbles coursed down his wrist. 'There were no wildflowers this summer, were there? Just the bones of my countrymen. All those lives . . . gone.' He threw the glob of mud aside and wiped his tears with the back of his hand.

Roland longed to give them both a chance to air their emotional laundry. However, the hard laws of the trenches hung like a vulture over his mind. Already, they had breached the unspoken rule and it had left Vernon in tears. It wouldn't do to push him any harder. At least, not now.

He put a hand on Vernon's shoulder and gave him a little shake. 'Come, Vernon. Crying won't help.'

Vernon's blue eyes turned to ice. 'What?'

Roland quickly withdrew his hand. 'I mean . . . it won't bring them back.'

Vernon put a shaky finger right in Roland's face, which had the same effect as a loaded pistol. 'Let me tell you something about crying, Roland Hawkins. It's not cowardly; it's human. Maybe if more people had a good cry, we wouldn't be in this mess.' He gave Roland a hard glare. 'You'll understand when it's the bones of *your* countrymen, and it will be very soon, from what I hear.'

He threw his spade down and lumbered back to the trench. His work detail was over.

Roland watched after him. Vernon, more than any man he knew, was brave. Because unlike the rest of these hardened men, he wasn't afraid to cry.

FOURTEEN
Ilse

There were no names next to Ilse's.
Again.
She checked the ambulance run sheet one more time just to be sure, but there was only the same haunting blank space. The same empty slot. For at least the fourth or fifth time in the last week, no one had signed up to partner with her, and in the recent heatwave, she could have really used a partner.

Ilse sighed, wiping a little bit of sweat off her brow. Perhaps it was exhaustion. Weariness. Because there was a time when nurses lined up to do ambulance runs with her. Even if they weren't all that close to her personally, they had at least respected her skills. They wanted to learn, and they could certainly do so while watching her drive those big, burdensome vehicles around like a champ.

Lately, however, that hadn't been the case. Everyone had taken an exceptionally cold attitude toward her, although she tried to pretend not to notice. She tried to ignore it when people whispered and pointed at her. Tried to pass it off when they didn't sit with her at meals. Tried to keep going despite her ever-increasing loneliness.

Ilse sighed, beckoning to one of the other nurses who lingered nearby. 'Excuse me.'

'What?'

There was no mistaking the tone. Cold and impatient. This woman didn't want to be near Ilse for more than five minutes. Just like so many of the others, and Ilse just couldn't understand it. What had happened over the last few days to make everyone so cross and snappy with her?

'I noticed there's no one signed up to do the next ambulance run with me. Given the weather, I could sure use help—'

'Well, there is no help.'

Ilse put her hands on her hips. 'Things are actually pretty quiet right now. I don't see why just one person can't come along with me and help out.'

'Maybe they just don't want to.'

'Don't want to? Why wouldn't they want to?'

The nurse just let out a haughty huff. Then, with a turn of her heel, she vanished into the sea of cots. No explanation. No apology. No nothing.

Ilse watched after her with alarm, trying to understand this most recent shift in the winds. What had she done to make them so hostile? She bit her lower lip in consternation, trying to work it all out. That's when she noticed a letter in her mail cubby. With a smile, she walked up and fished it out of its tiny box. She turned it over to see the stamp.

Roland Hawkins. Perhaps the only friend she would ever have.

Clutching the letter tightly in her hand, Ilse walked across the spacious, busy exercise yard just outside the church. Patients hobbled everywhere on crutches or canes, quite the injury maze to navigate as she headed toward a lopsided storage shed out back. A little place where she often went for a few moments of privacy.

Her fingers itching to open that letter, Ilse was very close to the shed door when she found herself bottlenecked behind one particular patient. An airman. He stood out from the rest in his flying pants, heavy coat, and knee-high, beat-up boots. He busied himself with a leisurely (too leisurely) stroll around the muddied grounds, his hands stuffed in his pockets. From the back, he didn't look hurt at all. He limped a bit when he walked, but he mostly looked like he should be at a dinner party instead of a churchyard full of broken people.

Ilse tried to squeeze past him, but another patient bumped her, brushing her right up against his broad back.

She gasped. 'Excuse me, so sorry.'

The pilot slowly turned. When Ilse saw his face, she couldn't stop her jaw from dropping, or her stomach from tumbling.

The man's face was gone. Just . . . gone. Disappeared inside a scarred, shriveled, and scarlet lump of skin that didn't even look human – burned beyond all recognition. He had no lips, so his mouth permanently gaped open, exposing his chipped, broken teeth. Only a flap of peeled skin remained where one of his eyes used to be. The other blankly stared at her with no color in the iris, no emotion, and no hope. It was like the man inside had died, but his burned and broken body remained. A mere fragment of what it once was.

His facial handicaps didn't allow him to speak, so he just tipped his head like a gentleman. Then he took his hands from his pockets and made a reach for her. Perhaps he wanted to shake her hand or give her a pat on the shoulder. He wanted a gesture, a token . . . anything that would make him feel like a real man again.

But on instinct, Ilse took a violent step back. Because like his face, his hands were just blocks of seared, burned flesh. The fingers were mostly missing. The usefulness gone.

At Ilse's horrified face, the man drew away from her and buried his hands back in his pockets. He turned his back to her. His horribly disfigured face could no longer register shame, but his slumped shoulders and sunken head sure could.

Ilse bit her lower lip and held back tears. She could feel the hurt radiating from that poor wounded man, who had been through so much, just to have her back away from him like he was some kind of hideous monster. It made her feel extra guilty, since she herself had felt the sting of that recently, what with all the other girls at the hospital turning their backs on her for no real reason. At least not one she could make out anyway.

Ilse sighed, knowing she had to do something to make it right. War had taken too much from that man. He deserved nice manners at the very least, just like she did. So, she worked up the nicest smile in her arsenal. Then she gently touched the man's shoulder. When he turned back around, she curtsied, as if they were meeting at a formal ballroom instead of a blown-apart church yard. She gently lifted his hand out of his pocket. It felt soft and warm inside of her own, despite its grotesque appearance. She brushed her lips on the back of it.

The man's hand shuddered inside hers. A tear dribbled from his remaining eye.

Not letting that smile leave her face, not even for a second, Ilse squeezed his hand one last time, making sure to look him right in the eye. With honor and respect. Admiration even. They stood like that for several seconds before Ilse gave another gentle curtsy.

'A good day to you, sir.'

Unable to speak, the man just nodded back at her. But it was clear the gesture had done plenty to make him feel better. That, in truth, was all Ilse could do. Try to make him feel better. Because she couldn't fix it. Not his face, not his hands, not the horrible war that had done this to him.

Struggling to hide her tears, she gave him one last gentle smile, then she turned around and made swift haste toward the storage shed, refusing to look back.

She had developed an iron stomach over the last two years, and made herself able to face things that others wouldn't even dream of. But some things were still too painful to see up close, and war had done something awful to that man. It had killed him not by taking his life, but by stripping him of any sense of life being normal again. People would treat him like a hideous beast. Children would scream when they saw him. Gentlemen would avert their eyes. Women wouldn't give him a second glance. He would spend his days alone, no doubt, hidden away from polite society, watching as the world moved on without him.

What kind of life would that be? And what could Ilse do about it?

Nothing. It was the most helpless feeling in the world.

Ilse finally arrived at the storage shed, and she shouldered the heavy door open. The familiar, musty smell of moldy wood greeted her. There were no beds in here, no patients, and no medical personnel. No wailing screams. No injured pilots. There was only silence.

That, and clothes. Piles and piles of bloodstained, ripped, and muddy old clothes. Mountains of torn uniforms, worn-out boots, and scraggly puttees. Piled so high that they almost touched the ceiling. Another big pile, comprised of hundreds of broken and rusty pieces of headgear, sat there as well. All of them pulled from soldiers who had died or been evacuated right here at this hospital.

As gruesome as they were, the clothes had to be kept. Because U-boats had disrupted supply chains all over Europe. Authorities wanted every scrap saved, so it could somehow be repurposed into something new. But for now, these mountains only served as a staggering visual representation of the harvest Flanders Fields had reaped. They represented soldiers from all over the world, who had once lived and breathed, loved and laughed, held nurses' hands as they breathed their last. Those coats once kept a shivering boy warm in the biting cold. The boots used to carry rotting, tired feet through the soupy mud. Now they were all hollow and forgotten, left to rot out of sight and out of mind, much like the men themselves.

Ilse sat down on a stack of folded pants facing away from the door. She pulled a flickering oil lamp close to her, then she pulled her letter from her muddied apron.

She and Roland had promised to write each other when he left the hospital, and it didn't take long for his letters to pour in. Only a few days after he left, in fact. While they started casual, with just some updates on how he was doing, what he was up to, and how happy he was to see his friends again, the last few had taken a personal turn. They showed hints of flirtation and deep affection. After a few weeks of writing, he had started signing his letters 'affectionately' instead of 'cordially.'

As for Ilse, she still clung to some of that hard steel in her soul, refusing to lose her head, even when she read his letters alone in this room. When she wrote him back, she held her cards close, keeping her language more professional than friendly. Because she was still so scared, still a *Lusitania* survivor with only a few small remaining pieces of her heart. If she gave Roland Hawkins too much of that, she wouldn't have much left for herself.

It often made her wonder if he would stop writing her. He might tire of trying to pry affection from a woman so hardened by loss. He had to struggle through so many other things. Why should he struggle for her too? She became so convinced he would move on to someone else that she almost began to expect it. Yet the letters kept coming, sometimes every day. And Ilse enjoyed each and every one. They were a small piece of happiness in a world growing increasingly hostile. Small pieces of hope when there was so little of that to be found.

She cracked the latest envelope seal and pried the letter out. It surprised her to find just a single sheet, because normally he filled a few pieces of paper or more.

'Darling Ilse,' she read aloud. '*I need to see you. I'm arranging time off with my captain. A good meeting place would be Talbot House in Poperinge, I'll let you know more when I can . . . affectionately, Roland.*'

A deep frown rumpled Ilse's brows. She couldn't think of many reasons he would need to meet her in person. Something serious must have happened. She pocketed the letter and wrung her hands together with anxiety. It was the first time his correspondence had made her scared instead of happy.

Just as she tried to ponder what it could all mean, she heard the shed door open with its heavy, squeaky groan.

Her nervous hands froze and her heart locked in place. 'Hello?'

'Ilse? Are you in here?'

Ilse let out her breath. It was just one of the other nurses. No one who would give her much trouble for taking a few minutes of silent refuge. 'Hello, Emily. What is it?'

Emily shuffled her way around the clothes mountains, then appeared from around the corner. Like Ilse, she looked way too tired, but she had extra reason to be. A noticeable bulge popped out of her abdomen, pushing against her apron despite her best attempts to conceal it.

When she caught Ilse staring at the bump, she folded her arms over it. 'What are you staring at?'

Yet more coldness and attitude from women who used to at least respect her. Ilse rolled her eyes, deciding for the thousandth time to just ignore it, because she couldn't for the life of her think of any real reason for it. It couldn't just be her heritage. They had known about that all along, and they had worked alongside her anyway. This had to be something new that she had done. Or maybe it was just jealousy. Of her driving, of her talents, of her relationship with Roland. Anything could have been the culprit.

'Sorry, Emily. What do you need?'

'Marie wants to see you. Right now.'

Marie was the new matron at the hospital. She had arrived just a couple weeks ago, only a few short days after Roland had left. The old matron had to be rotated out due to exhaustion. Marie came in her stead, bringing with her a distinct shift in the winds for Ilse. Unlike her old matron, who had almost been protective of her, Marie carried a deep, ugly prejudice toward anything German. She spouted her hatred of the 'boche' whenever she got a chance. She bought into every single piece of anti-German propaganda the newspapers spewed out. She called Germans 'Huns,' 'squareheads,' and 'child killers.'

So, it didn't surprise Ilse when Marie began treating her badly as soon as she arrived. She made an annoying habit of watching Ilse like a hawk. She always hovered nearby when Ilse worked with patients – watching, waiting, practically begging for any tiny little mistake to occur. Then she stopped assigning Ilse any important jobs, like assisting in surgery or triage. She followed Ilse around the hospital as if she were a murderer, keeping tabs on her every interaction. Ilse had even caught her rifling through her mail and personal things when she thought no one else was watching.

'Just trying to keep you honest,' Marie had replied. 'There will be no funny business in my hospital, believe you me.'

Back in the present, Ilse sighed and put her hands on her hips. 'Did Marie say what she wants?'

'She didn't. But you know we can't keep her waiting, so you'd best come along.'

Ilse wasn't sure why. After all, Marie had summoned her to the office plenty of times already for some dressing down or another. But this time, she got a sinking feeling in her stomach. A warning shot from deep inside.

Reluctantly, she followed Emily out of the shed and made her way back toward the church. Of their own accord, her eyes searched the grounds for that poor pilot.

Like her confidence, he was gone. Vanished into the mist.

Marie was a muscular matron in both build and personality. She lifted heavy equipment without aid from anyone. She had a loud, commanding voice, garnering everyone's attention when she used it. She kept her hair pulled back in a rigid bun, which perfectly framed her red, puffy, and stern features. She reminded Ilse of a bitter old schoolteacher that no amount of hard work could please.

For that, and obvious other reasons, she liked to keep her facetime with Marie to a minimum. So, she had to force her feet to timidly step into Marie's office, which was just a sectioned-off corner of the church with a shabby wooden table.

'Matron,' Ilse greeted her with a strained voice. 'You wanted to see me?'

'Yes, *Chère-Amie*,' Marie said in her thick British accent. 'It's what some of the boys call you, isn't it?'

'Sometimes, yes.'

'Lovely. Please take a seat.'

Ilse's stomach tightened with nerves, but she managed a half curtsy before she took a seat in a wooden chair across from the matron.

Marie wasted no time, quickly taking the stature of a woman ready to pounce on her prey. 'You know, despite your fancy nicknames, I'm fully aware of your heritage, my dear. And I had my doubts about anything with German blood working in this hospital. I wanted you thrown out, I did. Right from the moment I laid eyes on you. But your old matron assured me you were one of the best. Convinced me to look the other way.' She shook her head. 'How foolish that I listened.'

Ilse winced. 'I'm *American*. And my mother was English. If you know so much about me, you know that too.'

Marie huffed. 'You can't prove it, can you? You haven't verified or even discussed any of your life before the war in the months you've been here. And in a war, you don't want people drawing their own conclusions.'

'I know. It's why we came up with the other name.'

Marie laughed, but certainly not in a friendly way. 'Oh, look at you. It's all part of the play act, I suppose. The innocent girl, who only wants to help out, and all those long ambulance runs by yourself. It looks so good on paper.'

Ilse didn't like where this discussion was headed. 'What is it you want, Marie?'

Marie leaned across the table, her bulging, brown eyes menacing. 'I've received alarming reports from staff members about your behavior with poison gas patients. Checking on them late at night when no one is around, extra examinations, even speaking German with some of them.'

Ilse drew in a sharp breath, alarm bells going off all through her body. She couldn't believe her bedside romance with a patient could have been misconstrued in such a fashion. She would have laughed if it didn't put her in such a bad spot. Besides, it hurt too much to laugh. Because the whole thing reminded her, once and for all, that she had no friends in this hospital, and she probably never would. She had lost their trust, lost their confidence, and even lost their respect. All because of where her father happened to be born. That, and a secret romance.

'What do you have to say for yourself on this subject?'

Ilse struggled to find her voice. 'What exactly are you accusing me of?'

'The ladies tell me you're experimenting on poison gas victims. Seeing if you can worsen their injuries, improve the effects of the gas, and sending the information back to the Germans. Despite the horror of it, I can't say it came as a shock.'

It was a serious accusation, flung at her by her own colleagues. Colleagues that she had tried so hard over the last several months to win over. My, how she had failed. Devastated didn't seem like a strong enough word to convey how she really felt.

She would have to wade fast through the sting though. Because Marie had of course fallen for the story. She probably welcomed it as the long-awaited excuse to purge Ilse from her prized ranks. She wouldn't likely accept a secret romance as an excuse either.

'Marie, I've worked in this hospital for almost two years. My loyalties lie with America and her allies. You can't really think I would do something like that.'

'You know, spying carries harsh consequences, and being a woman wouldn't save you. If you do have an excuse for all the secrets, I suggest you spill it, and I suggest you tell me the truth.'

'The truth . . .' Ilse sighed. What did truth even mean right now? Marie would spin her own version of the truth, no matter what came out of Ilse's mouth.

She didn't know how she had wound up in such a fix. She was one of the finest nurses at this hospital. Her life had gained purpose here, and she meant something to people. Now here she sat, kicked aside by everyone and left to rot in the gutters of warfare. Like the torpedo in the hull of the *Lusitania*, the shift knocked the breath right out of her.

'Ilse!'

'I'm not German. I'm *American*. How many times must I say it?'

'You've said that more than enough. What you haven't adequately explained is why you left America. No one would leave that fortress for this wasteland. Unless they were up to no good.'

'My father lost his job. We were going to England to stay with my mother's family and wait out the war.'

'And your mother was English, was she?' Marie crossed her arms. 'To which part of England were you heading then, my dear? Tell me all about it, right down to the color of the soil, so I know you aren't lying.'

'I don't know. I had never been there before.'

'How convenient. Can you even tell me your mother's family name?'

'Smith.'

Marie let out an obnoxious cackle. 'Of course you pick the most common name in Christendom, so it's virtually impossible to track your mother's family down. It's clever, really. Then your papers were "lost," from what I understand. That too is very convenient, isn't it?'

'It's the truth.'

'And where is your family now? Fighting on the German front?'

Ilse glared. The more questions Marie peppered her with, the more her temperature rose. Even now, despite all the trouble that had just come crashing down on her, she could feel the anger flush her cheeks and bristle the back of her neck. She thought of her father, and how many times he had decried the Kaiser's cruelty at the dinner table. How many times he had condemned the war. 'Not all Germans support this war, you know. Not by a long shot.'

'Why not? Too cowardly?'

Ilse's eyes flashed. Her shoulders went rigid and her breathing turned feral. 'Well, you don't have to worry about my family at any rate. They're dead, if you must know. Dead. Never coming back.'

Marie clearly hadn't expected a shot like that. Not just the words, but the overwhelming emotion in them. A rare hint of sympathy appeared in her hard eyes. 'Well . . . that's . . . my Lord, child. What happened?'

Ilse suddenly felt every ear in the hospital turn to her, and it made her stomach boil over with rage. Of course they wanted the gruesome details of her family's death, as if it were grand and illustrious entertainment for their war-fevered minds. Well, she wouldn't give Marie or anyone else the satisfaction. They hadn't earned it. So, she stood from her chair with her jaw clenched in fury. She didn't even fear Marie anymore. She was too angry to be afraid. If this was how they wanted to play, then so be it.

'My parents were killed in a U-boat incident. I survived. That's all you need to know. And the only part I've played in this war is right here, saving countless *British* lives. Which of these things, may I ask, is a crime?'

'And what of all your time with the gas patients?'

'I warmed up to one. A Yank from New York. We . . . became involved, I suppose. But before you accuse me of loose morals on top of everything else, you should know all the girls have done it behind your back. I'm sure you've noticed Emily putting on some extra pounds lately, all in her abdomen.'

Marie's brief compassion vanished like the ripples on a lake. 'Babies out of wedlock isn't a war crime, dearie. Experimenting with gas patients sure is.'

'You have no proof, which is what you just condemned me over. Sending me to the authorities would only make you a hypocrite.'

Marie's demeanor darkened. 'Something tells me I could convince them without proof, young lady. Unlike *you*.'

'Well then, I hope you'll reflect on losing one of the only competent ambulance drivers left in this hospital.'

Marie may not have been one to negotiate with underlings, especially Ilse, but it was a valid point, and she knew it. The hospital, and in fact the entire medical department, had hemorrhaged ambulance drivers lately. Many got pulled to different units or even different fields of service. Most of the male ones had abandoned them for the airfields. Losing Ilse and her skills would slow her hospital operations to a crawl, and she couldn't deny that.

She glowered. 'Well, you've got some nerve, haven't you?'

'I got it from my father. Thanks for noticing.'

Marie snorted. 'It's almost admirable, whatever it is. Enough to give you some time, at least.'

'What do you mean?'

'You caught me on two points. I don't have any drivers, and I don't have any proof. So, you can stay here until I decide what to do with you. In the meantime, you will work directly under my supervision. Don't even think about a transfer because you don't have a shot in hell. Do I make myself quite plain?'

'You're putting me on house arrest?'

'I would feel lucky about that if I was you.'

Ilse was too angry to answer. She gave a sarcastic click of her heels, then she stormed away from the desk.

FIFTEEN
Ilse

October, 1917

Ilse leaned against the side of her ambulance, her eyes darting around the muddy streets of Poperinge. The small Belgian village sat roughly ten miles from Ypres, rendering it *mostly* safe from the shells and bullets, but not exactly making it peaceful.

Throughout the course of the war, the little town had morphed from a quiet country settlement to a booming civilian refugee camp. Families loaded down with carts of meager possessions swarmed the place. Gaunt mothers with pale faces and penniless purses trudged through the street with children clinging to their torn skirts. New widows scoured the Red Cross tents and begged for news about their remaining loved ones. One shriveled old woman, for some reason, carried a parakeet in a birdcage as she wondered along the street. A roughed-up old war hawk in a torn overcoat limped down the sidewalk on a cane. Several young men hobbled on crutches with missing limbs and distorted faces.

Then there were the British troops. Rough-and-tumble soldiers from the trenches who spent their brief periods of leave in this village. A stark contrast to the somber civilians, those boys viewed 'Pop' as the land of plenty, plowing through the pubs, brothels, and beer. They shoveled down any hot meals their pitiful army pay could get them. They shouted and whistled while they terrorized the streets, singing jolly, crude songs with their blood pumped full of drink.

Those British Tommies. Ilse thanked her lucky stars for them – especially today. Because along with their fighting skill and bravery, they were also a perfect excuse. The main one she had used to arrange this visit to Pop in the first place.

A few days ago, with a letter from Roland in her trembling hand and a heart thumping with anticipation, she had planted the seeds among a few of the quieter, less hostile nurses about how long overdue for an outing they were. A day out, away from the hospital. How long since they'd had any leave? Wouldn't they like a day to enjoy Pop and flirt with the handsome soldiers? She'd happily drive them . . . if they could get Marie to let her. Which, after enough begging, Marie did, with a stark glare. 'Don't let her out of your sight,' she had said to the other girls when she thought Ilse couldn't hear her. 'She's trouble, that one.'

Ilse managed to crack a smile at the memory of her own cleverness as she probed her way through the chaos, stepping into a schoolhouse yard to take stock of her surroundings. Slipping away from the other girls had been easy enough. 'I must stay and check the ambulance engine,' she had told them. 'Didn't you hear that incessant rattling on the drive? No? Well, leave it to me. Go, have fun.'

She could tell they had a hard time buying it. They had looked at each other nervously, unsure they could trust Ilse. Because no one could trust Ilse. Yet one look at those handsome soldier boys had done them all in. Off they went, giggling, merry-making, leaving Ilse behind to her own devices.

Ilse pulled the letter from Roland out of her pocket. The very one that had inspired all this sneaking around and scheming. 'Talbot House,' she whispered to herself. She ran her finger over the address, and the date and time Roland had asked her to come meet him. The only leave he could procure with his officer. *Please come*, he had penned. *It's very important I see you, away from the madness of the hospital.*

With a sigh, she looked around at the schoolhouse yard, where she found shuttered windows and chained doors, but a class was still taking place on the lawn. A male Red Cross volunteer, sporting a heavy gas mask, held up the respirator box to a gathered crowd of small children. Each child had their own mask too, some fitting so big the kids practically disappeared beneath the sour rubber and buggy eye holes. It made them look frightening, almost like little monsters. The Red Cross instructor pointed out the various features on the respirator box, teaching his charges how to use it in an emergency.

Ilse skirted past the chilling demonstration, ducking into a Red Cross medical station. Shrieking civilians had inundated the place. One woman with a split-open eyebrow stared into nothingness while a Red Cross nurse stitched her up. Another woman, heavily pregnant, wailed for her dead husband while a nurse offered donuts, as if that would somehow help. Another nurse bore a shaking old man with sweats and a terrible cough.

Ilse swallowed hard to shut out the awful scenes.

Wounded soldiers didn't bother her like this. She was almost callous toward them. The way she looked at it, soldiers fought wars, and wars produced injuries. Sad but true. However, she had no such stomach for the sight of wounded innocents. People just trying to live their lives and stay out of a fight they hadn't started, and certainly didn't have the means to finish. This wasn't their war, yet they still had to die for it in spades.

As for those who lived, well, they suffered more than anyone. Homes sheltering them for centuries had been obliterated by wayward shells. Trenches and gun emplacements had torn up generational farming livelihoods. Blockades and war shortages had drained their food supplies. Fabrics and clothes became impossible to get. Disease made deadly house calls to many a poverty-stricken family.

No one should have to suffer war, but to Ilse, suffering civilians were the worst injustice of all. Besides, the scenes resurrected some of her own dormant ghosts. These battered, crying faces put her in mind of the *Lusitania*. As she wandered through the tent, those awful memories of screaming people in the water, bodies lined up in the morgue, and her father's frozen corpse forced their way to the surface. It stopped her in her tracks. She closed her eyes, put her hands to her stomach, and tried to block out the sounds of screaming children and sobbing people.

'Say, are you the lady I saw driving that ambulance?'

Ilse's eyes snapped open. A Red Cross woman stood in front of her. She wore a clean-cut uniform with a becoming black skirt and wool jacket.

Ilse blinked a few times to collect her thoughts. 'Yes.'

'Wow, ain't too many women drivers in the American Red Cross. We could sure use 'em though. The men keep running off to join the air corps. Or getting drafted into the trenches.'

Ilse smiled. 'You're American?'

'Sure am.'

'I grew up in New York.'

The Red Cross woman brightened. 'Fantastic! Gosh, look at all us American gals over here doing our bit. Wouldn't they get a laugh back home to see us beating the men into the war zone? Maybe they'll finally give us the vote in the end.' She took Ilse's hand. 'Listen, we could really use an ambulance driver to evacuate some of these wounded.'

'I wish I could, but I'm on special orders.'
'Blast it all.'
'Could you tell me where I can find Talbot House?'
'You mean that army club run by the minister? What in the world brings you there?'

Ilse didn't know her prearranged meeting place would be recognized, and she turned the wheels in her brain for an excuse. No need to draw any unnecessary attention to herself, if it could be avoided.

'An officer I tended before needs a medical exam. Lord knows why it can't wait, but orders are orders, aren't they?'

The Red Cross woman huffed. 'They act like we got nothing better to do.' She pointed her finger down the main street. 'Follow this street all the way down. You'll see the sign to Talbot House out front. Big white building, you can't miss it.' She grinned and gave Ilse a wink. 'Don't worry, the reverend makes honest men out of those boys, so they should keep their paws to themselves.'

Ilse giggled. 'Thank you.'

Talbot House. The cozy, white building stood three stories tall, beckoning to onlookers with its fresh trim and crisp paint. Cheery piano music spilled from the windows and into the street, along with the thunderous voices of laughing soldiers, singing and stumbling their way through 'It's a Long Way to Tipperary.'

A host of British soldiers also clustered just outside the door. Despite their various ranks, they passed cigarettes and biscuits around, carrying on joyful conversations like they were old chums from Blighty. A jolting sight, because normally, officers and enlisted men had nothing to do with each other. But a sign above the door suggested things were different here at Talbot House.

'Abandon Rank, All Ye Who Enter Here.'

Ilse smiled at the sign. She didn't know much about Talbot House, but if it encouraged people of all ranks to get along, then she already liked it.

Her opinion only improved when she timidly stepped through the front door. A fancy front parlor greeted her, with polished wooden floors, fluffy, comfortable chairs, and a handsome rug for bootless feet. A modest chandelier hung from the ceiling, casting a romantic, golden light over the soldiers lounging about in a haze of cigarette smoke.

Music from the adjoining canteen room created a joyful ambiance. A happy soldier, with his coat casually undone and his hair rumpled, pounded on the keys of an old piano. The boys huddled around him and bellowed through patriotic songs. A large cauldron of tea steamed on the table behind them, while more soldiers tackled a heap of freshly baked cakes.

Ilse bumped and jostled through the rabble-rousing soldiers, and accidentally thumped against a large parchment on the wall. A tack holding it in place popped off, and she scrambled to put the wrinkled, faded paper back in order. As she did, she took in the countless, handwritten messages of guests past.

Brenton Smith of Manchester, your brother Will was here on 6/2/17.
Dearest John Bloom of London, your brothers Sam and Tim were here on 22/7/17.
Willy Thackett, my boy! Your father Bradley was here on 31/7/17.

Ilse gently ran her finger over all the happy greetings and wistful notes. As she read, she realized the parchment was a message board, a place for family and friends to try to locate one another in a world that had gone completely mad. Next to it, there was a big map of the Western Front. A little knot of soldiers, boisterously shouting as they did so, pointed out their various fighting spots, bragging about their many war stories and battle feats.

'You must be Ilse Stahl.'

Ilse whirled to face a stocky, well-built man with a gentle smile and thick-rimmed glasses. Instead of a uniform, he sported a blue blazer with a telling white square on the collar.

A man of the cloth.

She quickly collected herself. 'Reverend.'

The man took her hand and gave it an old-fashioned peck with his lips. 'Please, call me Tubby.'

Ilse stifled a laugh at such a silly nickname, even if it did seem to suit him. 'Yes . . . certainly, Mr Tubby. Pardon my asking but . . . how do you know me?'

'You're here to see Roland Hawkins, yes? A charming American fellow, I say. He told me he needed a safe place to meet with you. I told him you could come here.' He gave her a stern, only half-joking wink. 'Provided we all behave ourselves, of course.'

Ilse couldn't help but giggle. 'Yes. Of course. Could you tell me where I might find him?'

'Roland usually prefers the quiet reading rooms over the ruckus down here. If he isn't there, let's pray he ventured into the third-floor chapel. It would do that boy some good.'

Ilse grinned. She didn't imagine Roland as the praying type, but she didn't dare say that to a minister. 'Thank you for your help.'

Tubby gave her a polite bow. 'Please come find me if you can't locate him. And do please behave if you do locate him.'

With that, Tubby stepped into the canteen room, joining in the boisterous singing at the piano. A somewhat filthy number about a mademoiselle from Armentières. Tubby may not have approved of naughty behavior in his Christian establishment, but he sure didn't seem to mind singing about it.

As for Ilse, she made her way to the rickety staircase and crept up to the second floor. There, she found the reading room Tubby had mentioned. Piles of books lined every single wall, the stacks almost touching the ceiling. Old newspapers were spread open across the long wooden table. A young boy, too young to enlist, sat behind a small desk, barely visible behind a mountain of army hats. The now-hatless men, who had exchanged their cap as a deposit for their books, lounged about the table with their chosen reading materials.

Just off the bookroom sat a little writing nook, housing various desks and piles of stationery. Men with cigarettes and fast-moving quills occupied every one of them. Their heads bowed in concentration as they reveled in scratching off letters on fresh paper, with real pens. They also sipped tea and munched on cakes from downstairs.

None of them were the man Ilse sought, though. She strolled past the reading room and found her way to another staircase. Unlike the main stairwell, it was steep and narrow, more like a wobbly ladder than actual stairs. She clung to the railings and stooped to avoid cracking her head on the ceiling as she ascended. Each stair moaned and creaked under her weight. Once she reached the top, she poked her head and shoulders through an open attic door.

There, she found a small but beautiful chapel. The ceiling sloped into a gentle point, supported by curving beams painted a handsome buttercream. A stylish maroon carpet adorned the wooden floor. Rows of nicely organized wooden benches faced a red-overlaid altar and a humble, wooden cross. Soothing candlelight from a chandelier made the entire place glow.

As Ilse took in the charming space, she felt her tense muscles stand down. For the first time in months, her blood pumped a little more smoothly, and she even felt the brush of a smile. She could see how war-weary boys found their salvation in a room like this. She hadn't even officially entered, but she already felt more at peace here than she had in years. Perhaps from the lingering energy of all those soldiers, from all walks of life, who had come here and found something to live for.

Ilse climbed into the room and took a few humble steps forward, trying not to disturb the frail wooden floorboards. After all, she wasn't the only one up here.

A pair of uniformed men sat toward the front. Sobs shook the shoulders of one of them, while the other whispered words of comfort in his ear. Another man bowed his head in the back corner, rocking back and forth and chewing his nails in a nervous fit.

Lastly, Ilse's eyes found a man in a clean, freshly pressed British uniform. His chestnut hair was washed, his skin scrubbed spotless. He had folded his hands in his lap, one of them with a visible scar from gas blisters.

Roland Hawkins: a much cleaner version of him than Ilse was used to. She tiptoed across the wooden floor. When he didn't turn around, she put a hand on his shoulder.

As soon as he looked up at her, his eyes lit up with tenderness, like the candles in this room. He reached out for her hand and kissed it. 'Ilse,' he whispered. 'It's so good to see you again. I'd give you a friendlier greeting, but it might not fit the surroundings.'

'So your friend Tubby tells me.' Ilse sat down next to Roland and pulled out a crinkled letter from her pocket. 'Meet me at Talbot House . . .' She mock-read from the letter. 'You didn't tell me the place was famous.'

'I thought everyone knew about Talbot House.'

'Everyone but me.'

'I'm glad you found the place anyway, and that you met Reverend Clayton.'

'Clayton . . . has a nicer ring than Tubby.'

Roland chuckled. 'Yeah, he's silly that way. Another reason so many boys love him.' He made sure no one was looking, then he gave her a gentle kiss on her lower cheek, just brushing his lips against the top of her flushing neck.

Ilse's stomach ignited as she breathed in his scent. Light hints of soap and even a bit of aftershave.

Roland stood up and took her hand in his. 'Let's go out to the garden and talk.'

She allowed Roland to lead her out of the quiet chapel and back down the creaky stairs. They swept through the noise and celebration of Talbot House's main floor, and Roland led her to a back door off the canteen room, opening it up to let her outside.

Just before she walked out, Ilse exchanged a glance with Tubby.

His eyes twinkled as he noticed her with Roland. He gave her another polite bow, then he went back to his boys. 'All right, boys. "Long Way to Tipperary," one last time!'

The piano came to life again, as did the voices in the canteen room.

Roland and Ilse slipped out the back door and into a spacious bit of green ground behind the house. The lush lawn came as a shock to her tired eyes. Months had passed since she last saw a clean-cut lawn, undisturbed by shell craters and trenches. And forget about flowers. She hadn't seen one in so long, she almost forgot they existed. Yet here, countless, tidy shrubs packed with purple, spherical blossoms hedged the place off from the entire world. A fountain trickled in the middle of the grass. A few men sat under swaying shade trees. A few more crowded around a small building at the far end of the garden, which housed a petting zoo. A host of barks, squawks, and meows emanated from it, along with joyful laughter.

Ilse took it all in with a smile. 'This is something Tubby has done, isn't it? Giving all these boys a nice place to get away from it all.'

'It's not his only virtue.'

'Oh?'

'He'll help anyone, regardless of rank. Rumor has it he personally intervened with the British army to reunite two brothers who hadn't seen each other since 1914.' Roland looked around the spacious yard and his face fell a little. 'I heard one of them died a few weeks later.'

Ilse felt the familiar blade of tragedy, and she forced a smile to sweep it away. She didn't have much time with Roland, and she didn't want to spend any of it sad. 'So . . . you seem to know your way around this place.'

'Oh, yes. I come every time I get leave in Pop.' He let out a sudden, raspy cough.

Ilse noticed. She also ran her fingers over the marks on his hands. 'You're feeling better other than the coughing, I hope?'

'I suppose, but I'm still not the same.'

Ilse sighed. She didn't have the heart to tell him he might never be the same again.

'You know I was so excited to have a real meal when I got here,' Roland said. 'Soon as I was cleaned up, I stopped at a pub, got their finest dish, and sat down to devour it. Damn it all, it tasted like wood.'

'Cheap rations?'

'Probably, but that wasn't it. Ever since I got gassed, everything tastes like shit.' He unbuttoned his jacket, exposing another gas scar on his collarbone.

A silence stole up between them. Then, Ilse put her arm in his and let him lead her on a stroll across the grounds.

'All right, Roland. What's so important that you had to drag me away from the hospital?'

He hesitated, as if he didn't want to bring up a sore subject. 'Yes. I um . . . I have something to tell you, and I wanted to tell you in person.'

Ilse suddenly felt like she'd swallowed a brick. Ever since she got that first letter, she had boiled with curiosity. She had plenty to distract her from the pestering questions of what it might mean, but the anxiety always hung over her like a monkey on her back. Now, her steps came to a halt and she looked up at Roland, with images of women in trouble from loose-moral soldier boys flashing in her head. Emily, pregnant and alone because her soldier had left her for a nurse who wasn't in a delicate condition. Mary, who fell for a well-to-do British officer, only to find out he was married. Louise, romanced by a wild pilot and dropped by him a few days later.

Had her turn arrived?

'Well, I guess there's no subtle way to put this, is there?' He ran a hand through his hair. 'Ilse, I'm leaving Europe.'

Her heart skipped a few beats. It was a blow all right, just not the one she expected. 'What?'

'I'm joining up with the Americans.'

She struggled to absorb the news, and what it meant for her. 'When?'

'I'm not sure yet, but soon.'

She tried to take it in stride, but that was a hard ask. Roland was the only friend she had. While most of their interaction was through letters, at least knowing he was nearby, that she had someone to run to if things got too terrible – well, it got her through her increasingly difficult days. It would be hell to lose that safety net, and it wasn't like she had another. None of the others at the hospital wanted anything to do with her. Especially these days.

Ilse hadn't told Roland about any of this. She had wanted to write him, but Marie censored her mail. Besides, she probably wouldn't have even if she could. Because she didn't want to burden him in the trenches. He had plenty to worry about just trying to stay alive. But now he was leaving, which changed things enough that it meant the time had finally come to tip her hand.

'Roland . . .'

'Please don't be sore. I didn't want to go at first. I thought it would be better if I just stayed here. But, well, let's just say I've turned it over and I have my reasons. Besides, I might be able to get a commission. I could get out of those damn trenches, Ilse.'

'The doughboys will go to the trenches too.'

'The doughboys, perhaps. Not the air corps.'

Ilse froze. Images of that burned pilot invaded her mind. His twisted face, his gaping mouth, his missing eye.

Her lower lip trembled. 'You want to join the air service?'

Roland beamed. 'Yes.'

'Why, Roland? Why would you do that?'

He must have turned it over in his mind more than she thought, because his answer was immediate and unflinching. Yes, Roland had thought this over a great deal.

'Because I have to make this mean something, Ilse.'

She hesitated, unsure how anything could mean something in a war like this. 'Mean something?'

'My brother's enlisted now. He'll be heading to this hell soon enough.'

'Yes, I know. What has that got to do with the air service?'

'Then there's you, me, and the countless millions of other people caught up in this mess. All those deaths in the mud, Ilse. The throwing human beings at machine guns and hoping it will make a difference, when it obviously won't.'

'Roland—'

'We can never end the war this way. We can't crack those machine guns by just tossing more men in there. In an airplane, I can actually fight back. One airplane can do more damage than an entire regiment of men. They're the key to getting us out of this mess. Men aren't just numbers up there. Men can . . . well, make a difference. Bring some meaning into this madness.'

He turned away from her then, putting his fist in his mouth to keep from crying. 'I've already written some of my dad's old police pals for a recommendation. I figure I have a better shot getting in stateside, where at least a few people know me.'

Ilse stayed quiet for a long time, thinking the whole thing over, trying to process it all.

Watching her stew in her thoughts, Roland's eyes went dim. 'What's the matter, Ilse?'

She frowned at him. 'What do you mean, what's the matter? I work in a hospital, Roland. Those airplanes may be the key to your future, but they are no match for solid ground, are they? I've seen what happens to those men when something goes wrong up there.'

Now it was Ilse's turn to look away. The thought of that burned pilot was making her sick, and she couldn't stop her mind from putting Roland's face on his twisted body.

'Well, I won't go back to those damn mud pits. Something tells me I won't get so lucky in a second gas attack. And if I have to keep fighting, I'd rather do it in a battlefield where I can actually make a difference.'

Ilse wanted to argue more, but she couldn't think of a single thing to say. How could she? Instead, she just crammed the images of the burned pilot to the back of her mind. She would just have to keep him there forever, right next to her memories of the *Lusitania*.

'How long would you be gone?'

'I don't know. Probably several months at least.'

Ilse felt her emotions build like a tidal wave inside her, pressing against her organs and banging against her skin. For the first time in years, she couldn't control them. Her face turned to steel and her jaw clenched up tight. She felt her stomach tumble down, down, down. Almost into her feet, which suddenly felt very heavy. As if she didn't have enough to keep her up at night. Now she was going to lose her only friend, and in more ways than one.

'Well, wonderful. Just wonderful for you. Go back to America then, fly the airplanes, and I can stay here. Alone. And in the worst trouble I've ever been in since . . . since . . .'

She couldn't say it. She put her hands over her face and tried with everything in her to hold back the tears.

'Ilse, what are you talking about?'

'You're the only friend I have, you know. I thought I could at least depend on you in all this mess.'

'What mess?'

'Oh, this whole thing is a mess.' She whirled around and stormed off toward the petting zoo. Because if she kept looking at that wounded look on his face, she wouldn't be able to keep herself together.

Roland followed close on her heels and tried to keep up. 'Hey, start making some sense. What are you talking about?'

She came to a dead halt. Her pride begged her to stay quiet, but her wisdom urged her to show her cards. She had fixed all her previous problems without him, but this was one problem she just couldn't figure out on her own. She needed at least one person in her corner, and she needed him right this minute.

She sighed. 'Roland, I'm in bad trouble.'

His eyes filled with something that looked like worry, which was strange to Ilse. She hadn't seen anyone worry about her in quite a long time.

'What kind of trouble?'

'When you were in the hospital, some nurses got suspicious at all the time we spent together. They heard us speak German. They think I experimented on gas patients and reported it to the Kaiser. They think . . . they think I'm a spy.'

Roland's face went livid.

'My matron threatened to have me arrested. I'm on borrowed time.' Unable to meet Roland's eye, she focused on the rustling leaves to keep herself together. 'I need help, Roland. I'm not sure I can fight this battle alone.'

'Ilse . . .'

She let out a defeated sigh. 'What do I have to do to prove myself anyway? I didn't expect pity or handouts even when I deserved them. I thought if I got through it without any help, if I stayed on my feet no matter what, someone would finally let me into their world, or any world.' Tears brimmed in her eyes, but she fought like hell to keep them there.

Roland saw her coming unglued, and he snatched her in his arms and pressed her against him. Before she knew what was happening, tears, so many tears, were spilling out of her eyes and soaking the front of his uniform. Tears she had refused to cry for so long, but now could no longer hold in. As for Roland, it didn't seem to faze him. He just cradled her face against his soapy-smelling chest and let her cry.

'There now,' he whispered to her. 'Let it all out. Just let it all out, Ilse.'

Ilse, tucked away in someone's arms for the first time in years, flashed back to that hug with her father aboard the *Lusitania*, when he had promised she would always belong to him. Minutes later he was dead, and she hadn't belonged to anyone since. Now, in a quiet garden at Talbot House, Roland Hawkins held her in the exact same way.

She exhaled from deep inside and released years' worth of tension. Her shoulders relaxed, and her body sank into the embrace. She laid her head on his shoulder, and she let his comfort pour into her skin and penetrate down to her deepest layers, moistening the drought inside of her soul. She had forgotten the power of human touch. How good it felt to be held, how safe it felt. How loved she felt . . .

Roland ran his hand over her hair. After a few minutes, he felt her heavy breathing slow down. 'Tell me now, how serious is this?'

Ilse reluctantly pulled out of the embrace to lay it all out on the table. 'Well, I think it's bad. Marie hates anything German.'

'Tell her you're American.'

'I tried that. She doesn't believe me.'

'Don't you have a passport?'

Ilse felt renewed frustration bubble up in her stomach. 'No, Roland. I don't.'

He frowned. 'Well . . . sheesh, Ilse. How the hell did you get over here without a passport?'

The spark of frustration quickly fanned itself into a flame. A fire so strong she had to turn her back on him, before it spilled out of her mouth in a string of curse words.

Roland put a hand on her shoulder. 'Let me talk to her. It sounds like this was my own damn fault anyway. I can clear it up for you, can't I?'

Ilse just snarled to herself. 'You'd be wasting your breath. These days, once someone gets an idea in their head, it takes artillery and millions of deaths to talk them out of it.'

'Then how can I help?'

'I'm not sure you can, especially if you're leaving.'

'Don't you have parents that can help?'

She shook her head and wiped tears away before he saw them.

'Why not? Where is your family? Are they . . . are they in Germany?'

It was the thousandth time she'd been asked the question. Only this time, because of that warm embrace, she knew his motives. He didn't want to abuse her or beat her down. He just wanted to help her.

There was only one way she could do this. She had to detach from it all, not tap into her grief. She had to tell it like an impersonal narrator. There would be no pity and no consolation. She didn't want either. She just wanted to keep her life out of Marie's gnarled hands.

She steeled her soul and out it came. 'My parents are dead.'

Roland reeled as if he'd been punched. 'I uh . . . dead? Both of them? How?'

Ilse sighed. 'Back in America, my family, we never had it easy, but there was a lot of persecution once war broke out.'

Roland swallowed hard, remembering his own part in that.

Ilse continued. 'My mother's family lived in England, and they had a great deal of money. A safe place in the country where we could wait it out. We decided to go. We boarded a steamer . . .' She hesitated. She looked at Roland with pointed eyes. 'The *Lusitania*.'

His eyes went wide. 'Wait . . . you were on the *Lusitania*? The *Lusitania*?'

'That torpedo upended my whole world. Somehow, I survived. I kept going. And I've been trying to keep going ever since.'

Roland had no idea what to say, so he pulled her in for another hug.

She broke away this time. Affection would only break the dam she'd built against her grief, and now was no time for a breach. 'Save your sympathy, please. I've made as much peace with it as I can. Besides, I have to focus on living. Right now, I think that means going home. To my real home. America.' She folded her hands like an employer at a job interview. 'So, let's talk about that.'

Roland looked intimidated by her business-like tone, but it also helped him focus. 'Why don't you just write immigration? Tell them what happened?'

'It was a Cunard liner, so my mother used her maiden name to get our tickets. "Stahl" won't match the passenger list. They wouldn't believe me.'

'They might.'

'Please. A girl like me in a time like this?'

Roland sighed. 'I'm going to fix this, you hear me?'

'Good luck.'

He grabbed her arm. 'I mean it. I can help. My dad was on the police force in New York. Well respected. They can help me find birth records, employment records . . . something to prove you lived in America. Besides, everyone back stateside has immense sympathy for the *Lusitania* victims. For heaven's sake, they were ready to go to war over it right then. You need to tell people what happened to you, Ilse. Tell them. You might find more help than you think.'

'Maybe if my father wasn't German.'

Roland sighed. 'I promise you we can get the wheels rolling, but it might take time, so you'd need to lay low for a while.'

Lay low *how*? Ilse scanned her brain for ideas, knowing her options were limited. Marie wouldn't let her go to another hospital. Too much time had passed to find her mother's family. Besides, she doubted she could even get back to England.

The rattlesnake of Ilse's anger coiled inside of her and prepared to snap again, but then her eyes suddenly lit up. The Red Cross girl flashed in her head, reminding Ilse she had a skill many women didn't. She could drive, and she could do it extremely well. It meant Ilse had something valuable to offer.

'I can drive . . .' she mumbled to herself.

Roland raised his eyebrows. 'Sure . . . but I don't know how that will—'

'What about the Red Cross? The American Red Cross?'

He turned the thought over, nodding as he silently worked through the pros and cons. 'Well, it's a good idea, but how would we get you in?'

'They need women drivers.'

Roland winced. 'Yes but . . . American women drivers. You can't prove . . .'

She waved her hand through the air. 'It would be a problem stateside in a lengthy application process, but not over here, where they're short-handed and desperate. I saw a Red Cross woman on my way here. She was ready to put me to work on the spot. All I need is someone to get me out of Marie's hands. It's a privately run corps so technically she can't order me to stay, but she would probably have me arrested if I tried to leave on my own.'

'What can I do?'

'Like I said, technically they don't have to answer to the military, but if the military was on my side, I doubt she'd push it.'

Roland's face fell. 'I'm a private, Ilse. I can't pull that much weight.'

'But you've made some friends, yes? Any officer friends?'

Roland ran a list of his commanding officers in his head. He also ran a list of anyone else he knew. His eyes drifted toward the window of Talbot House. Inside, he saw Tubby at the piano with his boys. His booming voice floated out into the yard.

Roland grinned. 'You know, I think I do know someone who can help.'

Ilse followed his gaze. 'Who? Tubby?'

'I told you he's intervened in certain cases before. Maybe he'll help us too.' He smiled and grabbed her hands. 'Just stay alive until then. Can you do that?'

With that one question, with that one heart-rending yet hopeful look, Ilse mentally put back on the armor she had worn for so long. If she could survive the *Lusitania*, she could survive stuffy Marie and her band of treacherous staff. It would take a lot of resolve, but that was one thing she never ran short on. She nodded at Roland.

'I'll also get things going stateside,' Roland said. 'I know you're strong enough to take care of yourself, but I'll take care of you too, my Chère-Amie. Always.'

Ilse wasn't sure why, but something about this man made her remember how it felt to be loved. Really loved, like her family had loved her. She didn't have the words to thank him like a lady, so she planted her hands on him and kissed him on the lips instead.

The boys by the petting zoo gave them a hearty round of cheers.

SIXTEEN
Roland

November, 1917

A crisp, autumn morning had descended on New York City. The sky was clear, with the sun glaring down on the busy, bustling harbor. Steamer whistles and bells underscored the surge in outgoing ships. Seagulls squawked around more vessels sloshing around in their slips. Hordes of military men and women swarmed in between them like ants, barking orders at one another, heckling people who passed by, and heaving crates and boxes into ships bound for overseas.

Toward the end of the docks, a small, beat-up steamer had just arrived. Weary passengers walked down the planks and eventually stepped onto the solid ground of the United States. They wore gaunt and humorless expressions along with tattered uniforms or rumpled medical gear: US service personnel returning from foreign regiments to answer their homeland's call.

Roland Hawkins stumbled along behind them, dressed in his cleanly pressed uniform of the British Expeditionary Force. He had re-sewn his divisional patches onto his shirtsleeves, and the polished brass buttons and buckles gleamed in the morning sunlight.

But he felt far from polished, as evidenced by the pale green hue in his cheeks. He pushed startled, irritated passengers out of his way while he scampered to get around them and onto solid ground. 'Excuse me, I'm sorry, pardon me.'

At last, Roland hopped off the plank and stepped onto his home turf. It should have been a glorious homecoming, but his stomach lurched like the swells on the ocean, which left him no time to celebrate. He wanted one thing and one thing only – a private place to empty his stomach. His frantic eyes quickly spotted an abandoned trash pile, and he made a mad dive for it. Ignoring all military honor or manners, he dropped to his knees, grabbed an empty wooden barrel, and barely got his back turned to the masses before he tossed.

Roland couldn't believe he still had fluids left after all the vomiting he'd done on that damn steamer. He spent almost the entire Atlantic crossing leaning over the rusty railing of the flimsy merchant ship turned military transport. Now, after heaving a few more times, Roland's butt thudded onto the dock. He took a cleansing breath of fresh air, hugging the barrel against him like a drunkard. He looked around at all the soldiers and wondered how many of them saw his embarrassing display.

As the swells in his stomach settled, he at last found the strength to smile. It took months of training, weeks in the terrible trenches under gunfire and artillery, poison gas, and days of puking over the side of a steamer, but Roland had finally made it home.

Although, this New York was vastly different to the one he had left behind. Patriotic fever had struck the entire island. American bunting draped every window. Extra American flags adorned the harbor and the city streets. The familiar melodies of patriotic songs like 'The Star-Spangled Banner' and 'Yankee Doodle' poured out of the saloons.

The people had transformed too, now so boisterous and determined. Newspaper boys hawked the headlines from 'over there.' Excited women flocked around the countless military men. Army recruiters strolled the crowds and prowled for any man not in uniform. Even a Red Cross booth occupied a tucked-away harbor corner, where pushy women tried to recruit anyone who walked within ten feet of them.

The sight of the Red Cross turned Roland's thoughts to Ilse. He had hated to leave her in such a fix, although he at least knew Tubby was on the case. Roland and Ilse, meek and blushing, had approached him at Talbot House after their discussion in the garden. While they shuffled their feet and clutched each other's hands, Tubby's graceful eyes shimmered. He stroked his chin for a brief, torturous moment, then he gave them a smirk.

'Ah, to be young and in love. It reminds us what we're fighting for. I suppose I shall just have to see what I can do.' He put one warm hand on each of their shoulders, and he promised to straighten it all out. There would be some red tape, he was sure, and some tangles along the way. After all, these things always took time.

Time indeed. None of that red tape had budged by the time Roland left, and he couldn't stand stepping away. And it wasn't like Ilse was the only thing he was stepping away from. Vernon had been almost heartbroken when Roland's transfer out of the British

As The Storm Clouds Gather

Army went through. It had been easier than he thought it would be. Since no one wanted to get in trouble for taking him when the US was still neutral, a lot of the British paper pushers seemed almost glad to be rid of him. Which left him a free agent to go home and join the US forces.

Saying goodbye to Vernon had been difficult. Yet his goodbye with Ilse was ten times worse. He could see how hard she had tried not to cry. How bravely she held her head up and promised to take good care of herself. 'I always have, haven't I?' she had said.

Fair enough. Even so, Roland spent every minute of his downtime on that journey contemplating how to help Ilse once he got home. He had originally planned to ask the New York City Police Department for help, because they had always been there in the past. Sam Hawkins' old friends checked on his family regularly after his death. They applauded Roland's decision to make some waves overseas, thinking it brave that he had gone over 'off the books' when President Wilson refused to fight. So now, when he announced his intention to enlist in the air corps, half the force offered to write him recommendations. The police commissioner himself even wrote one. Roland adored the outpouring of support, and he had hoped they would grant him just one more favor.

But his first glimpse of this new New York cast a dark cloud over that notion. In his absence, a seismic shift had taken place toward Germans. Signs that read 'Hang the Kaiser' and 'Kill the Huns' hung all over the harbor. Vibrant army recruiting posters portrayed the Germans as evil people who would come for the innocent Americans in the night. Dark signs warned citizens to beware of German espionage lurking right on their doorsteps.

One poster in particular chilled Roland to his seasick bones. It showed a wounded soldier laying on the ground and crying for water. Nearby, a vixen German nurse poured water from a canteen and onto the ground, denying the dying man the small pleasure of wetting his lips. The caption read: *The Cruel Little Hun.*

Roland averted his eyes, trying to ignore the tickle of dread behind his neck as he staggered to his feet.

Straightening his jacket and brushing dust from his pants, Roland started trying to push and shove his way out of the harbor. He noticed many admiring gazes as he did so. Ladies batted their eyes at him and giggled. Gentlemen lifted their hats when he walked past. Little children, including the newsboys, gazed at him with wide eyes and grins. They pointed their chubby fingers and whispered about him – a brave defender of their beloved democracy.

Roland didn't get much pleasure from the attention. In fact, it almost annoyed him. He wondered if any of those ogling faces and flag-waving patriots knew what kind of hell they were sending their sons to with such fervor.

Besides, it stung him too much that he wouldn't find a familiar face. Not in this crowd. His parents were both dead, and his brother had joined the army. He had written Bernard and detailed the day he was due in port, and what ship he was coming in on, but he didn't expect his baby brother would be able to leave his base on Long Island. There would be no welcoming committee for Roland, other than these strangers who all thought war was some glamorous adventure to salivate over.

Roland heaved a gusty sigh and started contemplating where he might sleep, but a familiar voice stopped him.

'Roland Hawkins, don't I even get a hello?'

Roland spun around, his eyes scanning the crowd. When he saw the man who had greeted him, his eyes flew open wide.

Bernard Herald Hawkins had come to welcome him after all. Roland just didn't notice, because he was a mere shadow of the boy who had once been a baby brother. The younger Hawkins had filled out and formed some muscles, and he even looked a little taller. Remnants of facial hair had sprouted on his chin. An impressive uniform decked his manly build, with a matching hat and light-brown puttees and boots. His rusty hair was straight and set, and his hazel eyes had shed their boyish innocence. While Roland fought a cruel war on foreign soil, his brother had grown into a man.

'Bernie?'

Bernard grinned. 'You think I'm too good to welcome my older brother home? Shame on you, Roly.'

Roland let out a shriek of joy, and the brothers fell into each other's arms. Which gave Roland a second jolt. When he left, he could pick up frail Bernard over his head and throw him across a room if he wanted. Now, it was Bernard who lifted Roland off his tired feet, and he didn't even break a sweat.

Roland buried his face in his brother's strong shoulder. He drank in Bernard's scent of woolen army uniform and pomade.

The one-man-welcoming-committee was better than the finest Manhattan parade.

After a brief tour through the familiar streets that had changed too much, too fast, two long-lost brothers found a small table in an out-of-the-way pub in Manhattan. They sipped mugs of beer and caught up on all that had happened since they separated. Bernard regaled his brother with stories of his early military career. He had done well in training. He loved his life on the base. The boys were real swell. All in all, he thought he would make a fine little soldier.

He also told Roland more about their mother's death. 'It was a small funeral service. A few of dad's old police buddies and some of her friends from church.'

'And the house?'

'It sold fast. I hope you're not angry, but I had no choice. Answering Uncle Sam's call bought me some respect, but that doesn't put money in the bank.'

Roland gave his brother's rosy cheek a playful pat. 'Hell, boy. You did a bang-up job with the hand you were dealt. Better than I did anyway.' He gave him a weary smile. 'I guess that means we're the last of the Hawkins family, aren't we? We'll have to live up to that somehow.'

Bernard hissed into his beer mug. 'Well, we'll see what happens when I get my hands on those filthy Germans. I'll make them pay for all this; you better believe it.'

The words peeled a harsh bell in Roland's heart. With a shudder, he recalled his own arrogant zeal for German blood. He remembered his loud crows in training, his arrogant blusters to hardened soldiers, and his reckless behavior on the battlefield. Such grim pleasure he once took in hating other humans.

It disturbed him to see his younger brother on the same vengeful path. But he didn't know how to talk him out of it. Because he would have to share horrifying things in order to do so. Tales he had vowed to keep from his brother, no matter what. Because Bernard was already enlisted. He would go to Europe, and there was no way out of it. Scaring him would just be cruel.

Roland raised his mug in a half-hearted salute. 'Well, good on you, Bernard. I can tell already you're a real fighter. You stay on the base, then?'

'I'm crammed in a tiny barrack with about twenty other guys, but it beats the hell out of sleeping on the street.'

The two sat back in their chairs and shared a brief silence – the first since their reunion in the harbor. The happy tinkle of silverware and lunchtime chatter helped Roland relax. Until he noticed Bernard's fingers twitching and his eyes burning with questions.

'You got something on your mind, brother?'

Bernard slowly slid his beer mug to the side. 'You going to tell me what's it like?'

Roland choked a little on his own beer before he thumped the glass on the table with authority. 'No.'

'Why not? I need to be prepared.'

'That's what your training is for.'

'Roland, this isn't just your war to fight anymore. I'm going to see it with my own eyes soon enough.'

'Then let your own eyes tell you when you get there.'

Bernard slumped into his chair and crossed his arms over his chest. 'What about you then?'

'What about me?'

He beckoned to his brother's uniform. 'How much longer you planning to fight under that silly Union Jack, you traitor?'

Roland smirked. 'That's exactly why I've come back here. I'm joining the Americans now.'

'Excellent.' Bernard slapped his palm down on the table. 'Come with me over to the base and speak to our CO. They're dying to get their hands on experienced types. Hell, I bet they even commission you. You can boss me around just like you did at home.'

Roland sipped a bitter froth of beer over his tongue as another somber shift clouded the table.

Bernard frowned. 'Why so quiet? You don't think they'd pair us up together?'

'I'm sure they would, but I don't plan on going to the trenches.'

Bernard just laughed. 'Don't be silly, Roland. Where else would you go?'

'The air corps. I've got a recommendation from the police commissioner, and I'm meeting with them tomorrow morning.' He took a final gulp from his mug.

He waited with bated breath for his brother's reaction. He thought

Bernard would be excited. Airplanes and air power were going to be what won the war, after all. Surely Bernard would see that. Instead, his baby brother went still. He took a long sip of his own beer to hide his grim face.

'What's the matter? You don't like airplanes?'

'Roland, you can't sign on with the air corps.'

'How the hell do you figure?'

'It isn't the bull they print in the newspaper. Those pilots got about as much chance of surviving as a hailstorm in hell. You know how long they say airmen live on the front line?'

Roland just shrugged. He wasn't sure he wanted to know.

'Three weeks, Roland. And I'll tell you something else. You'd be up against a lot of dirty fighters in Europe. Have you ever heard of this German pilot they call the Red Baron?'

Roland slammed his fist on the table, rattling their mugs and displacing their silverware. A few curious heads turned and stared.

Roland ducked from their gazes and checked his shaking hands. 'God damn it, Bernie. I know what I'm in for, all right? But I tell you I won't go back to those mud pits. You're upset about three weeks? Those shit trenches won't buy you much more than that. That's why your CO wants me so bad, Bernie. He can't find anyone else still alive.'

Roland suddenly remembered who he was talking to. He snapped out of his angry haze and rammed his fist in his mouth to make it stop.

But it was too little, too late. Bernard's eyes were wide with fright. When he reached for his mug, his hand trembled.

Roland cursed under his breath. 'I'm sorry, Bernie. I didn't mean it.'

Bernard huffed. 'Oh, yes you did, Roly. Yes, you absolutely did.'

SEVENTEEN
Roland

Roland, dressed in all his military finery, stood at the front desk of an Army Air Corps recruitment center, located in the middle of New York City. He had made sure to crease his uniform to perfection before he arrived. He had also polished his boots to smooth down all the wear from the trenches, and had wound his new puttees tightly and smartly around his ankles. It made him look all shiny and new again, as if the trenches had never happened.

But looks could be deceiving. All the spit and shine in the world couldn't polish over Roland's brewing nerves. He drummed his fingers on the wooden counter while trying not to look so wound up. He darted his eyes back and forth. He nervously tapped his foot. Standing at this counter, listening to the clock tick past the anxious seconds, he suddenly felt very small and powerless. Like he wanted to disappear inside his uniform or run home to his mother like he had the night Black Tom blew up. Probably because the uniform, as fancy as it looked, symbolized a total and complete lack of control. It symbolized the trenches, where he was just another number to throw at the hungry guns. A life he didn't think he could ever go back to. Yet he would be forced to if this didn't work out.

As for the officer across from Roland, he gave nothing away. There was no shift in his posture or telling look in his eyes. He just kept his face glued to the papers Roland had given him. A letter of recommendation from the Police Commissioner of New York City, and another from little Corporal Vernon back in Belgium.

At the time Vernon gave it to him, Roland wasn't sure how a corporal could help. Now, as he stood in this stuffy room with all that intensity bearing down on his shoulders, he felt glad he had it. Vernon may have only had one stripe on his uniform, but he also had a complete record of Roland's fighting ability. A record that put Roland at least one space above the many hopefuls vying for a spot in the air corps.

And there were many hopefuls indeed. Men occupied almost

every available seat in this makeshift office. They whispered amongst each other, swapping stories and legends they had read about pilots and the air corps. They bobbed their knees up and down while they wrung their hats in their hands. Some of them looked at Roland with envious eyes, knowing his fancy uniform would probably move him up the line ahead of them, whether it had British markings or not. Experience was experience. That was how Uncle Sam seemed to feel about it these days.

Unwilling or unable to look any of them in the eye, Roland distracted himself with all the recruitment posters adorning the cracked, cream-colored walls of the office. *Uncle Sam Wants You*; *It's up to You*; *Fall in and Answer the Call.* The vibrant slogans, printed in large block lettering, splashed across brightly colored pictures, showing finely dressed soldiers pointing fingers at viewers, fancy military men blasting trumpets on horseback, and unfurled war banners waving over a glorious battlefield.

They made Roland snort with laughter. It would be more appropriate to paint a picture of a mud pit filled with bones, and a slogan reading: *There's room for you in the graveyard.*

A shuffle of papers turned his attention back to the officer.

The boy's carefully combed hair, spotless olive-green uniform, and smooth, pink cheeks showed he had never been near an actual battlefield. This rankled Roland. He didn't think it was fair that this fresh little piece of meat would be the one who decided his fate.

The boy handed Roland's letters back and folded his hands.

'Well?' Roland asked.

'Those are two fine recommendations, Mr Hawkins. The police commissioner is certainly respectable enough. And time on the front lines puts you above every man in this room.'

Some grumbles came from behind him at that remark, but Roland ignored them. 'So, where do I sign up?'

'There's just one problem. I don't see a single mention about actual experience in an airplane.'

Roland felt his stomach wind up tight like the alarm clock that used to sit next to his bed, but he didn't miss a beat. He just glowered at the recruiter. 'I see. Have you been in an airplane?'

The boy shifted in his seat. 'Well, no, but . . .'

'And you've been to the front lines, have you? You know all about what it's like over there?'

'Not yet, but that doesn't mean—'

'And you're the pony boy calling the shots, huh?'

The boy let loose a disgusted sigh. 'You've got it all wrong, Mr Hawkins. There's a long list of people wanting a crack at those planes. Some of them quite prominent. A president's son, for God's sake. I have explicit instructions on who to send through for testing.'

'And I don't make the mark? Pray tell what does? A president for a dad?'

The officer sneered. 'An American uniform, for starters.'

Roland looked down at his British dress and chuckled. 'Well, shoot. You think I can't handle an outfit change? Give me a little more credit, why don't you?'

'Why were you in such a hurry to sign on with a foreign army during a time of neutrality, Mr Hawkins?'

Roland scoffed. 'I was bored.'

The officer glared, and Roland sighed.

'I didn't think it right to sit here and twiddle my thumbs while everyone was dying over there and over here. I wanted to fight. So, I went and got in on the fight.'

'That's commendable, I suppose, but you have no time in an airplane and no higher education.'

Roland leaned over the officer's desk and did his best to look menacing. 'Come now. Learning to fly isn't the trouble. You either got a brain for learning or you don't, and I certainly do. Or I wouldn't be here arguing with you, not after what I've been through. What you boys need, what you really want, is experience. Believe me. It's a whole other world over there, and I'm here because I don't crack up. Not cracking up will get your precious little air corps a hell of a lot further than West Point protocol.'

'So, the trenches were their own graduate course, were they? Did they hand out diplomas in smart-mouthing while they were at it?'

'Nope. Just pounding little pony boys into the dirt.'

The officer laughed. 'All right, then. Don't get your knickers knotted up.' He reached into his desk drawer and pulled out some forms. He slid them across the desk to Roland. 'Fill these out. If we like what we see, you'll get an examination.'

'What, like a written test?'

'No, a medical test. Pilots have to be in top physical form. Are you in top physical form?'

Roland felt a telling prickle in his lungs, and a familiar sting on his scarred skin. Most of him was healthy. Soldiering in the open countryside had ironed the weakness from his lanky city body. It had turned his scrawny limbs into muscles, and it had improved his eyesight and mechanical skills. But it had also doused him with poison gas, and his lungs had never fully recovered. He still carried faint but visible scars from the blisters. No way to hide them. Not during a medical exam, at least.

The officer sensed Roland's hesitation. 'If you're not in top physical form, you're wasting both our time, soldier.'

Roland hardened his eyes and shook his head. 'The hell I'm not. I'm fit as a damn fiddle. Just watch me prove it.'

It took Roland forever to fill out the required forms.

First, he had to detail his service abroad and list any family member that had served in the US military. Which was easy enough.

Then came the medical questions. Lists of any diseases he or his immediate family may have had, past or present. Which forced him to spill the beans about his mother. It was too risky to lie about it, since all of it went on record somewhere. He supposed that would red-flag him, but even if he dodged that, he would have a hard time dancing around his own problems . . . and not just with the poison gas. These people wanted any and every minuscule problem he might have ever experienced in his life. Pain, stomach trouble, bowel complaint, fainting spells, bleeding disorders, skin trouble, heart trouble, acne, eye problems, hearing disability, and more. Anything he might have felt or experienced, they wanted to hear about it.

Roland felt invaded just checking off the boxes, and that wasn't even the worst of it. Once he completed the medical section, the air corps asked him for the details of his personal life. He had to check a box for his marital status. He had to identify any current or past sweethearts. They wanted to know if he'd had sex and with how many people. They asked if his childhood was happy or turbulent. They wanted to know if he had too many friends or not enough.

It put a blush in Roland's cheeks, to say the least. He wondered why in the world they could need such personal information.

Once he'd completed the mountain of paperwork, he plopped it down in front of the officer. 'Here you go, but you forgot the question about the size of my manhood.'

'Oh, we'll let the doctor decide if you fill that requirement.'

'You mean I'm not done for the day?'
'Lord, Mr Hawkins. You've only just begun.'

With those telling words, an orderly came out of nowhere and whisked Roland into a dimly lit back room, which had been hastily converted into a medical office. A tiny, cramped space, with various unpleasant-looking instruments scattered on hosts of silver trays. Reading charts glared from the far wall, and there were various needles and probing tools that would put the fear of God into anybody.

A stern man in a white coat greeted Roland with a friendless handshake. Like his recruiter counterpart, he was young. In fact, he could easily pass for a medical student. Obviously an Ivy League medical student, given his arrogant personality. But Roland had to rub elbows and play the game anyway. After all, his fate in the air corps rested in this boy doctor's pristine hands.

He was in an awful hurry to decide it too. The doctor waved any formalities or small talk, and he began his tests by seating Roland in a swivel chair and instructing him to read the eye chart.

When Roland aced that test, the doctor turned him around and around in the chair for several seconds, until his head spun with dizziness. Then he made Roland's blurry eyes follow his finger as he moved it all around. He made him read a few more lines from the chart.

After that, the doctor pulled out a water pump and flushed Roland's ears with scalding hot water, the steaming liquid gushing through his narrow canals. Then he chased it with a shot of cold, which made Roland so dizzy he thought he might throw up. He bore the feeling with clenched teeth, and denied it emphatically when the doctor asked if he felt sick.

Once that torture was done, the doctor made Roland strip naked, so he could examine every square inch of his body. He checked over his hands, his feet, his back and shoulders. He looked for signs of old injuries, and he prodded every little cut and bruise. He took special interest in the faded scars on Roland's chest and hands, lingering over them for several, uncomfortable moments.

'What's this? A nasty fall?'
Roland gulped. 'Something like that.'
The doctor glared at him. It made Roland so nervous, he worried heart trouble would concern the doctor next.

After the doctor moved on from the scars, he checked Roland's teeth, and he tapped his knee for reflexes.

All went well until the cough test. When the doctor turned Roland's head to the side, his cough came out garbled and filled with fluid.

The doctor narrowed his eyes and made a fast reach for Roland's paperwork. He thumbed through the forms while his patient tried to restrain his emotions.

'Your mother died of consumption, did she?'

'I don't have consumption.'

'That cough says otherwise, so you're unfit for the air corps. Can't have you spreading that around.'

'Listen, Doc. I said it's not consumption and it sure as hell isn't contagious.'

'How do you know?'

Roland sighed. He hated to reveal the extent of his injury, but mustard gas had to be better than consumption. At least that's the way he figured it, anyhow. 'I fought in the Ypres trenches, and you know what weapons they have.'

The doctor put the forms down. 'You were gassed? I suppose that explains the marks from that "nasty fall," doesn't it?'

'Yes, sir.'

'Why didn't you put that on your form?'

'Because it isn't relevant. The eye test proved I'm not blind, and the rest proved I'm not an invalid. I have scars and a cough. That's all.'

'Was it Chlorine? Phosgene?'

'Mustard.'

The doctor frowned. 'Mustard gas has long-term deteriorating effects on the lungs. It's just as bad as consumption.'

'But it won't spread to the other boys, so I don't see the problem.'

The doctor's stern glare showed he didn't care for the attitude. 'I'm sorry, but we can only accept candidates in the best of physical health.'

Roland's hands balled into angry fists. He decided right then and there that he had earned his place in the air corps, through blood, sweat, tears, and all kinds of misery, and he wouldn't let some snotty doctor, safe from the trenches because of that white coat, cheat him out of it. He stood to his full height and towered over the medical practitioner.

'And what about you? Will I see you in the trenches? Because I got some connections in the army. I'm sure they'd love another whip-smart field doctor like you, and I'm also sure the artillery could work some wonders on that handsome face.'

The young doctor's arrogance took a fast and sharp hit. 'I serve the cause by helping Uncle Sam get healthy pilots.'

'Well, aren't we lucky to have heroes like you.'

'What are you playing at, soldier?'

'Look, I don't need a stuffy doctor who's never seen the war telling me what I'm capable of. There's no gas in my brain, which means I can learn to fly just fine. Besides, if I die from bad lungs, that sounds like my business and not yours.'

The doctor, not used to such an attitude from air corps hopefuls, stifled a laugh. Then, he picked up a big rubber stamp and brought it down hard onto Roland's papers. When he removed it, the word 'Approved' shone out in bright red letters.

He put the papers into a file and handed it to Roland. 'Good luck, soldier. If you survive ground school and training with those lungs, you're OK in my book. But I'd keep that "nasty fall" to yourself, all right?'

Roland smiled and took the paperwork. 'Thank you.'

The next several weeks passed in a blur for Roland Hawkins. There was a lot to be done and so little time to do it. After he got approved for the air service, he formally enlisted into the United States Army. He purchased his new US uniform, and he flew through an expedited course of basic training. After that, he barely had time to pack a few things before they sent him to New York University to attend something called 'ground school.'

Roland had never heard of ground school before, but he got the gist of it pretty quickly. From sun up to sun down, army instructors crammed his brain with anything and everything he could need to know about airplanes. He learned all about wind, weather patterns, and the best type of skies for flying. He learned new terms like 'lift,' 'headwind,' and 'tailwind.' He learned about plane parts like propellers, rudders, and tail feathers. He sat in a makeshift cockpit and learned basic flying maneuvers.

The massive amounts of information fried many of the air corps hopefuls. Some of them dropped out in the end, but not Roland. He became the top of his class instead. He asked the most questions and got the best marks on tests. He often took extra reading to his barracks after hours. He wound up so busy that he had little time for friends.

He carved out time to write letters though. Some he wrote to Bernard and Vernon, but most went to Ilse. He got a few flowery letters from her in return, but they didn't bring much comfort. She reported that the other nurses had grown even colder, and Marie appeared to be moving in on her threats. Which certainly didn't help him sleep any better at night.

It was also why he worked extra hard on her citizen status back at home. Despite his full plate at ground school, he braved any German prejudice and turned to the police department first. He told them all about Ilse, how she had saved his life in Ypres, and her *Lusitania* survivor status.

Respect for Roland's father, and therefore his son, still ran high on the force, as did the sympathy for a *Lusitania* survivor, so they agreed to help. While they couldn't turn up any birth records, they found an old employment record at a clothing factory. It wasn't enough to prove citizenship, but they decided it was enough to take Roland on his word. So, they contacted immigration services and started the wheels rolling to reinstate her papers. It would be a long road ahead, but it was started, and that was a good thing.

Roland grinned from ear to ear when he put all that information in a letter for Ilse just as he finished ground school. *I will soon report to Kelly Airfield in Texas to continue my training*, he wrote. *Please write me there at the enclosed address and let me know you are safe. Affectionately, Your Roland.*

He sealed the letter into an envelope. Then, with a kiss, he dropped it in the nearest mailbox.

A thrill went through his fingertips as he did so. Next time he got a letter from her, it would be at a real-live airbase, where he would be flying real-live airplanes.

Roland spent his last night in New York City with Bernard.

After tearing up the town with pub visits, drinks, and all the food they could eat, they sat on Bernard's cot in his small barrack. They kept quiet at first, partially because they weren't alone. A few other recruits lounged about the place, reading books by candlelight or playing quiet games of cards.

Roland finally nudged his brother. 'Bernie, there's something I want to tell you.'

Bernard looked up at him with nervous eyes. 'What? Something about the war?'

That settled any questions of what was on Bernard's mind. Roland just smiled and gave him a wink. 'I've got a girl now.'

Bernard raised his eyebrows. 'Oh?'

'A nurse. American.' He smiled. 'Beautiful, and kind. I met her in the hospital.'

'You mean after you were gassed and barely escaped with your life?'

There was an edge in his brother's voice that couldn't be denied. Roland pressed his lips together in angst. 'Do you have something you'd like to say to me, Bernard?'

Bernard let out a shudder. 'Naw. It's just . . . well, I hoped you would change your mind about the airplanes. After all we've lost, what would I do if you go too?'

'I'll be fine. I've got an edge over anyone else, remember? I've already been to the war.'

'And it must be awful.'

Roland sighed. 'Don't put much stock in that nonsense I said at the pub that day. I was strung out from being so seasick. Don't worry about it.'

'I've got no choice.'

'Why?'

'Because if you would chance those planes over the trenches, the trenches must be really, really bad.'

Bernard's shrewdness cut Roland to the quick. It was so poignant he couldn't even argue with it. He just looked down at his folded hands, unsure what else to do or say.

To break up the heavy silence, Bernard reached into his pocket and pulled a familiar little box out.

Roland smiled. He remembered the Christmas morning all those years ago when he had given that harmonica to Bernard. His brother had been so happy, so excited. His eyes gleamed as he took in the polished silver, running his fingertips over it. How long ago it all seemed now. Part of another life. A far more innocent life.

'You still have that old mouth organ, huh?'

'I'll never part with it.' Bernard opened the box and took the familiar harmonica out. It shone even in the low lighting, begging to be played.

Bernard covered his trembling lips with the instrument and played a few somber notes. They bounced and echoed off the barrack walls. The other boys turned to watch at first, but then quickly went back to their various activities.

Bernard paused, letting out a boyish giggle. 'Remember when Pa used to take us to the park? And that time he stuck his foot in the lake, and that wild goose almost bit his toe off?'

Roland snorted a laugh. 'That god-awful honk it made, chasing him all around.'

'An investigator dealing with criminals and thugs, yet he screamed and ran away from a silly goose.'

Still shaking with laughs, Roland nudged his brother. 'Remember Mother at the piano?'

Bernard sighed, a dreamy look in his eyes. 'My gosh, a voice like an angel.'

'And so damn good with that piano. She made it look easy.'

Summer joy turned to winter chill in Bernard's gaze, and he ran his thumb over his little mouth organ. 'We started playing duets together after you left. It was the only time she let herself cry. She said music was the key to her locked-up heart. It made her feel things nothing else could. She said . . .' He paused to swallow a lump of oncoming tears. 'She said she talked to God all the time, and music was how He talked back. Whether it was at that old piano or just the little birds outside.'

Warm in his brother's barrack, Roland suddenly flashed back to the cold and gray of Ypres. He again heard that songbird and its call across no man's land. It made him realize there was a strong truth in what his mother had said. But then again, she had spoken a lot of powerful truths during her short lifetime.

It hit Roland just then, how he had never really processed his mother's death. How he would never hear that singing again. Never watch her fingers move so gracefully across the piano keys. She would never again light a candle for him to call him home after a long day. Like so much else lately, his mother was gone. His family was scattered by death and destruction. All he had left was the boy-turned-soldier who sat next to him, playing those sad notes on his sad little mouth organ.

Roland draped his arm around his brother and pulled him in for an embrace.

'You take good care of yourself over there, Bernie.'

Bernard kept on playing. Because goodbyes were just too hard.

EIGHTEEN
Ilse

Ilse stood once again in Marie's pretend little office, only shut off from the rest of the hospital by a thin, flimsy separator. Aside from the typical wailing of patients and clatter of harried medical personnel, she also heard the echoes of the record player. The last strains of 'Roses of Picardy' bounced around the chapel, which reminded her so much of Roland.

Ilse looked around while picking at her nails. Not so long ago, she sat in a wobbly chair across from Marie and bore the worst accusations ever thrown at her. Now, it was the judgmental matron who stood on the wrong side of pointing fingers. Reverend Clayton towered over her desk, making the most of his bulky frame, which was actually quite intimidating when he paired it with a booming voice and a stern, spectacle-enhanced frown.

It was an odd transition for Ilse, who had only ever seen Tubby's face with a gentle smile. She had only seen those teddy-bear arms hugging people in pain, only heard that voice consoling hurting humans with prayers. She had no idea that her single remaining friend in Europe, normally so warm and friendly, could throw out such an imposing air of authority.

'I've told you repeatedly what I requested and have been granted, my dear matron.' Tubby tossed a bundle of paperwork onto her desk. 'The American Red Cross needs drivers, and Ilse here is an American citizen. She will be moved at once to their station in Poperinge.'

Marie, never one to back down from a fight, shot up from her chair and stood her ground. 'American citizen, my foot. The girl is Kraut down to her core. I won't turn her loose on an Allied hospital to bring down hell on these poor American boys.'

'Ah yes, the infamous spying accusations. Do you have any proof to back up these claims? Have you actually seen Ilse act with anything other than compassion in this hospital? Or are we taking at their word a group of gossipy nurses who didn't like Ilse from the start?'

Marie shot him a glare that could break through glass. 'Are you suggesting that I lack any modicum of control over my own hospital?'

'Actually, I am.'

Marie let out a gasp that was almost comical. 'That is absolute rubbish. One of the girls reported Ilse's activities to me personally, and I launched my own investigation from there.'

'Yes, as I already mentioned – accusations that are highly suspect, when looked at through a lens of prejudice against a nurse of German descent.'

Marie's face went red with rage. 'If you are daring to insinuate I've been made a fool by a bunch of gossipy, squabbling girls—'

'Yes, I do understand the sting of wounded pride, Matron. Believe you me. Well, if that will be all then . . .'

Tubby picked up the bundle of paperwork, then made to reach for Ilse's arm, but Marie rammed her way in between them.

'And I suppose these papers of yours verify Miss *Chère-Amie*'s identity then, Reverend? A passport perhaps? Or even a birth certificate?'

She made a firm reach for the papers, but Tubby backed quickly away.

'Think of Miss Ilse what you will, Matron. Some stubborn minds even God can't penetrate. But I have signed documents from the American Red Cross accepting her into their employ. I also have a signed letter of intent from US authorities, who are restoring Ilse's citizenship after her papers were lost aboard the *Lusitania*.'

The word dropped like a land mine on that little office. Marie's eyes went wide and she flashed them from Ilse to Tubby. 'The *Lusitania*, did you say?'

Ilse glued her eyes to the floor while Tubby just barreled onward. 'You will release Miss Ilse to my custody at once, Matron. I won't ask nicely again.'

She let out a piercing guffaw. 'You and what army is going to make me?'

'What a silly question, considering the circumstances. I've had the British Army's ear on more than one occasion. I won't hesitate to get them involved again.'

'We're a civilian corps, Reverend. Privately funded. I'd like to see you try it.'

Tubby may have been a man of God, but even he had his boiling point. He took a menacing step toward Marie and drilled his stern gaze right into her skull. 'Oh, *would* you?'

At long last, Marie shrank back just a little. 'Well, I just mean they can't interfere with our business here.'

'I see,' said Tubby. 'And you're confident enough to test that theory, are you? Confident that I won't go to the military medical board and tell them that not only have you interfered with a direct order from a highly regarded Allied medical team, but you have also born false witness against one of the most hard-working nurses under your employ? That your own prejudice has left you unfit to handle this hospital? That perhaps it's time for the army to step in and set things right around here?'

Ilse could barely suppress laughter as Marie transformed from a hard-knock, steely matron to a trembling, red-faced, agitated pile of nerves. 'Well now, I don't suppose—'

'And you wouldn't mind then if I contacted the investors of your little private operation here, a wealthy family of some nobility, I understand, and told them of all the shenanigans afoot in this office, which could spoil your reputation amongst the elite of Britain?'

'Reverend Clayton—'

'And I suppose you believe that if I suggested the total revocation of your license to be a nurse, given your unstable and overt bias against non-British medical personnel, that the entire British medical community would rush to your defense then?'

Marie had paled to dangerous, ghostly levels and she took a big step back. The realization that she'd been beaten washed over her broad shoulders. 'All right then, Reverend, you've made your point. You've got more clout than I do, anyway. I suppose it's just so in a man's world.'

A man's world. The remark struck a chord with Ilse. She too had faced her own many problems in a man's world – men telling her she couldn't drive an ambulance, couldn't work in a war zone, couldn't practice medicine, couldn't fight in her own way. And she so often had to get men involved if she really wanted to solve a problem. Case in point, needing Tubby to fight a battle she wished she could have fought herself.

A man's world. It almost made Ilse feel sorry for Marie.

Almost.

'Well then, now that's all squared away, Miss Ilse and I will just be leaving.' Tubby tenderly took Ilse's arm and tucked it into his elbow. He nodded his head at Marie before exiting. 'Thanks for your cooperation, Matron. Do come by Talbot House for service if you wish. You'll find it the best medicine for wounded pride.'

As soon as they stumbled down the front steps of the church-turned-hospital, Ilse finally allowed herself to exhale. After months of walking on eggshells, questioning every sideways glance, enduring nightmares about going to prison, and nursing a terribly wounded heart alone on a smelly cot every night, Ilse Stahl had escaped. She wouldn't go to jail or to the gallows. She would go to the Red Cross and serve alongside her own countrywomen. The people she grew up with and shared a homeland with.

Of course, those same people had run her from their shores and onto the *Lusitania* in the first place, but maybe things were different now. That Red Cross girl from before certainly didn't seem to mind her heritage, so long as she could drive a car. And serving with the Red Cross would bring her one step closer to returning home. Maybe with Roland someday . . .

She let out a spirited giggle at the thought. 'Goodness, Tubby. I didn't think you had it in you.'

'I burn with the spirit of the Lord, Miss Ilse.' He gave her a wide smile and a nod of encouragement. 'Now let's get your things. Time to move on from this mess once and for all.'

'Wait just one moment, Reverend.'

'Yes?'

Ilse nervously shuffled her feet. She didn't want to pester a man who had already gone so far out of his way to help her. 'These papers you have.' She made the gentlest of reaches for the bundle of papers under Tubby's arm. 'How did you get them? What are they?'

With a mysterious smirk, Tubby handed the papers over.

Ilse took several moments to scan them, then looked up at Tubby with shock. 'Why . . . this is just a copy of the Bible!'

Tubby laughed and took her arm back in his.

'You were *bluffing*?'

'There's one sure-fire way to handle a bully, Miss Ilse. Bully harder, and bring props.'

'But . . . but . . .'

'I had a letter from Roland that the process is being started to reinstate your papers, but these things do take time, Miss Ilse. I know you understand that, but I didn't dare think that Marie would. And it's high time you got out of this place, no questions asked.'

'So you *lied*?'

'It was a bend of the truth. The papers are coming sure enough, and the Red Cross has agreed to take you, given some strings I pulled at the embassy. I just don't have any physical paperwork yet.'

Ilse crossed her arms and gave him a playful glare. 'Lying. Isn't that a sin?'

'And which is a bigger sin, my dear? A little white lie, or abuse against an innocent?'

'How about a war? Where does that fall on your scale?'

He sighed. 'Don't *even* get me started.'

NINETEEN
Roland

Spring, 1918

Roland first heard of Manfred Von Richthofen, better known as the 'Red Baron,' while he fought in the trenches at Ypres.

Even back then, the aviation ace had made a name for himself. He racked up more kills than any pilot on either side, commemorating each one with a hand-carved silver goblet, made by a jeweler in his hometown. He received fan mail from all over the world, had ample female admirers, and got every decoration the German military could bestow. People dubbed him 'the Red Knight of Germany.' All over the Western Front, eyes peeled skyward when any plane flew over. Every soldier wanted a glimpse of that famous scarlet plane.

It had been an Albatros biplane in Roland's trench days. It saw the Baron through most of his eighty kills before he switched to the Fokker triplane in 1918, a plane that would forever be tied to his career and legacy. Whatever he chose to fly in, Richthofen and his infamous flying circus created terror in the skies over Europe. Until one day in April of 1918, when it all came crashing down to earth.

Roland was training hard in Texas at the time, preparing for his own career in the cockpit. His first time up in the air had completely knocked his socks off. He had plopped himself in the observer seat of an open-cockpit, wobbly biplane, while a fully trained flying officer took the actual controls. Roland laughed out loud when his stomach dipped from the plane leaving earth. It thrilled him to watch the buildings, trees, and people shrink beneath him. His adrenaline pumped when the wind blew against his face and made the wires on the wings whistle.

It wasn't long at all before he went up by himself. How nervous he had been too. He had craved to go solo for so long, yearning to be rid of the pesky instructors scrutinizing his every move. But when the machine roared to life and he rumbled toward the take-off strip, the empty instructor seat haunted him. A terrible dread started in his shoulders and worked its way down to his toes.

Thankfully, that all vanished once he was airborne. Roland's training kicked in, as if his hands and feet had acquired a life all their own. He got a strong and irresistible surge of power sitting behind those controls by himself. No one could tell him what to do up here. No one could order him over the top, or into the mud, or at a machine gun. No more instructors pointed out his every flaw and failing. Fellow soldiers couldn't nag him; superiors couldn't judge him.

Up here, Roland was free.

He peered out the side of the plane, watching his little shadow careen across the wide-open expanses of emerald green, and vast purple patches where the bluebells bloomed. He gave the wings a wobble, and he giggled when his shadow waved back at him.

Once he landed his plane in perfect order, and jumped triumphantly from the cockpit, his commanding officer pinned a fresh set of pilot's wings on his breast. The silver trinket marked his acceptance into the elite pilot squad.

Celebrations followed when he returned to his barrack that night. The boys pulled out smuggled flasks and bottles. They started poker games and playful stunts, and they bellowed raunchy songs passed on to them from the foot soldiers.

Roland grinned as he watched from his cot. It felt like the dawn of a new age. He had officially graduated from those lousy trenches, and he could soon blaze his own trail through the history of aviation.

Moments later, a stern-faced captain barged into their barrack.

Boys snapped to attention, stuffing contraband liquor under their pillows and hiding any evidence of their card-game shenanigans.

The captain just rolled his eyes. 'Like I don't know you idiots have been raising holy hell in here since sundown. Smells like you have enough liquor to start a car engine, for Christ's sake.'

One of the boys opened his mouth to explain, but the captain shushed him with a hard glare. 'Now listen up, all of you. I came to tell you the Red Baron has been killed.'

The short announcement packed a huge punch. Innocent smiles morphed into terrified gazes. Jaws dropped. Hearts beat faster. One boy's lower lip began to tremble.

The captain awkwardly cleared his throat. 'Jury's still out on credit. They're thinking a British pilot, but ground troops are also trying to claim it. I'm . . . sure we'll know more in a day or two.' The captain gave them a firm salute, then he turned and left them to their thoughts.

Once his footsteps faded away, the pilots in training grappled with their newfound sense of vulnerability. The Red Baron was the kind of pilot they all aspired to be. To them, he was a true knight. A warrior. Untouchable. If the war had gotten bad enough to claim him, it didn't give them much hope for their own skins.

As for Roland, the Red Baron's death reminded him exactly what was at stake. It wasn't just about being the best flier, making a difference, and ending the war faster. He wasn't just risking a plane or a reputation. He would risk his very mortality. His life would hang in the wires of those wings. Death wasn't some kind of nap he could wake up from either, with medals pinned to his chest. It was permanent. A darkness no hero status would save him from.

After that sobering night, Roland became much more fatalistic. His dream of being a knight of old slipped into the nightmare of a sheep headed for slaughter. He held back on wild stunts during training exercises. He took the pesky notes from his instructors more seriously. On days off, he kept to himself instead of living it up with wild boys and their drunken antics.

One thing gave Roland hope, and that was the outpouring of respect, and legitimate mourning, that came from all fronts after the Red Baron passed. Commanders raised toasts to him at mess. They sent up an honor formation to fly around the entire base. They closed down classes for a day, so pilots could reflect on a legend vanishing away.

The gestures did more than honor a fallen pilot. They proved to Roland that some people still respected death. Probably because on the airbase, death stalked their outer parameters, but it didn't penetrate their personal lives. Pilots didn't live among human carnage. Bodies didn't speckle their barracks or dot their green airfields. Rotting faces didn't stick out of craters, and human bones didn't trip up their feet. They could take deaths one at a time here, which made the whole thing a bit easier to process.

The mourning for the Red Baron revealed a different side of the war too. The air war was a human war, not a numbers game. If he did plunge into that eternal darkness, someone would know. They could tell Bernard and Ilse exactly what had happened. His gravestone would have a name on it.

Yet, the Baron's death ushered in a darker era too. It somehow set the sun on the age of the old warrior and spread the disease of mass killing to the airplanes, putting innocent civilians directly in harm's way. Sometimes, they were even targets. Zeppelins flew over London on bomb runs. Then came the large Gotha bomber planes with no other purpose than bombing – cities, airdromes, and even medical facilities if the mood struck the pilots right.

Knights of the air had all gone west. Something darker and uglier cropped up in their stead. Despite Vernon's many wishes, there was still no color in the soil – unless he counted the crushed scarlet wings of the dead Red Baron's triplane.

By the summer of 1918, Roland was back overseas, and there was one thing he learned very quickly: the training field and flying school at Issoudun, France, was a world away from Texas. Pilot hopefuls absolutely swarmed this muddy, overcrowded place, with barely enough housing to accommodate them all. Flight instructors came from all over the world to try and teach them. Which was why this place had a staggering eight training fields instead of just one.

These eight fields represented eight different stages of flight readiness for pilots in training. The first three fields were for refresher courses for the basics, which grated on Roland's nerves something awful. He was sick of the damn basics. His head hit the roof when he finally got shipped overseas, only to spend weeks at Issoudun driving 'penguins' – planes with clipped wings – across a muddy practice field. Instead of learning combat maneuvers and acrobatics, he wasted precious time re-learning everything he had just finished in Texas.

His French instructor tried to quell his restlessness with an explanation. 'The French Nieuport planes are a lot different than training. We can't afford to break them up with careless accidents. So, you refresh on the ground, then we'll move you to the air.'

In other words, no matter how much he hated it, Roland would have to grin and bear it. But he did much more than that. He pushed those plane controls to their limits, and he dazzled every instructor on the base when he did so. Roland, just like he promised that pushy recruiter back in New York, quickly showed everyone what he was made of.

They advanced him to field six almost immediately. All the pilots drooled over this field, because there they learned the acrobatic maneuvers that would be used in real combat. Through warming days slowly melting into summer, and with arrogant, condescending combat pilots watching with skeptical eyes, Roland learned how to barrel his plane, dip it, vrille it, and peel it up into the atmosphere to outrun lower-flying German planes.

Once he polished off those skills, he moved onto field seven, where he learned to fly in formation with other seasoned fliers. They took off for a designated rendezvous above the base and flew around the field, practicing tight protective formations for escorting observers and photographers over the lines. They learned how to split off into attack formations. How to bunch up to protect a crippled plane. How to dive, lunge, and surround their prey as a group.

After Roland mastered all that plus some additional gunnery school, he advanced to the hardest and final fields at Issoudun: fields eight and nine, where pilots and their trainers simulated real combats.

Every day, while envious flying students watched on the ground, Roland went up in one plane while a fellow trainee took another. Cameras had been mounted on their wings. The boys 'shot' each other by clicking a button on their control stick that activated the camera, while an instructor observed the entire thing on the ground. Later, each pilot sat through a debriefing with their instructor, who showed them the developed photos from their flight.

On yet another cold, gray morning, Roland dipped his clunky fighter plane, painted dark green with a French tri-circle, over field eight.

In the other plane, a nineteen-year-old wild pilot named Elliot gave Roland a run for his money. He was an adventurous little youth who cussed hard enough to put sailors to shame, and filled his downtime with hard liquor and mushroom hunting.

He was also a hell of a pilot. Every time he got the wild youth in his sights, Elliot pulled some hairbrained stunt or another to escape. He dove down and turned into a loop. He dropped his plane sideways to choke Roland's engine. His favorite trick was buzzing the mess hall, taking his plane so low over the building that the people inside scattered in all different directions.

Roland had to push every inch of his flying muscles to keep up with that boy. He edged up hard on Elliot's tail feathers, but Elliot swung around, pulled straight up into the air, and did a fast dive. A fancy bit of flying, but a stupid combat maneuver. Because now, Elliot had nowhere to go but down. Roland edged up on his tail and got him right in his sights. He flirted with the shutter button, sitting where a real trigger would someday.

Click click click click.

Roland hoped it was a good shot, because he was tired of the non-stop pace of Issoudun. The place kept him so busy he barely had time for anything else. He had only managed one letter to Ilse, a quick missive to let her know he had safely returned to Europe.

Thanks to Tubby, he knew she had been successfully transferred to the American Red Cross and now worked happily as an ambulance driver in France. And she must have been just as busy as Roland, because he didn't hear from her often. When she did write, she signed her letters, 'affectionately yours,' which felt a lot more romantic than her usual 'sincerely.'

Which gave Roland something nice to think about during his very busy days.

A few hours later, after he finished his own training for the day, Roland stood off to the side and watched as two more planes went through a dizzying array of stunt work and combat maneuvers over field eight. Their engines rumbled loud and faded in and out with the numerous spins and turns. Both pilots were much further along in their training than Roland. He encountered them often on various fields, and he knew they were some of the best. One of them, Tommy, was already emerging as one of the biggest air stars on the base.

Roland felt his envy boil as he watched Tommy bank and dip his Nieuport like it was effortless. He longed for the day when he could be that good in the cockpit.

Elliot stepped up beside him and brushed a lock of silky brown hair from his innocent chocolaty eyes. He put his youthful, pink face toward the sky. 'Who's coming out ahead here?'

'Who do you think?'

'That Tommy is a fancy son of a bitch, ain't he?' Elliot spat on the ground. 'Bastard. Wish I had half his luck.'

'Me too. Especially after I saw our pictures.'

Elliot winced. 'Was I a dead duck or what?'

Roland huffed. 'Hardly. I would have been lucky to clip your damn wing tip.'

'You always were a lousy shot at gunnery. It must be that city upbringing.'

Roland suppressed the urge to tell Elliot he was a decent enough shot in the trenches. He didn't keep his mouth shut to avoid an argument either. He just hadn't told anyone about the trenches, and he didn't plan to. He had followed quite strictly that doctor's tip to keep his medical condition to himself. To keep people from poking in any soft spots, he kept his entire trench life under wraps.

Which wasn't easy. He worked very hard to silence his coughs after a long day in the air. He concealed his burning chest pain from all the other pilots. He never undressed in front of them, so they wouldn't see the red splotches from the gas burns. All strong smells at the airbase made him nauseous, yet he dared not get sick in front of the boys.

Secrecy kept him going in the corps, but now it left him with no defense against Elliot's insult. 'Well . . . I'll get the hang of it in no time. Then you better watch it.'

Elliot gave Roland a slap on the back, and the two returned their attention to the sky.

As the two pilots swirled around each other like vultures, Tommy's opponent jerked his controls a little too sharply. His wing clipped against Tommy's. A horrible crack echoed across the field, and Tommy's wing split up and the wires came unraveled.

Elliot gasped. 'Oh, God!'

Roland's heart stopped as he watched Tommy struggle to recover control. His wing crumbled, then ripped from the side of the plane, fluttering down like the feather from a shattered bird. His Nieuport went into a deep spiral and fell through the air like a stone. Then it disappeared behind one of the barrack buildings. While the wreck couldn't be seen, pilots all across Issoudun heard the smashing of plane parts and the snapping of wires.

Roland, Elliot, and the rest tore off toward the wreck. Instructors stumbled out of their quarters, and the ringing of a fire siren cut across the field.

Roland arrived at the crash site out of breath, where he saw that Tommy's plane had been reduced to a flaming pile of rubble. He felt the heat blast even from several feet back. The charred body remained tightly strapped into the cockpit, the skull grinning back at Roland.

Roland felt his stomach lurch, while images of the flamethrowers in Belgium seared across his memory.

Elliot's face went pale. 'Lord . . .'

Roland clenched his jaw to toughen himself up, then he put his hand on young Elliot's shoulder, turning him away from the awful sight.

The fire truck and ambulance arrived a few moments later. The medic climbed out of his rickety ride and approached the wreckage. 'Another for field thirteen, gents.' He turned to the pilots. 'All right, fellows. You've seen enough to scare you straight, I hope. Off you go now.'

One by one, the shaken-up pilots went back to their training.

Elliot leaned into Roland. 'What's field thirteen?'

Roland swallowed hard to will away his nausea. 'The graveyard.'

TWENTY
Roland

Roland rapidly climbed the ranks at Issoudun to become one of the best pilots. He got better with the mounted guns. His stunts got smoother and attracted big audiences. People began to whisper his name in the barracks and the mess hall. Younger pilots looked at him with admiring eyes. Higher officers acknowledged him with nods or quick salutes.

By the end of August, Roland was deemed a good enough pilot to finally receive his combat orders. He and a few others, including Elliot, would join the prestigious First Pursuit Group as members of the 27th Air Squadron.

Roland and Elliot arrived at their new airfield after a brief train ride across France. It was a big contrast to his train ride to Ypres. Back then, barking officers had crammed him into a wooden boxcar with about a hundred other men. This time, a second-lieutenant's rank assured him space in a real passenger car with real seats and fresh tea. When the new pilots disembarked, they walked to the airfield just outside a village called Rembercourt.

The place was small compared to Issoudun. It had a single, wide open, sodded green field. Two temporary hangars, where mechanics worked in oil-stained coveralls, occupied the fringes of the take-off strip. A long row of green and gray planes, French SPAD biplanes and the familiar Nieuports, sat in a tidy row on the grass. Deep, freshly dug trenches tangled with barbed wire surrounded the entire field, manned by enlisted men and dotted with anti-aircraft guns. Nearby, a large, tawny mess tent flapped beneath the swaying shade trees, surrounded by neatly spaced rows of other, smaller tents – the living quarters to accommodate four entire squadrons, including Roland's 27th 'Fighting Eagles.'

Roland was anxious to tour the space and meet his fellow pilots, but he and Elliot had just enough time for a fresh meal, and a minute to drop their things in their assigned quarters. Then, they marched into the pursuit group commander's office.

On trembling legs, Roland found himself face to face with Major

Harold E. Hartney. The older man's eyes twinkled with mischief, and his smile, crowned with a neatly combed mustache, put everyone's nerves at ease. He didn't give off the stern, strict aura that a lot of officers did. A few medals commemorating his time serving with the Canadians, and his stint at the head of the 27th Squadron, hung proudly from his breast. A polished Sam Browne belt over his broad shoulders and his hands stayed folded behind his strong back.

Looking at him made Roland feel very . . . well . . . lucky. To be serving under such an experienced commander, but also to be serving in such a prestigious corps.

Hartney greeted his new recruits with a bark of a salute and brief introduction. 'Gentlemen, I won't sugar coat a thing. School is all over. You have a man's job now. I'm sure you have many questions, but I have only one piece of advice. If you get up there over the lines and find that all you want is to come back, that means you're yellow.'

Some of the boys threw nervous looks at each other.

Elliot clenched his fists, as if the mere thought that he could be yellow was a personal affront.

Hartney continued. 'I won't ask you to go over anyway. Instead, I want you to tell me, so you can get the hell out of this outfit. Yellow pilots are a danger to themselves and all the pilots around them. So, do us all a favor. If you're yellow, at least have the guts to say so.'

Roland looked at the floor, while Elliot let out a quiet huff.

'For now, anyway, you are members of the 27th Squadron in the First Pursuit Group. This group is the finest flying outfit on the front. Back home there are fifty thousand young men learning to fly and eager to be where you are, so congratulations. But be warned, you're fighter pilots in name only. When you have shown your buddies that you play the game without cracking up, they'll let you stay. Probably. You'll know without my telling you when you are members of the gang, and that is up to you. That's all I have to say. You're dismissed.'

That was that. With no pomp, circumstance, or ceremony, Roland and Elliot were official combat fighters with the 27th Squadron. They would now have to earn the approval of the battle-tested pilots of their outfit. If they couldn't, it would be back to the trenches.

And after just a day of wandering around the base, checking out his new airplane, exploring the airmen's mess hall, and wiling away the long hours, Roland spotted his name on the list for the next morning's patrol. It meant that he would get up before the sun the next morning, and these tough pilots would escort him on his first combat mission. It would be the real thing this time, with live ammunition and everything.

A lump grew in Roland's throat. He ran his fingertip over the large, courier font that spelled his name on that list. He wondered if that same name would appear on a casualty list at this time tomorrow. Or worse, a wooden cross. Maybe it would appear on a roster of names that had been scrubbed out. Only time would tell, and it would be a miserable wait.

After a restless night tossing and turning, thinking of Bernard and longing for Ilse, Roland dragged himself out of bed while darkness still covered the airfield. He ate a hurried breakfast of eggs and overcooked bacon, then he went to the take-off field. His flight leader, a beefy and weathered pilot named Norman, waited there for him.

Norman was a tall, muscled man with hard brown eyes, jet-black hair, and a stern, brown face. War had prematurely aged him. He had stress lines on his young forehead and a few gray hairs in his scalp. Perhaps he'd had a sense of humor once upon a time, but it was all gone now. He had no encouragement to offer Roland. Just a nod filled with doubt.

'We go up in ten minutes. Let's see what you're really made of, pretty boy.'

It was the longest ten minutes of Roland's life. He suited up, then he sat to one side while his mechanic made some last-minute adjustments to his plane. The flimsy biplane had a drab, olive-colored paint job and red, white, and blue tri-circles on the sides and wings. A serial number was scrawled on the back end. Evidence of hard use sprinkled the cockpit, with chipped paint, splintered wood, and cracks in some of the gauges. After the mechanic oiled the machine and checked the petrol levels, he assisted Roland into the pilot's seat.

Roland almost wished the mechanic had found a problem, because his heart was thudding inside of him and his hands had gone cold and clammy with nerves. It wasn't just the thought of maiming or death that scared him either. He knew that if he didn't do well on this patrol, he would wash out. They would boot him into the trenches. The thought gave him an uncontrollable urge to urinate. He wouldn't be able to though, not with the dozens of pounds of pilot gear currently weighing him down into his seat.

The mechanic gave him a nod, then he jerked the prop into action. 'Contact!'

Roland answered him with a yell muffled behind his flight gear. 'Contact!'

The prop sputtered around to full speed, and the engine roared to life. Roland steered his plane to the grassy take-off strip, lining up behind his patrol mates. He felt the sizzling, piercing eyes of the other pilots on him as he did so. Many of them gave him a smirk, as if they knew he would fail and scrub out.

Roland tried to ignore them as he pointed his machine at the horizon. Just like they did on his first solo flight, which felt like a lifetime ago, his arms and legs took it from there. His hands dropped to his controls, and his feet fumbled over the rudder bar. Like it was second nature, Roland brought his plane up to speed and glided down the runway. Hangars and barracks sped past him in a blur. He felt the familiar surge as his wheels lifted off the ground.

Normally, he relished that feeling. This time, it made his entire stomach flip upside down. He felt his cheeks tingle and flush. He suddenly regretted that heavy breakfast. What would his squadron mates think if he stumbled out of his plane with vomit all down his front?

He tried not to think about it, but the harder he tried, the harder the nausea hit him. With each bank on the wind, bump of turbulence, or shriek of the plane wires, his insides jostled. His loose, wobbly wicker seat shot spurts of pain up his back. Thick, black petrol fumes and oil spray slapped against his green cheeks. The heavy smell of burned castor oil invaded his nostrils.

Roland battled the gag reflex, forcing his brain to focus on the controls instead. He leveled into an arrow formation with his fellow pilots and they started for the lines, with France drifting past underneath them.

Roland struggled to breathe, angry beyond belief that his stomach chose now to get airsick for the first time. Although he supposed his nerves had something to do with it. Which certainly couldn't be helped.

A wag of the wings from Norman snapped Roland to attention. He looked over his plane, and for the first time, he saw the Great War from an entirely different vantage point.

From way up here, the trenches looked like the harmless, long wormholes that he sometimes saw in the trunks of trees. The barbed wire was like pencil scratches on a piece of brown paper. Tiny puffs of smoke and flashes of light shimmered like jewels. It almost reminded him of the electric Christmas lights he had once seen in New York City, glowing and twinkling in the night. The war appeared so serene from this angle, but Roland knew damn well there was nothing peaceful down there. Against his will, his mind flashed with the grotesque images of squishing mud, relentless machine guns, and of course, the poison gas.

None of which did his churning stomach any favors. He let out a few raspy coughs, then he zeroed in on keeping his plane in formation. He prayed hard to the God above, who had to hear him now that he was so much closer. *Please, if I get shot that's fine, but don't let me get sick on my first sortie. Those boys will never let me hear the end of it . . .*

As he kept his head bowed in prayer, he suddenly heard a loud bang and felt a violent thud beneath him. His tail heaved up into the air, shaking the hell out of his entire machine. Other jolts and bangs quickly followed the first. They sounded like loud claps or even an extra-loud sneeze, and they tossed his plane around like a rag doll.

Roland clamped his sweaty hands over his controls. He wasn't sure what the noises were, but he figured it might be engine trouble. Just as he began a frantic hunt for a place to land, he noticed black smoke puffs popping up all around him like lethal party balloons.

It wasn't his engine. 'Archie,' the German anti-aircraft guns, had him in their sights. They hurled everything they had at the bundle of biplanes too. The shrapnel puffs spread out like polka dots in the blue sky, and the thick, black smoke soon smothered Roland's entire formation.

Another loud clunk came from right in front of him. This time, small shrapnel pieces collided with his plane. His wing fabric ripped in a few spots.

The jostling spiked Roland's nausea something awful, and he put a hand to his stomach in alarm. Thoughts of the crashes at Issoudun began to haunt his memories. He saw the graves in field thirteen, the splinters of plane parts in the field, and Tommy's charred corpse. An overwhelming urge to fly far away from here, as fast as he could, seized control of his brain. It pulsated through his whole being. He even put his hands on the controls and prepared to turn around, no matter what anyone had to say about it.

But then he glanced at the planes beside him, where he saw no signs of distress amongst the veteran pilots. It annoyed him something awful. These fliers had probably been through a plethora of Archie before, so of course they wouldn't be scared. And like hell he was going to let them show him up. He would stay. He would face it all. He would prove himself.

Roland groaned as more rattles and shakes came from his plane, and more Archie burst around him. He felt like a sitting duck with twenty guns pointed at it. Artillery was a weapon that he couldn't fire back on either, not from an airplane anyway. There was so much that he couldn't control. Nothing he could really do except endure.

Perspiration poured down his back despite the frigid temperatures in the dome. He struggled to steel his eyes and keep his plane steady. Then, after what felt like an eternity, Norman wagged his wings, peeled off, and headed back toward the airfield. Roland's body filled with relief as the other planes did likewise.

The patrol was short and he hadn't spotted a single enemy plane, but that was fine by Roland. He only longed to get on the ground and settle his nerves and stomach.

It wouldn't be an easy ride back though. For some reason, Norman did a series of banks and turns as the formation headed for home. Every few minutes, he flew off in a dive or shot for the blue dome like a bat out of hell. Roland couldn't figure the cause for such wild maneuvers, so he supposed the veterans just wanted to test his mettle. Give him a bit of proper hazing. Well, he showed them. He kept up with every stunt, right up until they landed safely at their own field.

Roland never felt more relieved to have his plane bump gently along solid ground. As soon as he was out of the air and back on land, the horrible nausea began to subside. His breathing returned to normal, and the sweat faucets turned off. He exhaled deeply as he taxied over to the field to line his plane up with the others. Then he shut down the engine. Once the prop went still, he sat back in his wicker chair and reveled in the silent cockpit. He mopped the oil and soot on his face with his equally oily and sooty coat sleeve. When he finally jumped out of his plane, he tore his leather helmet off and inhaled countless gulps of the refreshing air. With each deep breath, his nausea faded even more. His body chemistry leveled off. A grin even worked its way across his face.

He felt like hell and had almost tossed his breakfast, but he had survived his first combat patrol.

As he peeled his sweaty gear off like the layers of a banana, Norman strolled over to him and leaned against his plane. While he had removed his outer coat and lining, he still wore his bulky flying pants and heavy boots. Sweat stained the white shirt pressing against his skin. He watched Roland dress down with an eerie smile on his face.

He pointed to Roland's wing. 'Lookie there, your first combat badge.'

Roland followed Norman's gaze. Sure enough, a gaping hole peered at him from the bottom half of his biplane wing. The size of a fist, Roland couldn't believe it hadn't caused him a whole other bag of troubles up there. And he was painfully aware that if the shrapnel had landed just a few feet over, it would have gone right into his cockpit and killed him.

The close call gave his nausea a fresh boost, but he continued stripping off his heavy pilot gear in determined silence. He couldn't let Norman smell his fear.

'So, how did you like your first time out?'

Roland just shrugged. 'It wasn't so bad. Maybe Archie rocked me up a bit, but I didn't see a damn thing to scare me.'

Norman's eyes went wide. 'You didn't see a damn thing to scare you? Do you mean you didn't notice the four German planes giving us hell the whole way home?'

Roland halted. 'What?'

'They tailed us from the trenches, hanging back about a hundred yards away. I had to bank all over hell to shake them off. It's a good thing they don't go over the lines looking for a fight.' Norman laughed. 'Here you didn't even notice. Some pilot you are. Although you kept up nice, didn't you?'

Roland's heart screeched to a halt inside him. He had no clue how he could have missed four enemy planes tailing him almost the entire way home. 'I . . . I don't understand . . .'

Norman just waved his hand through the air. 'Relax, kid. It takes a few patrols to acquire flying eyes. You don't look for planes when you're up. They're too far away for that. You look for specks or unexpected movement. Sometimes you don't even notice them until they shoot out your damn windshield.'

Roland just gulped.

Norman smiled to put his nerves at ease. 'I'm trying to say you did a bang-up job for a first-timer. Get your flying eyes, and you'll be a solid fighter. I'm sure of it.'

Later, as the heat of late summer crept over the airfield, Roland accompanied Elliot to a nearby bubbling spring. The boy lay barefoot in the grass with a fishing line tied around his big toe. He watched the gurgling, clear water while he shook his head at his buddy.

'You mean to tell me you didn't see a goddamn thing?' He let out a bellow. 'Four Germans, and you didn't even take a crack at one?'

'They could've shot me out of the sky, and I wouldn't have even seen death coming.' He turned to his side and coughed. 'It scared me a little, Elliot.'

'Well, sure. Holy Mother.' Elliot bobbed his toe up and down to entice fish for a bite. 'At least you survived your first Archie blast. I hear that's half the battle right there.'

'Norman said he took me over the front lines on purpose. Because that first dance with Archie either makes or breaks a flier. Some crack up so bad they get reassigned. I guess he wanted to see which I would be.'

'So, you're a real fighter then, hey?'

Roland smiled. 'Not until I get the first black cross by my name. According to Norman, anyway.'

Elliot laughed and went back to his fishing.

Roland watched him for a moment and frowned. He stepped up to the stream's bank and took off his shirt. Next, he peeled off his pants.

Elliot gave him a sheepish chuckle. 'Save it for a girlfriend, city boy.'

'Oh, can it. You see more man ass in the barracks. Besides, you'll never catch fish with that lousy toe line. Let me teach you how to fish like a man.'

Elliot squealed with laughter. 'The city boy says he'll teach me to fish! Hell, I'd like to see that.'

'You will.' Roland jumped into the frigid water. He thrashed his arms and legs every which way. Big splashes and loud thumps shattered the silence by the stream.

It was an uproar the likes of which Midwestern Elliot had never seen. 'They didn't teach you how to swim in NYC? Holy hell, Roland. Come on out of there. No fighter pilot wants to die by drowning.'

After a few more seconds, Roland's head broke the surface of the water. He gave his wet body a shake, flinging water droplets everywhere. To Elliot's shock, he held a shiny and plump fish in each hand.

Roland dropped his catches in the grass. 'How many more you want?'

Elliot stared at him, dumbstruck. 'Where in hell did you learn how to do that?'

'Central Park.'

TWENTY-ONE
Ilse

September, 1918

Ilse, with a band of Red Cross personnel behind her, trudged through the foggy French countryside. The train, overcrowded with soldiers going to the front, and nurses going to their hospitals, had dropped them off a few miles back in the nearest town. As for the rest of the way to her new post at a casualty clearing station near Saint-Mihiel, she and her fellow nurses would have to walk. For the journey, she sported a dark skirt with a matching jacket. Red Crosses adorned each shoulder. She was proud of them, but she also kept them concealed when she left the hospitals. The war had become cruel, supplies reaching critical lows. Red Crosses became targets instead of deterrents. Germans would stop at nothing to get more supplies.

Perhaps another reason why Ilse looked so frail. It took a lot of effort to lift her black, mud-caked lace-up boots through the soggy terrain. She struggled to hoist her knees over the dead leaves and underbrush. Her cheeks were sunken, and her arms sagged with weight loss. Her hair hung in frizzy strands from her head, since she had little time or water for bathing. Exhaustion had moved in on her green eyes too, dulling them to a mossy gray.

A beige medical bag filled with bandage wraps and small stores of morphine rested over her shoulder. A bulging brown pack weighed down her back, stuffed with every piece of medical equipment she could carry. Behind her, about a half-dozen other ladies also hauled large packs. A wooden cart pulled by a lanky old mule creaked along beside them. The poor beast's hooves squished and suctioned in the mud.

Ilse hoisted her pack on her shoulders as her boots crunched through the dead leaves. She and her group had entered a wooded area, blanketed in a haunting silence. No animals fettered about in the underbrush. A ghostly, gray mist permeated the trees – trees that looked very odd. The leaves had disappeared, the trunks were an unnatural copper color. No wildflowers or grass grew on the ground, which only boasted withered leaves and ashen earth.

Ilse paused to sniff the air. Something wasn't right about this place.

She knelt next to a nearby shrub, examining its strange, scaly outer layer. Burned to the core, it was rough and coarse to the touch. Her fingertip brushed a solo, faded leaf hanging from one of its twigs. On contact with her skin, the leaf dissolved into dust. The particles slithered through the air and drifted among the human corpses scattered in the mud.

Ilse gasped and jumped up. With a hand on her fluttering heart, she took in the sight of the stiff bodies. They looked more like skeletons with taut, shriveled, and ugly gray skin attached. The mouths hung open in eternal trauma. Eyes bulged out of sockets. Bony hands stretched out for help and mercy.

The nurse beside Ilse couldn't hide her horrified sob. 'What the hell happened here?'

'Phosgene gas.' Ilse brushed the dust from her hands.

'My God . . . Do they suffer?'

Ilse drew her lips into a thin line. She couldn't tell the nurse that Phosgene gas was one of the worst ways to die. It was also one of the most potent gases on the front. It had surpassed even mustard to become the most lethal chemical agent of the Great War. Medical personnel estimated it had claimed about eighty percent of gas fatalities.

Ilse shuddered and took in the burned terrain. Much like the men the gas had scarred, she wondered if this barren landscape would ever heal and produce life again. She patted the nurse on the shoulder and motioned her forward. The two fell into step with the other girls.

'Come along,' she said to the other nurse. 'We don't want to be caught out here after night fall.'

These were scary and dangerous times.

TWENTY-TWO
Roland

September, 1918

Roland sat on a wooden barrel in the shadow of his freshly painted plane wing. He stretched his stiff limbs to air out some sweat, which pooled inside his full pilot gear. He hated wearing the heavy coat, boots, and scarf for hours at a time like this. But full gear was mandatory on 'morning alert,' a type of patrol where pilots had to fully dress for take-off, hang around the base, and wait for the sharp blast of the alarm bells – the signal that enemy planes had been spotted. Once they rang, morning alert had to be airborne in ten minutes or less.

Roland's first few times on morning alert shredded his nerves like a cheese grater. He trembled under his airplane, jumping at the slightest noises, pacing in anticipation of those bells. Embarrassing, but he knew he didn't suffer alone. All the new pilots struggled with morning alert. Just one of many emotional adjustments they had to make in a hurry.

It got easier though, after enough practice. Just like most anything in his short time as a pilot thus far.

Except kills.

Roland drew in a deep breath to settle his nerves, rustled by the knowledge that after his first full week at Rembercourt, he still had nothing to show for his many patrols – other than a ripe stench from all the sweat. With no real bathing facilities, the smell clung to him. Just like his flying record that was still devoid of any kills.

However, September had brought relief in other ways. It had slightly faded the oppressive summer heat to a refreshing autumn crisp. Clouds covered the French skies on a lot of days, blotting out the blinding hot sun. Although it was still quite warm this morning, which left Roland slightly uncomfortable as he sat by his plane and waited to see if those alarm bells would ring.

While he waited, he glanced over at another thing that September had brought him: his new friend – a jet-black stray feline that he had met a few days back.

She randomly showed up at his tent one morning, crying for something to eat. She was down to skin and bones, fleas clumping her fur. Roland, who could always use extra company, left bowls of leftover breakfast outside for her and tried to make friends.

And make friends they did. She became a regular visitor after that, following Roland all over the airbase, winding in and out of his feet for pets, food, and tummy scratches. When he went on patrol, she sat outside his tent and watched him go with her piercing, protective eyes. She didn't move from that spot until he returned safe and sound. She became his official mascot and he named her Jewel, despite the howling of his fellow fliers, who stormed that her black coat would curse them all.

Roland, who happened to like black cats, reached out and gave Jewel a scratch behind the ears. She purred and rolled over on her back, inviting her human to scratch her tummy.

Meanwhile, Norman and Elliot sat in the grass and played with their own pets – a passel of baby bunnies they had discovered in the bushes, the war having left them motherless. The baby animals sure brought out a softer side in their bristling owners. The boys scrounged up a wooden crate, stuffed it with hay, and gave it to the babies as a bed. They fed them scraps of vegetables from the mess, and provided countless cuddles and pets. Even now, the boys giggled like children as the bunnies hopped in and out of their laps. They picked them up and nuzzled them, tickling their cheeks with furry noses and whiskers.

'You close in on them from high up,' Norman said to Elliot. 'That way you avoid Archie on the ground.'

Elliot guffawed. 'Sure, because you exchange it for the hornet's nest of fighters in the air. You know how they guard those spy balloons. The information they get is too damn valuable.'

Norman leaned back on his elbows and watched one of the bunnies crawl around his legs. 'I know, which is why I'd give anything to take one.'

Suddenly, a rough growl came at them from behind. 'You want an observation balloon? Attack it head on.'

All three heads turned.

Before them stood a tall, husky young man with tanned skin and electric blond hair. His blue eyes glinted like ice inside of his stony, fierce face. His stance was borderline menacing. His manners quite rough. Even so, the stranger knelt down and held a hand to the baby bunnies. One eventually hopped in and sniffed his fingers.

Norman frowned. 'You attack them head on, they'll kill you head on.'

'Bull. Germans are all defense who put no stock in theatrics. If you go at a balloon head on and make it look good, they'll be caught off guard. Especially if one of you distracts them while the other goes for the bag. One shot with some incendiaries, and it's done.'

Elliot laughed. 'Sounds pretty damn reckless to me. Not to mention incendiaries are illegal. You get caught with them, they'll kill you.'

The other pilot shrugged. '*C'est la guerre.* You want a balloon, you fly head on and take it. Simple as that.'

Norman released an annoyed snort. 'That's pretty tough talk from a guy with no kills.'

A streak of anger crossed those burning blue eyes. The pilot lumbered to his feet and towered over Norman. 'I got a kill. Ask Hartney.'

'Hartney only says that because you're his little pet. No one else saw it. And if you ask me – no record, no kill. Which makes you a liar.'

The pilot glowered in a way that made Roland shrink inside his flight gear, praying he would never be on the receiving end of that look.

But the mystery pilot just stormed away, heading for the edge of airfields.

'Who the hell was that?' Elliot asked.

Norman returned to the bunnies. 'Name's Frank Luke. Some hothead out of Arizona. He's always running his damn trap about how big a hero he is, but he's late for half his patrols and hasn't downed a single plane.'

Roland watched the angry blond man as he arrived at the trench parameters, making his way over to the enlisted men. 'He really lied about a kill?'

'He says he went solo against a pack of Germans deep in enemy territory and downed one. Not a single person backed it up though. Except Hartney, who thinks he's a standout for some stupid reason. From where I'm sitting, Luke's a miserable asshole with no friends, no kills, and on the verge of washing out.'

Roland watched as Luke crouched by the defensive trenches, an odd place for him to be. Because they were all buck privates over there. The pilots usually didn't mingle with them. Yet this didn't

As The Storm Clouds Gather 161

look like Luke's first visit. The enlisted men scrambled out of their dugouts to greet him. Then he began handing out cigarettes and other treats he had swiped at mess.

The gesture rustled something in Roland's heart, tapping into some painful memories. He was an enlisted man once. He could only dream of being a pilot while he spent his days like a pig wallowing in mud. He had hated the officers who treated them like numbers instead of living, breathing men. Seeing Luke give them treats to cheer them somehow put a bandage over that old hurt. Made it sting just a little less.

Before he could think more on it, a hiss and a loud squeal yanked Roland from his thoughts.

Norman roared. 'Damn you! I told you to keep that witch's charm away from our bunnies.'

Jewel had swiped at one of the little creatures, which put the fear of God into all of them. The bunnies squeaked and hopped in a panicked frenzy while Jewel sat back on her haunches, an honest-to-God snicker escaping her jaws.

Roland swooped his ornery pet into his arms while Elliot and Norman scrambled after theirs.

And, of course, the alarm bells chose that moment to clang across the airfield.

Roland jumped, poor Jewel shrieked and vanished across the field, and Norman and Elliot cursed the high heavens as they flung baby furballs back into their box.

Roland bundled up his flight gear and climbed up the side of his plane, where his mechanic was already halfway through the required checks. In less than a minute, Roland taxied down the sodden runway and was airborne. Norman, Elliot and the rest of the patrol followed close on his tail flaps. Once safely above the airbase, they tightened into formation and flew over the fields in search of the enemy planes that had set off the alarms.

Worry seeped into Roland's body like a dripping tap as he did so, because he wasn't any different from Frank Luke. He hadn't bagged a German either. He had flown close to a dozen patrols. He had been under fire from both machine guns and artillery. His plane had sustained some first battle scars. Yet, he still hadn't downed any pilots. The way Norman talked about Luke gave him some not-so-pleasant things to think about. Like maybe that was how people talked about him behind his back. And if that was so, it meant he had little time left to prove that he deserved a place here.

The formation buzzed through the gray dome, punching through the thick, foggy blanket of cloud cover. Once they made it through the blinding mist, the sun blasted down through the crystal atmosphere, bouncing its harsh light off their gauges and windshields. Roland squinted, his body rigid with alert.

Then came the attack. Almost as soon as the formation broke above the cloud bank, a half-dozen German triplanes swarmed on them like buzzards. They were brightly colored, marked with hostile black crosses, remnants of the deceased baron's flying circus. They jetted down in a tight arrowhead formation, flashes appearing in front of their planes as they opened fire.

Roland didn't have time to be afraid, because the Germans were already on him. Bullets zinged through his cockpit. He heard loud cracks as they webbed the glass on his windshield and punctured his instrument panels. Wing fabric tore and wires screeched.

Forcing himself to focus, Roland banked his plane into position. After a few rolls and turns, he got one of the twirling German planes in his sights. His hand went for the trigger of his gun. The synchronizer gear clicked in place, and the guns burst to life. A cloud of black powder and smoke blasted against his cheeks, while a slew of red tracer bullets snapped from the gun, like sizzling nuts over a toasty fire.

Roland was a good shot, but the tracers swerved up and just missed the enemy plane.

He didn't panic. There just wasn't time for that. He turned his face down, following the enemy pilot through a dizzying maze of acrobatic escape stunts. He again lined his machine up and released a burst from his guns.

More red tracers zipped through the air. This time, a few of them pumped into the German's plane. Roland saw holes open up in the fuselage. A solid hit, but this pilot was cool under pressure too. He banked his plane right for another escape maneuver.

Roland curled his lips into a snarl and kept on target, slowly closing the gap of air space between himself and this enemy pilot. Then he let loose a final stream of bullets, which pierced his opponent's fuel tank. A brown fluid sprayed through the air. A few flames belched from the engine, followed by a trail of thick, billowing smoke. The pilot struggled in his cockpit. He tried a few times to resuscitate his dying machine. Then, he unstrapped himself from the seat and stood up.

Roland curled his hand tighter around his gun, wondering which was more humane – shoot a man leaping to his death, or let him free fall through the atmosphere. A question which sharply reminded him, yet again, what was at stake up here in the air. He had wanted to fly airplanes to make a difference and help end the war faster, but he would still have to take lives. And this time, it would be a hell of a lot more personal.

Before Roland could decide his fate, the German pilot stood up tall in his own cockpit. He threw Roland a firm salute. Seconds later, his plane burst into a ball of flames.

Roland yelped and jolted his own plane down to avoid the concussion and debris. Meanwhile, the skeletal remains of the German plane vanished into the cloud bank, leaving an ominous trail of smoke behind them.

Roland breathed so heavy his face tingled. A kill. Surely someone saw that . . .

He craned his head around each shoulder to locate his comrades.

They had done equal damage to their own opponents. Another German plane had just spiraled out of control and sank back into the thick cloud layer. Still another had taken a bad hit, and now it was limping away through the clouds. The rest had seen enough, and they took off in a mad dash for the horizon.

Norman gave a triumphant wag of his wings and dove down through the clouds. The rest of the patrol followed suit.

Roland was still in shock as he dipped his machine back into the fog, the image of that salute fused into his brain like a photo print. He once again stewed on the thought that he hadn't just shot a machine; he had taken a human life. He had killed someone. And unlike with Luke, there were plenty of witnesses. His kill would go on record. His name would be put on that chalkboard in the squadron mess, a cross etched next to it.

That German pilot's death had made Roland a real fighter. But it also probably broke the hearts of real people back in Germany. Or wherever he had come from.

That cooled Roland's pleasure considerably. In fact, it almost made him think that the numbers game in the trenches had its merits. Because back there, his enemies had no real face, and no real form. He shot at machine guns and trenches for the most part, with no way of knowing if his bullets ever found the mark. Which made it a bit easier to absolve himself.

Not in the air war. Here it was real. Here, there was no escape from what he had done.

Roland sighed with misery as he headed for home.

The grass is always greener on the other side of the fence.

TWENTY-THREE
Ilse

Ilse's new post was a casualty clearing station, one much closer to the danger zone than any other place she had worked thus far. Brown and olive medical tents covered an area the size of a city block. Even that wasn't enough space, as surplus wounded had been heaped all over in the mud. As Ilse's team arrived, huffing and puffing from another cross-country jaunt, she observed the chaos of the place.

The first stop on the road to recovery, casualty clearing stations housed soldiers just pulled off the battlefield. Harried military doctors performed emergency surgeries, slapped on bandages, and tied tourniquets. Men too broken to return to the front were loaded into medical trains and shuttled to the more permanent hospitals further back.

Being a qualified ambulance driver, Ilse had seen plenty of casualty clearing stations, but she had never worked at one full time. The first thing she noted was the danger. Many of the tent sides were shredded to Swiss cheese from stray bullets. Water-filled, foul-smelling shell craters lingered nearby. A cabinet filled with gas masks suggested she wouldn't be safe from the deadly fumes. The rumbling artillery, its flashes clearly visible on the horizon, forced people to speak in raised voices.

Ilse also spotted something she had never encountered before. A few arrowed signs sticking out of the mud, pointing the way to bomb shelters that were the only refuge from the giant, lumbering Gotha bomber planes, another weapon in the German air arsenal.

And the wounded were much gorier than Ilse was used to. Many hadn't even been cleaned yet. Trench slime reeking of decay plastered their faces, their clothes, and even their injuries. Wounds were crusted with blood and filled with the greenish ooze of infection. The entire station stank of blood and rotting flesh, the crackles of gas-gangrene wounds filling the air. Many of these boys would die before they made it to any hospital. It would be Ilse's job to raise the odds where she could.

A Red Cross nurse with fawn-colored hair and pale-gray eyes approached Ilse. 'You're my reinforcements?'

'Yes, ma'am,' Ilse said.

The frazzled woman held out her hand. 'We couldn't be more grateful. I'm Llewellyn, the matron here.'

Ilse shook her hand. 'Ilse. Or Chère-Amie, if you're in a friendly mood.'

Llewellyn laughed. 'I'm *always* in a friendly mood.' She waved her hand about the crazed facility. 'Living quarters are in the west block. Take whatever cot is open. We'll put you on the dawn shift, so you can have the evening to get settled.' She patted Ilse's shoulder. 'There's hot soup and crackers in the kitchen tent, if the soldiers left anything for you.' With that, she disappeared back into the chaos.

Ilse and her team dropped off their things in the nearest living quarters. The soldiers had indeed cleaned out the last drop of soup and cracker crumb, so Ilse and her cohorts contented themselves with lukewarm tea. They were too exhausted to speak, so they just listened. To the moaning of injured men and the shouting of frantic medical personnel. Doctors' voices from the surgical ward echoing across the block, along with the clattering of trays filled with tools. And the guns. So close, so thunderous, so frightening.

It must have been awful for someone new, but Ilse sipped her tea without a flinch. Until she heard a sound she wouldn't expect in a place like this . . . laughter. She perked up her ears and flashed her eyes to the tent opening.

One of the other nurses got up and poked her head out. 'Oh my,' she said with a giggle. 'There's some fly boys here.'

The other girls barely took notice, but Ilse sprang to her feet and pushed aside the nurse at the open tent flap.

Ilse at least knew Roland was well, for he wrote her often enough. But she had long since tired of only experiencing his love through letters. She longed with every bone in her body to see him, but she had no idea where he was stationed. Security and censoring had tightened their grip. He only addressed his letters from 'Somewhere in France,' and black blobs covered over a lot of his words, anything that might give away his location. Through all the letters he sent, she only knew that he was alive, and that he thought about her often.

It made her miss him entirely too much. At night, she thought about him while everyone else squeezed in some sleep. She imagined him right next to her. She tried to remember the weight and warmth of his arms around her waist. She thought back on their embraces with a strong, hot flutter in her hips, struggling to recall the feel of his dry, salty lips against her own.

For a woman who was once all business, it was awfully sentimental.

Ilse slipped out of the tent and filed through the swarms of nurses and injured men to catch up with the aviators.

The two boys were pretty typical pilot specimens, young and full of life. They had wild eyes and, more often than not, they had a wild personality to match. They laughed and joked while they stepped over hordes of broken men. Their loud, boisterous manners were symptomatic of recent alcohol consumption. Another thing pilots were famous for.

Ilse observed their features from a safe distance, trying to find traces of the brown-haired New York City boy she had last seen in Belgium. Her heart sank when she realized neither of them was her Roland. She tried to hide her disappointment, as it felt wrong to nurse a broken heart with all these broken men around.

She began the retreat to her barrack, but a voice stopped her.

'Hey, blondie!'

Ilse rolled her eyes. Busted. She turned back the airmen. 'What?'

The pilot grinned from a face not older than twenty. He had reddish-colored hair and turquoise, sparkling eyes. Ilse would have thought him handsome if her heart didn't belong to someone else.

He looked her up and down with very invasive eyes. 'So, this is where they keep all the pretty girls.' He held out his hand. 'My name's Calvin.'

Ilse allowed him to kiss her hand, but she jerked it away fast. Those mischievous, prowling eyes made her uncomfortable. 'Chère-Amie.'

'That's French, isn't it?' He grinned. 'I've heard loads about French girls and their hospitality.'

Ilse put her hands on her hips. 'Are you looking for something?'

'Yes. Girls.'

She glared.

'Oh, I'm not so fresh as you think. The boys and I are throwing a dinner party tomorrow night at a chateau down the road. We want company is all.' He winked. 'I'd like to cordially invite you.'

'As what? A waitress?'

He laughed. 'My word, you're mouthy. I love it. No, my dear. I'd like you to accompany me as my . . . well . . . company.'

Ilse's cheeks blushed. 'Flattering, but you see all the work to be done here.'

'Come now, don't be such a canceled stamp. It will be a gas.'

'A poor choice of words in a hospital, sir.'

He nodded. 'Right. Loads of fun, then.'

'Then I suspect you would have a fine time without me.'

She turned to go, but the pilot pulled her back by the wrist. 'Boy, you're a minx. I like it though. Means you've got morals.'

'Then I'll take the moral high road. You're wasting your flattery. I'm spoken for.'

The pilot snorted his disapproval. 'No fair. A doctor?'

'A pilot, actually.'

His eyes went wide with surprise. 'At least you know how to pick them. What unit does he fly for?'

Ilse's eyes gleamed. Here was an opportunity, and she went for it head-first. 'I don't know. Your censors don't even let a boy tell his sweetheart where he is.'

'Well, maybe I can help. What's his name?'

'Roland Hawkins.'

'Roland Hawkins . . .' The boy searched some files in his memory bank. 'Doesn't ring any bells.' He snapped his fingers in a mocking gesture. 'Darn it all. Guess you'll have to forget him for one night and come to our party instead.'

Ilse felt a second shot of stinging disappointment. If she knew where Roland was, she could find her way to him. But she couldn't even glean that much. She put her hands back on her hips and chewed her lip to keep from crying.

The pilot softened at her clear pain. 'You might try over at Rembercourt though,' he whispered, so the other pilot wouldn't hear.

Ilse perked up. 'What?'

'About ten miles yonder. The First Pursuit Group is over there, one of the biggest American aviation divisions. It's a good chance your boy will be there.'

Ilse was so happy she stood up on her tiptoes and kissed the pilot on the cheek. 'I appreciate it. You'll never know how much.'

'Enough to go out with me tomorrow night?'

She crossed her arms. 'What, are you deaf? I'm *spoken for.*'

He beckoned to her barrack tent behind her. 'But I assume they aren't.'

Ilse turned and saw the girls from her team, all poking their heads out of their barracks, giggling amongst each other, pointing at the handsome pilot.

TWENTY-FOUR
Roland

Roland's hands shook, fighting to control his plane after one of the worst fights he'd ever been in. Norman flew next to him, black smoke pouring from his engine. His plane made terrible coughing noises, rattling and shaking as he tried to keep it airborne.

Roland flew tight on his wing to protect him, hoping to get both of them home before the German fighters they had barely beaten off returned to finish the job. A fight that had already forced down the rest of their patrol. Germans were probably shoving the pilots into filthy, disgusting war prisons at this very moment. If they had even survived the landing.

Roland edged his plane closer to Norman's, his eyes darting all over the place, scouring the skies for tell-tale specks on the horizon, or any unnatural movements. He knew those Germans would come back. He wasn't sure why they left in the first place. Probably just to re-arm or get new planes.

He tilted his plane to use the landscape as navigation, but he couldn't find much to guide him. Just random splotches of green and brown, intercut with dirt roads that looked like tan ribbons from up here. Hazy pillars of smoke obscured a lot of the earth, while lightning-bug flashes indicated where there was active artillery inside the mist.

Roland tried to ascertain how far they were from Rembercourt. Before he could finish his calculations, he saw the anticipated four specks approaching from over the lines.

Roland cursed under his breath and signaled to Norman.

Norman also noticed the specks, shifting uncomfortably in his seat. He knew he would be easy prey, unlikely to survive the fight ahead.

As for Roland, just like his many combats before, he had no time to be scared. The German planes were upon him before he could even truly prepare himself. With an angry roar, he rammed his plane in front of Norman's. If they wanted to pick off his buddy, they would have to get through him first.

And they weren't afraid to do so. A stream of red tracer bullets spilled from the lead German plane, zipping past Roland with deadly pops and hisses.

Roland positioned himself and returned fire. The tracers blasted hot from his guns, but suddenly, the machinery above him clicked and fell silent. He pushed the trigger again, but no tracers appeared. Just that helpless clicking.

Roland's insides completely bottomed out. High above enemy territory, surrounded by Germans, and with only busted-up Norman to assist him, his gun had just jammed.

'Goddamn it . . .' He fumbled for the hammer he always kept in his cockpit. All the pilots were issued one, gun jams being a frequent problem. He picked his up and banged on the ammunition chamber. He tried the trigger once more, but only that pathetic click came out.

'Come *onnnn* . . .' Roland tried a few more bangs with the hammer, then he wrapped his nervous fingers around the trigger.

Click. Click.

While Roland struggled to right his guns, the four Germans formed up for their killing stroke. They melted into a neat point formation and wheeled in to take aim.

Hope deserted Roland. He would be forced down like the others, or he would explode into a ball of flames over France. Neither were good prospects. He flinched, feeling death's icy-cold fingers on his cheeks, but they didn't close their grip on him. Instead, a fresh stream of tracers blasted from somewhere up above and behind him. So close he felt the heat as they whooshed past his head and into the German planes, scattering them like a flock of pigeons.

Roland shouted with surprise and whipped his head around.

A fast-flying biplane, with French markings, roared onto the scene, tearing at the Germans with all the ferocity of a wild beast, banking and spiraling all over the place. Behind him flew a wingman, his engine screeching like a pterodactyl.

It was like watching two ferocious lions fight against a pack of scared house cats. One German plane caught fire and dipped to the ground in a blaze of smoke. Another's wing started to crumble, and the pilot made a mad dash for home. The remaining two scrambled to shift from attack to defense, completely caught off guard by this surprise attack.

Roland tried to identify the mystery pair of planes, but they were moving too fast. He couldn't make out the pilots, but he did note the serial number on the lead plane.

Twenty-six.

Frank Luke.

The Arizona hothead, bane of the squadron's existence and one of Norman's chief rivals, had made quite a name for himself lately. Mostly by targeting the coveted prize of German army observation balloons. He and his wingman, Joe Wehner, fought the behemoths head-on, just like Luke had once said they should. The rest of the squadron could only watch in a befuddled stupor as what started as a ludicrous bid for attention erupted into a dizzying array of kills over just a few days. Neighboring squadrons had taken to calling Luke 'the Balloon Buster.'

Now, it was looking like Luke would add a few more victories to his growing roster, and save Roland's ass in the process.

But Roland wouldn't get to watch. Because just then, his engine sputtered and belched out some black smoke. After a few jerks and rattles, it went ghostly silent.

Roland gasped and checked his gauges, quickly noting the fuel had dropped to empty in all the excitement. He clamped his hands and feet down and tried to restart his plane.

While he tried to remember any forced landings that didn't end in a ball of fire, the plane dropped altitude at an alarming rate. When he exhausted every trick to start the engine and save his life, he began the battle to keep the plane upright instead. Because it was crucial for him to hit wheels first, and that would be hard with a totally dead control stick.

Roland fought, pulled, and yanked, smoothing out his flight path just in the nick of time. The wheels thudded to the ground, the impact jolting him down to the skull. More jerks and thumps tossed him about as his wheels skidded and scraped through the deep mud. Stringy wheat stalks wrapped around the wheel axles and yanked the plane every which way. The left wheel snapped off. The plane tipped sideways, the wing dragging along in the mud, crumbling to pieces as it did so. Roland's body slammed into his instrument panel, which sent a burst of bright colors through his head.

The plane let out a final, monstrous groan before coming to a stop in the middle of desolate France, settling into the mud with a series of squeaks and groans. Roland leaned back in his broken wicker chair. With violently trembling fingers, he ripped his helmet off and pumped some air into his severely shook-up lungs. His ears caught the distant growls of shells and artillery. He also saw a curtain of smoke on the nearby horizon. He was dangerously close to the front lines, yet he had no idea which side he was actually on.

He unstrapped himself from the seat. His knees wobbled with shock, but he managed to stumble out of the open cockpit and splat into the mud down below. He stayed on his hands and knees for several moments, trying to catch his breath and reckon with the close call he just had.

He also looked around the small farming village where his plane had happened to land. There wasn't much left of it. People had long since fled. Flooded, sloppy shell craters spotted the parameters. Buildings had been reduced to mossy piles of stones. Only the village chapel remained intact, the unstable skeleton of a spire teetering above it.

Roland let out a raspy cough, then managed to wobble to his feet. He limped over to his ruined plane, rummaging for the flare gun in the cockpit. He yanked it out from under his smashed instrument panel, and checked the chamber to see if it was loaded. With downcast eyes, he aimed it at the beloved plane that had seen him through so much.

'Farewell, old girl.' He screwed his eyes shut and fired.

In a shower of red and orange sparks, one that he feared would give away his location, the single flare burst open in the heart of the cockpit. The fabric and wood went up like a haystack. While the flames crackled and burned, he searched his pockets and threw in his maps, guides, and even a few letters from Bernard. It felt cold and heartless, but it was protocol. Nothing, especially not his damaged plane, could fall into the hands of the Kaiser.

When he had destroyed everything of value, he turned and hobbled toward the church, the only place he could think to go for protection. He pulled on the heavy wooden door, and it opened with a painfully loud creaking noise. He stepped into the musty-smelling sanctuary, the door slamming shut behind him, wrapping him up in total damp and darkness. He took a few nervous steps forward, tripping over piles of stones and rubble.

'Hello?'

The only response was the nearby trickling of water, coming from somewhere deep within the badly damaged structure. On the roof, two big shell holes spilled some daylight on a wide sanctuary with high, looping ceilings. Hand-carved angels, saints, and doves peered at him from dusty stone walls. The stained-glass windows, once quite a work of art, now lay in pieces on the sanctuary floor. At the front of the room loomed a large altar covered in mud-splattered silks. A statue of the Virgin Mother lay on her side behind it, her face smeared with mud.

As Roland surveyed the empty space, a bright light glinted in his eyes. He put his hand up to shield his face while he stepped toward it, careful to avoid the many piles of stone and debris in the process. The light was coming from a crooked back door, partially blasted off its hinges. He gave the handle a jiggle and it easily swung open.

Roland found himself back outside, standing in a muddy, ravaged church graveyard. The iron-gray headstones towered around him, covered in moss and decay. They looked hundreds of years old. Maybe even more, and they had suffered accordingly. Many of them were cracked, split, or even broken in two. Pieces of them and their aging coffins lay scattered everywhere.

Even the dead couldn't rest in the Great War.

As Roland chewed on that, he noticed a newer grave along the crooked picket fence. A wooden cross, with a fresh heap of dirt piled in front of it.

Roland strode over to investigate. He knelt at the cross's base and scraped the mud off the epitaph.

'Unknown US Soldier.'

The words cut him deeper than the biting French wind, and memories of a somber day in Flanders Fields forced their way out from the rubble in his mind. The day he dug trenches in reserve with Vernon, and the corporal cried at the sight of all the bodies.

'You'll understand when it's the bones of your countrymen . . .'

That's what Vernon had said. Now, it rang painfully true and clear, punching Roland in the gut like a fist.

He tried to keep his jaw from trembling as he peeled more goo off the cross.

He had seen mountains of corpses, villages forever ruined, and innocent civilians ravaged by death and destruction. He had seen poison gas, humans torched to ash, and soldiers pushed to the brink. All so awful, but at least it was contained to Europe. Across the Atlantic, Roland thought America would always be safe, that it would always be home. But the disease had spread again. The Unknown Army had found new victims. Nowhere was safe now.

Tears built up behind Roland's tired eyes. A tidal wave of tears, ones that had waited for years to fall. Just as he prepared to let them, something caught his eye at the foot of the cross.

There, half-buried in the mud, sat a patch of mint-green growth. Nestled inside was a tiny scarlet poppy. Its blossom was young, not even strong enough to open yet. A bead of water was enough to almost completely weigh the poor thing down. What a sight to see here, especially so late in the season.

A single tear slid down Roland's cheek as he again flashed back to Flanders, and Vernon's somber, exhausted face. He heard again the wistful prediction that when color appeared in the soil, maybe the war would end. Roland had looked for color every day since. And here, at the foot of his millionth wooden cross, some had finally managed to poke through.

He reached out his finger to gently caress the blossom, allowing faint trickles of hope to break through the dry desert of his insides.

'Hawkins.'

Roland scrambled to his feet and turned around.

Frank Luke stood before him. Black powder and oil residue had smeared his entire face. His skin still pulsated with the thrill of the hunt. He gripped his helmet under his arm and stared at Roland with those piercing blue eyes.

'I saw you go down.' Frank stepped up to Roland and noticed the cross. Something like sadness appeared in those eyes, but it was hard to tell behind the fierceness.

'Norman?' Roland asked.

'Safe. Joe's guiding him home.'

Roland nodded with relief. His wasn't the only life spared by Luke then. 'Listen, what you did back there—'

'Spare me your poetry. Just back me up for the kill this time.'

Roland fiddled with his hands, unsure how to respond to such a sentiment.

Frank observed the wooden cross with his steely eyes. 'You know, I'm not half as brave as the infantry.'

Roland suppressed the sudden urge to cough, and the desire to tell Frank he didn't know the half of it. 'Is that why you spend so much time with the enlisted men?'

'They get treated like dogs and it's not right. They sacrifice more than any of us.'

Roland went to agree, but only a deep, raspy cough came out.

Frank glared at him, with a hint of suspicion that couldn't be denied. 'You should get that checked.'

'Yeah . . . maybe.'

'And those burns on your hands too.'

Roland looked down at his gas-scarred hands, then quickly shoved them into his pockets. He avoided Frank's knowing gaze, but he still felt it drill down to his deepest layers. When he did look up, Frank was looking at him in a new way, with something other than that cutting fierceness. There was something softer there now. Compassion. A hint of respect.

Somehow, as they stood at the foot of that cross, an understanding passed between them. Frank had guessed his secret, but both boys knew he wouldn't tell anyone. Without another word, Frank unwound the silk scarf from his neck. He knelt at the cross and tied the garment around it.

'For those boys in the mud.' He looked up at Roland. 'All of them.'

Roland just nodded and looked away. He knew everyone hated Frank Luke. Even though the boy had proved his mettle, he still didn't have many friends. He had a hard way about him that turned up a lot of noses. He was too hot-headed, too full of himself. But Luke's soft spot for the army's lower calling spoke volumes to a former infantryman.

Frank paused when he noticed the flower. 'What's that?'

'The end of the war.'

Frank frowned. 'What the hell do you mean?'

Roland just smiled. 'Come on, Luke. Let's go home.'

TWENTY-FIVE
Ilse

It was late September when Ilse saw the first flu patient. She was loading up other patients into a rickety ambulance at the time, preparing to take them to a safer hospital further back from the lines. The casualty clearing station where she worked had been bombed twice in the last month, not to mention the constant stray artillery shells that had torn up the ground around the tents. They had been lucky a shell didn't land directly on a tent yet, but it was probably only a matter of time. So, military medical orderlies had deemed that it was time to move the entire station, starting with bringing patients to hospitals further back.

That's when Ilse saw him. The sick one. She had wondered why he was so quiet, lying there in his cot without making a single fuss. This despite a gruesome shoulder injury which looked to be growing gangrenous. It would put anyone in immense amounts of pain, but he didn't say or do anything to indicate that. He just stared off into space, a telling sweat sheen over his forehead, and a dull look in his eyes.

Ilse slowly approached him and put her palm on his forehead, mopping away some of his sweaty hair. Even from several inches above him, she could feel the fever radiating from him, searing his insides, burning his flesh. She quickly examined his forehead, but there were no markings there to signify any treatment. No yellow tag around his neck. He had been laid off to the side, in an isolated place all his own.

Ilse found that very odd.

'Ilse.'

She turned around to see Llewellyn, her Red Cross matron, standing a few feet behind her. She gave her a quick nod. 'Matron.'

'There's a new batch coming in that needs to be triaged.'

Ilse frowned. 'Why do they keep bringing them here if we have to evacuate everyone?'

Llewellyn shrugged. 'There's just too many, and not enough places to bring them. It has to be here for now. Come along, we do what we're told.'

At the sound of a horribly raspy cough, Ilse turned and looked back down at the sick soldier, sitting there alone in his cot, so far away from everyone else.

'Water . . .' he choked out. 'Water, please.'

Ilse reached down for the canteen on her waist. She went to share it with the soldier, but Llewellyn's voice stopped her.

'I wouldn't do that.'

Ilse gave her matron a tired smile. 'It's OK. There's nothing else to give him and he clearly needs it.'

'You should never share your canteen, Ilse. Especially not with him.'

Ilse corked her canteen and shot Llewellyn a curious glance, because it was a far more callous attitude than she was used to out of her matron. 'What do you mean? You want me to let him go thirsty?'

Llewellyn considered her words carefully before answering. 'It's flu season, you know that. I don't want you picking up any germs.'

'So that's what's wrong with him? The flu?' Ilse looked around, trying to locate any other sick patients. 'Why is he over here all by himself? Shouldn't he be in the sick ward?'

Llewellyn drew her lips in a tight line. There was more to this story. Something she didn't want to say. It was painfully evident by the strain in her eyes. The blush in her cheeks. The nervous way that she fiddled with her hands.

'Come, Ilse. We need to triage those new patients.'

Ilse wanted to argue, or at least ask a few more questions, but she just nodded. She knew Llewellyn's words were code for 'this conversation is over.' So she went with Llewellyn to triage the incoming patients, which was an especially bloody and dirty job, because these were boys fresh from the battlefield dressing stations, covered with mud and screaming in pain. Coughing up gas. Squeezing bandages against fresh bullet holes.

It made for a long afternoon, which Ilse spent mostly on her feet, running back and forth between triage tents and surgical wards. Ambulances and sick rooms. Dining quarters and supply stockpiles. By the time the new patients were finally triaged and settled, darkness was falling over the clearing station, bringing a chaotic end to yet another chaotic day.

Ilse sighed, wiping sweat and dirt off her hands and face, making her way slowly to the small tent that served as her living quarters.

She stopped when she noticed that single cot, still sitting there by itself, still holding the same pathetic soldier boy.

Ilse looked around at all the busy personnel. Surely someone else could see to his needs, yet no one else seemed to even notice he was there. And he deserved some care, damn it. They all did.

Groaning under her breath, Ilse walked over to the cot. She bent over to examine the soldier. But, with a start, she quickly drew her hands back. Her mouth fell open. Her heart skipped a beat.

The soldier was dead. His face had turned gray, with a bluish tint to his cheeks. His lips were blue as well. His eyes were glassed over and devoid of color. Which meant it wasn't his wound that had killed him. It was his illness. He had died by drowning in his own fluids. Died of . . . the flu? A seasonal flu?

Ilse darted her eyes this way and that, searching through the maze for Llewellyn. Yet the matron was nowhere to be seen.

She looked back down at the dead boy. Not knowing what else to do, she took his hands and gently folded them over his chest. Then she pulled the blanket up over his head.

She had a very sinking feeling as she did so.

TWENTY-SIX
Roland

Roland stood in a vast, misty field, ankle deep in mud. Broken trunks that used to be trees clawed at the gray sky. At his feet sat a winding set of abandoned trenches, filled with yellow-tinted water. Rusted barbed wire and rotting corpses stuck out from the sludge. Empty ration tins and overturned helmets, picked clean by the rats, lay scattered in between. The thick stench of the place wobbled his stomach, which produced a guttural cough.

It wasn't just the smell that bothered him. This haunted place stirred up a lot of memories, none of them pleasant. Except Vernon, although even that brought him pain now too.

Roland reached into his breast pocket and retrieved a small envelope. He had received it just the day before, postmarked from a small village in England. It had taken some time to reach him, since he'd been on the move so much, and it was from Vernon's sister. Not only had she lost her father in the Somme, but also her brother to Flanders Fields.

Roland's jaws clenched as he ran his hand over the cursive writing on the flowery English stationery. It contained the story of Vernon's death, during an assault against a firmly held German pillbox in Flanders. He had been promoted to lieutenant, so he could have sat out the attack, but he demanded to lead his men into battle. A mortar went off in the middle of his company, and they never found his body. Vernon, everything he was, all he did for his boys, and the friendship he showed a stranded American, had simply disappeared into the mist.

Roland carried the letter in his breast pocket. He couldn't let Vernon just disappear. He wanted to remember that pleasant, gray-eyed face until the end of his days. And if the letter was near him, so would Vernon be.

As he slipped the letter back into his pocket, Roland coughed again, covering his urge to cry. Yet he couldn't cover the severity of the damage to his lungs, not this time. His body racked so hard he had to bend over and put his hands on his knees. A little bit of fluid came up, which he quickly wiped away with a handkerchief.

'You all right over there?'

Roland snapped his head up and saw Elliot watching him from down in the trenches. The wild boy pilot cradled a slew of war souvenirs in his arms. Most were indiscernible hunks of metal, but a German pistol stuck out from the mess. Of all the war trophies the boys lusted for, those pistols topped the list.

Norman rifled his hands through the gooey mud right beside Elliot, muttering under his breath. 'I come out here how many goddamn times and never get a pistol. The boy takes two steps into a trench and one practically throws itself at him. That's some shit, ain't it, Hawkins?'

Elliot snickered. 'Lay off it. There's bound to be more in here anyway.' He turned back to Roland. 'You going to look or what?'

Although he wanted to hurl a string of curse words at his mates, Roland just shook his head and scowled. 'No looting for me, boys.'

Norman held his hands up in defense. 'Whoa, fella. Souvenir hunting. Not looting.'

Roland just crossed his arms, silently challenging Norman to explain the difference between the two.

He knew he was the odd man out. Most soldiers lived for souvenir hunting, particularly in the air corps. Pilots got little exposure to the ground war, and trophy hunting was the only way to satiate their morbid curiosity. On their days off, they piled into base cars or hopped on rumbling motorcycles. Then they tore off into the horizon and scoured the terrain for keepsakes.

Roland never took part, no matter how much the other pilots teased him. He wouldn't dare disrespect his own time in the trenches, or those mud-coated boys who suffered, died, and slipped away from time in the depths of these mud pits. Boys like Vernon, who gave his life to lead his men into battle, only to disappear and never get his name carved anywhere. Not into any annals of history, not even on the front of a cross.

Roland seethed to think of Vernon's pack, his correspondence, his treasured family photos, falling into the hands of such looters and souvenir hunters. Pieces of his life stripped from the mud and toted around as trophies. As if the person who found them deserved them more than Vernon, simply because they had the sheer stupid luck to still be alive.

Elliot whistled to get Roland's attention. 'Did you hear me, Hawkins? There's plenty to go around. Quit being such a stuffed shirt and get in here.'

'No.'

'Why not? You think yourself so far above us, do you?'

'Hey, look at this.' Norman held up a split-open shell casing, one that had clearly failed to detonate. While the casings were normally filled with steel balls or shards of metal, some German had stuffed this one with any random objects to be had. Nuts, bolts, nails, washers, and rusty dials from a small clock.

Elliot squished through the mud for a closer look. 'What the hell is that?'

'Are the Heinies stuffing their shells with watch dials?' Norman cackled. 'They really are a sore lot these days.' He thumbed through the junk for anything salvageable.

Roland looked on with disgust. 'Are you guys done yet? I'm hungry, and that pub could get bombed any second.'

Elliot thumbed his nose at him. 'Easy, Hawkins. Let us play here, and I'll fry you up some mushrooms later.'

Roland grunted in response, leaning against the black car they had borrowed from Rembercourt.

'Hey, you'll never believe what I heard yesterday,' Norman said as he examined the shell casing. 'Uncle Sam is gassing the Boche now.'

Elliot whistled in approval. 'Good! Give them a taste of their own nasty medicine. How did they like it?'

'Not well. Their faces turned all sorts of weird colors, and they coughed up parts of their lungs.'

Elliot burst out laughing.

Roland's stomach lurched again, and his veins tingled. In his book, gas was the cruelest weapon of the war, best deployed by cruel enemies. He never imagined that his own United States would use such a weapon. Clearly, he shouldn't have fooled himself. This was the 'Great War,' after all. Nothing was beneath anyone anymore.

Norman grinned at him. 'What say you to that, Hawkins? Fancy spraying some Germans with gas?'

Roland shot him a look. 'No, goddamn it. I wouldn't fancy spraying the Kaiser himself with that lousy shit.'

He stooped over for another loud cough.

Elliot narrowed his eyes.

Later that night, Roland sat in a small, makeshift bar just down the road from his airfield, a popular hangout for First Pursuit Group pilots. They had set up the place themselves, keeping it well stocked with pilfered liquor. A few splintered wooden tables and chairs served as furniture. Someone had constructed a bar with rummaged, rotting planks. The boys even put a stolen piano in the corner. They splashed the bare walls with photos of famous airmen from all the different armies. There were also news clippings from back home, and some pictures of pretty girls. Woodrow Wilson sneered from a portrait in a darkened corner.

Behind the bar, planted front and center, hung a big, black chalkboard. Each squadron at Rembercourt had its own column on it. The columns listed the highest-ranking pilots, their scores marked with German crosses.

Roland hadn't made the board yet. Only aces, pilots who had downed five or more planes, got their names up there. Besides, normally he didn't come here enough to care. But Vernon's death had put him in a stupor, ripping away a dangerous chunk of his fading humanity. He felt more like a machine. Fitting, perhaps, since a machine now did most of his fighting.

At first the thought killed Roland, yearning to hold onto his human side. But sitting here sipping his drink made him wonder. His plane didn't cry over lost soldiers. It didn't lay awake at night hurting or afraid. No matter what happened the day before, it started up for every patrol without fail, especially after spending a night with mechanics. Perhaps that's just what he had to do to survive a war. He had to become like a machine. And damn, the soothing burn of the liquor felt like an awfully good mechanic.

Behind the bar, an enlisted man shook up another drink for him, using a cleaned-out shell casing as a mixer. He poured brown liquid into a glass and slid it over to Roland.

Next to Roland, Elliot also enjoyed a nightcap, or several. A collection of cracked shot glasses had already piled up in front of him. While he drank, he sorted through his pile of stuff from the trenches. One was a pair of daguerreotype photos framed in a tin fold-out. It showed a handsome woman with dark hair on one side, and a flaxen young maiden on the other.

'Look at this little lady.' Elliot held the picture of the blonde out to Roland. 'You suppose she's spoken for?'

Roland buried his nose in his drink. 'Why don't you go to Germany and ask her?'

'I just might, wise ass. She'd be lucky to have me.' Elliot put the picture down and rifled through the rest of his stuff. 'Look at this compass I found. It looks old, doesn't it? I bet it's worth a fortune.'

Roland took the compass and examined it. He rolled his eyes and clunked it on the table. 'It's a standard issue, Elliot. They give these to every lousy private on the line. It looks old because it's been buried in the mud for too long.'

Elliot took the compass, gave it a frown, then chucked it across the room. It clattered against the back wall and shattered into pieces.

'There was no call for that,' Roland said.

'You said it was worthless.'

'Yes, but it meant something to somebody once. You shouldn't just—'

A booming voice cut Roland off. 'Well, well! My boys from the twenty-seventh. Just the men I wanted to see.'

Roland whirled around to face a tall, light-haired young man with shimmering baby-blue eyes, a thin mustache, and a friendly smile. A mighty host of military medals weighed down the front of his crisply starched jacket. On his sleeve, he bore a hat-in-the-ring 94th Squadron symbol.

Roland knew him well, as did most people at Rembercourt. Even before the war, Eddie Rickenbacker had made a name for himself driving race cars. When the war broke out, he traded his race car for a cockpit and quickly made ace there too. Even the wild parties he hosted at the base garnered their fair share of headlines.

Roland greeted him with a handshake. 'Hello, Ed.'

Eddie took the open seat next to Roland and patted his back. He also observed Elliot's stack of trophy potentials. 'Lord, kid. Leave some for the looters.'

'Go to hell.'

'Where's your boy Luke? Everyone's looking for him.'

Elliot grumbled. 'Did you check the holding cell? Captain Grant says he'll arrest him if he keeps flying off by himself.'

Eddie laughed. 'He wouldn't dare arrest him now.'

That perked Roland's ears up. 'Why's that?'

'Five kills in about five minutes. Two balloons and three planes. It just came over the wire from the balloon company in the hills.'

Roland reeled with a gasp, while Elliot's eyes flung open wide. He tipped one of his empty shot glasses over in his shock.

'Hogwash,' Roland said. 'Not even the Red Baron pulled a stunt like that.'

'May he rest.' Elliot snickered.

Eddie nodded. 'True, but those balloon boys don't make mistakes. And that's why they tapped it in right away. They think it's a record. Press was on the scene in minutes.'

Elliot grumbled to himself. 'That son of a bitch. Such a little hothead and we all hate him. So of course he's the best damn pilot in the squadron.'

'If you hate him so much, give him to us,' Eddie said. 'He can add his kills to our score.'

Roland nudged Eddie. 'Why don't you worry about your own kills? He keeps up the rate he is and he'll smash your long-standing first place record.'

'So long as he's on our side, I don't give a shit.'

'What about Wehner?'

The twinkle in Eddie's eye faded just a little.

Roland didn't miss that look. 'Oh brother. What happened?'

'He's missing.'

Roland returned to his liquor glass. A missing pilot was usually a dead pilot and everyone at Rembercourt knew it. 'Luke won't take that well. Joe was the only one who could stand him.'

'And you, from what I hear.' Eddie jabbed at Roland with a smile.

Roland shrugged. 'He saved my hind end in a scrap a few days back, but we haven't spoken much since.'

'I should think you two would find common ground in your high regard for the infantry, since you did time in the trenches yourself, no?'

Elliot shot Roland a befuddled, almost accusatory glance.

Roland just swirled what was left of his drink, then downed the hatch.

Eddie saw that he had strayed onto unstable ground, so he got up from his chair with a polite bow. 'Well, if you see Luke, tell him I'm looking for him. We're hosting him a party tonight.'

'Forget it. He spends his nights with the US balloon units,' Elliot said.

Eddie gave him a nod, then he strode off across the bar.

Once he was gone, Elliot bored his eyes into Roland. 'You did time in the trenches? Why the hell didn't you say anything?'

'Don't get your knickers twisted up. I didn't tell anyone, so you're not special. Hell, I don't even know how Eddie found out.'

'Why would you hush it up?'

'It was a long time ago. It doesn't matter anymore.'

Elliot frowned, unconvinced. 'That explains that cough all right, doesn't it? And also why you got so touchy when we talked about gas earlier.'

Roland focused on his empty glass.

'What did you swallow? Phosgene?'

A shake appeared in Roland's lower lip. He put his glass up to his mouth to smother it. 'Mustard.'

Elliot's face went pale. 'Jesus . . .'

In a flash, Roland grabbed Elliot's arm and gave him a violent shake. 'You tell anyone and I will wring your scrawny little neck. You hear me?'

Elliot, who never backed down from a fight, actually cowered under Roland's murderous gaze. 'Hey, take it easy.'

'I mean it, boy. You swear on it or I'll knock you across this room.'

Elliot wrenched free from his grasp. 'I swear it. Lord, get a hold of yourself.'

Roland banged his empty glass on the counter and signaled the bar tender.

Elliot rubbed his sore arm. 'What's got into you, anyway?'

While the bar tender topped his glass off, Roland shuddered. The secrets he had to keep for so long threatened to burst from the seams of his mind, breaking through in individual, horrific images. The rat with red eyes as it hissed at him. Vernon's pale, drawn face and honest tears. Roland's gas-burned fists clenching sweaty sheets in the hospital. Ilse's green eyes. Her kiss. *'If I were the only girl in the world, and you were the only boy . . .'*

Roland thought about telling Elliot everything right there, but he didn't think he could get through it. Not without losing control of his emotions, and he simply couldn't afford to do that yet. Too much depended on him holding himself together . . . Vernon, and his memory, would just have to stay buttoned up in his breast pocket. For now, anyway.

He took a sip of his fresh drink. 'If they find out my lungs are half rotted, they'll kick me out of the air corps.'

'Oh, hell. If they let Mick Mannock fly with one eye, they'll let you fly with gassy lungs.'

'That was the old days, when pilots were harder to come by. You heard Hartney the day we got here. There's fifty thousand men stateside, any one of whom could take my place. That means you keep this to yourself, or I'll snap off your head. Got it?'

Elliot nodded. 'Yeah, of course.' He rubbed his arm for a moment more. 'So . . . you say your lungs are still bad?'

'I'm no doctor, but my cough isn't getting any better.'

'Will it . . . kill you?'

Roland held his glass in an icy grip. He didn't know if the mustard would eventually kill him or not, but he had long since been afraid of that. Because he had never fully recovered from that attack. Sometimes, he felt so sick he could barely get out of bed. On certain days, the cold air made his whole chest burn and his body ache. He coughed up fluids that a healthy man wouldn't. The doctor at his air corps entrance exam had warned him of a shortened life span. Of gassy lungs being similar to the consumption that had killed his mother so young.

He sighed. 'Well, *c'est la guerre.*'

Elliot's face fell. He drummed his fingers on the bar, looking at his war trophies with different eyes. They were treasures moments before. Now, they seemed more like relics of violence. Something that played a part in a slow-moving, excruciating death sentence for his friend. With the arm that Roland had just roughed up, he slid them off the bar and they tumbled to the floor.

Roland knew what the gesture meant. It softened him up so much he felt like hugging the boy. 'Don't throw away that pistol on my account. It's worth a lot.'

'Someone else can take it and put it to better use than me then. Like Luke, for example.'

'I thought you hated Luke.'

Elliot twiddled his thumbs. 'You know I went to church service last Sunday.'

'What the hell were you doing at church?'

'Luke and Wehner were there. They made a killing at poker last week and what do you think they did with it? Dumped it in the church collection plate.' He looked over at Roland with a sad glint in his eyes. 'I hope Wehner's OK.'

Roland drained the last of his liquor and thumped the empty glass on the bar.

'Why are you drinking so much anyhow?' Elliot asked. 'I thought it wasn't Christian enough for you.'

'I got a lot on my mind.'

'Like a girl named Ilse Stahl?'

Roland pounded his fist on the bar and rattled Elliot's empty shot glasses. 'Damn it, Elliot. Stop going through my stuff.'

'Who is she?'

Roland just cowered inside his empty glass.

'Oh, suddenly you're bashful. Is she cute?'

'She's cute. She's kind. And she saved my life. For heaven's sake, I might marry her, if the war doesn't kill me first. You got a problem with that, pipsqueak?'

Elliot giggled and gave Roland a nudge. 'Women and the things they do to us. You marry her, if that's what you want.'

'Well, who the hell asked for your blessing?'

'No one, but sometimes, the validation feels good. It's why I go to church, since you ask. When I'm up there after a machine, it's easy to think that it's just a machine. But it ain't, is it? It's a human in there. When I take him down and try to be an ace, I'm taking away a husband, a father, or a son. I need the validation sometimes, Hawkins.'

Roland shot Elliot a stunned glance. This was a side of him he'd never seen before. A frail little spirit hiding behind all that drinking, cursing, roughhousing and trench looting.

Roland's shoulders slumped. The enlisted man behind the bar went to top up his empty glass, but he shook his head and slid the glass away. 'No thanks, kid. I'm done.'

As for Elliot, he let out a gusty sigh. 'Goddamn. I hope Wehner is OK.'

The next morning, while Elliot slept off his hangover and the base awaited afternoon patrol, Roland crept out of his barracks and over to the airfield. At the end of the airstrip, a brand-new biplane sat there, freshly fixed up, and with a crisp new paint job.

It brought a badly needed smile to Roland's face. He had been without a plane ever since he'd had to torch his own. He had had to borrow planes from other pilots when he went on patrols. There was something unsettling about using another man's plane to do his dirty work. It almost felt like using another man's wife. Probably because pilots bonded with their machines. Especially Elliot. Sometimes, he popped up a tent and slept under the wing of his plane at night, unable to bear being away from it.

It put extra pressure on Roland's shoulders. If he wrecked a borrowed plane, he would break another pilot's heart. So, it made him extra giddy when he beheld that brand-new plane, all squeaky clean and freshly polished. Sitting there on the sod, just for him.

The mechanic rubbed the last few oil stains off his hands and smirked at Roland. 'I got that stuff you asked for.'

'Thank you.'

Roland pulled on a pair of leather mechanic work gloves. A few buckets of vibrantly colored paint sat just under the nose of his plane.

'You like the colors?'

Roland patted his mechanic's shoulder. 'They're perfect. Thanks again.'

The mechanic gave him a nod, then retreated into the hangar.

Roland leaned a wobbly ladder up against the nose of his new plane. He dabbed scarlet paint onto the machine and swirled it into a poppy bloom. After that, he drew a name in looping, black cursive.

'*Chère-Amie.*' So now his plane could remind him of two things – his girlfriend, and dearly departed Vernon.

TWENTY-SEVEN
Roland

September 29, 1918

Roland hunched at the steering wheel of his captain's base car, the engine rumbling on idle while he sat at a dead stop. The fumes drifted into his face and agitated his cough something awful. Above him, a sky thick with rain clouds threatened to burst at any moment.

Even if it did rain, Roland wouldn't move any time soon, because the muddy road was an absolute logjam of traffic. Horse-drawn carts carried heavy artillery guns. Swarms of downtrodden refugees hauled their meager possessions through the chaos. Ambulances honked their tired horns, and medical personnel shouted back and forth to each other. Military police blasted their whistles and pointed people in this direction or that. An occasional observation plane rumbled over, shaking the ground below.

Roland sank into his seat and tried to keep comfortable. He hoped his fuel supply would hold out through the mess. He had his orders, after all.

Captain Grant, his squadron's commanding officer, had sent him in the car to hunt down rogue Frank Luke. When located, the Arizona Balloon Buster would be brought back to the airbase and immediately placed under arrest.

The boy had gotten in another infamous row with the captain. Both young men had such terrible tempers, and they clashed repeatedly as tensions rose and more pilots dropped into early graves. After this most recent tussle, Luke took off alone in his plane for the wild blue. No one was sure where he went, but it was Roland's job to find him.

He decided to check the balloon units first, since Luke spent most of his time there lately. Probably because they were the only friends he had left. Wehner had been confirmed killed the day before. The Arizona Balloon Buster had been in a foul temperament ever since.

Roland sighed and drummed his fingers on the flimsy steering wheel.

Next to him sat Elliot. A big burlap sack rested on his lap, overflowing with freshly picked mushrooms. One at a time, he gave each of them a thorough examination. If the specimen met his standards, he slipped it back into the sack. If it didn't, he tossed it into the muddy countryside. He let out jolly whistles as he did so.

A unit of muddy, bedraggled American doughboys marched past the idle vehicle. Their heavy boots squished in the mud, and their rifles and accouterments clanked against their bodies. Their eyes didn't leave the ground. Despite their already frayed appearance, they marched toward the rumbling guns of Saint-Mihiel instead of away from them.

Elliot took his hat off and waved. 'Give them hell, boys!'

A doughboy in the back of the line snarled. 'Fuck you.'

Elliot's eyes flashed with anger. He made a move to get out of the car and throw the gauntlet down.

But Roland grabbed his collar and pressed him back to his seat. 'Leave him alone.'

'You heard what he just said to me.'

'Well, I said leave him the hell alone, Elliot.'

Elliot muttered but decided not to argue. Not with Roland's firm tone and stern glare. He returned to examining his mushrooms, but he no longer whistled.

A military police officer stepped up to Roland's side of the car. They saluted each other. 'Where you headed?'

'Murvaux,' Roland said. 'Can I get through?'

'Not on this road. You'll have to take the back way.' He pointed down the jumbled highway. 'There's an open grassy space up ahead. Use it to turn around and go back the way you came. You'll see the turnoff a little ways down. Good luck.' With that, he moved onto the next car without allowing any questions or concerns.

Roland could only grit his teeth and obey.

Dusk had already descended when the monster-sized dirigible of the Murvaux American Balloon Corps loomed into view. The ropes holding it down squeaked in the oncoming wind, straining under the weight of the behemoth floating balloon.

Roland couldn't help but admire the courage of those balloon observers. They went up every day in those flammable gas bags that swung them around like a rag doll. With nothing but some flimsy ropes to keep them tethered to earth, balloon observers ran the constant risk of their mount snapping loose. If it did, they would sail the skies at the mercy of the wind, and fire from the ground, until their bag ran out of air or they got shot down.

And balloons were an enticing target to enemy pilots. When they came under attack, an observer's only option was to abandon ship, which came with plenty of dangers. Although, balloon observers had one luxury the pilots didn't have – a parachute.

Roland pulled his mud-splattered car up to the makeshift base. As soon as he came to a stop, one of the balloon sergeants rushed out to greet him. He was a boyish-looking soldier with frizzy hair and a devilish grin. A heavy pair of binoculars hung from his neck. His windblown hair suggested he had been up in the balloon at least once already that day.

He noted Roland's markings and greeted him with a salute. 'Lieutenant. What brings you here?'

Roland and Elliot climbed out of the car and stretched their aggravated limbs.

'Lord, you got a pub around here?' Elliot asked.

The sergeant pointed the way to the mess hall. 'No, sir, but I'm sure those cooks can whip up something to start your motor.'

Elliot sauntered off without another word.

Roland gave the sergeant a much friendlier greeting. 'Never mind him. A shot of spirit will straighten him out.'

The sergeant chuckled. 'Well, he should find some in the mess hall. I wasn't kidding about those cooks. They brew up moonshine that could wake the dead.'

'I'm Lieutenant Roland Hawkins. We came from the Twenty-Seventh Squadron over at Rembercourt.'

'Welcome, Lieutenant. I'm Sergeant Harvey Smith.' His eyes lit up with mischief. 'The Twenty-Seventh, you say? Let me guess. They've sent you for Luke.'

Roland laughed. 'They have, and it was a hell of a drive. So, please tell me he's here.'

'Well, he does come by quite often, but we haven't seen him today.'

Roland let out a grumble. He had suffered through that horrible drive only to get back in the car and drive some more. 'Wonderful . . .'

Harvey put a hand on his shoulder. 'If there's one thing I know about Luke, it's that he'll keep. Why don't you take some air?'

'I believe I just might.'

'I'll show you around the base.'

Harvey beckoned toward the elevated balloon and led Roland to it. As they got closer, Roland's step wavered. The balloon looked a lot larger up close. The way it swayed in the breeze made him think of giant mythical beasts. The swarm of anti-aircraft guns planted beneath it also chilled the blood, forcing the question of how anyone would have the guts to attack one of these things.

Harvey craned his neck up to the balloon's wicker basket. 'Hey, Ned! Are you up there?'

There was a slight rustle, then a young, spry private poked his head over the side of the basket. He gave a friendly wave. 'Greetings, there!'

'This here is Lieutenant Roland Hawkins. He's visiting from the aero squadron down the way.'

'Good to have you, sir.'

Suddenly, all of them heard the low drone of a plane coming over the hills.

Harvey's friendly manners transformed to alarm, and his eyes scanned the heavens. 'Who the hell would put out a patrol this close to dark?'

Roland's sharp eyes struggled to penetrate the purple dusk. 'It wouldn't be one of ours. We've been grounded all day for weather.'

Harvey turned his binoculars toward the foreboding dome, barking orders to the people around him. 'All right, gents, ship inbound! Man your posts and bring the balloon in.'

The quiet base burst into action. Privates hurried to cord stations and began winding loud cranks. Inch by inch, the balloon dropped to safety while gunners swung the artillery pieces into attack position. They loaded up bullets and shells, pointing the muzzles at the darkening sky.

'Fire at my signal, boys.'

Soon, a single plane wobbled into view. Roland narrowed his gaze but, in the dark, it just looked like a black silhouette against the thick, scruffy clouds.

Harvey took another peer through his binoculars, and his shoulders relaxed. 'Thank God.' He again shouted to his troops. 'Stand down, boys. It looks like one of ours.'

'We're six miles from the enemy lines,' Roland said. 'You sure about that?'

'See for yourself.' Harvey handed him the binoculars.

Roland took them and glanced through. Sure enough, the plane was a single-engine biplane, marked with a US 27th Aero Squadron symbol. The ID number was Twenty-Six.

Roland shoved the binoculars back to Harvey. 'Jesus Christ.'

'Look out!' Harvey pushed Roland out of the way and both tumbled to the ground in a heap of limbs, just as a heavy metal object fell from the cockpit of the plane, landing with a loud thud at their feet. A few inches closer, and it would have put one of them in a coma.

As Roland screeched out some of his most colorful language, Harvey picked up the mysterious object. When he was satisfied it wouldn't explode, he turned it over and found a folded note taped to the bottom.

'*Watch for burning balloons*,' Harvey read aloud. Beneath the hasty note was a series of coordinates, scribbled in faded lead.

Harvey jumped to his feet. 'Ned! It's Luke! Look alive up there.' He turned to Roland with an excited grin.

'He must be attacking thirty-five, the German balloon unit just over those hills.' Harvey again turned his glasses to the sky. 'He also must be nuts. No wingman or anything.'

'His wingman is dead.'

Harvey threw Roland a surprised glance. 'Not Wehner?'

Roland nodded. 'I'm afraid so.'

The booming of artillery sounded over the hills. The Germans had obviously seen Luke and were ready to knock him from the sky.

'Well, God be with him is all I can say,' Harvey said.

'Who? Luke or the Germans?'

Harvey chuckled.

The shells got louder, and the rattling of machine guns soon joined the fray. A few strings of green fireballs flung up into the air, sizzling and popping as they streaked toward Luke's plane. Dubbed 'flaming onions' by the pilots, they were one of the biggest nuisances of the air war, because if they happened to collide with a plane, it instantly burst into flames.

Soon, a bright orange flash, followed by an ominous flicker, lit up the horizon. A cloud of smoke went up too, and the smell of burning canvas wafted toward them.

'There's one.' Harvey whistled up at the balloon basket. 'Did you get that, Ned?'

'Yes, sir. He's attacking thirty-five all right.'

'Well, keep sharp; he gave two other coordinates.'

Harvey had barely completed the sentence when another illumination joined the first. The popping of machine guns intensified, and countless more green spheres flared upward. Black smoke choked out the rest of the dome, along with the puffs and flashes of Archie. A third orange glare soon flashed through the sky, partially blotted out by all the smoke.

It made for quite the fireworks display. Roland didn't know how anyone could survive it.

'Holy Mother!' Harvey exclaimed. 'Did he just fry three sausages in one pass? Ned! What the hell's going on? Can you see him?'

'Just a moment.' Ned didn't sound as excited as Harvey. 'Heinie's sent up fighters. They're right on his tail. This damn smoke! I'm losing visibility.'

After he returned to the airbase, Roland joined the enlisted men in their barracks, set up in a small tent near the Rembercourt airstrip. The sky was pitch black now. Other than some frigid raindrops, and a handful of whistling night birds, it remained still.

Roland and the enlisted men kept their eyes glued to it anyway, waiting and hoping for any trace of a returning airplane. Some of the privates sent crimson, shrieking flares into the darkness, hoping the lighted beacon would elicit Luke's return. Luke, who always treated them with decency. Who brought them treats. Who made them feel like men.

Norman stumbled onto the scene after a while, dressed down for the evening and scratching his scalp with nerves. 'How you finding look-out duty?'

'Not very profitable,' Roland said.

Another flare arched into the sky, casting an eerie glow over the empty airstrip. The place looked so much different in that harsh, devil-red glare. Like something from a demonic story or a tortured fever dream.

Norman also searched the dark skies, the gleam of flares illuminating his pupils. 'Three balloons in one patrol? And it's been confirmed and everything?'

'It ain't official confirmation yet, but I'm sure that will come.'

As the late hours approached, curiosity rose amongst the rest of the squadron. Men in groups of two or three trickled onto the airfield.

Their eyes pointed skyward, waiting for something they knew wouldn't come.

'If he's hanging over at that damn balloon base while we're all worried sick, Grant will have him arrested,' Norman said.

Roland huffed. 'Yeah, but if he comes back, he should give him a Medal of Honor.'

Another flare bathed the field in its satanic red glow.

Although the enlisted boys kept up their vigil all night, Frank Luke never returned.

And it wasn't the only bad news. When Roland finally did return to his barrack, feeling more dejected and discouraged than ever, he found a stack of torn, muddied envelopes on his pillow. Each one stamped 'Return to Sender' in terrible, blotchy red ink.

His letters to Bernard.

TWENTY-EIGHT
Ilse

October, 1918

Another day of the war, another day at the frantic casualty clearing station. Another mass load of patients hauled in from the trenches. Another pile of admitting paperwork, death certificates, letters home to loved ones who would never see their soldier boy again.

Ilse, like she did every single day, did her best to keep up, and normally she was one of the fastest workers in the station. But today, something wasn't right. There was something off in her body and in her mind. She felt more tired than usual, like all her limbs had become heavy. She had to drag her body around like it was lifeless, forcing her arms and legs to do their jobs. Her breathing also felt a bit labored. Probably because of the cloth mask over her nose and mouth.

All medical personnel had to wear them now, because of the mysterious flu outbreak that was taking down everyone from patients, to doctors, and very overworked nurses. So many people had gotten sick that it whittled the medical staff down to the bare minimum. It delayed the station evacuation they had all been working so hard on. And it absolutely terrified the medical support team, watching what started as a typical, albeit severe, flu season morph into anything but.

Cases were mounting up among the patients as well. A slow trickle of sick soldiers had ballooned into entire hordes of them – coughing and hacking, burning with fever, ripped apart with fatigue. A tent, with big black Xs on the flaps to keep everyone out but the essential personnel, had been set up on the far edge of the property, so all the patients could isolate in their illness and hopefully keep their germs away from everyone else.

And the graves. No one really discussed the fresh batch of holes that had appeared in the middle of the field nearby, but everyone at the hospital knew what they were for. They also certainly knew to stay the hell away from them.

Whatever this flu was, it was far from ordinary.

Ilse swallowed hard at the thought, and as she did so, she noticed an alarming twinge of pain in the back of her throat. The same one she'd noticed when she woke up that morning. A slight burn and tingle, right over her left tonsil. She had swallowed a sip of tea to chase it away, thinking it was nothing more than a dry throat. But as the morning pressed on, the pain spread to her other tonsil. Then to her palate. Then to the roof of her mouth.

Soon, she could no longer deny it. She had a sore throat.

She was getting sick.

Ilse took a deep breath through her mask. Most days, she didn't mind wearing it at all. Whatever she could do to keep herself and others safe. But now, it felt aggravating. Like it somehow made her tired lungs have to work that much harder. Because they felt a bit fuller and tighter than usual.

'I heard that doctor died last night,' one of the nearby nurses whispered.

'What?' her companion said in a squeak. 'He took ill only yesterday, and he was healthy as a horse before then!'

The first nurse shook her head. 'He's gone now. Rest his soul. Along with about a dozen soldiers that came down with it as well.'

'For heaven's sake. What the hell are we going to do?'

Ilse closed her eyes, trying to shut out the burning pain behind her eyelids. Yes. What the hell were they going to do?

Forcing herself to keep busy, to keep moving, she finished up with her patient and moved onto the next one. Shrapnel had torn him up pretty good, but that wasn't what most alarmed her. Instead, she noted the sweat poking through his shirt. The telling blue tint already appearing in his lips. The gray shade of his cheeks. The blood trickling from his nose.

He was sick.

So sick . . .

Ilse's breathing went raspy and dry through her mask. Her body locked up. She felt a chill start at the base of her neck and roll its way down her entire body, hard and fast like a wave. The nurses next to her looked up from their work, taking note of her struggle.

'Ilse?'

She ignored them. She had to. Because she couldn't face the reality of this. Couldn't admit that what she had lain awake fearing for several nights had come to pass.

Ilse had caught the flu.

'Ilse?'

This time, Ilse turned around. It was the last thing she remembered before she let out an exhale of an exhausted breath, then crashed to the floor in a heap.

TWENTY-NINE
Roland

Roland never saw so many flowers. Especially this late in the fall. High above France in the cockpit of his plane, he took in the sweeping patches of golden buttercups and swaying pearly white blossoms. Green sprung up everywhere through the cedar-colored mud. Like an artist had taken a bucket of vibrant paint and splashed it onto the brown canvas of war-ravaged Europe.

The superblooms made him feel like the circles of life were turning again. Time wasn't frozen in this madness after all. Time, somehow, would move them all forward.

Roland hoped it would be soon, too. Because piece by piece, the war had begun to pick him apart. The biggest worry being Bernard. After repeated inquiries and investigations, he still didn't know what had become of his brother, or why all his letters had been sent back. Roland tried not to assume the worst, but it was difficult during a war like this. His brother could be anywhere. The only thing his investigating had turned up was that Bernard's unit had been sent into the Argonne Forest. What had become of them after, he had no real idea.

But if it was anything like Flanders, he could guess.

In the meantime, Roland had been promoted to squadron leader at Rembercourt. Some would consider it an honor, but he only felt extra pressure. On top of his own survival, he was now responsible for everyone else in his patrols. He had to wear the mask of fearless leader and take men to places he had no desire to go himself. He had to make the fight-or-flight decision in an instant, with the consequences of either option landing square on his exhausted shoulders.

The extra strain put nervous ticks in Roland's face and hands. His lungs burned a lot more than they used to. He was only in his twenties, but gray hairs already peppered his scalp. He tossed and turned at night instead of getting much-needed rest.

He wasn't the only one buckling. Boys all over Rembercourt had begun to feel the hard hand of war. Pilots tapped their last energy reserves and crashes had become more common. Illnesses swept through the barracks like a tidal wave. Especially the new, and very virulent influenza strain that found ample victims in worn-out war personnel. The squadron had sent a half-dozen pilots to the hospital with flu symptoms, and none of them ever returned.

Yet another reason to soak in those flowers, and hope that Vernon was right all along.

But the war wouldn't end today, as evidenced by a stream of tracer bullets that flew past Roland's wings and snapped him out of his daydreams.

Roland flinched and craned his head around.

While he had lost himself in flowers and visions of peace, three German triplanes had crept up behind his patrol.

Roland's reflexes kicked in, and he banked his plane, stealing a glance at the rest of his patrol.

Elliot flew on his flank today, along with two new pilots fresh from flying school, looking especially rattled.

Roland flipped his plane around and nudged up beside Elliot. He gave the hand signal to engage the enemy, and they split off from each other into attack formation. Once they were set, Roland zeroed in on his first German enemy. A colorful triplane with a gorgeous wolf painted on the side. If he put this man down, it would be his fourth kill.

He hadn't chosen an easy target though. The Wolf quickly dodged Roland with a peel into a loop, his plane engine roaring with the extra workload.

Roland stayed right on his tail. Even with his head almost completely upside down, he squeezed the trigger of his gun. A stream of red tracers whizzed by the German's plane.

The Wolf made a hard bank to avoid them, but Roland stayed on him like glue. He glared in focus and tried again. A few bullets thudded into the enemy plane, but not enough to put him on the ground.

Ever the pro, the Wolf flew in a tight circle to get into Roland's flank. Meanwhile, Roland kept in an even tighter circle to stay on the German's tail. A terrifying game of cat and mouse that would end with someone falling to his death over France.

Roland forced his plane to bank tighter, pushing the engine for all it was worth. While the machine clunked and shuddered with the effort, he curled his fingers around his gun. His eyes squinted through the wind. He wouldn't miss this time.

But suddenly, he found himself at the wrong end of an ambush. While he was distracted with one plane, another enemy plane had suddenly jumped onto his tail. A hot stream of red tracers fizzled over his head and right into his cockpit. He heard the cracks and snaps of bullets picking apart his machine. There came a loud clunk from the front of his plane. More oil than usual sprayed across his face. Extra-thick black smoke made him erupt into a coughing fit.

Roland tried to mop his face and force his control stick at once. But the plane lost altitude fast, a few sad sputters coming from the wounded engine. After a few seconds, it went silent for good, leaving Roland with nothing but the howling wind in his wires.

He peeked over the side of the cockpit. The flower fields were long gone. He now saw streaks of trench systems and scratches of barbed wire, along with constant puffs from artillery. He had caught up with the ground war, and the nose of his plane was headed right for it.

The howling wind whipped his silk scarf across his caster-oiled cheeks. He didn't have a prayer at making a safe landing. With a completely shot-out engine, he could only watch as the battle-scarred earth came closer and closer to his plane, where he knew one of two things would happen. Either his plane would burst into flames on contact, or she would break apart and he would have a shot at survival. If he did survive, his reward would be every gun in the German army pointed straight at his head.

And he didn't have much time to plan for either scenario. Because his plane had already plunged low enough for him to make out panicking foot soldiers, scrambling up and down their trenches to get clear of the plane. German machine gunners manned their positions. Soldiers standing there pointed their rifles.

This could be the end, but somehow, Roland wasn't scared. Peace swept over him like a warm cloak. In his mind's eye, he went back to that chaotic night in New York City. He saw the candle go up in the window and break apart the darkness. The orange flame reached across an ocean and two years of time. Everything would be OK . . .

His plane smashed prop-first into the rim of a shell crater, the plane's tail whipping into the air and flipping the whole machine over on its back. Roland saw the earth turn up on itself, with the noise of tearing fabric and screeching wires in his head. When it was over, the plane lay belly-up in the middle of no man's land, the wheels still spinning.

Roland's flimsy seat strap somehow held during the crash, leaving him suspended upside down in the crumpled cockpit, his head hanging directly over the nasty shell crater. The piercing odor of stale gas fumes, coupled with the shock of the crash, made his weak stomach surge with nausea. Before he could right himself, his mouth opened and vomit tumbled out.

Just as he predicted, German artillery quickly pointed their shells at the heap of his wrecked plane. Explosions soon pummeled him with debris and plastered him with globs of mud. Machine guns joined in the fray too, their bullets making the ground look like a pot of boiling water.

Roland finally managed an agonizing scream, but it was lost in the sea of shell concussions and machine guns. No help would come for him in this racket. His only chance was to get the hell out of there, as quickly as possible. He squirmed in his seat and tried to move his legs and arms. Blood dripped down from his chin and leaked into his goggles. Movement of his right leg sent shots of pain up and down his body.

He bent his knees to at least right his head, while stretching his arm to pry loose his seat strap. As he did so, a shell exploded so close that his plane groaned in protest and teetered precariously over the rim of the crater.

Roland gasped, anxiety ripping through him. He couldn't fall into that shell hole. If he did, the plane wreckage would pin him into the water. He would die by drowning in a lake of Great War carnage.

He gave a hard pull on the seat strap, pain be damned. 'Come on, damn you, let go!'

He halted when he felt a warm flow of liquid pour down his pants. At first, he thought it was blood. Then, he detected the sharp scent of aviation fuel. His broken fuel line had begun dousing him with highly flammable petrol.

As if he didn't have enough problems . . .

Roland screamed again, but this time with determination. Like hell he would die in the mud after all he had done to avoid that. He lurched his body forward, banking on the momentum for a ferocious pull on his seat strap. At last, the material ripped loose, and his body tumbled out of the cockpit. He landed in the mud with a splat, covered in fuel and his own blood. He dragged himself to his hands and knees and took stock of his position.

The American trenches lay a mere fifty yards away, but getting there wouldn't be easy. Shells were exploding everywhere, and the machine guns had drawn a sharp bead on him. It wasn't like he could fire back either. The only weapon he had was camouflage. His brown pilot gear blended in with the mud, and the smoke from the artillery provided a little bit of screen. It wasn't much, but his life would now have to depend on it.

Roland gathered his courage, dropped to his belly, and began picking his way through the muck toward the trenches. It would be the hardest fifty yards of his life. As he crawled, he had to vomit more than once. Not just from the pain, but also from the wretched reminders of trench life. Countless blackened and bloated bodies in the mud, piles of picked-clean bones, heaps of barbed wire, dead horses, broken carts, ravaged tree stumps, and wooden crosses.

By the time he finally made it to the edge of the American line, his strength had dwindled to nothing. He collapsed over the side of the trenches and landed in the arms of three stunned doughboys. They yelled as Roland's dead weight knocked them with a splash into the bottom of the trench.

'Sweet mother of God,' one of them said. 'Where the hell did you come from, fly boy?'

'I suppose he's from that wreck out there. A lucky bastard if you ask me.'

'Not for long. He's barely alive . . .'

The voices went mute, and Roland's vision grew fuzzy.

The last thing he saw was Ilse. Her blonde hair, her green eyes, her warm smile. She held a candle in a large window, placing it gently on the sill. Watching him, waving at him. Calling him home.

'Ilse . . .'

THIRTY
Roland

When Roland's eyes opened, he lay in the streets of New York City, just across from the brownstone he used to call home. Darkness covered the streets, much like that night from another lifetime ago. Only this time, there were no people. No broken glass. Nothing stirred.

Roland sat up to get his bearings, and he noticed his leg didn't scream with pain anymore. No blood leaked from countless lacerations on his skin.

The upper-story window of the brownstone suddenly opened, and a single candle came out. The orange flame cast an eerie glow about the street. It wasn't as peaceful as he remembered. It felt jarring and eerie. Disconcerting . . .

Roland crawled to his feet and frowned at the window. He waited for his mother's face to appear, but it didn't. The hand holding the candle didn't belong to her. It belonged to Ilse. She leaned out the darkened window and smiled at him.

His heart swelled at the sight of her. Yet, something was off. She had a gaunt, sunken look. Her wrists were bony and frail. An unnatural glaze coated her eyes.

She looked like a ghost.

Roland took a few cautious steps toward her. 'Ilse?'

This time when she smiled, it looked gruesome, like a grinning skull. 'Time to go home,' she said in a croaking voice.

Alarm settled over Roland. Something was definitely wrong. 'Ilse? What happened to you?'

'Time to go home.'

'Ilse!' Roland made a frantic dash for the door and tried to pull it open. It didn't budge. He gave several hard tugs on the handle. He kicked and punched the door to force it open, cursing when it didn't move an inch. 'Ilse, let me up to you!'

'Time to go home.'

The wind began to whip up around him. Dry, crusty leaves swirled and crackled down the street. Goosebumps cropped up across his arms. The gust picked up until it began pulling everything away with it, like some sort of other-worldly vortex. Glass windows shattered. Paint peeled off buildings. Streetlamps bent and snapped at their bases.

Roland gripped the door handle to stay in place. 'Ilse, let me in!'

No answer except the howling wind. The brownstone above him began to crumble away, brick by brick.

Roland let out a scream, and Ilse's orange candle flame went dark.

Roland awoke with a gasp, his mind and heart racing. A cold sweat glued a flimsy hospital gown to his ravaged body. He tried to open his eyes, but his lids were too swollen. So was his face. In fact, his whole body felt like it had been kicked and bashed across no man's land like a soccer ball. Panic spilled over him. Flashes from his past flickered through his confused mind. Burning lungs, a bloody cough, burned hands . . .

Gas . . .

'Help me! Please, someone help!'

'Easy, fly boy.'

The voice froze Roland solid, his breath coming in tight bursts. 'Who's there? Where am I?'

'You're in a casualty clearing station on your own side,' said the soothing female voice. Her warm hand came to a rest on his quivering shoulder. 'Try to stay calm. You were in a terrible accident. Control your breathing, please. Nice and steady. That's it.'

Although Roland's mind seared with a thousand questions, her voice and gentle touch removed the weight from his chest and blocked the flow of anxiety, just like Ilse's had once done in another hospital. Although he knew this new voice didn't belong to her, it made him think of her, and for the moment, that was enough. He laid his head back, tilting it to try and take in his surroundings.

For the second time in this war, Roland lay in a flimsy cot in a sea of others. The deep, rich scent of muddy, torn-up earth invaded his nostrils, suggesting his cot sat in the grass. Only a moldy medical tent shielded him from the elements. Some of the olive-colored sides had been frayed with shrapnel holes, which did little to keep out the cold.

A handful of women worked their way through the cots, their boots squishing in the mud, bending over to administer to countless crying patients. They sported dark blue and gray skirts. Red crosses adorned the sleeves of their long black coats.

The Red Cross.

Roland tried to sit up, but the woman's hand pressed him back to his cot. 'Easy there, mister. You can't sit up yet.'

'How long have I been here?'

'Two days. One of the frontline units brought you in.'

Roland turned his puffy eyes to the woman by his bed. Like the rest, she wore a Red Cross uniform. She had piled her long hair into a loose bun. Her eyes were blue once upon a time, but exhaustion had turned them to a cloudy sky.

He peered up at her. 'And just who the hell are you?'

She gave an exhausted chortle. 'Such nice manners you pilots always have. My name is Llewellyn. I'm the matron here.'

Roland tried to sweep the cobwebs from his banged-up head. 'I'm Roland Hawkins . . .' He tried to tell her more, but another cough pulled at his lungs.

Llewellyn helped him into an easier position. 'Easy, Mr Hawkins. No need to talk. We have all your basic information from the unit that brought you in.' She tsked as she rubbed his back. 'That cough sounds right nasty.'

He whooped a few more times before he could catch his breath and speak. 'I guess I've got used to it. How bad is the rest of me?'

'You have quite the goose egg on your head. Your leg is sliced up real nice too. The doctor cleaned it and stitched it up, but you're still at risk of gangrene. We can't let you go until you clear that hurdle.'

A knot appeared in Roland's stomach. He knew what gangrene was all right, and he knew the answer to his next question before he even asked it. 'What if I get it?'

She hesitated for a split second. 'Well, your leg would need to come off. I'm sorry.'

He rolled his eyes and dropped back onto his pillow. 'Lovely.'

'We'll do everything we can to prevent that, I promise. Including evacuation if we have to. But for now, with how swollen you are, we think it best you remain here.' Her face suddenly shifted, and she nervously folded her hands in her lap. She obviously had more to say. 'Mr Hawkins, I'm glad you're finally awake, because I really need to speak with you, and I'm afraid it can't wait.'

Roland glared at her through his swollen eye lids. 'Well for heaven's sake, am I in trouble or something? What is it you think I did?'

'No, you're not in trouble. But . . . well, we have a situation here. I think it's one you would want to know about.'

'OK . . .?'

'Are you aware of the outbreak going on?'

He let out another cough. 'Which one? The trench fever? Trench foot? Lice? Or just the ever-tanking morale problem?'

Llewellyn didn't crack a smile. Deadly serious. 'Influenza.'

The one word sucked the smart mouth right out of Roland. He knew about that outbreak all right, and he couldn't joke about it. Just the mention of it made him pull his blanket up to his chin, as if that would somehow shield him.

Llewellyn nodded. 'You've heard of it. It's pretty bad. It's put more people in the ground than bullets, including half of my staff.'

Roland clutched his ratty blanket into his fists. Memories of the ill pilots sent away from his base, never to return, flashed in his head. 'You think I have it or something?'

Llewellyn just narrowed her eyes at him. 'I bet you're pretty handsome when your face isn't so torn up. Do you have a lady friend roaming around these parts with blonde hair and green eyes? Answers to the name Ilse?'

That got Roland's attention. His eyes snapped open as far as they would go. 'How do you know that?'

She sighed. 'You're not sick, Mr Hawkins, but one of my prized nurses is. She's from New York. Sometimes uses a French nickname to hide some German lineage. Sound like anyone you know?'

Roland's mind reeled as the realization sank in. He hadn't seen Ilse Stahl in over a year. They barely even wrote each other because of all the censors and secrecy. He knew little of how she had fared, even though he thought of her almost every minute of every day. Now, this matron had suggested that in all the hospitals in all of France, where Red Cross personnel were scattered all over the place, seeing to the millions of wounded, he had somehow landed in the same one as his sweetheart.

It was a lot to wrap his foggy head around. 'Ilse . . . My God, Ilse! She's here?'

'Yes, she's here.'

He tried to bolt out of bed, but Llewellyn pushed him down. 'I said you aren't ready to get up yet.'

'Please, you have to let me see her.'

'I might, but there's something you need to know.'

He tried to wrench free of her grasp. 'Now, you listen here. If this has anything to do with those rumors from the other hospital—'

Llewellyn cut him off. 'Oh, please. I don't give credence to that kind of gossipy hogwash.'

'Then why won't you let me see her?'

'Well, I told you she's sick. She's in bad shape too. I have to be honest, I don't know if she'll . . .' She drifted off with a tiny sigh.

Roland went from absolutely elated to feeling like an artillery shell had landed right on his gut. For the last several months, he had wanted nothing more than to see Ilse. Now, he shared the same hospital with her, but only because she was very ill, perhaps mortally so.

'She keeps asking for someone, a pilot she knows.' Llewellyn let out a tired giggle. 'You can imagine my shock when she said his name, and I knew exactly who he was – that busted-up pilot in my own ward. She says she loves him. This pilot.'

That was all he needed to hear. Roland kicked off his twisted covers and whirled his feet over the side of the bed. 'Take me to her. Right now.'

Llewellyn tried to hold him down again, but this time he nudged her away from him. Then he stood up for the first time since the accident. As soon as he did so, the pain smashed into him like a train. He put his hand on his head and felt his legs wobble. He stumbled right into Llewellyn's waiting arms.

She caught him and managed to keep both of them on their feet. 'What did I tell you about getting up?' She wrapped her arm around his waist and helped him balance on his own two legs. 'There you are. Have you got a hold of yourself?'

Roland tapped into his last reserves to stop his legs from quivering. 'Yes. I can walk now.'

He pulled away and stumbled toward the open tent flaps.

But Llewellyn's voice held him back. 'Stop. I mean it.'

The firmness halted Roland's long strides, but he kept his back to her, unwilling to show her the brewing emotion in his face.

'You have to understand, Mr Hawkins. If you see her, it will expose you to a very contagious illness. And if you get it, especially in your condition . . . Do you understand what I'm telling you?'

Roland smacked his face into his own palm. He couldn't believe the gut-wrenching decision that had just been tossed in his lap. Ilse was in this hospital, just yards away from him, fighting an illness that could take her life. Yet, if he spent her last few hours with her, he would risk joining her in death.

He tried to muddle through his flooding emotions. 'You can't bring her to me?'

'And expose everyone else? Besides which, she can't be moved. There are some protections I can offer, but they won't guarantee anything. Think about it real hard, Mr Hawkins.'

The nightmare he'd just had came back to him in a flash. Somehow, through time and space, Ilse had sent him a supernatural call for help. Since her gentle, sweet voice had once pulled him back from his own death, he couldn't ignore the call to guide her through her own. Besides, he had to see her one last time. He had to gaze upon those sparkling eyes and that angelic face. To stamp it forever into his memories, so he had something to take back home with him when all this mess was over.

His eyes welled with tears, and he turned to look at Llewellyn. 'She was the first thing I saw after days of blindness. The first taste of humanity in a horrible war. The first time I ever felt . . .' He stopped himself before he revealed too much of his broken heart. 'Please, I don't care about the risks. Take me to her.'

THIRTY-ONE
Ilse

Ilse lay on a hard, wooden table, the only thing this place could give her for a bed. Her tattered Red Cross coat served as a blanket. Not very comfortable, but it would have to do, because all other cots and bedding were taken up with other patients.

So many other patients. There wasn't an inch of space between the cots inside this stifling, suffocating medical tent. Nurses had propped yet more makeshift beds into every corner. More people writhed in agony on the ground. They coughed up blood. They sweated with fever while convulsing with cold. They gasped for air in their fluid-filled lungs. Ashen faces, with blue lips and red eyes, stared into the next world from bloodstained sheets.

The doctors, outfitted in floor-length robes, masks, and gloves, comforted seizing patients, holding bloody rags over gushing noses. They massaged backs to help patients cough up phlegm. They held out trays to catch the bloody mucus coming from so many mouths.

And the dead . . . More robed personnel stacked the gray, shriveled corpses in the back corner of the tent, where they would be collected for burial in the morning. Mass burial, of course. It was the only safe way. Besides, there simply wasn't time to bury them one by one. Not when thousands of people were dying within a day or two, sometimes hours, of falling ill.

Ilse, her vision wobbly with fever and her head swollen with pain, turned her head to the side to take in the people around her. Victims of a whole other enemy. All condemned to a terrible death inside this tent, where candles turned black shadows into demonic, frightening figures. Where ghosts of medical orderlies scuttled between the cots, robed and masked, more afraid than their patients.

The patients, just statistical numbers to so many, but each with their own page in the big book of the human story. A young soldier, someone's son and sweetheart, who wheezed with pneumonia and stank of fever. An officer, who once led screaming troops across a shell-riddled battlefield, now so shriveled and shrunken he no longer filled his uniform. A child from the nearby village, the precious darling of her parents, inches away from her early death, blood trickling out of her little nose. A nurse's body, a woman who worked so hard to put back together what man had torn apart. Now she was hard with rigor mortis on a cot, and doctors covered her ravaged body with a sheet.

Look what something so tiny had reduced all of them to. Utterly destroying them when even world war had not. A whole other army of wooden crosses for the people back home to cry over.

Ilse drew a tortured breath into her ever-tightening lungs, filling with fluid at an alarming pace. Her cheeks felt sunken and flaming to the touch. She tasted bitter bile and blood in her mouth. The skin on her trembling hands had turned a chilling shade of gray-blue from the serious lack of oxygen in her blood. And her lungs took on less and less with each breath.

Ilse wondered what it would feel like to die. What would happen after she closed her eyes for the last time. Would it hurt? Would anyone walk her over the bridge to the next world? Could she see the living from the other side?

And what about Roland?

Ilse closed her eyes. She would have cried, but her taxed lungs and exhausted body simply wouldn't allow it. All she could do was try to keep breathing. No matter how much it hurt. No matter how hopeless it felt. No matter how few people were left in this world who would really mourn her in the end.

As she tried to force more oxygen into her chest, to just stay alive a few minutes more, she heard a voice. It sounded muffled, like the voices did when her head was under water in the sea off the Old Head of Kinsale. She couldn't pinpoint whose it was.

'She got sick the same day you came,' the woman's voice said.

Another voice answered. Strong. Male. So familiar it pierced Ilse right in her center. 'How did she get so sick so fast?'

'She was under a lot of pressure. We all are. The last big push took up most of our manpower and resources.'

'Thank you. I'll take it from here.'

'Mr Hawkins—'

Mr Hawkins. Roland. He had come for her. Or had he? Perhaps this was just a fever dream. Some type of hallucination God had allowed her. A goodbye of sorts.

The thought sent a sharp pain spiraling down her gut. She didn't know what happened after a person died. If it was just an eternal blackness, or if she would be reborn, or if there truly was a spiritual plane that would hold her soul indefinitely. What she did know was that all of it sounded bleak without Roland.

'Roland . . .' It took everything she had in her to choke out the name.

Once she did, the voices above her stopped. She wondered if she had indeed dreamed the whole thing. Until the warm touch of a human hand enveloped her own. A rough, calloused hand covered in burn scars. A hand she would know anywhere, because it had held hers so many times before.

'Ilse . . . My darling, look at me.'

Ilse blinked a couple of times to break the heavy shackles influenza had put over her eyelids. When her blurry vision cleared a little, the flickering candlelight poured in and burned right into her brain. Her head throbbed. Her ears felt like they would bleed. Her breathing picked up, but her lungs turned it into pitiful wheezing.

But through it all, she saw him. Or at least half of him. Someone had tied a mask over his face and put a strange gown over him. But it was definitely him. Those beautiful coppery-brown eyes cracked through her fever. So clear where everything else felt hazy. Yes, those were her Roland's eyes . . .

She narrowed her own to take a closer look, and it was then she noticed the bruises. The swelling. A cut across his forehead. Another across his cheek. War had beat up on Roland, just like influenza was beating up on her.

'It can't be . . .' She choked out.

A single tear managed to roll down her hollow cheek. Because it just wasn't fair. Their reunion should have involved flowers, kisses, and embracing. They should have been laughing and jumping for joy. They should have held each other in a marriage bed. Not a death bed.

White-hot anger flashed through her in bolts. Similar to what she had felt beneath the waves of the Irish sea. This war had robbed her of so much already. Now it would strangle those precious sparks of love that had kept them both going for so long. It would take something that beautiful and cast it asunder. Just because it could.

'It's me, Ilse. I'm here.'

When she managed to speak again, it came out in tight gasps. Painful wheezes. Like a weight sat on top of her chest. 'No . . . no, it can't be.'

'It's true, Ilse.' His warm hand squeezed hers. She felt a soft brush of fingertips on her sweaty brow. 'I'm here now.'

'Oh, God.' Ilse felt nausea grip her innards. An icy-cold sensation moved in on her throat. So unfair. She had so much left to do in this world. So much life to live. So much love to share. 'Will I die very soon, Roland?'

Roland fiercely shook his head. It was clear he held back tears. She wasn't sure for whose benefit. 'No, my love. You are very much alive.'

'What . . . happened to you?'

'A plane crash. But a godsend. Because look where I am now. Right next to you.'

Ilse took several breaths to muster her strength. So little strength she couldn't lift her head, but she managed to reach her feeble hand up to touch his mask. 'I was . . . going to come . . . to your base.' She paused for a horrible cough. This time, she definitely tasted blood. She didn't have much longer and she knew it. 'I was . . . just waiting . . . for the best time . . .' Tears dribbled down her cheeks, which intensified her struggle to breathe.

He squeezed her hand again. 'Ilse, please don't cry. Just try to rest, darling.'

'R-Roland, I'm . . . I'm going to die . . .'

He shook his head. 'Like hell you will. You're too damn stubborn.'

Her breaths came even tighter. Blackness started moving in on her. She heard death whispering in her fever-riddled ears. 'It's OK, Roland . . . I'm not scared really . . . I'll get to see my family again . . . My father . . . I've missed him so much . . .'

Roland put his hand in her damp hair. His skin felt cooler this time, slick with anxiety sweat. When he spoke again, his voice cracked with emotion. 'I know you miss him, sweetheart, but you have family here now. You won't leave me behind, will you?'

The thought stopped Ilse cold. Family, he said. He saw himself as her family. A found family that could never replace the one she'd lost, but who would love her just the way they had. Hold her up. Help her through. Walk beside her hand in hand, come what may.

A vision dribbled into her mind. It was blurry, like looking through bifocals too strong for her. But she still saw it – a candle in a window on a busy street in New York. In the German neighborhood where she had lived with her parents. Her mother always put out that candle to signal her home after an evening gossiping with her girlfriends, or chasing the boys through the alleyways, or rambling about the market arm-in-arm with her closest friends. A candle that always reminded her, no matter what people said about her, no matter what names they called her, that she had a place to belong and people who loved her.

'*You will always have somewhere to belong*,' her father had said on the bow of the *Lusitania*. '*To your parents, who love you*.'

Who *love* you.

A smile flickered across her cracked, blue lips. 'Roland . . . do you love me?'

His eyes went misty. She couldn't see his lips behind his mask, but she knew he was chewing on them. He always did when he was nervous or contemplating something serious. A small little tick about himself he never noticed, but she always did.

He squeezed her hand. 'Very much.'

She again choked for air. Another gurgling cough came out. 'It's time to . . . go home now, Roland . . . Time to go home . . .'

Roland's hand shook as he touched her face. 'Please don't give up yet. Please stay with me.'

'I'm not afraid . . .'

'I know you're not. You never have been. But I am. I need you, Ilse. I love you. Stay with me.'

Her eyes filled with tears. 'I'm so tired . . . Roland. Tired . . . of the war. Tired . . . of losing . . . everyone. Tired . . . of having no home . . . with a candle in the window . . .'

Roland's eyebrows flew up sharply at the mention of a candle in the window. 'Ilse?'

'Oh, Roland . . .'

Ilse watched as his steel exterior cracked. Frantic hopelessness flickered in those brown eyes, making them duller and sadder than ever. But then they came to rest on the candle by her bedside. The flame danced merrily in the chaos of the tent, which almost felt like a slap in the face. But he picked it up from its holder and flashed it in front of Ilse.

The glow was so bright it almost killed her, but she could still see him just behind it. Those eyes of his, imploring her. Loving her. Begging her to stay.

'Let me be your home now,' he said, his eyes glowing in the candlelight. 'I'll do anything if you stay. Just stay with me.'

Ilse tried to speak, to tell him she loved him too. To tell him she was so very sorry to break his heart this way. But all she could do was struggle to suck in more oxygen.

'Don't try to talk,' he said, resting his hand over her forehead. 'Just rest.'

'Roland . . .' Her chest made a horrible wheezing sound, and more blood escaped with her deep and rasping cough.

'No talking. Not now, Ilse. Tomorrow, when you feel better, you can tell me what you need to say then.'

'T-Tomorrow . . .'

She felt gutted. She had already accepted that she probably wouldn't see another sunrise. And it would hurt Roland terribly, but someday he would move on. There would be more sunrises. Gorgeous red and pink ones. The world would keep turning and he would keep walking in it. Without her. She opened her mouth to tell him so, but no words came out. Her lungs were too full. Her mind locked up. Her hand turned to ice inside of his.

Roland moved his hand from her forehead to her cheek. He didn't take his eyes from hers. Although death had cropped up between them, he clearly wouldn't let it take her without a fight. He leaned down close to her, putting his masked lips just centimeters from her ear.

'Tomorrow the sun will rise,' he said. 'It will be beautiful, and you will be here to see it. I promise. And I'll be right here waiting for you so we can watch it together.'

This time, Ilse couldn't hold in the sob. It broke out of her with a loud wail, then her eyes shut of their own accord. Just when she thought she couldn't feel any sicker, nausea jolted her from her stomach down to her toes. She actually felt her face turn green. With animal instinct, she rocketed upright. Before she could finish the thought, a stream of red-tinged vomit spewed from her mouth.

Roland jumped back, his eyes wide with terror. 'Llewellyn! Help! Somebody get over here, quick!'

Suddenly, the low rumbling of plane engines grumbled just outside. Medical tools rattled on their trays and fell into the grass. Some of the patients ducked under their cots.

A host of soldiers from outside burst into the tent with a clamor. 'Gothas overhead,' one of them yelled. 'Better button up this place good and tight.'

Nobody needed to be told twice. Doctors covered patients with extra blankets while trying to shove them under their cots. Some sick people tried to scramble for the bomb shelters, only to be pushed back by frantic orderlies.

'Don't let them out,' a nurse yelled. 'They'll infect this whole hospital.'

Outside, the first explosion clapped like a peel of thunder. Every loose object and person tumbled to the ground. Patients screamed and collapsed in their weakness. Nurses and doctors dropped to their knees and covered their necks.

Another explosion rocked the night, the flashes glaring all through the tent. Roland threw his body over Ilse's to protect her from the wrath to come, just as a bomb burst right outside the tent. The concussion knocked everyone still standing off their feet. Equipment crashed to the ground, and the tent roof collapsed under the impact. Screams rent the air, and everything went dark.

THIRTY-TWO
Roland

The next morning, Roland found himself on a cot back in the regular ward, with a throbbing headache and no clue what had happened to Ilse, because at some point the night before, orderlies had dragged him from her side. He had thrashed them good in his efforts to stay close to her. Punches and kicks. Yells and curses. Even a scream or two. But all the orderlies had to do was slap a cloth over his face. After that, he remembered nothing.

He got little help from anyone the next morning either. 'Excuse me,' he murmured to a passing orderly. 'I'm looking for someone. A nurse.'

'Well, who isn't?' The orderly said in a snappy tone.

'Please, I need to find a flu patient. Her name's Ilse. She's a nurse here. Please.'

'Forget it. Most of them didn't survive the bombing.'

The orderly skirted away after that. No words of comfort, no hand-holding, not even an apology. Roland felt his nerves ratchet up, right along with his temper. Someone would answer his questions, damn it, come hell or high water. He swiped at a nurse here and another orderly there. He asked for Ilse in a booming voice. He demanded information on who had survived the bombing and who hadn't.

'Someone talk to me!' he cried. 'Someone tell me where Ilse is!'

Another orderly arrived at his bedside, wearing a stern glare. 'Don't make me knock you out, fly boy.'

'Guess you'll just have to give me what I want and tell me *where Ilse is*.'

'I don't know any Ilse,' the orderly said. 'But I do know that if you don't hush up, I'll hush you up myself. With my fists to save on chloroform.'

'All right, that's enough.'

Both men turned at the sound of Llewellyn's voice.

The orderly glared. 'This one's a bit too feisty for my taste, Miss Llewellyn. He's yelling and cursing and smart-mouthing everyone here. We haven't got time for it.'

Llewellyn patted the orderly on the arm. 'Why don't you let me take it from here then?'

He growled in response. 'My pleasure.' With that, he was gone.

Llewellyn pulled up a wooden chair and plopped down next to Roland. 'And how are we this morning, fly boy?'

Roland's only response was a hand to his pounding head. 'Lord, my head.'

Llewellyn chuckled. 'That's the chloroform. You know, you shouldn't treat those orderlies so rough. They can outwit anyone with those cloths. Even a hot-headed fly boy.'

'You'd think they have better people to use it on. Someone actually in pain, for example.'

'Well, you've got me there.'

'Where is Ilse?' Roland asked. 'Tell me what's happened to her. Please. I promise I'll behave from here on out if you just tell me what's become of her.'

Llewellyn sighed. 'She's alive.'

Roland let out a tense breath, but her somber expression suggested he shouldn't celebrate prematurely. 'Why the long face then?'

'Ilse's condition has taken a nasty turn. She's vomiting up everything we give her now, even water.'

Roland bowed his head into his sweaty hands. It was all he could do to keep his tears in check. His tears, the oceans of them that he would cry if what he dreaded most of all came to pass. 'My God, Ilse . . . She's really going to die, isn't she? I really thought she could pull through it. She's got such a will about her. I honestly thought . . .' He couldn't say more, because he couldn't stomach crying. Not because he was embarrassed, but because if he started, he knew he would never be able to stop. Not after everything he had been through, and definitely not if Ilse was just about to leave him for good.

'Now, Mr Hawkins, Ilse's condition is very serious. What I'm about to tell you doesn't change that.'

Roland frowned at her. 'What the hell is that supposed to mean?'

'I'm not . . . entirely sure she will die.'

'Interesting theory, since you just told me she's not even keeping water down.'

'Which is bad, yes. It's a struggle to keep her hydrated. But all the vomiting, you could say it means there's a bit of hope now.'

More than just a bit of hope shot through Roland's stomach,

along with confusion. A lack of clarity. He sat up straighter in his flimsy cot and tried to make sense of it. Ilse was very sick, but she might not die. There was hope now, despite her being even sicker.

'How? How is there hope?'

'Some people do get better, Mr Hawkins. It's rare with this illness, but it does happen. I've seen it. And of those who did get better, many of them vomited up everything first.'

Roland gasped. 'But . . . why would that help?'

Llewellyn shrugged. 'Throwing up is how the body purges poisons. It's not pleasant and could kill her on its own, but it will also help get rid of everything in there. If we can get her past this phase, she just might recover completely. But like I said, Mr Hawkins, it's a big if.'

Roland grumbled and ran a hand through his sweaty hair. The war had taught him one thing. 'If' was a sneaky word, with sneaky intentions. 'If' just couldn't be trusted. But he had to cling to something, and 'if' might have to be enough for now. As much as he didn't like it.

Llewellyn gave him a nod, as if she saw right inside of his mind. 'It's not much, I know. But take it for all it's worth, Mr Hawkins. Ilse needs it.' She stood up and gave his hand a squeeze. 'I'll be back when I know more.' With that, she vanished into the busy hospital.

That left Roland with nothing to do but wait. Wait for Ilse to die. Wait for her to get better. Wait . . . A terrible thing, especially with so little to keep his mind occupied.

As he lamented how in the world he could possibly fill the time, he noticed a banged-up letter at the foot of his cot. Someone had ripped it open and re-sealed it, probably army censors. Mud stained the outside along with some old raindrops. He reached over and picked it up, turning it over to inspect the postmark. When he read it, his jaw dropped open.

Bernard.

'Oh my God . . .' Roland tore at the letter like a hawk would its prey, unfolding the single sheet of paper that was, to his great dismay, mostly blacked out. However, he recognized his brother's distinguished writing swirl, which always stood out given his left-handed penmanship.

As The Storm Clouds Gather 221

My dear brother,
 I'm so sorry it's taken me so long to write. My regiment *************** but I came out all right. We got put in reserve while command worked on boosting our numbers back up. Good luck with that.
 It will be back to the line before long. Can't say I'm looking forward to it. I expect a posting somewhere around ****************. I'm a sergeant now too. Surviving the wreck of ************* I guess makes me worthy. Did you ever imagine that? Your baby brother leading men into battle.
 I guess that's all for now. I'm sure the censors (hello boys!) have had a field day with this letter as it is. Just wanted you to know I'm OK. I hope you will write me soon, Roly. I haven't heard from you in so long and you know how I feel about those airplanes.
 Love,
 Bernard

Roland actually laughed, he was so happy. He also exhaled. A powerful, long, cleansing one. An exhale that took all his troubles and fluttered them away on a breeze.

His brother was alive. So alive, and that was a miracle. A stroke of luck.

So much damn luck. No wonder Vernon had always called him Lucky.

With shaking fingers, Roland folded the letter back up and slipped it into its envelope. His brother was alive. Now, he just needed Ilse to get better.

Ilse . . .

Roland squeezed his eyes shut and held the letter close to him. If he could just keep his lover, and his brother, he could figure the rest out. He could make it through.

He could live.

THIRTY-THREE
Ilse

Ilse lay in a real cot now, in a much quieter part of the station. No more gray corpses stacked in the corner. No black Xs on the tent flaps or eerie, long white robes on the doctors. No more sick patients crammed into every corner. No more coughing, no more blood.

She was glad to be out of that sick tent, although she wasn't entirely better yet. Weight loss had ravaged her frame down to a skeleton. Her skin remained ghostly pale. Her limbs still trembled with weakness. But she was alive. Her eyes glowed green again, as if her soul had been safely returned to her body. Her stomach took food again. She could breathe again, and how she relished that easy flow of oxygen. In, out. In, out. She allowed a smile to flicker across her thirsty lips. In fact, she could barely hold in a giggle.

'Roland Hawkins,' she said, this time in a stronger, clearer voice.

The bruised eyelids in the cot next to hers fluttered open. Those brown, melted-chocolate irises gazed at her for a long moment. Taking her in. Making sure he wasn't dreaming. He propped himself up on his elbow, staring at her, slack-jawed and relieved at the same time.

'Oh my God . . . Ilse?'

She laughed. 'Surprised to see me this side of the pearly gates?'

Roland let out a gasp and reached his hand out for hers. 'Ilse! You're . . . you're alive. You're OK. You're OK, right?'

She took his gas-scarred hand in hers and kissed it. 'Yes, Roland, my dear. I do think I'll be OK now.'

Those brown eyes glittered with relief. Emotion. Joy. With the knowledge that he wouldn't have to finish this war alone. 'You're OK . . . Oh, Ilse, my darling.' He bowed his head with a sharp exhale. She thought he heard him thank someone. God, maybe. Then, without letting go of her hand, he crept up from his own cot and sat down on the edge of hers.

'I feel like a real sap saying so,' she said. 'But I missed you. So much that as soon as I got well enough, I made Llewellyn move me in here so I could surprise you. Isn't that sappy?'

He laughed in an attempt to hide his tears. 'And other than sappy, how do you feel?'

Her smile vanished and her heartbeat slowed. A terrible wave of sadness washed over her as she remembered how ready and willing she had been to die. To let all the pain fade away into nothingness and let death carry her away on its wings. Because she thought she wouldn't leave anyone who really cared behind. She hadn't realized, until it was almost too late, that her life might be worth fighting for. If not to her, then to someone else.

She swallowed a bitter lump in her throat. 'I was ready to die, Roland. So ready to die.'

His face dissolved, as if the words were an actual knife to his heart. 'Ilse, why in the world would you want to—'

She cut him off. 'A lot of those patients who didn't make it had families. Loved ones. With my whole family already gone, with so few friends around, I didn't think it was fair for me to live and them to die. I thought I should trade myself for them.' She smiled. 'But when you came, when you told me you loved me and called me your family, it was a reminder. Me dying wouldn't save anybody. And you gave me what so many others have had this whole time and I didn't. Something to fight for.'

As the words escaped her, words she had wanted to say for so long, she felt a flutter in a place that had been dormant for years. Her most guarded, vulnerable place. Where a shoot of green now popped up through mounds of ash. Through all the horrors the last few years had flung at her, no matter what roaring fires raged through her soul, there was still a woman in there who could feel things. Who could love and be loved. Who wanted to know Roland, really know him, deep in the night with no one else around. It was a relief, really. Realizing that no weapons of war, no virus, no bullets could reach that precious place inside her.

Roland squeezed her hand in his. 'You said something about a candle in the window the other night.'

She nodded. 'My mother always left one in the window for me. Back in New York. It was always such a welcome sight after a long day at the clothing factory.'

Roland's eyes shimmered as he kissed her hand. 'Mine did too. Another way we're so deeply connected, Ilse. I've always thought of that when I feel hopeless or afraid.'

She raised her eyebrows. 'Really?'

He smiled and nodded. 'And I realized something when you were sick. You've become my candle in the window, Ilse Stahl.' He took the candle from his bedside and put it next to hers instead. 'Maybe you'll let me be yours?'

Before she answered, he leaned down and gave her the gentlest kiss on her forehead. She soaked in the warmth of his body, the damp of his sweat, the smell of his hair. She heard his heart beating inside his strong chest, and it made her feel more connected to him than ever.

'There's something I didn't get a chance to tell you, Roland.'

'What's that?'

The candlelight gleamed in his eyes and it dissolved any resistance she had left. 'I love you too.'

Roland sat her up in her cot. He took her head in both his hands. Right in front of God and everybody, he kissed her right on the lips.

And he didn't stop.

THIRTY-FOUR
Roland

Ilse mended fast after that. Just a few days later, she left her bed and went walking around on her own. She even donned her Red Cross uniform and insisted on helping around the station. Ambulance runs were out of the question, but Llewellyn at least let her comfort patients and help them write letters to their families.

She spent the rest of her days with Roland. They often stayed up whispering to one another after hours. It reminded him so much of when they met in Belgium, all that time they stole with one another, and those sweet songs playing on the record player. This time, he swore he would never leave her side again . . .

Until the war found him. Early one morning, Elliot strolled in with his typical swagger, decked in his full dress, holding a bundle under his arm and grinning like the ornery devil that he was. He even swatted a helpless nurse on her backside when she walked past him.

Then he zeroed in on Roland. With a happy wave, he crossed the busy tent and dropped down at the foot of his friend's cot. 'Well, well. Roland Hawkins, in the flesh.'

'Elliot!' Roland laughed as he shook hands with his favorite wingman. 'What in the hell are you doing here?'

Elliot gave him a too-rough clap on the back. 'You think I wouldn't visit my favorite squadron leader?' He laid his bundle, a full sack of fresh-picked mushrooms, in Roland's arms. 'Here, I pulled these up on the way over. You won't believe how many there are. All that damn rain and . . . well . . . fertile soil.' He pulled a flask from his jacket pocket and took a long swig. There was a noticeable tremble in his hand as he did so. His nervous eyes darted across the harried nurses and personnel. 'Where's that dishy lady of yours anyway?'

Roland gulped at the sight of Elliot's tremors, and the other strains that had begun to show. He cleared his throat, trying to choose his words carefully. After all, boys didn't like to be accused of cracking up. 'How's things at Rembercourt? Any big news from patrols?'

'Are you asking me if I got the son of a bitch that landed you here? I'm afraid not.'

'Well, how's everyone else then? I mean . . . has anyone . . .?'

'Gone west? Well of course. *C'est la guerre*. No one you know, at least. Norman's still kicking, and most of the new boys in our squadron are hanging in there.'

'And they're doing well? Feeling good and everything?'

Elliot ran a hand through his hair. Another tremor jolted his wrist. 'Well, now that you ask . . .'

Roland looked sternly at his fellow flier. 'Elliot . . . I thought you looked a little under the weather. Are you cracking up, boy?'

'I wouldn't call it that.'

'What would you call it then?'

He sighed. 'I get dizzy spells, and I'm hard of hearing all of a sudden. Norman says his eyesight is gone to hell and he loses his balance a lot. Then there's the boys that get mood swings out of nowhere. One minute they're fine, the next they're busting up the bar and maybe someone's head. Everyone's so erratic these days.'

'What does the cap say?'

Elliot shrugged. 'He carted in some doctors to check everyone out, but they can't figure what the problem is. Airplanes are still so new. The effects of extended flying aren't fully understood, I guess.'

'So, what now?'

'We still fly. What else can we do? Cap tries rotating us out more, but most boys go up anyway. We all want this over with.' He winked. 'It'll be nice to have you with us again.'

'Well, I'm working on it.'

'You better work faster and harder.'

'What do you mean?'

'You've been cleared for duty. Thank Christ, too. Because we'll murder your cat and eat her if she doesn't stop her damn whining.'

Roland felt his heart skip a beat. Cleared for duty. He would be back up in the air in a day or two, maybe less. He was surprised Llewellyn hadn't given him a warning.

He chewed his lower lip in angst. 'They really think I can fly when I'm half busted up?'

'Oh, hell. They're so desperate for seasoned fliers. They'll at least put you on training duty until you can sit your busted-up ass in a plane again.' Elliot squeezed the ankle on his friend's injured leg, which sent a shot of pain through Roland's calf. 'I better get back, but I'll fetch you first thing tomorrow.' His eyes scanned the room for a nurse he had hoped to meet. When he still didn't spot her, he glanced at Roland. 'So, uh . . . your friend's here?'

Roland just nodded with a sly smile. 'Working right now – but yes, she's here.'

'Well then, make tonight count, you scoundrel.' Elliot winked and got back to his feet. He staggered a little from the booze, then lumbered toward the door and was gone.

Almost as soon as he left, Ilse appeared from around the corner. Still in recovery from her illness, her walk was slow and stiff. She carried a pile of fresh clothes for Roland, and she sat in the place Elliot had just occupied. 'I saw a pilot with you.'

'Yes. Elliot, my wingman.'

'I suppose he's told you the news.'

While Roland did want to return to his squadron, he hated the thought of leaving Ilse here. Being apart from her yet again, and for who knew how long this time. Perhaps forever, the way things had been going. But then the candle in between their cots caught his eye.

He reached out and took her wrist. 'Ilse, look at me.'

When she did, tears glistened in those green eyes and made them sharper than ever.

He picked up the candle and put it in her trembling hand. 'Remember where your home is,' he whispered in her ear. 'Just because I'm not here, doesn't mean I won't be with you.'

She smiled. Then she put the candle down and kissed him right on the lips. Roland put his arms around her waist and kissed her back.

For now, they were alive. And for now, that was enough.

THIRTY-FIVE
Roland

As soon as Roland returned to the airbase, Major Hartney summoned him to his office.

It threw some cold water on Roland's excitement to be back on the airfield, because a summons from the major meant one of two things – promotion, or he was in big trouble. Since he had been in hospital for the last several days, he didn't figure he'd earned the former.

Now Roland sat in his full-dress uniform, in a freshly polished wooden chair in a large, intimidating office, right across from the head of the entire First Pursuit Group. His own squadron commander, Captain Grant, stood firmly behind the major. Roland bobbed his legs up and down as Hartney went through a thick stack of papers spread out on his fancy desk.

Roland's complete medical records. Detailing not only his recent crash, but also his troubles at Ypres. Records he had managed to keep sealed . . . until now. All the energy he had wasted keeping those damn things a secret. He had threatened an army doctor and struggled through rotting lungs and cough attacks without help. He had spoken sparingly about his experience in the trenches. About Vernon's death. All to keep his secret, and his spot in the air corps. But somehow, they'd found out anyway. Now would come the consequences.

From the look on Hartney's face, they would be grave. 'So mustard gas, eh, Hawkins? What's that like?'

Roland gave him a deadpan stare. 'Unpleasant.'

'That's all you have to say about it?'

'Yes, sir.'

'What about lying on your entrance exam?'

'I didn't lie. It just got left off there. Some paperwork mistake, *obviously*.'

Hartney glared. 'One that worked out awfully convenient for you.'

Roland shifted in his seat and gave a revealing crack of his knuckles. The only prayer he had was that Elliot could be right – maybe they were that desperate for seasoned fliers.

As The Storm Clouds Gather 229

'So, you've been flying around with rotting lungs all this time? Putting yourself and the rest of your squadron in danger?'

'Seems like more of a danger to all the Germans I've shot.'

Captain Grant stifled a laugh, but Hartney wasn't amused. 'There's a reason pilots need to be in top form, Hawkins. A squadron is only as strong as its weakest pilot. If something happens to you up there, it isn't only your life at risk.'

'Sir—'

'Not to mention all the flying could severely aggravate your condition. It might shave a few golden years off your life.'

Roland just shrugged. 'I'd shave a lot more off in the trenches, and I'd score a lot fewer hits for God and country.'

Grant wanted to laugh so badly his face turned red.

Even Hartney saw the humor in that response. 'Well, it's hard to argue with that, isn't it, Grant?'

Grant at last burst out laughing. The tension in the room dissipated, and Roland smiled, looking down at his twitching fingers.

'You know I was prepared to give you hell,' Hartney said. 'Maybe even toss you out of here. Lying on your paperwork is a big problem, Hawkins. But I suppose you've handled yourself well enough. Only one forced landing and one crash, which is far and above some of the other wild types around here.'

'So, I'm not in trouble?'

Hartney chuckled. 'For now, anyway.'

'Do I get a new plane then?'

Hartney stacked Roland's medical records and put them down. 'In all honesty, it might not matter.'

Roland looked from Grant to Hartney. 'What do you mean?'

'We've got word in from top brass. The Germans are teetering bad. Peace delegates are negotiating an armistice as we speak.'

Roland's eyes went wide and he fell back into his chair. An armistice. Peace. After four long years, this all might end – and soon. The idea flitted across his mind like a dragonfly over a pond. He hadn't thought about life beyond the war in so long, because he feared 'after the war' was a pipe dream. Especially for pilots. But peace meant he could go home. Maybe even find a new place to call home. He could choose anywhere he wanted. The United States was so big, after all, with so many different lifestyles.

A sudden flash in his head saw him sitting on a porch somewhere quiet. At a house all his own, with wide open fields and woods nearby. A windmill turning in the breeze. Ilse sat next to him, bouncing a baby on her knee. Their baby. A life so blissfully normal.

Hartney's voice cut into the fantasy. 'It's not signed and sealed yet, *obviously*. We're keeping up our normal patrol schedules in the meantime. So, you'll have to borrow planes until a new one comes.'

'Yes, sir.'

'And for God's sake, see the medic regularly for those lungs.'

'Yes, sir.'

'And one more question.'

'Yes?'

Hartney grinned. 'Is that little black feline witch's charm happy to see you?'

Roland snickered. 'Always, sir. Always.'

Roland stepped out of the major's office, where the late-October nip bit into his cheeks and nose. Winter wouldn't be long in coming now. If there was indeed an armistice in the works, Roland hoped it would be settled before then.

He rubbed his hands together for warmth, strolling across Rembercourt toward his old barrack tent. Little Jewel patiently waited for him at his barrack, and when he arrived, she sprang to her feet and weaved in and out of his ankles. He knelt down to scratch her behind the ears while she purred.

'Hey there, you. Looks like you're a lucky charm after all. I get to stay.'

He stopped petting his cat when he heard the sound of inbound planes up above. The morning patrol, and it didn't look good. Of the five planes that went out, only three now floated above the airbase. The one in the rear limped, leaking clouds of black smoke.

Roland's jaw hardened. Elliot and Norman had both been on that patrol. He forced his sore legs into motion and took off in a hard half-sprint toward the landing strip, limping on his bad leg as he did so.

Despite their beat-up condition, the remaining planes all came down smoothly, one right after the other. As the lead plane touched down and came to a stop, Roland banged on the fuselage to summon the pilot out. He also leaned down to cough, his lungs unprepared for such strain after all they had been through lately.

The pilot crawled out of his plane, still wrapped in an oversized, full fur suit the pilots had dubbed a 'teddy bear.' The pilot was burrowed so deep inside it, Roland didn't recognize him until he took his hood down.

Norman. He leaned over to assist his choking buddy. 'Lord, Hawkins, listen to that cough. You ever going to get that checked?'

Roland stood up straight and grabbed Norman by his fur collar. 'Thank God you're all right. What happened?'

'Fritz must have smelled us coming. We weren't up fifteen minutes before six of them came right at us. Tough bastards too. Busted up my engine, my wingman's leaking fuel, and another went down in enemy territory.'

Roland scanned the other planes for Elliot, but he saw no sign of the boy. 'Elliot?'

Norman drew his lips in a tight line.

'All right then, time to go.' Roland left dumbfounded Norman by his plane and sprinted toward the nearest vacant airplane. He grabbed the shocked mechanic by the arm. 'Get this plane ready for take-off. Right now.'

'Y-yes, sir.'

Norman caught up with him and tried to block his path. 'You're going up now? Your lungs are a mess. Besides which, rain is coming in. You'll never make it.'

Roland grabbed a flight coverall draped over the side of the plane's cockpit. He stumbled into the pants and wrapped the beat-up fur around his shoulders. 'Where did he go down?'

Norman rolled his eyes. He clearly wanted to argue more, but he didn't dare provoke Roland's temper. So, he just bent over and helped him into the coverall. 'It was that damn field just shy of the lines. I think he was alive when he landed.'

'Thank you.' Roland pulled the damp rubber headgear over his head and strapped on a pair of goggles. Without another word, he climbed up into the aircraft.

Norman looked up at him and sighed. 'You're too busted up for much stunt flying, Hawkins. You won't stand a chance if you get in a fight.'

'Either start me up, or get the hell out of my way.'

That settled it. Norman nodded and beckoned to the mechanic. The startled mechanic put his hands on the propeller. 'Contact!'

With one flick of his arms, he pushed the prop into motion. It coughed a few times, then rumbled to life. The wind off the prop blasted Roland back into his seat, but he still managed to clamp his hands and feet over the controls.

It was like riding a bike. His ligaments, although sore and stiff, still knew exactly where to go and what to do. The plane rolled across the grass and approached the take-off strip. Across the way, he caught a glimpse of little Jewel. She had resumed her guardian position in front of his barrack. There she would stay until he returned. Hopefully when he did, Elliot would be with him.

Roland turned his eyes back to the runway. Without even waiting for clearance, he sped off down the take-off strip and his wheels lifted off the ground.

If he wasn't so terrified for the safety of his pal, he would have been extremely happy to be reunited with the sky. The fierce wind blew past his cheeks and rejuvenated his spirit. The expanse of the sky felt like freedom after his long imprisonment on the ground.

He lurched the wobbly plane up through thick, heavy swirls of gray rain clouds. A few big drops pelted his windshield, and he saw distant, thick rain bands in the distance, struck through with golden sun pillars, reaching for the ground like big, long claws. It actually looked like something from heaven, but Roland knew he damn well better avoid it, since it could be deadly enough to send him there. Storms and flying simply didn't mix.

After a few minutes, Roland approached the farm field Norman had mentioned. It was filled to bursting with thick, golden grass and scattered, yellow fall blooms. Which made it a bit hard to examine, but even through the maze, Roland quickly noticed a large man-made object. A pile of fabric and wood hunkered in amongst the natural environment.

He dipped his plane lower and circled the object.

It was definitely an airplane. It still sat on its wheels, and the wings looked intact. If it was Elliot's plane, he had done a nice job of landing.

Roland's stomach jolted as he put the plane into a sharp descent. He straightened it with the horizon, then he cut the engine, floated on the breeze, and let his wheels thud to the ground. He struggled to keep the plane from buckling on such uneven turf. Grass blades tugged at his wheels. Lumps and pockets in the ground rattled and jarred his teeth. At last, the plane slowed down and skidded to a stop just across from the other plane. At much closer range, Roland confirmed it was Elliot's.

'Elliot!' Roland unstrapped himself from the hissing, clicking cockpit. He scrambled out of his machine and jogged toward the other plane while low-pitched, threatening thunder signaled the storm's fast approach.

'Elliot!'

No answer. The plane remained still and silent. Almost ghostly. The grass swayed and yellow blooms dodged from his path as Roland's legs crunched through the field. Crunch, crackle. One heavy footfall after the next, until at last, Roland stood right next to Elliot's downed plane. A hasty examination showed him that one of the wheels had snapped on landing, listing the machine slightly on one side. Other than that, and a couple of random bullet holes, it had escaped any real damage.

Roland fumbled toward the cockpit while a few hard raindrops smacked against his hot cheeks, and a pickup in the wind sent rippling waves through the field. A creamy wool collar came into view. As did the brown, beat-up leather sleeve of a flying coat. Then, a stiff and still body. Elliot remained strapped in his seat, his eyes straight forward. Crusted brown blood plastered the side of his face. His skin matched the gray skies above.

Roland whipped his legs up onto the wing and hoisted his body up.

'Elliot, boy . . . answer me.'

It was no use. His little wingman was long gone, evidenced by the gory bullet hole in his chest. He could have been shot in the air, but Roland had to doubt it. The plane had been landed too neatly. No one struggling with a mortal wound could have done it.

Anger brewed deep in his gut like the storm brewed in the sky. Pilots were so often dubbed 'Knights of the Air.' But shooting a defenseless pilot on the ground wasn't anything a knight would do. Elliot had died to satisfy someone's damaged ego, or boiling war prejudice, or plain and simple killer instinct. A way of thinking that Roland had learned, the hard way, just didn't live up to what it meant to be human. It wasn't fair. It wasn't right. Just like all the rest of this mess.

And yet . . .

Roland's grip turned to a vice on his dead comrade's shoulder. His eyes flickered along with the lightning up above.

He couldn't stop the old familiar monster from moving through his blood, consuming everything he thought he had learned during his terrible time in this war. Gobbling it up. Wiping it out. Roland knew there would be no tears, not this time. There would be no crying over another wooden cross. There could only be revenge . . . and Roland would have it.

Right now.

THIRTY-SIX
Roland

Thunder roared in the distance, just like Roland's plane engine roared as he moved further into enemy territory. Crackling forks of lightning lit up the horizon. Warnings to high tail it home flashed through his mind. If it started raining too hard, it would dissolve the fabric on his plane wings like a piece of paper in a puddle.

The weather wasn't the only danger, either. Roland had never gone this far into German territory, especially not alone, and it was bad judgment for a pilot to go anywhere without help. But in his blind rage, Roland didn't care about any of it. He wasn't afraid. He only lusted for payback – the same animal instinct that had overpowered him when his father died.

Through the thick clouds, the German airdrome finally appeared in Roland's windshield. A simple place, with a barn for headquarters, some grassy airfields, and a makeshift mechanical hangar or two. The colorful planes lined the airfield, covered with tarps to brace them for the incoming storm.

Roland's anger burned like acid in his blood, and he tilted his plane, taking dead aim at that airfield. The wires in his wings screeched with fury, a bird of prey on the hunt. As the talons of his machine approached the German take-off strip, he fired his clunky machine gun.

Sizzling tracers blasted across the fields, and German mechanics scattered like a flock of frightened pigeons. They covered their heads and ran toward the hangars. Shards of wood splinters puffed from the planes as Roland's bullets shredded them to ribbons.

The ruckus eventually rousted the pilots from their barracks. They stumbled about, pointing at Roland and yelling at each other. A few made mad, heroic dashes for the planes.

Unafraid of either them or their planes, Roland banked his own plane up into the air and whipped it around for another pass over the field.

Below, panicked anti-aircraft crews manned their positions. There came a few loud thuds and echoes, then black puffs of smoke began peppering the sky.

It still didn't stop Roland. Or his gun. He kept flying, and he kept firing.

The pilots on the ground began running, ducking, diving, and barreling for cover. One even splatted belly-first on the muddy ground and covered his head in fright. Yet one brave pilot ran for the closest airplane and ripped the tarp off. It didn't take long for the colorful machine's engines to roar to life.

Roland just laughed. A second bidder in his dangerous gamble just pumped his ire up even more. As another peel of thunder rumbled through the heavens, and a few more raindrops splatted on his windshield, he wheeled his machine around for a third time, and streaked his plane over the German take-off strip. He had to move fast. He was running out of time, and for more reasons than one.

The German triplane positioned itself at the end of the runway. When he got a few feet off the ground, still at a severe disadvantage, Roland dove in on him from above. More red-hot tracers whizzed from his gun, and the German machine jolted with a hit. The nose dipped and smacked into the grass. It sent the entire plane somersaulting down the rest of the landing strip. Although there was no one around to observe it, Roland was certain it counted as a kill.

He wheeled his own ship around for a fourth time, while another German pilot struggled to get airborne. Just as his wheels lifted off the ground, he got the same treatment – a waterfall of Roland's bullets right into the engine of his machine. It burst into flames and crashed to the ground in a pile of wood chips.

This time, a duo of German planes started their engines. Each pilot went for opposite ends of the airstrip, where they would take off at the same time. It was smart really, as it ensured at least one would get airborne.

Roland just circled back around and readied his guns. But as he prepared to open fire, a loud burst clapped over his head. His plane jerked with a heavy concussion. Some fabric on his fuselage ripped.

Shrapnel.

Roland tested the controls on his wounded aircraft. So far, they held, but he couldn't guarantee for how long. Especially with those bands of rain clouds inching ever closer.

Then there was the other problem: those two German planes were both gaining speed. With a growl of his engine, Roland pumped the first one full of lead. It screeched to a halt, skidding every which way, before the wheels even left the ground. The other used the distraction to gain speed. A few seconds later, its wheels split from the turf.

Meanwhile, an entire artillery bombardment had zeroed in on Roland's plane, and he scrambled to keep her steady in the constant blasts. Puffs of black smoke and streams of green flaming onions hissed and popped all around him.

Roland gritted his teeth. No plane could take much more of this. Besides which, he wasn't alone in the sky anymore, and the rain was coming closer. The first warning drops of the storm were pelting Roland with ever-increasing frequency. The time had come to run for home.

He yanked back on his control stick, pulling the plane further up and deep into the swirling rain bands. The clouds pulled him into their chilling embrace, which would conceal him from the other pilot, but they also hid the ground and concealed his land markers. He didn't know what direction he was flying in, but he didn't care, so long as it was away from that airfield.

He craned his head for a glance behind him.

The threatening rain hadn't deterred his German counterpart. The pilot still pursued him, his machine struggling in the turbulent storm system, lingering too far behind to be a threat.

At least for now.

Roland pushed his plane harder than ever before. The engine coughed in protest and secreted puffs of smoke. The artillery had mortally wounded her. She wouldn't be able to stay airborne for much longer. Certainly not long enough to make it home. He cleared nervous steam from his goggles and tried to look beyond the thick clouds for a place to land.

Through patches of fog and swollen rain clouds, he spotted an open and abandoned beet field below. It no doubt would be a soggy, soupy mess, but he couldn't afford to be choosy. Not with the rain splattering hard against his plane now. Mopping the oil and water from his face, he aligned with the landscape and prepared for landing.

Just like before, his wheels impacted hard, his plane bouncing and slipping across the field. In the quagmire of mud and slimy tubers, the wheels snapped from the fuselage and the plane flopped down on its belly. It slushed through the beets like a sled, mashing and bursting them in puffs of red, before coming to a hard stop, somehow without tipping over.

A bloodied Roland sat by himself in the wrecked cockpit, taking in the irreparable damage to the wings and fuselage of his plane. Meanwhile, the rain hammered him from above, the cold drops dampening his anger and bringing him back to his senses. Returning him to reality and reminding him that he had just killed at least two people. All in cold blood. The same cold blood that had killed Elliot and so many others in the first place.

Roland put his hands over his face. He couldn't believe what he had just done, or that he had made it out alive. Alive, but in much rougher shape than before. Blood covered his hands and ran down his face. His left arm hung limply at his side. Minor injuries, really. He was lucky to be alive. So damn lucky . . . even if the people he loved and cared about were not.

Roland ripped at his seat straps. Even with just one good arm, he tore himself out of the banged-up cockpit, flung his body out of the plane, and spilled onto the ground below. He rolled onto his back while beets squished and burst beneath him. The rain splashed against his face, and the thunder mirrored the turmoil in his soul.

'Elliot . . .'

His hot tears mixed with the cold rain drops. While his body heaved with sobs, the thought suddenly came to him. Once he got back to the airfield, there would be some additions to his kill list. Enough to earn him a new nickname, since his total was now over five.

Ace.

THIRTY-SEVEN
Roland

The next day, Roland Hawkins again sat before the formidable Major Harold Hartney. This time, Captain Grant had left him to his own devices, and those devices were few. In fact, it would take a miracle to get through this meeting in one piece.

Which would have been hard even if he did have support. Roland's attack on the German airfield had taken a toll on his body. Stress had poisoned and stiffened his muscles. Purple bruises sprinkled his entire complexion. The onsite medic declared his arm broken in multiple places, and wired it to his chest with an uncomfortable sling.

Roland's broken body matched his fractured soul, Elliot's death having torn something irreplaceable out of him. He may have got some vengeance, but it wouldn't solve the hurt. The hurt so heavy he could barely sit up straight under the weight of it.

Hartney's rage-filled face gave him other reasons to hunch over in shame. Roland couldn't even blame him. He had stolen a squadron plane, destroyed it, and mounted an illegal attack on an enemy airfield. Even though the kills were somehow confirmed, his brand-new ace status wouldn't save him from the wrath to come.

Hartney cleared his throat. 'Well, I guess you've always had a hot streak about you, haven't you?'

Roland didn't answer. He figured he was in enough trouble without adding his lip service.

'Yesterday, when we found out you covered up a serious dent in your medical history, I gave you the benefit of the doubt. Because I thought you were at least dependable. Do you call this stunt dependable?'

'Elliot would probably think so.'

Hartney slammed his fist on his desk. 'That's bullshit, Hawkins! These airplanes aren't here for you wild types to raise hell whenever you please.'

'He deserves justice.'

'So does every other pilot who dies over France. You don't see anyone else busting valuable planes over it.'

Again, Roland stayed quiet.

'Then the doc tells me your injuries will ground you for who the hell knows how long. What am I supposed to do about that?'

Another hot streak of anger shot through Roland. After all he had been through, and the friends he had lost, he had had enough. He looked dead into Hartney's stern face and didn't even blink. 'Look, I don't really give a damn what you do to me. Elliot didn't deserve what he got, and I'm glad I punished the people responsible. I wouldn't take it back for anything.'

Hartney wrung his hands. 'You got some brass, don't you, boy?'

'I'm a squadron leader. You put those boys in my hands, and I will fight for them to the bitter end. No matter how many of your precious planes I have to destroy in the process.'

'Well, then I guess you deserve this after all.' Hartney leaned over and opened his desk drawer.

Roland waited for him to bring out his dishonorable discharge. Maybe there would even be a court martial in there. Either way, he winced in pain. Bracing himself for the sting.

But Hartney only pulled out a small envelope. Much too small for any troublesome paperwork. He pried it open, and a bright, boldly colored ribbon spilled out.

Roland peered at it, trying to make it out. 'What the hell is that?'

'Stand up.'

Roland wobbled to his stiff, sore feet.

Hartney, with a sneer of a smile, strode up to him and pinned the ribbon to his breast. 'Distinguished Service ribbon. You can wear it until they send your medal. They'll put it on you in a nice little ceremony with brass bands and the like. Doesn't that sound nice?'

'No, it sounds stupid.'

'I quite agree. When I heard about your stunt, I was ready to have you discharged and shot in front of a damn firing squad. Top brass felt different though.' He clapped Roland on the shoulder. 'Pilots are a whole new breed, Hawkins. The Germans had their Red Baron, the British had their Albert Ball, the French had Guynemer. We got a couple of our own maestros, like Luke and Rickenbacker, but a few more couldn't hurt.'

'What in the hell are you saying?'

Hartney pulled one more thing from his desk. A newspaper, which he handed to Roland.

It was the Stars and Stripes, a military-run paper, sent to the troops all over France. It flabbergasted Roland to see a large black and white photo of himself on the cover.

Ace Pilot Launches Solo Attack on German Airdrome.

A severely inflated version of Roland's antics followed the giant headline. His brain spun cartwheels as he read through the piece. The article, the publicity, 'ace' written next to his name. It was everything he had craved in a time that seemed so distant. He had made a name for himself. He had become a hero.

It didn't feel very good though. Perhaps because of its cost. Human blood had paid for this. A lot of it belonged to people he knew and admired. His father, mother, Wehner, Luke, Vernon, and Elliot were all dead. Even if the flu hadn't killed Ilse, she was close enough to the front a bullet still might. Bernard had returned to the roaring inferno of combat after barely escaping his first go. And despite all the rampant rumors of an armistice, the war's ugly vortex still turned, ensnaring millions of people across the globe into its deadly pull.

All so he could be a hero.

He laid the paper aside and glared at his commander. 'So what? Now you need someone new to give the public?'

'Which is good news for you . . . *Lucky.*'

Roland started at the name. He wondered if Hartney knew of its background, or if it was just a fantastic coincidence.

Hartney pulled a notation out and read it with a smirk. 'For single-handedly mounting an attack against an enemy airdrome, and eliminating multiple German planes, we hereby award Lieutenant Roland Seybold Hawkins with this Distinguished Service medal.'

'That's a load of bullshit.'

Hartney folded the notation and slipped it into Roland's breast pocket. 'What you did was idiotic, but top brass loves that shit. It makes people back home who hate the war sing patriotic songs and hand over their salary for war bonds. Besides which, the boys were touched to hear what you did, all in the name of your buddy. You may not feel like a leader, Hawkins, but your actions paint a pretty darn good portrait of one.'

Roland looked down at the ribbon. A nice addition to his military dress, but it pierced him like a knife to the heart. To think this is what he had wanted, more than anything, once upon a time. 'What I did, it won't bring him back. It won't bring any of them back.'

'No, it won't. Elliot will get a good send-off though. The band and flag and everything.' He folded his arms across his chest. 'Then there's you. What do we do with you?'

'What good am I to anybody?'

'Well, we all know that mangy cat couldn't do without you.'

Roland would've laughed, but he didn't have the heart. 'I'm so busted up I probably couldn't even train.'

'You'll be better use here than rotting in a hospital. I'd like to keep you on. We could have you do additional ground school.'

Additional ground school. Roland would teach a class full of incoming troops the basics of aviation science. It would be more than unnecessary at a combat squadron, and he knew exactly what it meant. Hartney wanted him sidelined, away from his precious airplanes. But with his new hero status, they wouldn't dare cut him from the squadron's roster. It disappointed Roland, but he probably deserved a lot worse.

His eyes fell on the picture window behind Hartney. A crisp, cool morning beckoned. The sun had popped out of the clouds for once, bathing the airstrip and clean planes in happy yellow light. Beyond them stood a line of trees with bare, dormant branches.

They pulled at Roland's fragile heartstrings. He knew what Elliot would say if he was still alive.

Roland got up and limped toward the door.

'Where the hell do you think you're going?' Hartney asked.

'Out. It's a great day for mushrooms.'

THIRTY-EIGHT
Ilse

As October rolled into November of 1918, Europe devolved into chaos. Mutiny spread across battlefields like a disease. Russia had crumbled under the weight of the war, and been torn apart by revolt. Germany also found itself in the grips of revolution, starved half to death by the British naval blockade and buckling under the pressure of a failing monarchy and toppling army. Then came the new influenza that had almost killed Ilse. It spread like a shockwave over the continent, felling more people than the last several battles put together.

And still, the war raged on. Even after four years, millions of deaths, the collapse of empires, and the destruction of countries. Although peace rumors were prevalent, the shells kept screeching across no man's land. The bullets kept flying. Planes kept bombing. People didn't seem to know how to stop killing one another.

Which was why Ilse was glad to have a day off from it. Twenty-four hours, to be exact. A short leave Llewellyn had granted her when she asked, because she had never asked for leave before. This morning, she walked through a quiet field instead of a busy casualty clearing station. She had brushed up and cleaned her hair, tucking it neatly under her black cap. A fresh red cross on the sleeve of her uniform popped the blush in her cheeks.

She made her approach into a small, picturesque village with humble brick buildings and a lovely church spire. A place that had somehow avoided the majority of war damage. The extra-crowded graveyard, packed with mounds of fresh graves, was the only sign that fighting raged nearby. A small wooden sign, with 'Nancy' printed on it, swung in a chilly breeze.

Ilse roamed Nancy's small, homely town center, looking for a tucked-away inn that the letter had described so well. When she found it, she stepped around to the back of the building as she had been instructed to. A green door, with chipped and peeling paint, beckoned to her, just as the writer promised it would. It looked quite inviting in the gray-brown stone of the tiny building. She did a quick primp of her hair, straightened her jacket, then knocked on the door.

She heard a faint, muffled footstep on the other side. 'Go away,' said a tired, bitter voice.

Ilse only smiled. 'Let me in, Roland.'

A sharp pause. A drawn-out silence. Then the door opened just a crack. Eyes narrowed in suspicion sounded her out. Then they opened wide, along with the door. Roland stood there, dressed in simple trousers and a stained, cream shirt. His hair was rumbled and greasy. His face carried fading bruises and hollow cheeks. He looked dreadful.

'Ilse?'

She grinned. 'There's my Roland Hawkins.'

'What are you doing here? You said you couldn't meet me until tomorrow.'

'I had a special delivery.'

'For what?'

'This.' She reached into her pack, slung neatly over her crisp jacket shoulder, and handed Roland a bloom from the fields nearby. She placed it gently in the palm of his hand, and its vibrant color seemed to brighten his entire little room.

But it didn't put any color in his cheeks. He just stared at it, almost like it made him angry. Like he saw all of his dead comrades in it.

Ilse drew her lips in a thin line. Reaching into his war-hardened heart would be more difficult than she thought. It's why she had come to meet him earlier than planned. His last letter, detailing his leave and where he would spend it, had dripped with a bitterness he never had before. His language was curt. His words empty. He didn't spell it out, but Ilse knew. Roland had reached the end of his rope and she needed to get him back to rights.

She timidly swept past him and into the little room. Her eyes took in the flickering candles, the tiny writing desk, the welcoming feather bed. 'A charming room. Compliments of the air corps?'

He shrugged as he slammed the door shut. 'Of three months of back pay, actually.'

'You wouldn't believe all the flowers in the meadow outside of town.' Ilse beckoned to the tired blossom, still sitting in his trembling hand. 'I've never seen anything like it, especially this late in the fall. The girls say it's the chemicals in the gas. It reacts with the mud and causes some sort of superbloom. Maybe we should take a walk over there and . . .'

Ilse trailed off, swallowing hard, as Roland crushed the flower in his hand, mashing the petals against his dirty skin. When he looked up, he glared. 'I think it's all the good boys buried under the soil.'

The grim reply, and the newfound darkness in him, caught Ilse off guard. 'Yes . . . I suppose.' She looked around the room again to avoid his chilly gaze. That's when she noticed the black cat, curled in a ball, purring away on his pillow. The animal took in Ilse with suspicious, yet sparkling green eyes, daring her to do anything that would harm her human.

She looked at Roland and smiled. 'Well, look it here. I thought I was the only girl in your life.'

Roland laid the smashed blossom on his windowsill and managed a tight-lipped smile. 'That's Jewel. She's a little stray I took in.'

Ilse sat down on the bed and scratched Jewel behind the ears. The cat immediately flopped on her side so Ilse could get her tummy, while whistling purrs escaped her throat. She had decided, without a doubt, that this strange new lady was a friend.

Roland finally found a smile from somewhere within. 'She doesn't usually let anyone else pet her. She must sense you take such good care of people.' He sat down next to Ilse, shooing Jewel off the bed.

Feeling just slight relief, Ilse turned to Roland and took in his battered appearance. Really took it in. She brushed her fingers over a healing cut on his lip and ran her eyes down the bruises on his exposed chest. The remaining burn scars. Yes, the war had done a number on him, all right.

Roland smiled. 'You think I look bad, you should see the other guys.'

She sighed. 'I heard about your wild little antics at the German airbase. It made me think you could benefit from a medical professional.' She moved in to embrace him, but paused. She had caught sight of his jacket draped over the bed, and the military ribbon pinned to it.

Her eyes lit up with admiration. 'Is that . . .?'

Roland's face hardened again. His eyes dropped to the floor. 'Distinguished Service.'

She could see the subject pulled on a dangerous thread, but she also couldn't stop the pride from gleaming in her eyes or tugging at the corners of her lips. Roland, her Roland, had been decorated. 'Roland Hawkins, why in heaven's name didn't you write and tell me?'

'Because I'm not proud of it.'

'Why not?'

'I killed people and they gave me a ribbon. Seems a little barbaric, don't you think?' Roland didn't wait for an answer before plopping on his back on the bed.

Ilse took his hand in hers and cupped it into her bosom. 'Roland, you're no murderer.'

'Interesting sentiment, considering what I do every day. And what I did to earn that ribbon . . . Let's just say I wasn't sorry. Sounds like a murderer to me.'

Ilse leveled her eyes with his. She could see the path he had strayed onto, and she felt determined to shove him off it. It would do no good to him or anybody to dwell on the situation they'd been forced into.

'Now, Roland, you listen to me. You can't start spouting right and wrong in a war, because the whole thing is wrong. We're all victims of a game played by people safe in a mansion, far away from the reality of it. And that certainly isn't your fault or mine.'

Roland struggled to hold back tears. 'To think this is what I wanted when I came here. Medals, glory, honor. Like there's any honor in any of this.' He buried his face in his hands, and his body clenched and shuddered with oncoming sobs.

Ilse's heart locked in place at the sight of it. She'd never seen him like this. Not even when mustard gas had him in its terrifying grip. This was something newer and somehow uglier. She scanned her racing brain for something she could do. A magic spell to snap him out of it. To give him any kind of momentary relief. She stood from the bed and put her hands on her hips, slapping a smile onto her shaken face.

'Roland Hawkins, it looks to me like you need a bath.'

He glared up at her. 'What?'

She held out her hand, inviting him to take it. 'Come now. It's the best thing. And it looks like you haven't washed your hair in weeks.'

'Well, we don't have bathing facilities at the airfield, and I don't really give a damn what my hair looks like.' He rolled on his side and put his back to Ilse.

She wouldn't have it though. She had dealt with enough unruly patients to know all they needed was a metaphorical bend over the knee. She drew herself up to her full height and threw her daunting shadow over his balled-up form. 'Roland Hawkins, of the two of us, I'm the medical professional. And I'm ordering you into that washroom this instant. You're having a bath, and that's that. Argue with me one more time, and I'll leave. Do you hear me?'

It felt harsh coming out that way, but it worked every time, and so it did on Roland. Like a spurned child, he roused himself from the bed and allowed her to lead him into the cramped washroom. She ordered him to undress while she got hot water from the inn keeper.

Minutes later, naked Roland lay in a steaming bath, his pale, shrinking body barely filling the tub. Ilse, who no longer felt the slightest blush around nudity, removed her jacket and shoes to make herself comfortable. Then she gently ran a washcloth down his war-ravaged frame. Her fingers brushed the bruises and lacerations, speckled like pox, across his entire chest and back. She tenderly worked the stress knots out of his tired shoulders. She gently dunked his head in the water and washed all the oil and grease from his hair.

Roland stayed quiet the whole time, staring at her with tortured eyes that were begging her for relief. For the end of his suffering. Eyes that clearly reveled in the power of gentle, soothing, human touch.

Ilse knelt at the side of the tub and gently brushed his wet hair away from his face. She leaned in close enough to smell the fresh soap on his clean skin. 'You know something, my Roland? You are just like those flowers in the meadow. You might feel buried under the mud now, but you will grow back. And when you do, you will be more beautiful than before. Because you're one of the good ones. You always will be.' She took a flickering candle from the stand beside the tub and held it out for him. 'So, time to come home now, Roland. Come back to me.'

Roland's lower lip trembled. He bowed his head for a long moment, then ran his good hand over his broken arm. His back and shoulders rose and fell with big, whooshing breaths. He whispered a few things to himself – something about a boy named Elliot. Then, he looked up at the candle. He pushed himself to his feet. He stood naked before her, totally exposed, water dripping down his tired frame. Yet a fire had lit inside his eyes. A part of him had returned.

Ilse felt a butterfly swarm move in on her stomach. A woman who had grown completely numb to nudity now suddenly felt vulnerable in the face of it. Because she had just remembered that she shared something with this man that she hadn't with any of the others. She had given him pieces of herself. Now, he looked ready to do the same. So ready it intimidated her.

He stepped out of the tub and moved toward her. The tired muscles in his arms suddenly bulged. His shoulders tensed. He wrapped himself around her, and his bath water seeped through her blouse. It tickled her breasts and made her nipples poke through the thin material.

'Roland,' she whispered, sinking into his body.

Before she could say anything else, his lips were on hers. It was different than any other kiss. Harder. He used his tongue more. Her body went limp inside of his. Bursts of pleasure crept up from deep inside her stomach and thighs, rippling through her entire body.

Roland's lips moved from her mouth to her face, to her neck. Next thing she knew they were in his bed. All without him taking his lips from hers, not even for a second.

The heat inside her grew stronger. Hotter. Impossible to control. It turned her breathing wild and sent her hands up and down his face and into his damp hair. She suddenly found she couldn't get enough of his lips. His hands. His skin against hers. She began tugging fiercely at her own clothes, as if they would burn her if she didn't get them off.

Once she had freed her body from its fabric prison, everything happened fast, coming to her in bursts. Her back pressed against the cool sheets on Roland's bed. His warm, naked body enveloping hers. His strong arm around her, holding her, protecting her. A finger massaging a place no one had ever touched before. A brush fire catching in her stomach. He entered her, sending hot streaks all down her legs. His hands cupped her bare breasts. His lips pressed against the dip in her neck. Sweat. Heavy breathing. Entwined legs. Whimpering.

He moved against her in all the right places, then the brush fire in her stomach erupted. Her back curled up. She let out a cry. His hand clamped over hers. He groaned and shuddered.

Then quiet. Heartbeats slowed. Breathing turned down. Roland withdrew from her, then dropped his head into her bosom.

She wrapped her arms around him, pressed his head to her so he could feel her heart beating. Thudding. Calling out for him.

Then she lost her gaze in the flickering candle. Its warm glow. He had come home.

THIRTY-NINE
Roland

November 11, 1918

The morning was silent on the airfield. Pouring rain and swirling clouds kept all planes on the ground. Roland and the First Pursuit Group passed the dreary day in their little pub. Every seat was taken, with more men crowding in the doorway. Mechanics had wandered over, along with some high-level officers. Boys even made room for the scrawny, dirty enlisted men. There was no revelry, no playing on the piano, and no drinking. All heads remained bowed in a nervous silence. Only the distant rumble of artillery penetrated the thin walls.

The clock on the wall ticked away the seconds. As the hands slid into the armistice hour's position, everyone held their breath.

Right on cue, a single artillery blast rattled the walls. The window trembled, and a few glasses tipped over. Then the rumbles on the horizon halted. No machine guns popped in the air. No alarm bells for enemy pilots, no horrific plane crashes. For the first time in four years, silence ruled the Western Front. The war that had swept up everyone in Roland's time, that had destroyed lives and worlds, that would change things forever, was finally over.

It took a minute for the realization to set in. When it did, the bar erupted into chaos. Shouts, whistles, and squeals rent the air. Someone went crazy on the piano. Boys overturned the tables and smashed the wooden chairs to splinters. They threw glasses against the wall, shards of glass crunching under countless flying boots. The bartenders broke open the last of their bottles and passed them around in frenzied revelry.

The excitement, much too great for the bar to hold, spilled out into the pouring rain. The boys ran around like wild animals. They stripped off their shirts and held their open palms to the rain. They burst into wild fits of laughter. One or two broke into sobs. Some dropped into the mud and wrestled one another, while others started a conga line around the airfield.

As for Roland, he just stood under the pub's overhang and

watched, cradling his still-broken arm. Someone dropped the needle on a record player in his mind, and it showed him the same fantasy he had seen before. That quiet porch, with the sapphire-blue sky shining down on open fields. So much room to spread out. The turning windmill. The cooing baby.

Ilse's eyes . . .

Roland watched his boys and smiled. 'Home . . .' he whispered.

A week after the long-awaited armistice, Roland Hawkins flew his last mission with the United States Army Air Corps.

His injuries still kept him barred from the pilot seat, so he rode observation while another boy handled the controls. He had insisted on going, because he had a feeling it would be his last time in an airplane. After everything he'd seen, and the men he'd killed, he didn't think an airplane would ever excite him again. So, before his flying days came to a permanent end, he wanted one last flight. One last taste of the wind in the wires and the breeze on his face.

A peacetime patrol for photography and observation fit the bill perfectly. Top brass wanted pictures of all the abandoned German airfields for their records. So, Roland climbed into one of the tiny observation planes. This time, no fighter patrol had to take off with it. Which was something to get used to in the end.

The air felt so much different when the world wasn't at war. When Roland didn't have to watch for enemy planes, he could watch for beauty instead. Like the perfect way the clouds billowed and glowed pink in the sun. Or a flock of birds flying level with the plane, flapping their wings, gliding in the same rigid formation his combat patrols had once used. He marveled at the sunbeams bursting through the clouds, and the bold, fresh colors below, finally visible without the billowing screen of artillery smoke.

The patrol's first stop was the field Roland had busted up himself. The rickety plane came in for a bumpy landing on the overgrown turf. As the two boys climbed from the plane, a heavy silence greeted them. All the brightly painted German planes still sat in a neat, tidy row. Many had broken wings, crumbled control panels, and flat tires, a last act of spite from their pilots. The mechanical hangars sat empty of tools and personnel. The abandoned barracks howled in the wind.

While the photographer set up his equipment, Roland went exploring. His feet squished in the soggy grass, and the wind swirled cold in his ears. In his mind's eye, he saw the Germans running from him when he dove on them like a bird of prey. He saw a few brave pilots climb into their planes and start their engines. He saw balls of fire and splintered wood . . .

Lost in his thoughts, Roland walked over to a rickety shed. Bare except for a few windows with tightly drawn curtains.

Roland wedged the door open with his good shoulder and stumbled inside. Darkness and a musty smell hit him first. When his eyes adjusted, he made out what must have been a briefing room for German patrols. They had clearly left it in a hurry, since papers with footprints lay scattered over the floor. A wooden table had been turned over and the chairs knocked askew. A filing cabinet leered in one corner, the drawers hanging open. A large black chalkboard remained nailed to the far wall. It had various German names scrawled on it, with marks to show their kills.

Roland huffed. How cheeky to leave that in place . . .

Still, the motionless void of a room haunted him. He knew how hectic it must have been just a few days ago. He could see the ghostly images of German pilots, preparing for a morning mission, talking over semantics with new fliers, instructing them what to do if a solo flier madman came right at their airfield.

He also noticed a message on the blackboard.

Roland frowned and took a few steps forward to investigate.

When he got close enough to read the message, a feeling he couldn't describe poisoned his stomach. A tingling sensation, a sense of dread. It weakened his knees and pricked the back of his neck like icy needles.

He narrowed his eyes, rubbing his fingers across the words etched in chalk:

Aus der asche wird Deutschland wieder steigen. (From the ashes, Germany will rise).

Next to it, there was a very familiar drawing. A wolf, with golden eyes and a devilish snarl. The exact same drawing he had seen on a particular German plane.

The wolf nose art. The game of cat and mouse. Roland crashing into a shell hole in no man's land. Where he would have died without all that damn luck he carried around. Luck the Wolf pilot must have had too, since they had both survived the war. Yet one of them apparently had no peace to look forward to. No home in the countryside. No laurels. One of them, it seemed, had only bitterness. Only loss. Only anger.

Only the hope that his country would rise up and start this all over again.

As soon as he returned to airfield, Roland hid himself away in his barrack. The message in the German briefing room had left a cold sensation in his blood. Injected him with a foreboding feeling that despite everything he had been through, despite the trenches that crisscrossed France, and the millions of dead people beneath the mud, he hadn't heard the last of Germany.

The thought made him shudder. The future suddenly looked bleak and uncertain instead of peaceful. What he saw on that chalkboard was the deep, rankling bitterness of a defeated enemy, pulsating over that empty airfield, those silent trenches, and in all those empty, starving stomachs in the Fatherland.

No war could end all wars. Not with the complicated human race, with their fragile egos and their axes to grind. Roland didn't know how long it would take, but someday, those words would come true. Germany would rise again. They would reach for their guns. They would go to war. Maybe not in this generation, but soon. The children of today would be the wooden crosses of tomorrow.

Yes, lying there alone in his barrack, with purring Jewel curled up on his stomach, Roland Hawkins saw it all, and it scared him half to death.

'Hawkins, you in there?'

The voice pulled Roland back to the peace, however long it would last. He rolled his eyes and dragged himself up. 'I think it's time I told you boys I don't like to drink.' He flung his shabby barrack door aside.

Instead of more rowdy fly boys, Captain Grant stood before him. Roland straightened up and saluted. 'Sir!'

'Can it, Hawkins. You never respected superiors before, so don't bother now the war's over.'

'Well, what brings you here then, if not respect?'

Grant pulled a folded letter from his pocket. 'Some infantry dropped this off for you. I came over first thing, because I wanted to give it to you myself.'

Roland took the letter into his trembling hand. The scrawl on it was unfamiliar, and he didn't recognize the regiment number. 'What is this about?'

'Your brother.'

Roland's racing mind came to a screeching halt. He ripped the envelope open, unfolded the letter, and scanned through it. His eyes caught two terrible words toward the bottom.

'Wooden cross.'

FORTY
Ilse

Spring, 1919

Ilse and Roland, both dressed in civilian clothes, squished through an abandoned old battlefield near the River Meuse. Bird songs echoed instead of bullets. The warm sun emerged from its foggy curtain, its golden light spilling over decaying barbed wire. Fresh, mint grass invaded empty shell craters. Scarlet poppies fluttered where soldiers once stood. Quiet trenches snaked to the horizon, and undetonated shells stuck out of the mud. Shells that would wreak havoc on farmers for decades to come.

Ilse walked quietly beside Roland. She had tied her skirt just below her knees to keep it out of the mud. She gripped his clammy, sweaty hand as they stopped at various clusters of wooden crosses. Each time, Roland scanned them for one name amongst a sea of unknowns. He had yet to find what he was looking for, although they had been at it for hours.

They took a pause by a bubbling brook, a tributary of the hard-fought-over Meuse River. Roland cupped some water in his hands, drank it, then splashed his face.

Ilse looked on while her stomach churned. She felt his pain. His crushing disappointment. They both knew it would be a long shot, but that didn't make it any easier to bear. In this sea of dead, some marked with crosses but many vanished forever in the mud, how could he ever find that one name? The needle in a haystack? And how could he ever find peace if he didn't, never knowing what had really happened to his brother?

Ilse felt tears build behind her eyes. Just as they threatened to burst, a gentle bird coo cut into the silence. Roland's shoulders stiffened, as if someone familiar had just tapped him on the shoulder. He slowly looked up to find a single wooden cross sticking out of the mud. It had tilted in the wind, with scratches that looked like an engraving on the front.

Ilse got a funny feeling as she looked at it, somehow knowing already it was the one Roland wanted. She almost felt the dead boy's energy lingering nearby, beckoning to his brother from another world. She gave his shoulder an encouraging squeeze.

Drawing in a deep breath, Roland creaked to his feet and approached the cross.

Ilse followed him, slipping her hand in his again. They both looked down at the lonely grave.

Sgt. Bernard Herald Hawkins, the cross read. His unit sat beneath the name, along with his date of death. Roland reeled when he saw it: *November 11, 1918.*

November 11. Bernard Hawkins died on the morning of the armistice. He had missed survival by hours, maybe even minutes. It was simply too much after everything.

Roland choked back sobs as he knelt at the foot of the cross to straighten it. Beside him, Ilse laid down a bundle of wildflowers she had picked from the nearby fields.

'Hello, Bernard,' Roland said. 'Sorry it took me so long.'

A forlorn bird call sounded in reply.

'I'm glad they found a nice spot for you at least.' Roland's voice cracked, and he took a moment to look at all the battlefields, the blown-apart trees, and the soupy mud.

As for Ilse, she could barely contain her emotion. 'Nice spot' seemed too generous a thing to say. There was nothing peaceful about this place. No redemption or honor. Bernard's grave would be disturbed time and again by graves registrations and clean-up ops. Farmers would turn up this land for planting. Bernard's memory, and all the boys buried here, would be erased. By nature, by man, and by time. The years would crawl over them like a wet blanket, covering over everything they had sacrificed. Snuffing out all the flames.

The same horrible fate that had befallen her parents on a day that felt like ages ago. So many lives lost, forgotten, and turned over. Families separated for all time. Countless widows in mourning black. A generation of women who would have no men. And for what? Torn-up earth? Broken trees? Loaded cemeteries?

Nice spot, indeed. Ilse balled her hands into fists and tried to steady her breathing.

Roland couldn't keep a straight face either. 'November eleventh . . .' He buried his face in his hands. 'My God . . . he couldn't hold on one more day? One more hour?'

'One more minute . . .' Ilse shook her head in dismay.

Roland bowed his head. The tears sprang forth, although he tried to hide them by turning away.

But Ilse knew they were there. She always knew. They had given too much of their hearts to each other for her to not know. She put her hand on his shoulder to remind him she wouldn't leave him for baring his heart. Not now, not ever.

Roland stood up and wiped his face with the back of his hand. With a troubled sigh, he buried his teary eyes in the golden, setting sun. 'My God, I'm the only one left,' he said in a sad whisper.

Ilse gazed up at him. 'What do you mean, darling?'

'My whole family has disappeared. Been swallowed up. I'm all that's left of the Hawkins name.' He slipped his hands in his pockets and stared down at his brother's grave. 'The war took everything from me.'

Ilse squeezed his hand. 'It didn't take everything, Roland. We still have each other. And it's over now. No more killing. We can start over.'

He kept his eyes on the sunset. 'Start over . . .' He sniffled. 'Go home . . . I haven't wanted to go back to the city. Not for a long time.'

Ilse found that curious. Heartbreaking, really. No day passed without her thinking of New York. The little flat where she had grown up with her parents. Where her mother always put a candle in the window and her father always let her feel heard. It was dirty, cramped, and nothing to brag about, but it was home. Her own tree had taken root there. Everything that she was or would be – it all began in that dusty little hovel in the middle of a big, shining city. She knew she may never see it again, but she also knew it would always have a piece of her.

She turned to him with puzzled eyes. 'Then where do you want to go, Roland? What does "after the war" look like to you?'

He sighed, still lost in the pink sky. Something clearly captivated his mind though. He had a picture of home in there somewhere, but he kept it from her for now. 'You know, I wasn't sure there would be an "after the war." Not for fighter pilots.'

Ilse nodded. What he said made a lot of sense. More than once, she thought she'd never find a home again either. In America or anywhere else. She sighed and turned her gaze back to the grave at their feet.

'And yet here we are somehow.'

Roland looked at her. 'Yes, here we are.'

Here they were indeed. It reminded Ilse that she was a survivor, too, the last of her family just like him. Two orphans of the world, who somehow had to forge a path forward through the war's bitter and broken remains. She kept her fingers entwined in his, wanting to say something, but unsure what. After all, what exactly could she say to heal their hurts?

'I hope you know the ones we love never really leave us,' she finally said in a gentle whisper. 'They're always around, even if it's only in your memories.' At last, she looked up at him. She tenderly moved a lock of his brown hair out of his shimmering eyes. 'Is there anything I can do, Roland?'

He took her hand and kissed it. His brown eyes glowed copper in the golden light. His gaze turned hot, just like it did before he made love to her in a tiny inn in Nancy. 'Yes, Ilse. There's something you can do for me.'

Under that passionate gaze, Ilse somehow knew what he would ask her. She felt it down to her bones, like the stillness just before a summer thunderstorm.

And it caught her slightly off guard. Because a part of her never expected her wartime romance to end in marriage, just like Roland hadn't expected to survive the war. On the one hand, she knew it was him. It had always been him. Ever since she saw him in that clearing station in Belgium. Ever since she read him the letter about his mother's death. Since she held his hand for the first time. Kissed him in secret in a busy hospital. Bathed him in his brokenness while no one watched. Felt his body and his heart merge with hers.

However, Ilse had long since stopped trusting the world. She had a constant, nagging fear that all this would sink beneath her feet, just like the *Lusitania*. It still could, with such an uncertain future looming before them. But the way Roland's eyes pierced her, the way he held her hand in his, the way he stood so strong and fearless against it all, despite the shallow grave at his feet. He offered to build the solid ground she had craved for so long. To give her a place to belong. Their own home together. One that would always have a candle in the window.

She let out a nervous exhale and felt a smile tug at her lips. She knew what her answer was before he even asked.

As for Roland, a small cloud of hesitation cropped up in his eyes.

Just a split second of doubt. Then, he opened his mouth and out it came.

'Marry me.'

Ilse giggled this time, high-pitched and girl-like. She blushed so hard she couldn't even look at him. This man, who had seen every little part of her. Yet still she felt so shy and innocent standing before him. What a relief the war hadn't spoiled that.

She squeezed Roland's hand, beaming up at him like those golden sun rays. 'Yes, Roland. Always yes.'

FORTY-ONE
Ilse & Roland

Five years later

The sun beamed down on a golden wheat field rustling in the summer breeze. It sat under a crystal-clear sky in the heart of the vast, unbroken Nebraska plains. Only the sawing and hammering of tools disturbed the beautiful peace.

Those came from Roland and a host of construction workers, putting the finishing touches on a nice farmhouse. They painted it a buttery cream color with trim to match Ilse's eyes. A red shed went up just behind it, and a shining, squeaky windmill turned in the warm breeze.

Ilse Stahl Hawkins sat in a rocking chair on the wide, front porch. A golden wedding band shimmered on her finger. She cradled a baby boy fussing in the summer heat. When her cooing failed to silence him, she bounced him on her knee.

'Hush, Michael, darling. Mommy's here with you.'

The cries soon transitioned to squeals of happiness. He reached his tiny hand out, which came to rest on a soft patch of black fur – Jewel. She lay on the arm of Ilse's rocking chair. A shiny collar sparkled around her neck, and she nuzzled the boy's hand with her face.

Roland looked on and beamed with pride. The woman he loved, on their porch, with their child in his arms. His fantasy come to life.

Happy memories of their wedding day at a small church in France bubbled up in his mind. Captain Grant and Llewellyn had served as witnesses. Old Tubby Clayton of Talbot House performed the ceremony, while they stood amid broken windows, a shelled roof, and piles of dust. In a church broken by war, two people declared their unbreakable love for each other. How beautiful Ilse looked that day, in a simple lace gown. She carried a bundle of red poppies. Her green eyes gleamed behind an elegant veil.

Roland stood before her, dressed in his Army Air Corps uniform complete with his pilot's wings and Distinguished Service medal. He looked so polished, yet he felt inadequate next to his beautiful bride. So unprepared that she had actually chosen him.

They kissed to make it official, and they enjoyed a short honeymoon touring around England. They spent their days sightseeing in London, and they spent their nights making love in cozy little inns, just like the one in Nancy. Soon after that, Roland returned to the United States with Ilse on his arm and Jewel in a crate.

They went to New York first, where Roland got his discharge from the Army Air Corps, and Ilse hung up her Red Cross uniform. Then, they fled the busy city, never to return.

They wound up here in Nebraska. They bought their own farmland, and over time, they picked up the pieces from the war. They worked their land, they lived their lives, and they made friends amongst their quiet neighbors. The months turned into years, and new life joined their nest.

The precious baby boy was a sprig of new growth on their dead family trees. They were no longer the last of their blood lines. Their names, their stories, could live on.

He smiled at his wife and baby, then went back to work.

On the porch, Ilse settled the baby into a gentle nap. She turned and looked at the kitchen window, where a candle sat on the sill, its flame flickering in the breeze.

Home at last.

Author Note

World War I was a time of incredible upheaval in society – the most apocalyptic conflict humanity had faced up until then. While the guns from this globe-altering conflict went silent over one hundred years ago, the ripple effects can still be felt, and even seen, today. That's why it felt so important to me to write a book that took place in this period. To shine a light on the scars still visible in the terrain, on the countless gravestones that still dot the countryside of Europe, and on the monuments bearing the thousands of names of the people who were never seen again.

In my own telling of the story of the Great War, it was my honor and my challenge to always stick as close to the real history as much as possible. However, this is still a work of fiction. To bring attention to every angle I possibly could of this war, I had to bend some truths here and there. Timelines had to be stretched a bit, fictional scenarios had to be created, and many fictional people as well.

My favorite part of this process, though, was resurrecting some very real people who played a part in this conflict. Especially Frank Luke Jr. His exploits during the first air war made him a fitting personality to add to this narrative. Although he didn't survive the war, Frank Luke became the first American pilot to be awarded the Congressional Medal of Honor. He was the second highest-scoring American ace of WWI, and Luke Air Force Base in Arizona is named in his honor. Since history has in large part left him behind, I wanted very much to reintroduce him to you, and in these pages, I hope I have done him, and the many warriors of the first air war (such as Joe Wehner ((Luke's wingman)), Eddie Rickenbacker, Major Harold E. Hartney, and Captain Grant, also real people), the honor they deserve.

The other person I was absolutely delighted to bring back to life for this novel is Reverend 'Tubby' Clayton and his famous Talbot House – a historical site that still stands today in the town of Poperinge, Belgium. In a world that had descended into total violence and chaos, Tubby chose peace. He brought as much comfort and compassion as he could to the suffering soldiers of the Great War. It is true that he intervened with the British Army to reunite two brothers who hadn't seen each other since the war began, and it wasn't the only time he went out of his way to bring a little light into such a dark world. During his downtime, he brought a small, portable organ to the trenches and played and sang for the downtrodden soldiers. His third-floor chapel at Talbot House brought many broken people closer to God, and thousands of people took their first (and in many cases, quite tragically, their last) communion there.

I was lucky enough to pay a visit to Talbot House in the summer of 2018. I felt as welcomed into that house as any soldier would have during the Great War. Sitting in the sun-filled canteen room and having tea was one of the highlights of a whirlwind European tour that summer, and I will forever hold it close in my heart and memory.

In this story, I also wanted to bring at least some attention to the love songs and music that came out of this era, a true testament to the resilience of people to persevere in dark times. Two real songs quoted in the manuscript are 'If You Were the Only Girl (In the World)', first written by Nat D. Ayer, and 'Roses of Picardy,' first written by Frederic Weatherly.

While not everything in this book happened in real life, I wanted to write it to bring home a very real message. In a world of darkness and pain, love can still win. Sometimes maybe not as quickly as we'd like, and maybe not in the way we might have expected. But give it time. Let it grow. The light will shine again, and love will win. It's what I most firmly believe, and what I hope we can all work together to achieve.

Acknowledgments

Writing is often times touted as a solo profession – and in many ways it is. However, one cannot create a book without help. Lots and lots of help. I would first like to thank my agent, Lindsay Guzzardo, who keeps believing in me and helping me get my work out into the world. Next, I thank my editor Sara Porter, and all the incredible people at Severn House, who saw something worth fighting for in this story that sat in my files for many years, until these wonderful people helped me brush it off and make it shine.

A major thanks goes to my husband Joel, who has been there for me through the entire crazy journey of being a writer. The ups, the downs, the highs, the lows. He sees me through it all, and always hands me a glass of Scotch when I need one. I am also blessed with many friends who are always there for me, and I especially thank Erin and Liz for reading early drafts of this book, giving me notes, and not laughing in my face. And where would I be without my family? All of whom have been so supportive – with special thanks to my father, the aviation expert, who helped me navigate the airplane technology of the era.

I must also thank the various educators over the years who always encouraged me with my writing – especially at Alburnett Jr/Sr High School in Alburnett, IA, and the University of Iowa.

I also want to throw a shout-out to all the online writing communities who have given me so much support, especially my friends and fellow bloggers on Wordpress.

Lastly, I thank God – for making me just crazy enough to give writing a try.